BY LAUREN OWEN

The Quick

Small Angels

Small Angels

Small Angels

A Novel

Lauren Owen

RANDOM HOUSE
NEW YORK

Small Angels is a work of fiction. Names, characters, places, and incidents are the products of the author's imagination or are used fictitiously. Any resemblance to actual events, locales, or persons, living or dead, is entirely coincidental.

Published in the United States by Random House, an imprint and division of Penguin Random House LLC, New York.

RANDOM HOUSE and the HOUSE colophon are registered trademarks of Penguin Random House LLC.

Hardback ISBN 978-0-593-24220-9
Ebook ISBN 978-0-593-24221-6

Printed in the United States of America on acid-free paper

randomhousebooks.com

2 4 6 8 9 7 5 3 1

First Edition

Book design by Caroline Cunningham

For Amie and Grace

LAG forever

Contents

Small Angels

Mockbeggar

Tell it to the trees. This was once high praise in the village below the woods. It was what you might say at the close of a lively tale—told at dusk in late December, with a good fire snapping at the coals.

Not bad. You always were a dab at a story. You should tell it to the trees, see what they make of it.

If the mood was right—if there was a clear moon and no call to retire early, maybe you'd go further:

Let's do it, you'd say. *Come on. Let's go and tell them.*

If your companions were willing, you'd take up your cloaks and hats, fetch a lantern and stumble outside into the dark. You'd go softly through the dreaming village and the moon-shadowed fields, up the hill to Mockbeggar Woods.

By the time you reached the trees you might have begun to regret your earlier enthusiasm. The woods were an imposing presence by night. Nobody knew how old Mockbeggar was, or how big. The outside had been mapped and measured, but once you were in there it seemed to stretch much farther—fern and nettle, oak and beech, green on green for miles. Some nights, it was said, you might find yourself walking amongst trees that had fallen centuries before.

Mockbeggar grew by itself, hundreds of years before people took to tree-planting in this part of the world, and yet it was said that human beings had played their small part in its cultivation. In a distant time (the story ran) people cleared trees from the edge of Mockbeggar to make space for themselves, a place to build and farm. They moved in and stayed awhile, and then they were gone—wandering or dead, no one could say for sure now. But they left their relics behind: smashed pots, lost coins, assorted bones. And decade by decade, root by root, the trees moved back and swallowed it all. The saplings grew tall on a diet of history.

This would go some way to explaining why Mockbeggar was the way it was. Because it was widely agreed that the trees in that wood remembered; they could whisper to one another of things past and days long gone. They were hungry for human dramas, and they loved to hear stories from the village below.

If you whispered your tale by moonlight (the trees listened best by moonlight) you might hear Mockbeggar whisper back. The story would rustle from leaf to leaf, branch to branch, all the way to the shadowed, thorny heart of the woods where no human had ever ventured.

When the trees listened, a story *lived*—it became vivid, it took possession. You'd be there at its center, watching it all unfold. It was worth braving the dark and the cold for this subtle magic.

Sometimes the woods heard a story they particularly liked. The trees would listen in rare stillness until the tale was finished. Then a wind would move through the branches, making the leaves rustle. The old oaks and beeches would whisper: *This one we will keep.*

These were the stories that belonged to the tellers, that had their roots in village soil, stories with blood in their veins. Often they were stories of those who had been lost. (After a death it was custom to walk up the hill and entrust to Mockbeggar your memories of the one who was gone.)

The trees would listen, and sometimes they would whisper: *Yes. This one.*

Consequently it was not unknown for the dead to linger in those woods. Two hundred years ago, this was small cause for concern. In the village they were used to Mockbeggar and its ways. It was well known that a story told there—even a game of imagination played beneath its shifting, leafy shadows—might stick like a burr. The stories could cling in that subtle way that pollen clings, invisible in the throat, or showing at the sleeve as the faintest trace of gold dust. Sometimes the stories lasted too long or clutched too tightly.

Two hundred years ago, people had simple remedies for the woods' stings and snares, and they agreed that the dangers were a tolerable price to pay for Mockbeggar's gifts.

In the centuries that followed, the trees had a great deal to observe. The village never knew a lord or squire. Instead it was a refuge for those unwanted in other villages—the disappointed and the dissolute, the seduced and the abandoned. These burdens on the parish refused to decently shrivel and die. They drudged or poached or starved, clinging fast to lives that were only occasionally sweet, and all the while Mockbeggar watched and listened. The bells rang in the little church at the edge of the woods, and the trees saw the people come and go. Brides, biers and babies passed in and out of the dark oak door. Things were as they were and nobody wanted them different.

But all this was long ago. Customs changed and the village changed and perhaps the woods changed too. They were an object of suspicion in the village now; all wonder and reverence were gone. In these later years, Mockbeggar was left mostly to itself. The little church was quiet, and the paths through the woods were all shut.

CHAPTER ONE

The Albatross

It was Hag Night. The wedding guests—reluctant to part as stags and hens—gathered instead at the Albatross, the village's only pub. They came in laughing, throwing the door wide open and letting in a smell of late summer, of warm earth and dying grass.

At the heart of the group were the engaged couple, Sam Unthank and Chloe Day, whose happiness that evening had a glow like candlelight. Drinkers smiled on them from afar, and the waitress brought them complimentary cheese and olives.

Tonight's singer sat near the fireplace, a half-full glass at his elbow, his head bent over his guitar as if confiding something important. Still his voice reached every corner and curious alcove of the ancient pub. It was an old song—the Albatross made a specialty of old music—a story of long exile, lucky meeting, lovers reunited.

Most of the drinkers knew the tune well enough to hum along, chiming in for the chorus. Elizabeth Daunt, the village librarian, joined in without looking up from her book or setting down her gin and tonic. Even John Pauncefoot, the pub landlord—usually too shy to take part—sang a note or two, in a voice of surprising beauty.

Chloe—one of the few in the Albatross who had grown up outside the village—glanced at her bridesmaids (whose off-duty clothes somehow looked quite striking here, though they would have turned no heads in London). Her expression said, *what did I tell you?* She had promised they would find the village like this. There were so many quaint, lovely moments waiting to surprise a visitor. It was like tripping backward in time.

Brian Last joined them so adroitly that nobody noticed him setting his half-pint and packet of salt and vinegar crisps down on the table. As the song ended he turned to Chloe—who was radiant, ready to be feted, a bride already though the wedding was a week away—and said,

"You're getting married this Saturday, I hear."

"That's right."

"At Small Angels?"

Baffled, amused, Chloe hesitated, so Brian graciously enlightened her:

"I mean that place up by the woods. St. Michael and All Angels. Big name for a little church. People mostly just call it Small Angels."

"That's quite pretty," Chloe said. "If I'd known, I'd have put it on the invitations."

Her praise, though well-meant, seemed to infect Brian with gloom.

"Cake ordered by this time, I suppose?" he said. "Wine bought? Guests invited?"

"Ages ago. You have to be organized, you know, planning a wedding. I finished my first to-do list eighteen months ago yesterday."

Chloe waited for congratulations—on the wedding, if not the list—but there were none. Brian took a sip of beer and ate three crisps—all ominousness, all grim thought. The laughter of a minute ago smoked out and vanished.

"Good luck to you, then," he said at last. "I suppose you know what you're doing."

"What are we doing?"

"You're tempting fate. Don't you know the story of Small Angels?"

"No." Chloe glanced at Sam—a local, unlike herself. "Nobody's said a word. What's wrong with our church?"

"Anyone want another drink?" Sam said. "Brian, same again?"

But he was too late to save the evening. There was no distracting Brian when he had a tale to tell.

Brian was a local historian, a curator of gossip. He had run the post office for several decades, carefully noting the address of every letter he franked. He lived alone with a Jack Russell named John Aubrey and a freezer full of meals that his wife had cooked for him before her death—neatly labeled lasagnes and shepherd's pies on ice. The dog loved him and they were rarely seen apart. Tonight it lay quietly at Brian's feet, watching as he spoke. Besides Chloe, it was the only creature in the Albatross to listen willingly.

They did listen, though. The wedding guests listened, and the rest of the pub listened too, letting conversations lapse. John Pauncefoot leaned against the bar, concentrating with a resigned air. Elizabeth Daunt set down her book and sighed, but did not depart. A family of diners fell silent, the children twisting in their seats to stare, ignoring their mother's frown. The waitress set down her tray of dirty glasses and listened openly.

Brian had an earnest gaze, thin, restless hands that seemed made for dramatic gestures, and a long acquaintance with the acoustics of the Albatross. The singer by the fireplace—seeing that he had lost his audience for the time being—put his guitar to bed in its case and took his half-hour break.

"The thing is, Small Angels doesn't rightly belong to the village at all," Brian began. "It belongs to the Gonnes. Much good it did them."

"Do you have to do this now, Brian?" Sam said. "We're meant to be celebrating, and this is morbid stuff."

"I don't mind," said Chloe. Snug in the Albatross, in her circle of well-wishers, in her happy love affair, she was ready for a gloomy romance—something grim howling outside to make the warmth and bright warmer and brighter. Sam said nothing further, and Brian continued:

"So, there's a house out beyond the village. White walls, sitting by itself in the middle of nowhere—Blanch Farm. The Gonnes lived there for over a century. The family name changed from time to time, of course, but it was always the same people underneath. Ten years ago, there was a whole pack of them there.

"Selina—the old lady—was boss of the clan. I went to school with her husband, Paul. Not a bad sort. Quiet, mind you. Talked like words tasted bad. He and Selina had four granddaughters to bring up, and I never envied them *that* little task. You'd see those girls wandering the fields at all hours like they didn't have a home to go to.

"Maybe they'd have picked up better ways if they'd gone to school, but they never stirred from Blanch Farm. People used to say that the old lady didn't want to spend on the bus fare. Somebody should have stepped in, but no one liked to upset Selina.

"They were strange people. The thing was, they lived much too close to Mockbeggar Woods." He turned to Chloe. "You've seen Mockbeggar, I suppose?"

"Just from outside," Chloe said. "It's near the church"—smiling, she tried out the newly discovered name—"near Small Angels. Isn't it? I wanted to go in and explore but Sam said we couldn't."

"I should think not," Brian said, frowning. "Nobody with any sense goes into those woods."

Chloe looked around the Albatross, expecting a contradiction. But no one spoke. Sam had picked up the candle on the table and was tipping it so that the liquid wax threatened to drown the light.

"Only the Gonnes ever walked in Mockbeggar," continued Brian. "People used to say it was just them and the dead."

A sigh from Brian's audience. Here was the meat of it at last.

"So this is a ghost story?" Chloe said, pleased and surprised.

"I don't claim that part's true, mind. I wouldn't say *that.* All I know for sure is what the tradition is, and what I've seen and heard for myself."

He looked around the Albatross. "They'd rather I didn't tell you this stuff now. They listen, don't they, though? Can't help themselves. Because the thing is, we all knew that there was *something* going on. That's where Small Angels comes in.

"The Gonnes were at Small Angels all the time, back in their day. It's just up the fields from Blanch Farm, practically on their doorstep. God knows what they used to do there, but that church is more used to strange goings-on than it is to weddings, you can be sure of that. They kept the church key—had it for generations. The old lady used to wear it on her wrist."

"This must be hers, then," Chloe said. She took the key from her handbag and held it up so Brian and her guests could see. It was a gorgeous thing—dark metal, weighty. "They gave me it when I'd paid the deposit. Isn't it pretty?"

Brian looked as if he wanted to ask to hold the key but didn't quite dare.

"Yes," he said. "That'll be it." He gathered his story threads: "Once a month, when there was a full moon, you'd see lights in the windows of Small Angels, you'd hear bells ringing across the fields. That was the Gonnes. I passed them once, walking through the fields toward the church. It was dusk, but the moon was out already. They all carried lights and they were singing. I said, *Good evening* but they didn't answer. Paul Gonne hung back for a moment and he said, *Get out of it, Brian. Get home.* I didn't hang about to see any more.

"And then there were the beacons, too. Have you seen those yet?"

"I don't think so," said Chloe.

"There are four of them—metal brackets, you can't miss them, still standing at the boundaries of the Gonnes' land. The family would light them every evening. People used to get worried if they weren't burning by dusk. You could talk all you wanted about *quaint local superstitions*, but when night came you wanted to be damn sure those lights were lit."

"But you didn't know why?"

Brian shrugged. "Maybe our grandparents' grandparents knew. But the Gonnes kept their secrets very carefully. The old lady wouldn't even let strangers in the house. Fought tooth and claw to stop Small Angels reopening. Being turned into a *venue*." He looked darkly at Chloe and Sam. "Damn-fool idea, given what happened last time that place was used. I don't suppose they told you when you booked that Small Angels has been shut up for ten years?"

"No."

"Of course not. The last time the church was used was for Paul Gonne's funeral, and that wasn't an occasion you'd want to repeat."

He took a sip of his drink, and continued uninterrupted:

"Before things went wrong, the Gonnes were managing well enough, as far as any of us could tell. They walked in the woods and no matter what company they found there, it seemed to suit them well enough. They never had quite enough money, but they got by. They had a vineyard, and buyers would come from far off for the wine. Paid pretty well for it, apparently. There was something curious about the taste, something it picked up from the earth and the water.

"But one year there was a freezing spring. Vicious cold in May, just the worst time for a grape crop. Paul Gonne went out to the field one night to check on the vines and didn't come back. They found him curled up out there—stroke, the doctors said. But he was a strong man, never ill a day in his life. The attack came out of nowhere.

"After that, things changed at Blanch Farm. The Gonnes stopped coming into the village. You hardly saw them anymore. Especially the girls.

"I called round once. Just to see if I could do anything for Paul. Shouldn't have bothered. Selina told me to leave them in peace, said she was sick of me spying and I should mind my own business. I never spied, though."

"Of course not," Chloe said.

"Just kept my eyes open. Maybe if more people had kept a lookout, things wouldn't have happened the way they did."

Brian paused to finish his drink. Those who knew where this tale was tending were waiting for someone to intervene. But the story went on; it unfolded like a disaster, unstoppable.

"It took Paul a while to die. Can't have been pleasant for the family to watch."

He reached down and scratched John Aubrey's ears gently. The dog looked back at him—anxious, adoring.

"He kept going until late summer or the start of autumn—this kind of season, in fact. Weather was beautiful that year.

"I didn't find out about Paul dying for a few days. I don't think anyone outside the family did. Then Selina came to church—*our* church, I mean, the one just a spit away from this pub—one Sunday and summoned everyone to the funeral. Said she'd be glad of our company.

"It was tradition for the Gonnes to invite the whole village to their funerals, and it was tradition for everybody to go. After the service at Small Angels the family would have a feast back at Blanch Farm—wine, food, music. It was the way they always did things. Nearest thing they ever got to making merry.

"But at that time, after Paul's death, I didn't like how things were looking at Blanch Farm. There was a bad sort of atmosphere when you went by. Shutters closed all day. Mess in the yard. Lights in the windows at odd times. Seemed to me it was a bad idea to go off to Small Angels at dusk and then traipse back to the house in the dark."

He looked around his audience—most of them locals.

"You lot keep your eyes on the ground, don't you?" he said. "Don't like to mention what happened that night. But you all know.

"The church was full that evening. The Gonnes were in their funeral best, of course, and most of the village was there too.

"I remember darkness falling outside, night air coming in. It felt like we were in a lifeboat on the open sea. You understand what I mean? Better inside than out alone in the dark, but at the same time we were so obvious. One bright point in all that blackness. I had my prayer book open in front of me: *Defend us from all perils and dangers of this night.*

"And I thought: well, whatever we're in for, it's too late to get away now.

"I felt *watched* that night. In the graveyard, in the dusk—dusk burials were always the Gonnes' way, they'd bury by torchlight or moonlight—I felt that the woods had come very close. Small Angels always did look like it was going to be eaten up by the trees any minute. That night, it seemed like Mockbeggar had crept closer than ever.

"After they'd put Paul in the ground, the girls lit lanterns to lead the way back, and there were lights burning along the path to guide us through the dark to Blanch Farm. More of them outside in the yard. People said it was pretty.

"We were out of the dark, away from the graves now, and here was food and wine and a sight of the Gonnes. The daughters were all grown up by that point and people were curious about them and their strange ways. Most of the village drank and ate and stared, and started to enjoy themselves.

"All the time, I knew something was out of joint. I had a feeling of something coming, something about to go wrong and I couldn't stop it, couldn't leave. It got to ten, and then eleven, and the party—it *was* a party, though we were all supposed to be mourning—the party kept going. It was like nobody could drag themselves away.

"I went round the back of the house. There's an orchard there. I wanted some quiet, to clear my head a moment. Work out in my own mind what was going on.

"But I wasn't alone out there. Just beyond the orchard gate—just where the lantern light failed—I saw something moving close. A pale shape."

"A person?"

"No. I went closer to the gate, away from the noise of the party, and that's when I heard it—"

Here came a distraction: a late guest had arrived—a tall, dark woman, unperturbed by the stares of those around her.

This was Sam Unthank's sister, Kate. It was common knowledge that she had barely shown her face in the village for years, and it had been generally agreed that she would miss the wedding.

Chloe knew better. Months ago, she had pushed Sam into asking Kate to be his best man, despite his insistence that Kate would refuse.

He didn't say that he didn't want Kate at his side, Chloe noticed, only that Kate would turn him down. So she told him that they would visit Kate and issue their invitation in person.

During the visit she had been eloquent, stressing how happy Kate's presence would make them both, and how excited they both were about the wedding. Eventually she piqued Kate's interest. Before their departure, Kate had asked her if she and Sam were really proposing to clean and decorate Small Angels for the ceremony in the space of a week.

Chloe had confirmed that this was the plan, and Kate had said that in that case she had better join them to help. It was surely one of her duties as best man.

(Punctuality was also one of her duties, Chloe thought now, but she wouldn't hold that against her.)

Kate's gaze was on Brian—she had caught his last few words as she came in—and her expression was both somber and sarcastic.

"You sure you want to tell that story, Brian?"

"I've got a right. I was there."

"All the same. Isn't talking about Blanch Farm meant to be bad luck?"

The Albatross was quiet. All over the pub, eyes were cast down. John Aubrey sneezed.

"Brian?" Chloe said gently. "Don't leave us stranded. Even if it *is* an unlucky story. What happened next? What did you see at Blanch Farm?"

But Brian was affronted. His performance had been spoiled.

"Ask your fiancé," he said to Chloe. "I should be getting on." He nodded toward his dog. "This one needs a walk."

After he left, there was a few minutes' awkwardness. The locals looked uneasy; they clearly regretted allowing Brian to run on like that uninterrupted. Conversation returned only slowly.

Chloe wished it hadn't ended like that. She should have stopped the whole thing earlier, probably—only she had felt rather sorry for Brian, whose story was so unwelcome and whose grudge against the village clearly brought him no joy.

She put this thought aside. Here was Kate to welcome. She was still standing by the door, as if tempted to turn and leave. Chloe went to her and gently steered her to the place that had been saved for her.

When Kate and Sam embraced it was with a fractional hesitation, like two people jumping into icy water. The resemblance between them was a shifting thing—striking in some lights, invisible in others. They were made of the same stuff, Chloe thought, but made very differently. Both were tall, both handsome, but Sam had light eyes and a practiced, easy smile. Kate's eyes were dark, and she did not look as if she had forced a laugh in her life. The effect was a little intimidating. Still, Chloe would make a friend of her, and she would make her and Sam friends again, too. That would be her wedding gift to him.

"Thank you so much for helping out this week," she said to Kate, steering her to a chair. "I didn't realize how much I was asking until Brian enlightened me just now. Sounds like we've got ten years of dust to contend with."

"It'll be fine," Sam said. "Brian's a professional doom peddler, that's all."

"He's certainly given me a new perspective on our church," Chloe said. She was about to ask Kate what she had meant about Brian's story being bad luck, but before she could, Kate said something about checking on her car and slipped away outside.

Now the food arrived: searing-hot plates of steak and chips, one of the Albatross's specialities. Chloe was diverted, for a moment, in ensuring that each guest had what they had ordered and checking if anybody needed another drink.

Further down the table, Beth and Nicole, her bridesmaids, were both looking ill at ease. Nicole, who was forthright, would have almost certainly had something to say about Brian's story if she were sitting closer to Chloe. Beth, who was gentle about voicing her opinions, was staring down at her untouched steak with a little frown.

Neither of them had been enthusiastic about the village even before this disruption. Chloe had been excited to show it all off to them—the old village church, the small, neat gardens full of lavender and herbs, the Albatross with its bare boards and rag rugs and sloping ceilings.

She had expected them to be charmed, but something had failed to click. People watched them, Nicole said, frowning, as the three of them strolled through the village. Had Chloe noticed that?

It was a small village, Chloe reminded her. Of course they were going to look twice at newcomers. Especially the fiancée of one of the local boys.

Beth, politely, had said that she understood. And Nicole had said that she could always drive down and fetch Chloe back to London if she needed a break during the prep week.

They meant it kindly. But she was taken aback at her friends' reaction, because her own infatuation with the village had taken hold so quickly.

She had been here only once before, but the visit had made an impression. It was late June, and the weather had been blissful. She and Sam had spent most of their time out of doors—cycling between villages, stopping at odd pubs along the way, picnicking at the edge of green fields of wheat, dotted here and there with poppies and dog daisies.

Sam had preferred for them to spend their time out of his parents' house. She didn't press him on it. At this point, she had still been learning the Unthanks' history, the source of Sam's unease. Sam had told her briefly that Bill and Birdie—he never called his parents anything else—had reached an understanding after many painful years.

When Sam and Kate were in their teens, there had been a rift. Then a grudging reconciliation, then several smaller separations. Bill, Chloe gathered, had been more to blame. Perhaps even cruel. But Birdie had involved Sam and Kate in her unhappiness more than was strictly fair. Still, that was over and done with now, Sam said. Though things were not quite right with Kate. There were things she couldn't let go of.

Every family has its strange, painful place, Chloe had thought, just as every house has one drawer full of chaos, crammed with nails and knotted string, orphaned keys and half-burned candles. She wondered if there was a way to make things easier for Sam's family.

Away from Bill and Birdie's house, it was easy to put the Unthanks' mostly-buried history out of mind for a time. The village was so unlike anywhere Chloe had ever visited before. The white and pink painted houses (the pink was traditionally made by stirring in berries or blood, Sam told her), the little stone walls, the village water-pump (she was delighted to find that it still worked), the roses climbing over the garden walls, the lush grass verges, the narrow winding lanes. There were old-fashioned lamps set at the end of each lane, and when she and Sam cycled home at nine o'clock in the evening, they were all lit. Her lasting impression was of a place with its own kind of time, its own customs and possibilities.

She had discovered Small Angels by accident. She had left Sam behind on one of their bike rides, joking that she'd race him back to the village—only to take a wrong turn and find herself cycling uphill on a faint track that threatened to vanish into the grass at any moment.

Sam called to her to wait, and she stopped for him. But Small Angels was already in view.

It was simply built from oyster-colored stone, its size making it look like it was meant for children. There was no wall to the churchyard, nothing to mark it off from the fields on either side. There were graves jutting out of the grass at odd angles, and a cherry tree growing close to the path. Just beyond the graveyard were the woods.

"I've never seen such a tiny church. Did you come up here a lot as a kid?" she asked Sam.

"No. Why would I?"

"What do you mean, *why*? Look at the place." How could he miss so much beauty? "Besides, it's so quiet. Ideal place to come if you wanted to do your own thing without your parents breathing down your neck . . . What did teenagers do around here to rebel?"

"Me? Went to school every week. Got my A levels. Left."

"Seriously?"

"We weren't like your family. Bill wasn't reliable, you couldn't trust him to be kind. They're not bad people, my family, but it wasn't stable when I was growing up. It's better now."

"What about Kate? What did she do?"

"Kate's not big on confidences. Never was."

She looked away, sensing that he wouldn't thank her for further questions. It was unusual for him to share so much about his childhood without a veil of sarcasm.

A few yards from the farthest grave, a new structure was almost finished. She would discover later that this was the Tithe Barn—the innovation of a local entrepreneur, a reception hall built to ape the architecture of the little church. He had spearheaded the push to reopen Small Angels, and intended to market church and Tithe Barn together as a venue for concerts, weddings, and other events. A nice new stream of revenue for the village, he had promised.

"What are they doing there?" Chloe asked.

Sam shrugged. Later she would think that he *must* have known what was going on, but there was no one working at the building that day and they had the church and graveyard to themselves.

She wandered closer to the woods. The first trees were spaced far enough apart for her to make out a glimpse of ferns and flowers—small flecks of pink among the green. But they quickly gave way to close-growing trees and brambles, and what lay beyond these was hidden.

"We should be heading back," Sam said, hurrying to catch up with her.

"What's it like in there?"

"Never been in. It's out of bounds."

"How come?"

"I suppose the owner doesn't want to share." He took her hand. "Seriously, Chloe, we can't walk that way. It's not that sort of place."

"Not some National Trust idyll, you mean?"

"Exactly."

But she lingered, listening to the woods. She heard droning—bees or wasps—and the trees stirring in the wind. She had the feeling of something waiting to be discovered.

The woods and the little church had returned to her thoughts more than once afterward, tinged with a longing for something she couldn't articulate and didn't understand.

When their original venue—Bill and Birdie's village church—had fallen through at the last minute, she had made a spur-of-the-moment decision, booking Small Angels and the Tithe Barn at a bargain price. (Both would need a little help, the entrepreneur said, to make them ready. Some sprucing up. The Tithe Barn was very new, and the church was very old. But he was sure a young couple like Sam and Chloe weren't afraid of a bit of hard work.)

Sam had been surprised when she told him what she had done. It had taken a while for him to accept the new plan and concede that it ought to be fine.

Perhaps this was what he had been thinking of: the story of Small Angels, the bad luck. Perhaps this was what Nicole and Beth had sensed as they walked through the village. Some morbid history lingering like a bad taste in the mouth.

Rubbish. She put these thoughts away—always a knack of hers. She had a tidy mind. There was nothing to worry about in her church but grime and perhaps a few stray nails that the workmen had left behind.

Chloe started her meal, readying herself with questions for Kate.

Sam was always so reticent about his childhood. There were many things Chloe had planned to ask her. But Kate did not return.

Ten minutes passed. At last Chloe asked Sam if they shouldn't see what had happened.

Sam shook his head and said that Kate always did come and go when she pleased. She was back in the village and that was the main thing. One best man to check off the wedding list along with the rings, cake and flowers. Chloe could relax, everything was going to plan.

"Brian's a crank, by the way," he added, slicing chips, knife scraping his plate with a noise that made her wince. "Blanch Farm is a strange obsession of his. Don't let him infect you with it. Nobody else takes him seriously."

'Is that why you didn't tell me any of that stuff?"

"To be honest, I'd forgotten. Most people round here grow out of those stories by the time they're through primary school."

"So we're not cursed, then."

"Are you disappointed?"

"Slightly," she said, smiling. "I've never been haunted before. You'll have to put me out of my misery, at least."

"How do you mean?"

"The story. He was just getting to the good bit. What happened at Paul Gonne's funeral? And what about the family? Are there any still left at Blanch Farm?"

Sam sighed. "Do we really have to go into this?"

"I can go and find Brian, if you'd rather." She was trying to sound playful, as if it hardly mattered. In fact, being put off had only increased her curiosity.

"Can I tell you later?" he said. "It's not a nice story." He had lowered his voice. A couple of their guests were listening, she realized. "Not some big exciting mystery, or whatever it is Brian was trying to sell you. Just human sadness." He looked toward the door, which Kate had left open. "You don't want to give it much thought. It'll only upset you."

"Fine. Later, then."

They said nothing more about it, but she found herself thinking of little else that evening. She had been cocooned in joy only a short while ago; the world had seemed made for her delight and convenience. Now she had a new perspective on the Albatross—its jars of sunflowers, its gleaming horse brasses, its little lights. This was a pleasant place, but outside it would soon be growing dark. Her happiness felt like a very small island. Through the open door she saw that the sky had changed. A chill was creeping in like a touch of cruelty.

CHAPTER TWO

Mockbeggar's Children

Lucia tells a ghost story

In the beginning were the woods. They knew me before I was born. They saw my mother grow sick and heavy with me; they saw her discontent grow alongside me like a twin. When—in the weeks before my birth—she took to standing silent at the orchard gate, watching the autumn wind whirl dead leaves free into the sky, the woods saw that, too. From my earliest childhood they were a backdrop to my thoughts, even in the private and forgetful moments of sleep. When the trees moved in the breeze the sound was as familiar as the sound of my own breath.

Before I was six, I had learned how the seasons passed on the vineyard: the flowers, the fruit, red and yellow coming among the green of the leaves (traffic lights, Elphine used to call this effect). Then the pruning-back, the dead months when it seemed that nothing would grow again, and then the green-and-pink furred buds that always returned. I learned to enjoy watching my grandparents in certain tasks—testing the ripening grapes' sweetness, or making up Bordeaux mixture, that bright blue fungicide that looked like a bucketful of summer sky. I learned to look for the partridges coming home to roost in the pear trees in the evening, to listen for the owls returning to bed at dawn. But Mockbeggar was the most important thing of all.

The woods watched us work the fields in every weather. They watched Grandpa pruning for hours until his thoughts became a merciful blank and he saw vine branches whenever he closed his eyes. They watched Nan busy over our accounts, a shoebox of receipts at her elbow. They watched our father standing at the orchard gate, at the very place where our mother used to linger in the weeks before her departure.

With me and my sisters the trees were more than watchers—they were an audience. It was one of our oldest games, acting plays in Mockbeggar, and whenever we came to the woods tricked out for a new production—trailing cloaks of mildewed velvet, shedding glass beads with every step—I had a sense of the woods growing wakeful. We made them hungry. They wanted the story we were going to tell.

For a long time, I was too young to be involved in the plays, too young for anything but the very shortest visits to Mockbeggar. I would sulk when my sisters left me behind, but it did no good.

Then, eventually, there came a day when Ruby—always our leader, being the eldest—said I was old enough.

I was seven years old. It was late August or early September. The grapes were small and hard still, and very green. There were blackberries growing in the hedge.

"You can eat these," Helena told me, "but not the ones from Mockbeggar. Nothing from in there. Understand?"

I already knew that very well—Nan had told me dozens of times that it wasn't safe to eat things growing in the woods—but Helena still reminded me of the rules quite often. She said I obviously needed it, given how many I regularly broke.

I was about to tell Helena to mind her own business, but Elphine spoke first.

"Look, Lucia," she said. "These are dead-nettles. The petals are sweet."

She pulled up a nettle and showed me how to pull off the small white flowers and suck the nectar from their base. I didn't have to be afraid of the sting, she said. They were safe to touch.

Because it was my first real visit to the woods, my sisters had decided that I needed a proper welcome before we got down to the play. We halted at the edge of the trees. There were still ox-eye daisies left, and Elphine strung together a little wreath for me, then Ruby and Helena crowned me carefully, making sure the flowers were straight.

"Welcome, Lucia," Ruby said, mock-solemn, and the other two echoed her—*welcome, welcome.*

They curtsied, circling me, and they were joking, but not entirely. I knew not to laugh.

Then Ruby said, "What do you want to see first?"

It was almost awful, a question like that. Where could I possibly start? What if I chose wrong and missed something important or lovely?

I looked at the ground, and at the trees, and neither helped me.

"All of it," I said, finally.

"Oh, is that all?" said Helena—but with only mild sarcasm. She understood how I felt.

There was never a bad time to see Mockbeggar. But that season might have been the loveliest of all. There were sloes and raspberries growing, the clearings were bright with goldenrod. The sun came through the trees and the light seemed tinted green.

"It doesn't matter if you miss something today, you know," Ruby told me. "You can come back again. As often as you like."

As often as I liked. Such staggering luck. It was almost too marvelous to believe in.

We passed from silver birches to beeches, and the mild breeze made the branches rustle. *Welcome, Lucia,* I imagined them saying, like my sisters had done. *Come and look, come and see.*

Back then there were dozens of paths through Mockbeggar:

There were some that were very hard to find—stumbled upon once or twice and then never again.

There were a couple of bad paths. If the woods sometimes moved like one great mind, stirred by a single impulse or memory, then these bad paths were like trains of thought which led nowhere good, dark or dangerous ruminations. We avoided these paths and gave them no names.

Some paths were new—the trees shifting on a whim. Our ancestors wouldn't have recognized them.

Some paths had been there for a while and were now lost; the woods had swallowed them. Grandpa might have known them in his youth, when he still visited Mockbeggar, but he never talked to us about the woods.

That first day, my sisters showed me the easiest path to find, the hardest to lose—the Elbow, which runs straight for a while and then veers off without warning at a right angle, leading right to the heart of the woods. Or as close to the heart as any living person has ever been.

There were little streams of clear water running over the path. We were happy, excited, and so we talked very loud—Ruby explaining things, Helena clarifying or disputing, Elphine sometimes putting in something gentle or strange. We always listened when she spoke because she had a way of making things look different. Like a sudden shift in the light. I already knew that she didn't think like other people.

As we went along I jumped the streams, saying *look at me, look at me,* and because it was my day, my sisters did stop to look. They were glad of me just then, I think—pleased I was there to share their adventures. And I was glad of them.

Then we reached the bend in the track. Just before we turned away, deeper into the woods, the Elbow took us close to the river. The Fane runs deep and fast in some parts of the woods, but at that point it's shallow, and there's a brown rock halfway across. If you wanted, I thought, you could use it as a stepping-stone and reach the opposite bank without getting your feet wet.

The opposite bank was overgrown with corn mint, and beyond that were briars growing higher than any I had ever seen before, looming over the narrow path. The track advanced a couple of yards and then twisted out of sight. I had an idea that there might be a clearing beyond.

"What's that way?" I said, taking a step forward.

Ruby pulled me back from the water, her face so serious that I was alarmed.

"We don't go that way. Not *ever*. You understand?" Her fingers dug into my wrist. In those days Helena might pinch or kick me when I aggravated her more than usual, but it wasn't Ruby's way.

I shook her off and rubbed my arm ostentatiously. No one asked if I was all right, not even Elphine.

"Lucia," Ruby said. I had never heard her so stern. "You understand? Never go that way. You have to promise."

"Fine."

"Come on," Elphine said, taking my hand. "Let's go. This isn't a good place."

We didn't talk about it any more. From experience I already knew there were some questions that nobody would answer, no matter how often I asked.

Instead my sisters taught me to peel bark from fallen twigs to find the cream-colored wood beneath. They taught me to trace figures in the shapes of the branches: writhing limbs and wild hair, acrobats frozen mid-fall.

We came to a horse chestnut my sisters liked—a friend of the family, practically. Ruby lifted me onto the lowest branch and shook it so that it shuddered and jolted and I was in wonderful danger of being dashed to pieces.

"We'd better get a move on," Helena said at last, looking up at the sky. "The light's already going."

Mockbeggar didn't belong to us after dark. I was mostly ignorant back then, but I already knew this one thing very well: leave at dusk if you know what's good for you. The sunlight lies, it tells you everything's safe, it tempts you to outstay your welcome.

Time was slipping away, so we ran, our feet thudding like horses' hooves over the dead leaves. We *were* horses, briefly, in my imagination. (So easy to turn into a horse back then. You remember that?) I was the slowest. I could hear my sisters calling up ahead, I could see their costumes bright blue and red and amber against the leaves. By the time I reached the clearing, I was breathless.

This glade was called the amphitheater, Ruby told me. It was about thirty child-strides across, ringed by an audience of trees.

At the center stood a ruined beech. A storm had brought down one of its branches and it looked as if it was twisting in grief or pain. If it was a person it would be wringing its hands.

"That's the Dervish," Elphine told me.

"I don't like it."

"Of course you do," Ruby said.

And she was right, I realized. The Dervish was beautiful. Or at least hard not to look at. I touched its damp mossy bark and my hand came away greenish. If I rested against the tree for long enough perhaps I would become part of it, I thought. I wondered whether or not I would mind.

"Places, please," Helena said, her voice now brusque and official-sounding. "Two minutes to curtain."

I fussed with my red cloak. Like all our costumes, it had come from a trunk in the attic. The trunk was an heirloom with a cautionary tale attached. Nan told the story well: decades ago, the clothes had belonged to a relative of ours, a man who had—perversely enough—wanted to leave Blanch Farm. Even if this was permitted (and of course it wasn't) it seemed like a strange thing to want, I thought. Still, he had fled, and—remarkably—had managed to get away. He went to town to pursue the stage. Naturally he failed. His new friends forgot him, and he drank himself to death. This was what happened to you when you forgot your right place in the world, Nan said.

The actor was buried far from the village, and only his trunk made it home at long last. The silk and velvet and tweed, all tainted with mildew and disappointment, had been stowed in the attic until we had found them.

That afternoon, I thought of the poor drunk-to-death actor and I understood him less than ever. How could anyone want a better audience than this?

"Wake up, Lucia," Helena said. "We're starting."

I wish I could remember that first play better. Someone was poisoned, I think. There was almost certainly a rich merchant and a mad queen and a tragically-starved-to-death orphan (this would have been me.)

I had been told in advance what would come next. I had been promised. I had waited to witness it with almost unbearable excitement. Still, when it happened I wasn't quite prepared.

We set the story going, and the woods listened, and slowly the world shifted.

The story caught like a fir tree blazing up; it was all around us. Our voices didn't sound like they belonged to us anymore. When Helena, the cruel merchant, told me that I was no use to anyone and had better starve, it was as if I saw two people. There was Helena with glittering eyes, face pale and rapt—and there was someone else, not visible and yet there all the same. We had summoned something into the amphitheater with our words and careful gestures—the story gripped us like a spell. I felt as if I moved my hand very quickly, I might see sparks.

I would have felt drunk with it on my own, I think. The magic might have been too much. But the other three were there, and they had done this before, so I knew it was all right.

Dusk came on as we were acting, and we had to run for it when we were done—stamping through nettles and foxgloves in old velvet, costumes snagging and trailing in the dirt. When I struggled to keep up, Ruby and Helena each took one of my hands and pulled me along.

It was bewildering, to be dragged out of the play so suddenly. You know that feeling of putting down a book that's held you, or stepping out of a cinema after your film's finished? It was that kind of shock, only stronger. On my own I might have got completely disoriented.

We beat nightfall by five minutes. At the top of the field we paused to get our breath back. There was still light in the sky, and down the lovely orderly sweep of vines was Blanch Farm; the windows were shining bright in the dusk. The beacon outside the orchard wall was already burning. All was in balance, all was well.

When we got into the kitchen Nan was there, busy over her weekly budget. All the money in our house went through her. The income from the vineyard got written down in a big book, along with expenses, shop and restaurant orders, sales from country fairs and to other customers. She noted down the money our mother's family sent, too, and the money that trickled in from elsewhere. She was the only one who understood how much cash we had from one year to the next, and how badly we were doing. (We were always doing badly, it was just a matter of degree.) At Blanch Farm, the money you had in your pocket was the money Nan put there. Nothing was bought that she didn't know about.

"Did you behave yourselves out there?" she asked.

Ruby nodded. "We did, Nan, honestly. We remembered all the rules."

"Well, mind you keep on remembering. Last thing we need is you girls putting his back up—" Then she saw I was listening and told me sharply to go and get changed, I was deep in Mockbeggar dirt and looked a disgrace.

Even in those days, I knew that we were always only *just* safe. Nan impressed this on me more than once. If we didn't mind her, and mind the rules she had put in place for our safety, there was no saying what might happen. She understood Mockbeggar better than anyone, for all she was a married-in and hadn't grown up at Blanch Farm.

Nan told us that our riches—the beauties of Mockbeggar, its alchemy, what it did to our plays and stories—didn't come for nothing. The beacons were one duty we could never forget. All of us had to take our turn lighting them; Nan sent me out with Grandpa to do my part as soon as I was old enough to hold a match.

I remember striking the light, standing on a small crate so I could reach the fuel. In the dusk I thought I saw something in the flare of the match flame. A pale shape, at the edge of the circle of light, half-hidden in trees.

I gasped, and nearly dropped the match.

"Steady," Grandpa said, lifting me down. "Don't want to be making a fuss about that."

"But—"

"Often happens. So there's no need to get upset. Understand?"

I wanted him to think I was brave. I nodded.

"Good," he said. "Good girl."

He held my hand for a little while walking back, which helped. Then he took his hand away to adjust his hat and didn't give it back. I walked as close to him as I could and I thought *often happens,* over and over, until we were safe home.

You didn't get something for nothing. Nan was always saying as much.

The beacons were fueled with wood and gorse that we gathered from the hedgerow near the woods. This task was never completed. There never seemed to be enough cut to satisfy our grandparents, and we could never be certain that Nan wouldn't descend on us as we read or played and order us to go out and cut more.

I asked Nan what the beacons were for, of course—why one of us had to make the weary trudge to the four corners of our land every evening to light them—and I got the usual answer. I'd find out in good time. When I was older.

It wasn't just a matter of age, though. Nan was cagey about telling me things, even more than my sisters; she always found me a little suspect. It began from the outset: I'd been born wrong—outdoors, in

Mockbeggar itself. Who knew what other perverse things I might take it into my head to do?

Nan—who knew how everything ought to be done—said that the proper way was for our family to be born at Blanch Farm. Start as you mean to go on, Nan used to say, and stay out of trouble. Born here, live here, die here, and be buried at Small Angels.

Our mother had meekly gone along with this edict for the births of Ruby, Helena and Elphine—just as she'd dutifully gone along with every other rule at Blanch Farm. If she rebeled it was quietly, as in the matter of our names. (Much too fanciful for Nan's taste. She preferred to call us all different intonations of *girl.*) For a while our mother was happy—she loved Mockbeggar and our father. Ruby, the only one of us old enough to remember, was adamant about that.

But slowly our mother changed. Nan found her undutiful—skulking off to the orchard or her cello or her books when she ought to have been working. Small things—a favorite cup being smashed—upset her out of all proportion. She was always wanting to talk to people about Mockbeggar, inviting them over for coffee. Sometimes she verged on the indiscreet—though of course no one in the village wanted her confidences. She said she was lonely.

"She was from London," Ruby used to say, when she told me the story. "It wasn't her fault she couldn't understand this place."

Ruby thought that if she had understood—*properly* understood—she would never have run off. But that's what she did on the evening I was born.

She left it late to make the decision. Maybe she wasn't bold enough until labor forced her to show her hand. Then she announced that she wanted our father to drive her to the hospital. She didn't want Nan's help—she didn't want Nan to be the first person in this world to touch her baby.

Dad said no, of course. They had to remember the rules.

Nan and Grandpa had raised him carefully—just as they were raising us—and he knew his duty from a young age.

My mother, desperate now, got John Pauncefoot to drive her instead. John was working here in those days. This was the piece of kindness that got him fired.

They were halfway through the woods when my mother realized it was too late for the hospital. Instead I was born then and there, with John Pauncefoot's help, on the side of the road. Hedgerow child, Grandpa used to call me. He would say it kindly, though never when Nan was present.

Our mother never returned to Blanch Farm, though I was deposited there not long afterward. She went back to London, to her family—who were wealthy enough to pay Nan a large regular sum to maintain me and my sisters, on the understanding that none of us ever contacted them again.

It was probably for the best, Nan said. Our mother was only a married-in, it didn't matter so very much if she left. Better she went back to her own people than stayed at Blanch Farm practicing her tragedy airs.

Still, it was unsatisfactory. Nan feared our mother might set a bad example for me and my sisters. (Me especially, since I had almost escaped with her.) The desertion was bad for our father, too. He stayed devoted to our home—as hardworking as Nan and Grandpa could have asked—but some spark, always very faint, now died out of him altogether. His opinions withered to nothing. *Whatever you think best,* he'd say, when Nan asked him some question to do with running the vineyard. As I grew up I realized that she worried he lacked some crucial quality that would be needed for keeping things afloat when she and Grandpa were gone.

I wondered if Nan had been a fraction less careful in bringing up our father, whether he would have gone after our mother on the night of my birth. Ruby said that he had been halfway to fetching the car before Nan reminded him of his duty. I think that Nan saw all of this when she looked at me. Perhaps she smelled the woods on me, too. I'd got too close, even as a baby.

That was the beginning of it, I suppose. I was a discordant note from birth. As a child, I was Lucia-the-bad. I was the one they had to keep an eye on. Most of the family used to remember—sometimes laugh over—my small crimes. It gave them a sense of continuity, of knowing where everything stood in our small world. Sometimes I liked these reminiscences—as the youngest child, it was nice to stand out, even for infamy—and sometimes I didn't.

There was one story they particularly loved: the first harvest I was old enough to watch unsupervised, I'd never stop pestering the workers in the fields. I wanted them to talk to me, but they wouldn't. They were seasonal pickers who came from the village, and they wanted no conversation with any of us. But I didn't know that, and I took it personally. I didn't care to be ignored. I was mildly curious about these people from the outside. I wanted to know what it was like to be them. And they had snubbed me without any justification.

To avenge my dignity, I began a campaign against them—quite a clever one, Ruby would say, laughing.

"Do you remember *any* of it, Lucia?" she'd ask, and I'd shake my head.

That didn't matter, because everyone else did. I began small—sneaking off with people's water bottles and sandwiches. I was so quiet about it that people began to wonder what was going on. I enjoyed the sandwiches—I was always a hungry child—but it wasn't enough. They hadn't paid sufficiently.

I began hiding tools and crates. Then I started leaving things to replace the thefts. Small animal bones, bits of broken glass. People got very nervous—it was easy to make them nervous, this being Blanch Farm.

At last they complained to Nan, who eventually caught me and slapped me and dragged me out from behind a bush to apologize to them all. After that I shunned them as thoroughly as they shunned me.

Years later, I recall my family sitting at dinner, reminiscing over this. I saw Nan glance at me—born outside like an animal, I imagined her thinking. What more could you expect of a girl like that?

The time I really went too far was mostly an accident.

Everyone knows how our family used to visit Small Angels. But at this point, I was too young for that, as I was too young for so many things. Every month, by moonlight, my grandparents, father, and sisters would walk to the church, singing a song I didn't know, and wait the night out there. When I was very small, Nan would stay with me, but once I was six or seven, it was judged that I could manage well enough in the house alone. I'd be sent to bed early, barricading myself into my bedroom against Blanch Farm's emptiness. Then I'd be left with nothing to do but listen as the church bells rang—chiming through the silent village streets, through the paths of Mockbeggar. There was a challenge in the music. It sounded like *come and get us.* In the village, Ruby told me once, they used to hear it and lock their doors.

Can you blame me for getting curious? I wanted to join the procession, I wanted a candle of my own. I wanted to sit with my sisters at breakfast the next day, tired but full of satisfaction, importance, knowledge of a job well done. Because it was *important,* whatever happened at Small Angels. I was sure of that.

One vigil night, I decided I was at least going to hear the song properly.

Nan had already sent me to bed, and neither she nor any of the others would have expected me to be rebellious enough to stir. They were unlikely to notice or miss me. I slipped outside with a coat thrown over my pajamas and hid in the long grass of the orchard before the others came out.

October, it must have been. The sky was clear and the moon was out, smiling down like my accomplice. I got chilly but didn't move.

At last they came out. They lit the candles and began to sing.

The tune was familiar—"Maria Marten," or pretty close—but the words were new to me. The song was a conversation. I was too far off to hear everything but I could make out a quarrel, a fight, and a terrible threat:

—your heart will feed my hungry dogs
And your eyes will feed my crow
And your blood will spill on the thirsty ground
In the woods where roses grow

I saw Elphine's face grow tight in the candlelight. The story grew bloodier, and I saw her eyes widen. I heard her voice grow fainter, like she was suffering in the telling. I didn't understand why they wouldn't stop or comfort her.

At last they got to the final verse. Now Nan's hand was on Elphine's arm, warning her. They all had to keep going.

He walks among the whispering trees
And this will ever be so
No help of ours could set him free
From the woods where roses grow

Then silence. Elphine's eyes were full of tears.

They turned and went through the orchard gate one by one, and the song began again.

I already knew that Elphine—who felt things differently and deeper than other people—should be protected at all costs. I wanted to make her happy, and fix the song for her.

I was good at tinkering with stories in those days. I had a secret game where, if a book displeased me, I would doctor the ending—add a pencil line or two after the last paragraph. *But later the wolf got better.* That sort of thing. So why shouldn't I change this song story for Elphine?

That night, barricaded in as usual, I sat up and distracted myself from the quiet by stringing words together. I made a rough new verse for the old song. And the next day, when Elphine was back, I slipped into her room to sing it to her.

First I had to tell her about my spying, though. She was troubled about that.

"Nan would be so angry," she said. "She doesn't want you knowing about all that yet—"

I cut her off. I could tell that the song upset her, I said, but I had the solution. And I began to sing:

But maybe one day things will change
And he'll be free to go
And history will be laid to rest
In the woods where roses grow

It was marvelous, to begin with. My voice wasn't as sweet as my sisters'—nothing to Elphine's—but I was singing the family song all the same. More than that, I was improving it. Shaping it like warm clay into a friendlier shape.

But Elphine stared at me as I sang, eyes wide—and when I finished I realized she was terrified. I didn't understand why until I followed her gaze to see Nan, standing in the doorway.

She hauled me to my feet, stared into my face for a couple of seconds, and then slapped me.

"You stupid girl," she said.

"I was just playing," I said, trying not to cry. The slap had taken me by surprise. "It's only a song—"

"It's life and death," she said. "You've got no idea how much it means for us. And you've got no right to meddle with it."

Worse than the slap, worse than being locked in my room for two days afterward, was the general agreement that I had brought it all on myself. I had no business spying, Nan said, and no business at all messing with that song.

No one came to see me during my imprisonment. I had thought

that my sisters might, but they sided with Nan. Even Elphine wasn't defending me.

On the first day I spent hours staring out of my window, watching afternoon turn to evening. Outside, I could see Grandpa, just visible in the dusk. He was calling the hens in. The dark of the chicken shed filled with the sound of beating wings as they jumped one by one to their perch.

Most nights it made me melancholy and happy to hear him. Now I only felt lonesome.

Ruby came outside—just a little way into the garden—and said something to him. He answered, shaking his head, and she went in again, followed soon after by Grandpa. Now it was just me and the moon.

If they thought I was bad, I'd prove them right, I decided. Through the quiet week that followed—I was in disgrace even after Nan let me out of my room, nobody talked to me any more than was strictly necessary—I racked my brains for something awful to do, something to show them all.

At last I decided I would cross the Fane, at that shallow spot with the stepping-stone. I had promised Ruby not to, but now she wouldn't stick up for me when Helena said I was an idiot and a sneaking little spy besides. So I'd cross the Fane and follow that curving path and see what was waiting there.

It took me a day or so to find my moment. But I did manage to slip away at last, late one afternoon.

I used to have a secret game that I never told my sisters. Because I had been born in Mockbeggar, I used to tell myself that the woods might like me best.

I knew it was pretense. But that afternoon I almost believed my own lie. To begin with I felt so welcome. I had been to the woods several times by that point, but never alone. There had always been someone to follow. And yet I didn't lose my way now. I found the path to the Fane like it was nothing.

But before I reached the river it had already grown darker. I was beginning to wonder whether or not I'd make it back before dusk. But I went on. Stubborn, fighting tears. It felt too late to turn back.

There's no safe place to stand in a darkening wood. Even with your back to a tree, you're not out of harm's way, not really.

I sobbed once. A small sound in the deep Mockbeggar shadow. I heard myself and I didn't sob again.

He would have been following me awhile, I think. He would have crept along in my wake, almost as soon as I'd passed the boundary of Mockbeggar. Barely visible, a dark shape between the bare branches—disappearing when you turned your head or moved.

I crossed the Fane. The stepping-stone was as convenient as I'd thought it would be.

I'd already come too far. I struggled up the bank, crushing mint underfoot. I took the narrow path, rounded the bend so the river was lost behind me.

This path was out of bounds. None of my sisters—not even Ruby, who got to do everything first—had been this way before. I wanted to run back to safety, to find them even if they were furious with me. At the same time there was a thrill to that knowledge.

In a clearing, I found a house made of briars. That's how it looked at first glance, anyway. The old stone had crumbled to almost nothing; it would have made you grieve to see it. But the briars had grown up around it so that the shape of the building—which could only have been a hovel even in its heyday—was still roughly visible.

It was very quiet. No birds there, not the buzz of an insect. The only sound was a child crying softly.

A boy was sitting on the step, his knees drawn up, his head bent so his face was hidden.

When I took a step closer he looked up at me. He was thinner than a child ought to be—so thin that in some places he didn't seem to be there at all.

"Why are you crying?" I said.

"I can't find my brother," he said. "Why are you crying?"

My tears had returned without my noticing. When I tried to explain them to him, my words came out feeble and inadequate:

"Nan's cross with me. She hit me for no reason and locked me up. Nobody told her to stop."

He seemed to understand, though. He said, "You can stay here for a while, if you like."

There was no saying no, of course, even if I'd wanted to.

CHAPTER THREE

Plastic Bag Kite

The road to Blanch Farm couldn't be trusted, not even by those who knew it well. In some places it twisted back on itself in a way that felt like pure spite. You had to watch out for deer, too, or so people still liked to warn each other.

Kate had seen a deer only once—long ago, one dark afternoon on Christmas Eve. She happened to glance through the car window at the right moment and glimpsed a doe stepping through the trees, just visible in the twilight.

Nothing else stirred in the woods. The deer moved without haste, daintily picking her way between day and night. Her eyes were big and dark and there was nothing human in them. It seemed to Kate that she had glimpsed a mystery, serious and lovely, too precious to talk about.

But it had been years now since a sighting, years since an accident. Sometimes she thought the deer were all gone.

If you followed the road out of the village, eventually you would reach a place where the trees gave way to bare fields—and there Blanch Farm would be. It was a place you were most likely to see fleetingly, from your car, while bound for somewhere else. For an instant you would spot the house—the rain-stained white walls, the red vine creeping toward the roof—and twist in your seat for another glimpse, wondering at such curious isolation.

This evening, Kate thought that ten years had changed very little. The house looked exactly as she remembered—shabby and secretive as ever, still seeming to ask the same old question: *wouldn't you like to know?*

The track to Blanch Farm bordered a field full of dandelions where, when Kate was a child, a shire horse called Hector had lived. He was awe-inspiring in his size and also in his goodness, which gave most adults a fleeting sense of shame. Looking in his eyes recalled every mean thing you had ever done.

Children felt none of this. They loved Hector and he would take mints and apples gently from their hands.

There was another horse grazing the paddock now. This was Hector son of Hector—or Hector son of Hector son of Hector, for all Kate knew—there had always been a bay horse in this field and there always would be. He belonged to John Pauncefoot and was a beloved presence at village celebrations—no fete or festival was complete without him.

Kate had brought him an apple. He took the gift without ceremony and for a while there was no noise except the sound of the core breaking under his teeth. She stroked him briefly, imagining his thoughts—slow musings on hay and sunshine—and envying them.

Brian might have retreated for this evening, but he would be back holding forth at the Albatross tomorrow or next week or a month from now, scratching at the old history like a flea bite. No matter that nobody else wanted to hear his account of how Paul Gonne's funeral had dissolved into chaos, how during the confusion the Gonnes had suffered a second tragedy. How Elphine—sweetest of the four sisters, her family's darling—had been found dead in the woods.

Everyone had speculated over the accident. They still wondered, even ten years later. But they didn't wonder aloud. The usual village discretion about Blanch Farm and its people held good. Kate herself never talked about it. She had forgotten as thoroughly as was possible. She did not think Elphine would begrudge her this means of keeping on.

Lucia crept back in, though. At work Kate still found her attention snagging on things that would interest her: a cathedral grotesque, grinning and chewing its stone fingers—or a dandelion growing at the top of an old stone wall, born from a wind-sailing seed, cheekily out of place.

So you make tombstones, Lucia would probably say. *Suits you.* And Kate would explain that it was not quite this. She was attached to an ancient cathedral in an ancient city; she and her team had been hired on a project which would take a century or so, at the least. When you restored such buildings you thought in these terms. She worked in the stoneyard or above the city, scaffolding holding her high enough to see the fields beyond the houses. Office workers on their lunch break, small beneath her feet, would look up at her with envy before hurrying back to their desks. She grew strong, she found she had a good head for heights. She watched the stone turn dark gold in the rain, pale and warm in the sun. She went to the pub with her colleagues. She was not unhappy. Sometimes the bells of the old city sounded like the bells of Small Angels, but these nerve-jangling moments would pass.

During her ten-year exile she had heard from Lucia only once or twice, by letter. The notes were short, scrawled on odd scraps of paper—usually receipts. From these, Kate gleaned a little of how Lucia was living: she was wearing a secondhand coat and silk against her skin. She was taking long bus journeys after midnight. She was buying remedies for headache and insomnia. She was spending too much on wine and not enough on food. She ate chips drowned in vinegar, cheap donuts by the bag. Sometimes Kate found traces of these meals lingering on the paper—a mark from Lucia's fingers, a faint smell of sugar and salt.

Here was the everyday strangeness of relics. Lucia had lived with these bits of paper, she had carried them in her coat pocket. Now they were with Kate.

Do you still Lucia wrote more than once—not sober, perhaps, because the question was never finished. *Could you still possibly*

It was always questions that she sent. Never an explanation, never an apology. *Do you have a garden now? Do you remember Small Angels? Have you heard from Elphine?*

Lucia might have meant to trouble Kate with that last question. Or it might have been a plea. They didn't think about the dead like normal people, the Gonnes. Perhaps Lucia had looked for Elphine and not found her.

Kate's memory of the night of Elphine's death was uncertain. As years passed, she had become more convinced it was better left alone, better not to question the old village wisdom. Anything disconcerting or dangerous—anything to do with Mockbeggar—and the refrain was always *leave it to the Gonnes. It's not our problem.* She had left the letters unanswered.

A reply would have been impossible in any case—Lucia had never included a return address. It felt like a punishment, though Kate had never been certain for whom.

Three years ago, the letters had stopped. Most likely it simply meant that Lucia had grown tired of the game. She hated to be bored, Kate reminded herself. But occasionally, at times when she was forced to be idle, she would wonder with a lurch and a rush of blood whether something might have happened. She told herself that she would know.

She had intended to avoid Blanch Farm during this visit. But Brian had raked things up, startled her into the realization that the house and its history existed outside her thoughts. For the first time in years, the place was properly real to her. Now she needed to see it again.

There was no real harm in it. Everything was over and lost now. There was nothing left to dread here anymore.

Gravel crunched behind her, and Kate turned to see that she was no longer alone at the gate. Three small girls were watching her from a few yards off. Each was pushing a pink bike. They were almost certainly sisters—oldest, middle one, youngest—descending in height like three neat steps. They all wore pink-framed glasses and had fine, pale-blond hair. To Kate they had the look of three bright-eyed white mice.

"Hello," said the youngest.

Kate nodded. They continued to stare.

"You shouldn't feed the horse," said the middle one. "Our mum says he might bite your hand."

"Well, he didn't. So."

"Did you know the old lady's dead at Blanch Farm?" said the eldest.

Kate had heard as much from her mother. Selina Gonne had remained at Blanch Farm after Elphine's death, after her surviving granddaughters moved far away. Only her son Andrew had stayed with her, and after his death she lived alone. She had grown strange, brooding on her losses. In the end, no neighbor had dared go near her. She had died alone at Blanch Farm, and her body had not been discovered for days.

Birdie never ordinarily mentioned the Gonnes to her daughter, but she had made a point of sharing this news, with a clear unspoken coda of *thank goodness.* This was the last of the Gonnes, and good riddance.

"She used to talk to herself," said the middle sister. "I heard her once. She said *come back, damn you.*"

"Liar," said the eldest.

"I *did* hear her." The middle sister was adamant. "She walked up Crockery Hill into the woods. Right through all the nettles and thorns like it was nothing. And she was talking the whole time."

"You didn't see her," said the youngest. "You're just making things *up* again—"

"What are you doing here, anyway?" Kate said, nipping the argument in the bud.

The children shared a glance, apparently considering whether or not Kate looked like the kind of adult who would spoil their plans. The final verdict was that she didn't:

"We wanted to see the house," said the eldest.

"Because it's haunted," said the youngest.

"That's why the old lady went mad there," said the middle one.

They were talking themselves up, increasingly elated with their own daring. They'd be heading down the drive in a moment, eager for a sight of the ghost or at least a relic of the old lady who'd gone mad. They would shriek and laugh at every real or imagined danger, edging closer to the house and then away, daring each other to go near enough to look through the windows. Horrors or wonders, it hardly mattered. Lucia and her sisters must have gone to Mockbeggar with the same thrill, in their time. It seemed extraordinary now to think of them roaming there alone, barely older than these three. A little wiser, perhaps, but no less open to injury—falls and drowning and a score of other harms.

"I'd keep away if I were you," she told the children—hearing her own voice like a stranger's, detestably prosaic and grown up. She was letting them down; they had assumed she was a more interesting sort of person. "Nothing at Blanch Farm but dust."

"Don't you believe in ghosts?" said the youngest sister.

Ghosts? Kate didn't believe in them any more than she believed in small talk or shoddy craftsmanship. They were a dangerous diversion from sane, ordinary life. They were history pulling at your clothes like a whining child. Telling tales: *Someone hurt me. It's not* fair. *Do something.*

"Of course not," she said. "I'm not an idiot."

"It's true, though," said the eldest sister, frowning. "At school, I heard that Blanch Farm is too close to Mockbeggar, and—"

"All rubbish. Made up to scare little kids. You're wasting your time here. Better go home."

Now she'd offended them, taken all the bloom off their adventure.

They were daring explorers no longer—just three children who would probably be grounded if their parents knew where they were.

"We've got tea soon, anyway," the eldest sister said—ostentatiously ignoring Kate, chivvying the others back the way they had come.

They took to the road with a crunch of gravel, rounding a bend and vanishing from sight and sound.

There was no one but Hector to see Kate climb the gate and jump down on the other side. No one to witness this futile trespass. Coming back would change nothing. But she was here now, and in spite of all good sense she found she needed to go closer.

The drive was almost lost in grass and dandelions. Kate trod carefully, wary of stirring up memories like the dust which coated this road in dry weather.

At the end of the drive, where the road opened into the yard bordered by empty outhouses, she stopped and confronted the house.

She stared at Blanch Farm and Blanch Farm seemed to stare back from its blank windows and think that Kate was the one who had changed most.

There were lights from Paul Gonne's funeral still hanging up in the yard. Broken crockery on the ground, along with an empty wine bottle.

Had Selina never been able to bring herself to clear the party debris away? *The old lady went mad,* one of the mouse girls had said. Kate had an image of Selina then, so clear she could almost have mistaken it for a memory: Selina sitting out here in the gathering dark, watching the lights swaying in the wind, waiting for a family who would not return.

It would have troubled Elphine to see this mess. Selina's suffering would have hurt her terribly. She couldn't witness pain without doing something to take its edge off, or finding a kind, bright thing to say. She would talk so eagerly—breathless, always, from haste and her lungs which had never quite served her as they should.

It all seemed incredible now. Kate had been here, and Lucia and the others had been here, music and wine had been poured out into the night, there had been dancing and drinking and laughter, and Elphine was still alive. She had forgotten her younger self along with the other details of that night. She had a faint idea of someone brave and anxious, full of love. There was something important she had to do, though the prospect terrified her.

Better not to dwell on it. She had spent a long time trying not to think of this past-Kate.

A red hen scratched in the yard. She paused and studied Kate with curious orange eyes, before deciding she was no threat. The two of them seemed like the only living creatures left in the world. It was so still that it felt that nothing would ever happen here again.

It was getting late. But she could not leave without rounding the side of the house, wandering through the orchard—overgrown now, fallen plums rotting in the long grass, fool's parsley growing high. She couldn't leave without seeing Mockbeggar. If only to prove to herself that it was all done with, that she was not afraid to approach the trees.

She went through the orchard. A dull-red wall kept the half-wild apple and pear trees from the fields. Beyond the gate there were plowed fields, and beyond that were the woods.

Kate remembered these fields as measured rows of vines, aisles of grass, jars of honey and vinegar hanging at intervals—bait for wasps. Now there was only soft dirt. She sank with every step like the earth wanted her.

At the edge of Mockbeggar there were silver birches. This was a safe place, a halfway house. You didn't have to keep your wits about you here like you did in the woods proper. There were ferns and grass underfoot, foxgloves here and there.

The woods were not as they had been. Even from the field she could tell that. There had been an outrageous quality to Mockbeggar's blooming life, back in the old days. The colors of the leaves and flowers had had a rich, concentrated quality. Now the light was nothing special. The magic of the place was gone now, lost like Elphine.

Everything miraculous—both good and bad—had been stamped out long ago.

Still, Kate wondered, stupidly hopeful and stupidly fearful, if something might not have returned all the same. What if she were to go a little way down the path? Might she be able to sense the romance, the story magic, the terrible buried malice once more?

She had taken three cautious paces through the trees—enough for the silver birches to start to hide the view of the fields behind her—when she heard a crash, then the sound of a curse. And there was Lucia, only a few yards off, only now visible through the trees—a flicker of red among all the green. A small flame dancing at the edge of Kate's quiet world.

No good reason for Lucia to be there and yet there she was, slashing at one of the silver birches with a fallen branch. There was something white and fluttering caught in the tree above her, and she was vainly trying to free it.

The thing in the tree was a plastic bag, handles tied with red string and silver tinsel. Elphine's kite.

It should not have been possible. But Kate had made the kite herself, she recognized her own handiwork. Even now, with Mockbeggar dead or diminished, unlikely things could still happen here.

Lucia's branch snapped and she turned around, panting slightly. Her face was pale and still, her eyes glittered. She wore a red summer dress and her bare legs and shoulders were scratched—the branches had left marks like fingernail scrapes. Her boots were muddy, and there were dead leaves in her hair.

Kate remembered now that she had always loved red. Selina had favored browns and grays for her granddaughters' clothes—rabbit colors, hen pheasant colors, tones that blended in among the earth and corn. Lucia had always resented the enforced drabness. She had stolen a red jumper from Kate once and Kate had pretended not to know because she had liked to think of Lucia wearing it.

Seeing her felt like standing up so fast the world went dark at the edges. There were so many small things Kate had missed—the freckles on her arms and shoulders, her quick, humorous, hungry look. She had aged since their last meeting, and it suited her. There was a line where that uneven smile used to twist her mouth.

Kate reached down and picked up a stone.

"It won't—" Lucia began, but Kate threw before she could finish and the kite was knocked out of the tree like a shot bird.

Lucia picked it up. She put a hand to her chest—her hand clawed as if she were clutching something back—a word, a sob. It was the same kite without a doubt. Some of the blue-painted lettering remained. Half of Elphine's name was left. She had been so delighted with the simple gift. But then joy had come easily to her, it had been one of her gifts.

"You remember?" Lucia's voice was rough, like she'd been screaming.

"Elphine's."

Again she marveled at it. Ten years since that day. And the kite had been so thoroughly lost.

Lucia folded the kite carefully again and again, as if she could fold it entirely out of existence. As she did so, Kate got a closer view of her hands—bitten fingernails, grazed palms.

"What happened?"

"You saw. I fought a tree and the tree won." She licked the blood away.

"You should clean those properly. Looks nasty."

Years ago, Kate would have seized her wrists and raised the injuries to the light. (*What the hell did you do to yourself? Sit down, I'll get a plaster.*) She could see the same thought in Lucia's face.

"You shouldn't be here," Lucia said. "You know the rules."

She and her sisters had taught Kate so earnestly: *These are the things you have to know to keep yourself safe. Here are our remedies, here are our secrets.*

They didn't tell her every secret, of course.

"Story-rules," Kate said now (as if the kite was not there in Lucia's hands, giving the lie to this). "Superstition."

"Do you believe yourself when you tell it like that?" Lucia said.

Without warning she reached out and touched Kate's throat just above her collar, gently tracing the scars there—those delicate marks which had grown almost too faint to see.

Kate caught her wrist—quick but not brutal—and pushed her away.

Lucia took a step backward, breath unsteady. They had played around like this a long time ago, a game that was not quite a game. For an instant Kate caught her thoughts the way she used to do—she was thinking *good* and she was thinking *can't*, she was angry with both of them.

"Do you forget about them most of the time?" Lucia said, retreating into spite. "I suppose you must. Then someone notices—you're with some girl and she sees them and says *oh you poor thing, what happened* and you say *I fell through a window*. Or some other stupid fabrication. It must be exhausting; you never were much good at lying. But I suppose it's more comfortable in the long run."

It had never been about comfort. It had been about making a life that was tolerable and sane. After Elphine's death, Kate lost her taste for the incredible. She had lived quietly and worked hard to mistrust herself. Pain and fear had wiped out most of the details of her last night in Mockbeggar. As for the rest, she had invited doubts in and let them gnaw at her memories like mice running riot in an attic.

Lucia might understand some of this if she had talked to Kate properly after the night of Elphine's death—if she hadn't fled the village immediately afterward without a word to her.

She stood expectant now, eyes glittering. She was spoiling for a fight; she wanted Kate to lose her temper. But under her fierceness she seemed as desolate as Blanch Farm. She smelled of smoke and alcohol, sweat and earth.

"Are you all right?" Kate said.

Lucia scowled. "I'm doing fine. Don't judge my life and I won't judge yours."

"I'm not," Kate said, biting back anger. "I don't."

Even after so long, Lucia should know her better.

Lucia wiped her hands, still bleeding, on her red dress, and looked away from Kate—through the trees, as if someone was standing there, listening.

"Why did you come back, Kate?" she said.

As if Kate needed to explain herself. But she did want Lucia to know that it was not her own choice to return, and she had not come to Blanch Farm in search of her.

"It's Sam's wedding this weekend," she said.

Lucia looked surprised. Kate guessed the many questions that she wanted to ask. But when she spoke, she said:

"You said you liked me best, once. Better than anyone, you said. Remember?"

Of course she had it by heart. Kate said nothing.

"If there's a crumb of that left, then do me a kindness and stay away from here."

She was probably right. It had been a mistake to come here. Seeing her had brought memories flocking back like birds returning to nest. Lucia had never allowed her much in the way of peace and ease. She had changed the world at one time, troubling Kate's understanding of what was possible and what was not. No surprise, really, that she had that same knack still.

"Good luck, then," Kate said.

She turned away from the woods and retraced her steps down the field, feet sinking deeper into the soft mud. The night was coming on now, the cold too. It was almost dusk. She had stayed here too long.

She stopped halfway down the field and looked back. Lucia was gone.

CHAPTER FOUR

Harry Child's Dogs

Selina tells a ghost story

These are the dreg days now. Me and the year both past our best. The last of the fruit is rotting in the orchard. The birds have robbed the pear trees and the wasps have sotted themselves on spoiled plums. Now it's almost winter and soon I'll be carried out of here, dead or alive.

Not yet, though. Not tonight. The doors are locked and Blanch Farm is mine for a short while longer.

My silent domain. This kitchen was so full of noise at one time. Even now I seem to hear them upstairs, running up and down the corridors, calling to one another, just too distant for me to make out the words.

A long time ago I told Lucia:

"If you get lost, you get lost. No good making a song and dance about it. Just turn around and head back to the start. Step by step. Work it out."

In the days when I can't stir from my chair without staggering like a drunk, I tell myself the same thing: head back to the start. I sit and try and work out how we got from there to here. I retrace my steps to find the first one that went wrong.

We were at the edge of Mockbeggar when I gave Lucia that bit of advice. It was just her and me and the darkening woods ahead.

I'd known she was one to keep an eye on, even before that business with Harry's song. None of the others would have shown such disrespect, to go fooling around with the ending.

I said to Paul it was only to be expected, really. Look how she was born.

Paul said that nobody can help how they come into the world. As if that was the point. The point was she was born in the woods and she was born hungry. Her questions came earlier than her sisters' and there were more of them—why are the woods like they are, what do you do on moonlit nights at Small Angels, why do you ring the church bells? She asked like she had a right to know.

I remember one of our vigil nights. Our work on those evenings was second nature—the song and the lights and the long silent waiting at Small Angels. Still, those were always anxious times. That night the others were at the church but I'd stayed behind because Lucia was still too young to be left. I went up to the attic after they were gone, looked out of the window, over the fields to the church. Keeping an eye out for him, like always. It was clear and frosty that night, so cold even the moon seemed frozen.

Then there was Lucia pulling at my skirt, wanting me to lift her up and show her Small Angels with its lights shining, show her where the bell chimes were coming from. Excited like there was some treat to be had. No fear in her.

I lifted her up so she could see. I remember the solid weight of her. Five years old by then. Wearing Ruby's old pajamas, legs rolled up. I let her stare her fill and I didn't tell her that there was any danger in it, though I should have done.

When she was old enough to go to the woods, she got even hungrier. When it came to Mockbeggar, she could never have enough. She never got sick of the place, and it never seemed to get the better of her.

Every so often, the woods would get too much for the other three. They'd come back and their play would be hanging around them like fog. Something frightening in the story would have taken over and wouldn't leave them alone. They'd come home sick and dizzy, not quite sure what was real. Voices in their minds, talking and singing.

On those occasions I treated them with the same remedies people always used with Mockbeggar, the ones I picked up from Paul: bicarbonate of soda to wash the woods out of their hair. Mint tea to wash it out of their mouths and throats. A good story—something old and familiar—to steady their thoughts. Sometimes a knife under the bed as they slept, to keep their dreams safe.

They'd be peaky and miserable for a day or so, but it was just the way of the woods. It happened to all of them—but not to Lucia.

I don't mean that Mockbeggar was always kind to her. She'd come home scratched, bruised, wet to the knee, but she wouldn't seem to notice till one of us pointed it out. Then she'd just say *oh, that,* and shrug. Small smile. Like it was a joke between her and the woods. That sly look never sat right with me.

All the same she made me remember how I felt about Mockbeggar, when I first came here. The woods knew me and I knew them. And I loved them straight off, like I'd never loved anything or anyone before. I saw something like that in Lucia.

It might come in useful, I thought. When I was too old to manage, someone else would have to be ready to keep an eye out for Harry Child and make sure we were still in his good books. Maybe have a word with him if needs be.

Andrew would be no use, of course. Ruby and Helena were handy enough in most vineyard work—damn sight more help than Lucia—but not for this. As far as Elphine went . . . Well. It was never her job to be useful. None of us ever expected that of her.

But Lucia might be trained up, I thought. Though whatever knack or affinity for the woods she had needed to be kept in check. She was ignorant and full of herself where she should have been humble and cautious. So I decided it was time for her to know everything there was to know, including the price for stepping out of line. I decided to tell her earlier than the other three, and more directly. I brought her to Mockbeggar at dusk.

It was autumn then—late October, after the harvest. It had been raining all day, but the sky cleared as the sun went down. Paul had lit the beacons early, glad to get it done with and back indoors.

He never did appreciate the woods like I did. He never would notice that a downpour brings extra life to Mockbeggar. After the rain the trees are dark, the green pools deep in the woods are brimming, and the nettles are dripping under the weight of water. Even after the sky has cleared, the woods have their own rain. Whenever the breeze shakes the branches tiny showers fall from the leaves.

It was the same way the first time I came to the woods alone. All around me things were drinking, growing, all so strong and green. Gloss of rain on the leaves, moss bright under my feet. No sound but the breeze and the water pattering around me. I hadn't known there were places like this in the world. I hadn't known a way of living that wasn't drab and fearful. But in the woods in that instant I knew that other things were possible, and I couldn't ever go back to how I'd lived before.

I didn't usually let the girls in the woods so late. Lucia had heard my warnings. I could see her wondering whether or not to ask me what it meant—curious but not wanting to push her luck.

The moon was just rising. Mockbeggar was all shadows, pale light coming in faint through the branches, making odd shapes on the ground.

"I suppose you're wondering why we're out here at this time of night," I said. "Well, it's not a pleasure outing. You're here to learn."

Lucia jumped a splash of moonlight like it was a puddle. No fear to be seen, I thought, proud and irritated. I pulled her back closer to me, clutching her shoulder tight to keep her safe and hard enough to bruise.

"We go carefully in these woods. Remember that."

"I'm all right in Mockbeggar," she said. "I was *born* here, Nan."

"You were only born here because your mother was fool enough to put you both in harm's way for no reason," I said. "No call to think yourself special over *that.* If you don't keep in line you'll come to a bad end, same as anyone else."

I always had a knack for stories. Just as well, considering how many I had to tell as a child to people chasing my father for money (he'd pay them back soon, he was out and I didn't know when he'd be home). At Blanch Farm, there was one story that was the most important of all. I'd told it different ways in the past—sometimes better than I did that night, sometimes worse, sometimes more or less dreadful. For Lucia I told it like this:

"You know already that the trees of Mockbeggar love stories. You've seen how they get with those plays you and your sisters put on. That's the gift of Mockbeggar. That's the joy and wonder of this place.

"There are times when the woods take a special liking to a story. They brood over it and keep the memory close. That's how it was with Harry Child."

I saw her guilty look. She knew the name, of course.

"He's the one we ring the bells for every month," I said. "I suppose you've probably guessed that much already. Given all the eavesdropping you've been doing lately."

"I wasn't being bad on *purpose*. I just wanted to know."

"Well, after tonight you'll know. And I wish you joy of it. You'll have the bells of Small Angels with you all your life. The bells have to be rung every month without fail. They mean we're still here. They mean we remember, and we're sorry for what happened to Harry Child."

"What happened to him?"

"I'll get to that. First I need to tell you about Mockbeggar."

The path was narrowing, there was less light now. She wouldn't have been this way before. The ferns were high on either side of us, brambles running across the track, but I knew the way well enough not to falter. I waited for her to fall behind and call for me to slow down, but she kept up. Still that glitter to her, like we were off to the circus.

"Mockbeggar remembers a lot of things," I said. "Some of the stories it likes are strange true things that had happened—"

"Like what?"

"Well, the widow's goose, for one."

I looked back at her and she was smiling to herself. Laughing at the idea of a goose spirit, I thought at the time. Cheeky and full of herself as ever.

But I wonder now if it was because she'd heard that tale before.

"You can wipe that smirk off your face, Miss Lucia," I said to her. "It's a true story. Three hundred years ago, a widow in the village had her cottage go on fire one night. She'd have been burned up like dry grass, only she had this goose that was her pride and joy. She was afraid it might get stolen, so she used to let it sleep in the cottage with her. The night of the fire, the goose woke her up and saved her. Afterward, the widow would lead the goose about the village on a blue ribbon and people would come and look. She fed it dandelions and soft bread every day. When it died, she took the story to the trees, and the trees listened. Now you'll still see that goose every so often in Mockbeggar. Dead and still walking. It's given people a scare before now. But there's not much harm in it. Which is more than you can say for some."

"Like Harry Child."

I wondered if she'd noticed how the hush of the woods deepened when she said that name.

I wondered if she'd noticed that the trees were thicker here, hiding the moon. I had a torch but hadn't switched it on, I was waiting for her to ask me for more light.

"He isn't like the others," I said. "He doesn't just pass through Mockbeggar's memory from time to time. He's the one the woods love. He's the one they'll never let go.

"Two hundred years ago, give or take, a family called Hart lived at Blanch Farm. Your grandfather's ancestors, though the name's different. They were rich and they were happy. People thought well of them, they were the leaders of this village. They walked in the woods when they chose, and Mockbeggar welcomed them. They'd bring back firewood, baskets of blackberries and hazelnuts. They lived well, they were pleased with themselves.

"At the edge of Mockbeggar, bordering the Fane—far off from any other building, as far away from Blanch Farm as Blanch Farm is from the village—there was a tiny cottage."

She looked sharply at me and started to say something and then tripped, feet snarled up in the briars. I had to stop and help her up.

"Keep your eyes open," I said.

She nodded. Mud splashed across her forehead. Didn't seem hurt, just surprised, so I carried on:

"The cottage by the Fane wasn't much, but it went with Blanch Farm and so the Harts had possession, they could let it to whoever they wanted. Two hundred years ago, Harry Child lived there with his mother and sisters and brothers."

"Where was his dad?"

"Traveling. He was a ballad-seller, went up and down the country selling his songs at village fairs. You never knew when he was going to turn up next. Eventually he stopped turning up at all. The family had been poor before, but now things got desperate. The mother worked here and there—on the land, or taking in washing—and sometimes she poached. The oldest boy got taken on by local farms, a couple of the girls went into service. But there were too many of them, and never enough to eat. Every morning, Harry's mother would push the kids out of the house and tell them not to be back until dark.

"There should have been charity from the village. But people didn't care for Harry's family. Nothing respectable about them—and the worst of it was that none of the Childs seemed to care. Only Mr. Hart—the master at Blanch Farm—ever took an interest. Once or twice he came across Harry's mother with wire under her cloak and a dead rabbit or two under her skirts, and he let her go without having her prosecuted for poaching.

"That was as far as the village's kindness went. The family had a hard time of it, and Harry had it worst of all. He wasn't big enough to keep up with his brothers and sisters, and often they left him behind. Some days he'd find something to eat—blackberries or hazelnuts or wild raspberries—and some days he starved. All the while the woods watched him. I think they wanted to know what would happen next.

"At first he couldn't talk much—he was very young and nobody in the little cottage troubled teaching him—and when he did start to speak, the woods were the ones who listened. He said the names of his brothers and sisters. He told them little stories: *Harry fell, Mama gone.* And the trees listened and loved him because he was growing up in front of their eyes."

"What was he like?"

"How do you mean?"

"When he was a kid, my age. What was he like?"

"What do you want to know that for? All you need to know is that he loved the woods as much as they loved him. He was always off wandering these paths, he stopped caring about getting into trouble for being away too long. When he got older his mother got him a job crow-scaring in one of the Harts' fields. But often they'd find out that he'd wandered off, and no punishment seemed to teach him sense.

"One day, Mr. Hart's foreman noticed him trying to slip off and took him by the scruff of the neck to give him a good hiding—"

"What?" This, of all things, seemed to upset her. "You mean *hitting* him?"

"They were cruel times. That's beside the point, though. Harry was getting his beating when Mr. Hart—the farmer, the master—stopped by and asked the foreman what was going on. And when he saw Harry he couldn't stop staring, because Harry was so like his own son, Fred.

"The next evening he called round to see Harry's mother and the two of them talked awhile. The upshot was that he took Harry away with him, back to Blanch Farm."

"Why?"

"He was pretty sure that he was Harry's father. So he had a right to him."

"Didn't Harry's mother mind?"

"Why would she? One less kid to feed. He'd get three meals a day and a bed of his own. It was the best thing for everyone. Everyone thought that except Harry.

"He was miserable at Blanch Farm. It felt far from everything familiar. They wouldn't let him go to the woods. He knew the Harts had taken him on out of duty, not love. Mrs. Hart had no use for him. Fred didn't like him either: what was this cuckoo-child thinking, showing up at Fred's home and wearing his old clothes? How dare he?

"Mockbeggar grieved for Harry. For a month after Harry was taken away, the village had no rain. But Mockbeggar stayed lush and green. It was like the trees were draining water from the soil and sky all around.

"Mr. Hart didn't know what to do. He had parched fields, and a crying child upstairs. Harry was wretched, wouldn't talk, wouldn't eat. Stared out the window every chance he got, up toward Mockbeggar.

"The mood of this place changed. Anger and sadness wrapped around you whenever you stepped into the woods. Mockbeggar had never been like that before, not in anyone's memory. It stopped feeling safe."

I paused and looked at her. We were nearly at the Fane by that time.

"You paying attention?" I said.

She nodded.

"Messing around with the way things are meant to be never does any good. Mr. Hart learned that the hard way.

"It was his son, Fred, who found the remedy at last. Not that he set out to do that. Harry got too weak to stir out of bed—sadness and no eating and drinking made him ill—and one day Fred slipped in planning to tell him to stop making so much trouble for everybody.

"But when he saw Harry, white and miserable, he felt a touch of pity for him.

"*What are you making such a fuss about?* he said to him. Not as harshly as he'd planned. *Why don't you eat and sleep like a sensible creature?*

"*I can't,* Harry said.

"Is *it your family? Do you miss them?*

"Harry shook his head. *It's the woods.*

"Fred didn't really understand, so Harry explained it to him. The way you could live in Mockbeggar. How it tinted the whole world, made it feel like there were wonderful, strange things always lurking at the edges of your vision. Deep mystery just out of sight. He missed the trees bitterly, and they missed him.

"*You'd better go back to the woods, then,* Fred said. *Have a visit.*

"*Mr. Hart won't let me,* Harry said. (He still couldn't call his father by any other name.)

"*I'll manage* him, said Fred. *You can go back, and stop this stupid wasting away. And I'll come with you and see if it's as wonderful as you claim.*

"So they went back. The woods saw Harry, and it settled them, and he got well again. And Fred saw that the woods were just as Harry described them. He saw the little cottage in a clearing where Harry's family lived, where dog roses grew high even then.

"After that they went back again and again. They played there like you and your sisters do. Only I suppose it was even better for them.

You always saw something special if you went to the woods with Harry. They never forgot he'd been born here."

"Like me."

No doubt she said that to annoy me. At least partly. But the note in her voice was strange, wondering. It was too dark now to see her expression.

"Not like you at all," I said. "You already know that. The woods never loved anyone like Harry Child. They loved him more than the peace and happiness of the village, more than the peace and happiness of Harry himself. That's the way these woods love.

"In the woods, Harry was always the most important. But at Blanch Farm he was a duty and a burden. Mr. and Mrs. Hart put up with him, gave him a little bit of schooling—enough to make himself useful to Fred later. There was some talk of him working as Fred's foreman when they were both grown up. But he never had the expensive teaching Fred had. Mr. Hart sent Fred away for a year to study farming, and when he came back he was a young gentleman with a good horse and three pure-white, pure-bred dogs to run alongside him whenever he rode out. They were bull-baiting dogs—"

"What're those?"

"In Fred and Harry's day, people would sometimes set a pack of dogs on a bull. Just for the fun of it, you understand. Entertainment. You'd need a fierce animal to take on a bull. Good strong jaws. Fred's dogs were that kind.

"At first people were happy to see Fred back in the village. But slowly his old friends found he was different. He'd turned into the kind of person who likes it when you're afraid of them. The dogs went with him everywhere. Nasty things. Only Fred could do anything with them.

"Harry didn't care at first. He was just glad to have his friend back. He'd been lonely while Fred was away. The rest of his family had left years before. They didn't tell Harry where they were going, and after they'd left the cottage stayed empty. No one liked to take it on.

"Harry wrote and told Fred all about it, and Fred told him not to be sad. When they were older he'd give Harry the house to live in and the two of them would always be companions, their children would marry and live here for generations and generations.

"So Harry didn't pay any mind to the rumors and the changes in Fred at first. If people said Fred had got proud and his temper had turned mean, Harry would defend him. When they went to the Albatross, people would sit by Fred as long as Harry was there too, leading the singing. He had a lot of songs, Harry—his only inheritance from the ballad seller. He had a voice that could take you out of yourself. Whilst he sang, people forgot to resent Fred.

"The thing was, Fred saw that people liked Harry better than him. It didn't sit well with him. *He* was the finest young man in the village, the richest, the son of Mr. Hart. *He* was the one they should envy. He didn't like how easy Harry was in the woods, either. Fred was the real son, not the charity case. The woods should love *him* best, he thought.

"He was doing well in the world—he had a fiancée who was a rich factory-owner's only daughter, who dressed better than any of the other women in the village. But when Harry was with him, somehow none of that seemed to matter.

"When Fred looked at Harry he saw a kind of thinking about life that was different to his own, thinking in which Fred Hart didn't look so terribly lucky or important after all, where there was nothing that mattered more than Mockbeggar.

"When Fred introduced Harry to his rich and handsome fiancée, Harry was charming with her. But when Fred said, *I hope you'll be as lucky yourself one day*, Harry only laughed. He didn't want Fred's life, though he wished him joy of it. At the fiancée's request he sang a song—one of the ballad seller's—before he left, and when he was gone he seemed to take something bright away with him and leave their lives a bit drabber and more ordinary by contrast.

"Harry wouldn't envy Fred like Fred wanted, and he wasn't afraid of him either. When Fred bullied or frightened people in the village—

let his dogs hassle them, or made himself disagreeable on account of his money—Harry would always be there to tell him he was forgetting himself, to stand between Fred and his victim. It started to get on Fred's nerves.

"So it wasn't one big thing that made Fred resentful. It was dislike made of dozens of small grains, building up slowly, like dust. He felt less and less friendship for his brother. And Harry knew it.

"The next thing that happened was that Fred Hart's parents died unexpectedly. Fred took over Blanch Farm and Harry's childhood home.

"In spite of the new coldness between them, Harry still thought that the Rose House would be his. A promise is a promise. Maybe he told himself that this was the moment when they could be properly brothers again.

"But Fred announced that he was going to have the cottage pulled down. There wouldn't be a stone left to show the place where Harry had been a boy, where the woods had first found him and where he had last heard his mother's voice.

"They argued over it, and their words got ugly. Fred said that he didn't want Harry showing his face anywhere near Blanch Farm again. He turned him out of his place with nothing.

"*What will happen to me? What will I do?* Harry said, and Fred said that he wasn't Harry's keeper. He could starve for all Fred cared.

"So Harry left, and for weeks afterward nobody saw a trace of him. Fred was too busy to think of him much; he had to prepare for his wedding, which was happening at Small Angels. But every so often Fred wondered if Harry might not come to the wedding in spite of everything.

"They'd planned it all, you see, back when they were friends. Harry was going to be groomsman, the most important guest after Fred's parents and his new in-laws.

"It got closer and closer to the wedding. *I don't care where he is,* Fred took to saying.

"*It's clear that you do,* his fiancée said.

"*He'd better not come back here, that's all,* Fred said. *If he shows his face at the wedding, I'll horsewhip him. I'll set my dogs on him.*

"His fiancée raised her eyebrows but didn't look impressed. And in spite of all he'd said, when Fred thought of his wedding day—the bells pealing, his pretty bride on his arm—he couldn't imagine it without Harry there with him, the way they had planned it. It could still have been like that, he thought, if Harry had only known his place and hadn't gone and spoiled things. A bit of awe and envy was all he wanted—was that too much to ask from the family charity case?

"On the eve of the wedding, Fred set out on a walk. He took his dogs with him for company, and he went as far as the little cottage in the woods. There were flowers growing that evening—dog roses, which he remembered Harry saying his mother had always liked.

"And Harry was there, like he'd been waiting for Fred.

"First they looked at each other, and at the house, which was already falling down, neglected.

"*Are you going to warn me off?* Harry asked.

"*No,* Fred said.

"They paused and Fred might have said something then. Maybe he would have apologized. The wedding the following day had made him miss Harry more than before.

"*Tomorrow*—he began.

But Harry was looking at the house. The ruin Fred had made of his childhood.

"*Don't trouble yourself,* he said. *I'll be away from here by then. You can keep the affair respectable for all your new relations.*

"He said *respectable* and it sounded like an insult to Fred. He saw then that Harry would never envy him, and as long as Harry cast eyes on his life, there would always be one person who didn't think Fred Hart was a fine, enviable fellow.

"Fred told him that he was to stay away from the cottage from now on. Harry said he'd do what he liked.

"By that point, Fred wasn't used to being defied. Wasn't used to putting any curb on his temper, either. He called his dogs.

"Harry knew he wasn't joking. He fled through the woods, all the way to Small Angels. He locked himself in. The dogs raked at the door with their claws—you can see the marks even now—but the door didn't budge.

"Harry and Fred paused then, one on either side of the door. They could hear each other breathing, the way they used to when they were children, sharing the same bedroom when storms stopped them sleeping.

"At last Fred said, *I'm sorry. I didn't want it to happen like this. I wanted . . .*

"He hesitated, and Harry didn't say anything. The dogs were silent too.

"*I wanted us as we were. Soldiers, travelers, brigands. Remember that? Us, in the woods? The games that were real?*

"I think he meant it. At least partly. He was remembering the stories he and Harry had made up, before Fred decided he had other things to think about.

"*Please open the door*, he said."

I heard Lucia draw her breath in sharply. Afraid at last. The dark of Mockbeggar made it seem closer. And she knew what was coming, of course. No way of avoiding the end to this story.

"Harry believed him," she said softly.

"He did. And he opened the door.

"Maybe Fred meant to do one thing, and maybe he meant to do another. There was a moment when he might have just walked away. But there was Small Angels behind Fred, ready for Fred's day of triumph—and there was Harry, who took the zest out of all the fear and envy Fred inspired in the village. And the dogs were there, eager for the command.

"Fred said a word, maybe half a word. That's all it took.

"The dogs sprang at Harry, and by the time Fred had called them off it was too late. The dogs ripped his throat out as he begged Fred to save him. No breath, no voice left to plead after that. They tore at him, scattered his blood over the earth of Small Angels graveyard, over Fred Hart's fields, over Mockbeggar.

"Fred buried Harry Child as best he could. Found a secret place near the woods and hid his body in the earth.

"The next day, the wedding took place as planned. People noticed how strange Fred Hart looked—sick like he'd been poisoned. There was still no sign of Harry Child. People talked about that, too.

"The bells rang out like they always did, though—over the village and the countryside, peals you'd hear anywhere. Even underground you might hear them. Harry Child, murdered and hidden, heard the chimes, the happy din above him.

"There was a time of quiet after the wedding. Fred and his new wife lived contentedly enough at Blanch Farm, to all appearances. Then came a night of heavy rain. Washed a lot of soil away. The afternoon of the next day, Fred Hart's wife was sitting on the front step doing some sewing. There was one of Fred's dogs that she could just about stand—the smallest of the three. Sometimes Fred, joking, called it the runt. The dog had something in its mouth. The girl called it over, and it dropped a human ear into her lap."

"What did she do?"

"She buried it near the pigsty and didn't say a word to anyone."

"How do you know what she did if she didn't tell anyone?"

"Tradition."

I don't think it's a case of embroidering. I think the business with the ear really happened. It'd be like Paul's family. Every time I tell the story I see Fred Hart's wife (nobody seems to remember her name) scrabbling in the mud and filth near the pigsty, looking over her shoulder every other second.

I pressed on—the journey was nearly over, I'd have to be quick:

"Not long after that, somebody found Harry's hat at the edge of Mockbeggar, covered in blood. They searched the woods for him and found remains. Enough to call the village constable.

"People talked over what had happened. *Did you hear, did you hear,* walking up and down the road out of the village. They talked it over as they walked past Mockbeggar, and the trees heard what had happened to the child they loved.

"In the ruined cottage, roses started growing. Dog roses, a fine tree springing up strangely fast. Mockbeggar remembered and remembered and planted Harry's story at the very heart of the tree. And there was a sweet scent to them, though that sort of rose shouldn't smell at all. No one had ever seen the like. Strange, people said in the village. Bad business all round.

"Of course they guessed who must be to blame. Fred tried to run, but it was too late. The constable and some of the village men hunted him across his own fields, caught him and dragged him back to the Albatross, blood and mud all over his face.

"There were some in the village who might have been happy to skip the trial and go straight to execution. But the constable said he should be taken to town to be tried properly. It was late evening now and there were people outside the pub—it looked like a fight might break out—so they decided it was safest to keep him in the Albatross overnight and take him away at daybreak."

"What happened to the dogs?"

"They were shot."

"Even the runty one?"

"All of them. They might not have been able to punish Fred Hart straight off, but his dogs were the next best thing. They say that Fred heard the shots from the Albatross.

"After that they cuffed Fred to a bed upstairs so he couldn't escape, and set the constable to watch him until morning.

"In the night, Fred Hart woke up screaming—he sounded like he was being burned alive, the constable said later—and begging them to send Harry Child away, back to Mockbeggar. *He's outside now,* he kept saying. *He's come out of the woods. Can't you see him?*

"Fred said they could hang him or do whatever they wanted to him as long as they didn't let Harry in. They promised to keep Harry away, but it didn't settle Fred much.

"Next morning, when they set off in the carriage to town, it was as stormy and dark a day as anyone had ever seen. Fred kept trying to make them *promise* that he'd be hanged. That upset them all, even the constable. Given the choice they'd rather have hanged someone unwilling.

"They were on the road away from the village—the one that runs through Mockbeggar—"

"The one I was born on?"

"I suppose. Don't interrupt. Just as they were going through the thickest part of the wood, something ran out into the road and terrified the horses. Carriage went over and smashed. When the commotion was over, Fred Hart was gone.

"When they found Fred at last, it turned out that he'd been hanged after all, in a way. He was strung up among the dog roses close to the Rose House. Briars tight around his neck, like a noose. They had no end of trouble cutting him down."

"Was it Harry Child?"

"Who else would it have been? After that Fred Hart's wife left the village and things seemed to go quiet for a bit. People said to themselves—well, Harry's had his revenge. Maybe that'll be an end of it. But it wasn't. Harry wasn't gone.

"He was still angry, people realized. Someone would walk through the fields and come back with Mockbeggar dirt on their shoes and the next thing you'd know they'd be dreaming: Harry's pain, Harry's fate—or Fred's. They'd choke with a noose of briars; they'd feel their flesh torn and their face covered with dirt. Mouth full of earth so they couldn't breathe. The nightmares got worse—they took over people's waking lives, too.

"Harry took an interest in those who were celebrating. Maybe happy voices put him in mind of Fred Hart's wedding. He'd trail laborers out of the fields to their harvest supper. He followed at the heels of carol singers. He liked weddings and christenings above all. If there were people gathered for a party it might be that someone would see a shadow pass across the window, and later one of the guests would find horrors taking over. People found themselves choking as if something had pulled tight around their throats, or as if their mouths were full of earth. Several people didn't recover. Small wonder.

"Things got worse still. There was barking heard from Mockbeggar most nights. People began to see white dogs running between the trees in the distance—Fred Hart's dogs. Harry Child's dogs now, people said.

"Nothing but shadows, they told each other. But they were shadows with sharp teeth. There was a man—prosperous sort, not long married—chased from one end of the woods to the other, and when they found him at last he was dead of exhaustion and fear, and bitten to the quick on both hands, like he'd been fending something off.

"After that, the village put their heads together. He's angry, he wants his revenge still, they thought. Maybe, waking up the way he did, he doesn't know how to want anything else. Taking Fred Hart hasn't brought him peace.

"They decided to find a scapegoat. Fred's family were the next best thing to Fred himself. If Harry had them in his power, maybe he'd leave the rest of the village alone."

We were at the riverbank now. The moonlight showed the stepping-stone halfway across the gleaming black water. Easy crossing, even by night.

The bank was steep and overgrown, but Lucia didn't hesitate to follow me, I'll give her that. She struggled but she didn't complain.

On the other side of the river I saw her notice it—the smell of the roses. They didn't bloom out of season often, but when they did it was something to witness. Almost too sweet to stand.

At the top of the bank, we stopped. Thorns up ahead. You might think the path led nowhere.

"So they brought the Harts back," I said. "Fred Hart's wife was far away from the village by this time—she had sense enough not to stick around—and she had a little baby. Fred Hart's son, Harry Child's nephew. A group of men from the village tracked her down, and one day without warning they took the baby away with them.

"Fred Hart's wife came after them, frantic. They told her she would have her child back safe as long as she returned to Blanch Farm. If the family stayed there forever.

"So she said all right. I suppose she thought she'd make a run for it later, once the villagers had relaxed their guard. But by then it was too late. Harry knew she was back at Blanch Farm, with Fred Hart's son. He let the village alone now; all his thought was for them. He wouldn't let them get away a second time.

"They were his people. His family, and his murderer's family. His victim's family, too, I suppose. If you think what was done to Fred Hart counts as murder. In any case it was complicated, what he felt for the Harts. He wanted them wretched but he wanted them close by. He hated them but he craved their company. He was unhappy and he needed people here, and he wanted his blood. You understand?"

Lucia nodded. Quiet for once.

"In the village, people used to say that things would end badly before too long. Sooner or later, there would be no more sights of Fred Hart's wife nursing her child, wandering up and down the road to Blanch Farm. Harry wouldn't be able to help himself. In a month or a year he'd lose patience and he'd take them, and then there'd be no company left for him. And what would happen to the villagers then?

"But it didn't happen like that. Instead, there was an arrangement made.

"The story doesn't say how they reached their agreement. Maybe Harry crept close to the house one evening. Maybe Mrs. Hart left her child sleeping and went through the orchard and out into the fields to talk to him. Maybe she offered him something. Mourning, penance. The family would pay tribute to him forever, and in return he would let them keep their lives and leave the village alone.

"I think that's how it happened. Harry listened, and he agreed.

"Then Mrs. Hart invited a brother and a sister of hers to move into Blanch Farm. She filled the house with her family, and she set them to work—on the land, but in other places too. There were beacons set up at the corners of Blanch Farm's land, and they were lit every night as a memorial for Harry. The family visited Small Angels once a month to show him that they still remembered, they were sorry for what Fred had done.

"Sometimes they'd hear him come to the church door, listening. But usually he left them alone. If he harmed them too thoroughly he'd have no company left. Mrs. Hart must have pointed that out to him."

"That still sounds lonely, though. Just waiting outside, not talking."

"It's how he likes it. And you'd better not let me catch you seeking him out. Worst and most dangerous thing you could do. If we offend him, we're done for. The only thing to do is keep a distance, keep respectful. You understand me?"

She nodded. "It *does* sound lonely, though."

I thought, fleetingly, that she wasn't taking the point quite right. Worried over his loneliness instead of our duty. I pressed on, quickly:

"And it grew into a kind of bargain with Harry. As long as the Harts stayed, and remembered, Harry would leave the village alone—and he'd be merciful to Fred's family.

"The Harts made their pledge to stay, and they kept it. They lived quietly, always keeping Harry's story in their thoughts. Never laughing too loud, or forgetting how close he was. Him and his dogs."

"Are the dogs still here too?"

"Of course. Where else could they be?"

We were close to the Rose House now. Something small scuffled in the undergrowth, but Lucia didn't turn to look.

"Then what happened?" she said when I paused.

"Then nothing. The family promised to stay, and stay they did. Every so often one of them would be lost to Harry. The ones who tried to run, or the ones who neglected Harry's memory—sometimes just people who seemed too happy."

"You mean Harry took them?"

"He did. Sometimes a person would just be harmed. They'd wake up choking, odd marks on their throat. And someone would disappear and never be seen again. Then we'd have an empty-box funeral at Small Angels. That's what happened to your grandfather's brother, you know."

She'd have wondered about that. Impossible to be with Paul and not see his mourning. Sadness hanging about him like illness.

"He was high-spirited, your great-uncle," I said. "Careless. Didn't take as much care with the beacons and the singing at Small Angels as he should have done. Went poking around places he shouldn't have done. Talked stupidly about renovating, changing things at Blanch Farm. Once or twice he said he wondered if old Harry was as real as we'd all supposed. One day he went into the woods and didn't come back.

"He was one of the last we lost that way. But it could happen again. Nothing to stop Harry getting angry. If there was disrespect, say. If someone messed around with the way things are meant to be. His song, for instance. He doesn't care to have people disrespecting his history. So we pay our dues and we leave him alone. Let sleeping dogs lie."

We were quiet a moment. Then I went on:

"All the same, he needs us. We're his people, and he doesn't want to be alone. He can be kind, too. In the woods and the weather. We flourish here because of his goodwill. That's something to be grateful for. It's a noble thing, too, your grandfather says. Keeping people out of harm's way. Not that they seem grateful in the village."

"They don't remember, do they, though? Not any more."

I sang a verse of our old song to her:

Take comfort, neighbors, take your ease,
You need not choose to know

How murder was done outside the church
By the woods where roses grow

"Ignorant by choice, that lot. Only one or two of them wonder," I said. "The others don't want anything to do with us. Wouldn't walk here even if it was safe. I wouldn't live like that if I could. Would you?"

"No," she said. I saw it in her then—the same love and wonder I still felt after years. "This is better than anything. Isn't it, Nan?"

I nodded. Not often I could agree with Miss Lucia's opinions, but she was right in this.

"Some people don't know what's good for them," I said. And we walked quiet for a little way, her close to my side.

Then we came to the clearing. I have seen the Rose House countless times, but I don't think I ever saw it lovelier than that evening. The flowers were blooming—just a few, out of season, and so sweet it took your breath for a moment. There was a rain-shine on the wet leaves, the branches wound around each other like lace. It was all these things and it was more—a house made of flowers and memory, Mockbeggar's work of art.

"Don't you go close to the house," I said. "He won't be wanting visitors. This place is the heart of it, understand? Nobody goes in. I'm showing you this for once, so you know what it's like. But after tonight, you never come back."

She stared at me, eyes glittering, wide as if she wanted to eat it all up with one glance. She nodded, playing at obedience.

But not scared, I thought, dismayed. How could I not have scared her?

We heard the dogs then, not far off. I told her to listen. Hear that lonely, echoing sound and imagine it getting closer. The baying of dogs that never tire and are never satisfied.

"Remember he's always here," I said.

She nodded again, obedient as you could ask, but still with shining eyes.

"I'll remember," she said. "I'll remember for ever."

I told myself that she meant what she said, that surely I could set my mind at rest.

I wonder now what she was thinking, standing pale and rapt in the moonlight. I wonder whom she spoke to when she made that promise. If she had any notion of what she'd cost us all before the end.

CHAPTER FIVE

Three Copper Coins

OK, so there was this girl called Chloe and she was getting married.

When Chloe woke in her room at the Albatross—Sam a welcome barrier between her and the edge of the narrow bed—the words were already there in her mind, uninvited.

It was just past dawn, and the light was soft. Inside, all was still quiet. Outside there were pigeons calling. Last night John Pauncefoot had told her that they lived in the eaves of the pub, and had done for generations.

She lay still and struggled to get at a distant recollection—almost inaccessible, like something caught at the back of her teeth. Finally she had it:

Like most of her childhood memories, it was a happy one. She had been eight, staying at a friend's house with four or five others. They ate ice cream with chocolate sauce, played out a tangled drama with their hostess's dolls, and watched *Beauty and the Beast* in their pajamas. After that—once the nightlight was on and they had zipped and unzipped and half-zipped their sleeping bags until they were finally comfortable—came the ghost stories.

You needed an authoritative beginning. Something that set your victim up from the outset. *There was this couple driving home late at night. There was this man who lived near a graveyard.*

There was this girl called Chloe and she was getting married.

Driftwood, Chloe thought. Debris washed up at the edge of her waking mind, flotsam from some already vanished dream.

She sat up gently in bed, wary of disturbing Sam. Last night had been a late one. They had lingered downstairs at the bar after the rest of their guests departed, sitting up even as John Pauncefoot finished cleaning and locked the door.

They were tired and comfortable and full of wine and good food, and beyond this she suspected that they had both wanted to eradicate the slight coolness that Brian's story had left between them.

For half an hour after John went to bed they were content to sit and enjoy each other's company. She mentioned that she had finally broken in her wedding shoes before they left London, walking soberly up and down her office's corridors during her lunch hour—feet glittering, the rest of her ordinary in her work clothes.

"No blisters this weekend, then," Sam said.

Their bottle of wine was almost empty—he divided the remaining inch between their two glasses. Such steady hands, she thought, suddenly ridiculously affectionate over this small quirk. Every so often it struck her afresh how much she liked him.

She emptied her glass, sat back in her chair.

"I've got to have shoes I can count on," she said. "What if I want to run?"

Sam smiled. "Why would you want to run? Isn't John Pauncefoot driving you up to the church in his cart, decked out like the Queen of the May?"

"Even so. You should always be prepared." And now—judging that they were both relaxed and easy enough for the topic not to spoil the mood—she added:

"So tell me about Paul Gonne's funeral, then. What did Brian see out there in the dark? What happened next?"

He frowned. "I thought we'd had enough of all that for one evening."

"You said you'd explain."

She almost wished she hadn't returned to the mystery. All the ease and humor had gone out of him in an instant.

"It's just morbid. I don't know why you found it all so entertaining."

"I was *curious.* I don't understand why you're getting so upset about it."

"You really want me to go into this? Fine. A girl died that night. Elphine Gonne, one of Paul's granddaughters."

She stared at him. Somehow she hadn't been expecting it to end here.

"I told you it wasn't a nice story," Sam said. "All of that stuff—it's best left alone."

"Tell me how it happened, then, and I'll leave it alone." In spite of herself, she found she couldn't help asking. It was a craving. Best satisfied and then forgotten.

"You promise?"

She stared at him. He had never asked her to promise him anything before.

"Fine."

To her surprise, he stood and fetched another bottle of wine from behind the bar.

'Is this the Gonnes' wine?" she said, pushing the glass close to one of the candles, so that the wine tinted the light like stained glass.

"No. Theirs was white. Bacchus, I think. I doubt there's any of it left by this time. Good riddance." He took a breath. "You heard how Brian talks about Blanch Farm. People don't usually—no one round here except Brian really takes that stuff seriously, of course. But at Paul Gonne's funeral it was different. People got worked up, imagining things.

"It started at the service. The atmosphere was funny from the start—the family looked scared, even Selina Gonne. And she was as tough as they come; we were all terrified of her as kids. I suppose whatever was going on with the family infected the guests. At the meal afterward, people—a few people got upset."

"Upset how?"

"Doesn't matter," he said, frowning. "It was nothing. The drink and the dark. If you ask around now, most people will agree with me."

"So you didn't notice anything strange?"

"I wasn't there." He paused, then added reluctantly: "Kate went."

"And she didn't see anything?"

"Of course not. All that upset just distracted people. If there hadn't been all that freaking out over phantom shapes in the dark—white running things or whatever Brian likes to talk about—they'd have probably noticed a damn sight earlier that Elphine was missing. Maybe it would've helped."

"Where was she?" Chloe said. The room—cozy, before, lit only by the candles and the little lamp on the bar—was now a little too dark, too quiet. She wanted to get up to turn a light on, but was reluctant to move in case the distraction stopped Sam's flow of talk.

"In the woods," he said. "Her sisters found her just before dawn."

"What had—how did she die?"

"Something to do with her lungs. She'd had problems with them her whole life."

"Did they find out what she was doing out there that night?"

"I don't think so. Elphine's sisters all left soon afterward; it was only Selina left in that big old house with her son to look after her. Then he died, and it was just her until she died three years ago."

"Who's there now?"

"I heard that one of the granddaughters came back. But you'd hardly know it. No one sees her, and she's let all the traditions slide."

"So no more beacons and singing?"

"None of that. And yet Hell hasn't broken loose. So Brian doesn't have a leg to stand on with all his scaremongering. Everything's quiet, and it's going to stay that way."

That was that, then. She stretched, and emptied her glass. How had this new bottle disappeared so quickly? The candles were burning low. No sound from the village outside, or from the fields beyond—no dogs barking tonight.

"We should go up," Sam said. He got to his feet. "Come on. It's late."

He didn't remind her of her promise, but she could see in his face that he wanted to. Leave it alone, he was thinking, put this morbid bit of history to bed. Well, she'd had her curiosity satisfied now, mostly. She wouldn't push it further.

After they'd gone to bed, Sam had been restless. Chloe had woken up about two for some water and found him sitting on the edge of the bed, staring at the narrow patch of moonlight on the old floor. She had to touch his shoulder to get his attention. Even when he became aware of her, he didn't seem entirely present. He said that he was all right, only tired past sleeping.

He had been tired the day before, too. As the date of their return to his childhood village approached, he had seemed increasingly restless. It had once occurred to her to tell him they didn't *have* to go.

It would have been pointless to say it, though. Of course they had to go. The wedding was now larger than either of them. Family and friends had booked train tickets and annual leave. Money had been spent.

The wedding dress was hanging on the back of the door in its white garment bag, pale and strange in the dawn light. The shape, for a moment, looked like nothing familiar, nothing from the sane waking world. It hung there like a phantom, a hanged man, barring their exit. It took her eyes a moment to translate the sight into sense.

Then her vision adjusted and the shape was only the dress she had chosen so carefully. Silk bought at sixty percent off, swathed in thick plastic.

Still the voice nagged like a bad tooth: *There was this girl called Chloe.* Not a person worth getting to know. Destined for misfortune early on, best not to get attached to her.

She wished Sam would wake up. Then she could tell him about this dream that wasn't quite a dream, and he could laugh and say that they had enough to worry about wondering if the hog-roast van would arrive on time without worrying about turning into stories. Or whatever it was that was troubling her. This week would be their past soon enough; they would be back in their flat before they knew it, wrapped up in the comfort and joy of their familiar lives.

> She had fallen in love with the village, and with the idea of herself there, getting married in the old church with her hands full of sunflowers. And why shouldn't the wedding happen there?

She shook her head, impatient. The voice had buzzed too close. It felt like a trespass, like having a fly settle on one's face.

The movement disturbed Sam, who stirred, looked at her blankly for a moment.

"You're at the Albatross," she said.

"What time is it?"

"Half six."

"Wonderful." He closed his eyes. She thought he had gone back to sleep, when he said, "Were you crying just now?"

"No, why?"

"I thought I heard crying. Just before I woke up. Very soft."

"Must've been a dream. Or the birds."

"Bloody pigeons. John should put them in a pie."

"Sam," she began.

But he had already fallen asleep again. She curled up next to him and tried to do the same, but the memory of the story voice wouldn't leave her.

It was an hour later, and she was just beginning to doze off, when Sam's phone began ringing shrilly from the chest of drawers.

Swearing, he clambered out of bed and reached it just before the caller rang off. Weakly, selfishly, Chloe regretted that he had caught it in time.

The phone conversation was short. After the first greeting, Sam switched immediately to his work voice, Chloe's least favorite.

She had heard it more often than usual of late. Last year he had started his own marketing company with friends, and the business required careful nurturing. She had been proud of him, never doubting for a moment he would succeed. All the same, when she saw his face on hanging up, she sat up in bed, full of foreboding.

"What's happened?"

"It's all right. I think it's all right. Just let me—" He jumped up, turned on his laptop and began searching through emails. After a tense couple of minutes he sat back in his chair and sighed.

"OK. I emailed it to him. It's there. Thank God."

She stood up and went over to the desk. "Sam. Are you all right?"

"Think so." He took a breath. "Oh my God. I thought we'd lost the whole thing for a minute."

"Is this for the new account?"

He nodded. "Computers crashed in the office, they thought something important wasn't backed up properly."

"But it is. So you're fine?"

"More or less. I'm going to have to do some resurrection work to get this ready for Friday. I don't know how much time I'm going to have to help with the church."

"What? Can't the others manage?"

"No, it's not something either of them are equipped to deal with, and if we don't make our deadline—"

"Right. I understand." It was like a delicate plant, this business, she thought. It had to be tended carefully and seemed perfectly capable of dying of neglect. "How long is this going to take?"

"A couple of days."

The computer crash wasn't his fault. If the account was lost, the company would suffer. The life they were building would suffer.

So she wasn't angry, though she dressed without a word and spent the rest of the day choosing her words very carefully. He needn't have agreed so quickly, she thought.

After breakfast, he left for his parents' house to use their internet connection, which was a little better than the Albatross," though not outstanding. (Property prices in the village would be considerably higher if the internet speed and phone reception could only be improved, Bill had told Chloe. But people had been complaining for years, and no remedy had been found. They were in something of a dead area.)

They would begin tidying Small Angels later that morning—without Sam's help. At a loose end until then, Chloe changed and went for a run.

It should have been a respite. At home, a run always meant peace of mind, notwithstanding catcallers and pavement-mounting cyclists. She fell into the rhythm easily, quickly leaving the pub behind and heading into the village. The day was sunny with a bite of crispness. But she found herself uneasy. People turned to look at her as she went: level, troubling looks from the woman cutting roses, the man carrying a box of apples in from his car. *Where are you going so fast?* they seemed to wonder. *What's wrong?* They might have been thinking that she ought to run faster, or that she could never run fast enough.

She was losing her rhythm. With a deliberate effort she returned her thoughts to her breath, the strike of her feet on the pavement.

As she left the village she increased her speed. If she was running with Sam—a Sunday-morning ritual of theirs at home—he would be telling her to pace herself. But she was alone, and there was no one to slow her down as she pelted down narrow lanes, away from those steady, judgmental eyes.

She had intended to visit Small Angels, but now she realized that she was running in the wrong direction, along the road out of the village. She was reluctant to turn back, having come this far. She would keep going and see where she ended up. The woods the road skirted belonged to Mockbeggar, someone had told her last night. You couldn't get in or out of the village without passing under those trees.

It wasn't a pleasant route, she discovered. She had a choice between struggling through nettles or running on the road proper. But there were few cars this afternoon, so she chanced it—she was in that sort of mood.

When the trees ended, she was surrounded by fields. Ahead of her was Crockery Hill, a slope of rough grass leading toward Mockbeggar. She left the road and approached the trees, feeling like a disobedient child as she did so. She had promised Sam she'd leave it alone, and she would, really. She would go a little way in, that was all. Not enough for it to count.

At the edge of the woods, she halted. There were thick brambles ahead, but these weren't impenetrable. With a slight struggle, a flexible person could find their way in.

There was a certain satisfaction in pushing her way through, crushing nettles underfoot. The childish pleasure of doing something forbidden.

> She thought of how they'd all said don't go in, stay away. She thought about how people had looked at her when she ran through the village, like they were just waiting until she'd gone so they could start talking about her.
>
> The trees in the wood felt like that too. They watched her like they were waiting to see what she would do.
>
> She won't do it, they were thinking. She won't go on. She'll have more sense.
>
> But she went on, she went in.

It was stronger now, that sense of herself viewed from elsewhere, told from elsewhere. She could sense the tone of the narrative more clearly. It was hard to ignore that persistent little voice.

The phantom storyteller thought she was a fool to come here, and perhaps she was. Not because of whatever superstitious prejudice the village had against the woods, but because nobody knew where she was. Her phone, she realized, was back in the Albatross.

The brambles ended. She pushed through a patch of ferns and found herself on a path. Here she was in Mockbeggar at last.

A lot of fuss about nothing, was her first thought. She had seen prettier woods than this by far. The path was bordered by bindweed and more brambles, neither luxuriant. The younger saplings appeared to have reached a certain height and then failed to flourish.

She followed paths that led past blackberry bushes—all fruitless now—past pools livid green with algae. A frayed skipping rope hung from a low branch of a chestnut tree, a remnant of an ancient swing.

Hearing the sound of water, she pushed on ahead, and found herself standing on a steep bank above the river, gazing down at a rush of gray-blue-green-brown water. She stared for a moment and then took a step backward, unnerved by the speed and violence of the current, the treacherous rocky slope, the slippery moss.

There was no bridge, and the gap was far too wide to jump, even if she had been the foolhardy type. But as she wandered along the side of the water, the bank became less steep, and eventually she came to a place where the water ran shallow and gentle. At the center of the river was a flat brown stone.

She couldn't remember the last time she had used a stepping-stone. As she made the crossing she was half-laughing, feeling like a child escaped from school.

At the top of the steep opposite bank she hesitated. She could make out nothing but close-growing trees and brambles ahead. The path might lead nowhere.

But she pressed on anyway, and a little way from the river found herself in a clearing dominated by a mass of dead branches. A tree or bush had grown here once, before withering away. And beneath it—

The shape baffled her to begin with, just as the garment bag on her bedroom door had done. Then her eyes and mind translated it: the shape was a house—so small that it seemed like mockery to use the word—overgrown with dead branches. At one time there must have been a wonderful green profusion here. Now there were only thorns, and beneath that a pitiful rubble.

There was no such thing as a good or a bad place. She was patient with friends who believed in such things, but her own conviction had never wavered. You pass through the world and leave very little behind, and the little you do leave fades with every year. Perhaps people had been happy in this ruin at one time. Perhaps they had suffered. Either way, there was nothing left of them now.

She knew this. And because she knew this, she was irritated by her reluctance to stay in the clearing. Because the house—the almost-house, the house-that-once-was, the house built of thorns—frightened her, she went closer. She found a door—a space where a door would have been—pushed her way through brambles once more, went in.

It must have been a rose tree, she thought, studying the dead branches around her—proud, as a city girl, to have identified at least one plant. Wild roses. Dog roses. When living, the branches would have filled the house so that there was hardly any room to stand.

There were a couple of small green shoots poking through. Life was coming back, very slowly.

The roof had fallen in here and there, and above her she could see patches of blue sky, netted over with dead branches. With the leaves growing it would have been dark in here. Greenish dark. You must have felt like you'd been swallowed by a tree, if you'd stood here back then.

At the center of the small room, she found a strange thing: the tree's trunk had been roughly sliced through. It must have been a difficult business, because the trunk was surprisingly thick for such a tree—perhaps the width of a child's neck. Who would take the trouble to destroy such a unique curiosity?

They'd made a bad job of it, whoever they were. The strokes had been haphazard, like the axeman was in a hurry.

That wasn't the strangest thing, though. After cutting the tree down, someone had hammered coins into the wounded stump. Copper, she thought, with a dim memory, could kill a plant. Or was that a myth? It looked as if there had been dozens of coins driven into the tree at one time, but most had since come loose, worked their way out of their grooves, and now only three remained, and they too were loose. They'd be out in a short time, Chloe thought. It looked like the tree itself was working the metal free.

When she reached for the first coin it was without a great deal of forethought.

> She felt sorry for the tree. That's why she did it.
>
> She felt sorry for the tree because someone had hurt it. The cutting-down and the coins. Poor thing. It looked like an act of deliberate cruelty.

You don't give up, do you, she thought.

The tree looked like it was fighting back. As she looked closer, her eyes picked out a couple of little green shoots. It was doing its best, and she wanted to help.

She was surprised how easy the first coin was to prize out of the severed trunk. It was as if the tree had just been waiting for a helping hand. A minute's struggle and the coin was out.

It would make a fine souvenir, she thought. But the coin slipped through her fingers and was lost among the branches and leaves.

As she struggled with the second coin she felt like someone was watching to see what she'd do, though there couldn't be another soul in the wood. This coin was a bit harder. She had to dig her nails in. She felt a splinter pierce her skin, but that didn't stop her.

The third coin was the hardest. This time she ripped a nail and she had blood on her sleeve by the time she had the coin free.

There you go, she thought to the tree. Breathe. And she felt like the tree did breathe.

But now she started to look around and take in how strange the whole place was. Why was there a tree growing inside a house in the first place?

A new thought came to her. Sudden, deep knowledge—she should run. She should get out, as soon as possible, as far away as she could.

The branches around her seemed to shift—were they all breathing now? What was that whispering sound? Why were the leaves rustling so loud?

She scratched herself running through the thorns, crashing through dead rose branches. She forgot the copper coins, forgot all thought of a souvenir.

All the time she tried to be calm on the outside, and inside her thoughts were just oh my God, oh my God. Get out now.

She got out of the ruin and she ran—faster than she'd ever run before, back across the river and through the wood, not looking left or right. She didn't stop till she reached the edge of the trees and then she sank to her knees, shaking and breathless and almost fainting.

She felt the sun on her face and shut her eyes against its dazzle.

She told herself that it would all be fine, nothing bad had happened and she hadn't done any harm, or at least she hadn't meant any harm which was almost as important. Surely.

Back in her room, she found that she had a splinter in her palm that wouldn't come out. She didn't want to ask Sam for help, because then he'd know where she'd been.

She tried to soothe herself with a brief gloat over her wedding dress. The gown and veil ensemble had looked so effective yesterday against the backdrop of the Albatross's old beams. But when she had it out of its garment bag she found out that there was a tear at the hem.

That's impossible, she thought. I put it away so carefully.

But the rip was there all the same. It was a snagging sort of tear, like it had been caught on a thorn.

CHAPTER SIX

Brothers, Long Ago

Lucia in continuation

That first time at the Rose House, I wasn't quite sure who he was. Nan still hadn't told me everything at that point. I knew enough to be wary, and that I could never tell anyone that I'd broken my promise and crossed the Fane, but I didn't know enough to be as frightened as I should have been.

I could tell that he wasn't like me, that he belonged to the woods—but in the half-light he looked alive, and more unhappy than dangerous. I was unhappy too, so that was a bond between us.

I sat beside him on the front door step—the only part of the Rose House that's still intact and gives some clue about how it might have looked when people lived there. He scratched in the dirt with a stick, not looking at me as he spoke.

"You live at Blanch Farm," he said.

"Yes. With Nan and Grandpa and my sisters. And my dad."

"A lot of company." He sounded wistful.

"There's too many of them, sometimes. I never get any space to myself."

He looked at me shyly. "There's space here. Come and see."

I wanted to tell him that there was no way I could get into the house. The branches grew too close together, the rose thorns would cut me to ribbons.

But he'd ducked inside before I could speak. I followed him because already I didn't want him to think I was a coward.

The Rose House was marvelous in those days. The rose tree filled it from wall to wall, hiding everything in a maze of leaves and branches. Even when the roses weren't in bloom the sight was incredible—a twisting mass of briars, winding around and around each other and snaking through the glassless windows, over the earth floor. I never saw a rose tree to match it. No leaves greener, no thorns sharper.

It's a tiny place, of course. Before the dog rose took possession you could have crossed the room in five strides. But at that time, with the tree so full of life, the branches made a barrier that was almost impassable.

Without him I couldn't have made my way through. But he showed me, patiently, the places where the branches parted just enough to allow me to slip through unscratched.

"This way," he said, slipping under a low-growing branch. "Just watch." He looked back at me and we grinned at each other shyly. I thought then that it was settled, we were going to be friends. (I'd read about friendship. About how ordinary people had friends, I mean. Meeting someone at school or in your home village and seeking each other's company lightly, casually, out of choice. No pressure of shared history, no family resemblances, no blood. Elphine had several imaginary friends she would never tell me about. But I had never even had one of these.)

There's a clearing at the heart of the Rose House where the trunk of the rose tree stood. Overhead the branches made a canopy, wrapping around us like a cave or a cage. It was a secret place, just like Harry had promised.

"No one would find you here," he said.

It was wonderful. For a little while we lay back on the ground, not speaking, and looked up at the darkening sky, the net of brambles above us.

Then I heard a dog barking close by. Or did the sound come from the village? I told myself it was probably the village. Still, it brought me back to myself. I'd already stayed too late.

"I have to get back," I said. "They'll be mad otherwise."

"You can come back, though. If you need to get away from them."

"Will you be here?"

"Always."

I must have suspected who he was. Surely. I look back at my child self and I want to shake her till her teeth rattle. *Open your eyes. Be honest.* But at the time I didn't think too hard about what I was doing. There was less guilt that way.

When I got home from the Rose House it was teatime. My sisters were cooking—some new and daring combination of canned foods. Helena was just adding a tin of baked beans and sausages to a can of spaghetti shapes, Ruby was stirring in chopped onion and frozen peas, all three were laughing.

I thought of three good witches, stirring a cauldron. Heads bowed over some spell or other. They were indifferent to the darkness outside, they had their own light. And there was Harry, out in his ruin, with no one to talk to or laugh with. I could hear rain against the kitchen window. I wondered if he could still feel the cold.

Elphine was off to one side, chopping apples to stew. Ruby always tactfully gave her a separate task when we cooked because she worked so slowly. That evening, she was pausing every so often to admire the white flesh of the fruit, its sweet woodsy smell. I remember seeing it briefly through her eyes, being struck by the beauty of it all—the wooden board, the apples, her hands, the knife.

I was about to ask if I could join in when Elphine caught a glimpse of me and exclaimed in dismay:

"Oh! What happened to your face?"

"Nothing." I hadn't noticed being hurt. The thorn must have caught me slyly as I followed Harry among the briars.

"Did you fall? Is that why you're scratched?"

"Mind your own business. You're so *nosy* sometimes."

"Am I?" She looked more thoughtful than offended.

"It's all right, Elphine. You're fine," Ruby told her. To me, she said: "Do you have to be horrible?"

"Maybe she does," Helena said. She passed Elphine another apple.

"It's all right," Elphine said. "Lucia, we're nearly ready. Do you want something to eat?"

I shook my head. I was hungry—with that cold kind of hunger you get in the dead of night—but I couldn't eat with them. I left them to their meal, to the warmth and light of the kitchen. I went upstairs and curled up in bed like I was sick.

I could tell them what I'd done, I thought. I didn't ever have to go back to the cottage in the woods.

But I knew already that I would never tell them, and I would go back.

By the time Nan told me the whole story—Harry and Fred, and the murders, and the fate of the Rose House—and I realized who my friend really was, it was too late. He was a secret I didn't have to share, one thing that I knew and nobody else did—not my older sisters, who always knew more and better, not my grandparents with their endless rules, not the people in the village, who stared at us like unwelcome wild creatures whenever we went to the post office. Besides, he didn't have anyone except me. I could hardly abandon him now.

I knew that Harry had made bad things happen—but they hadn't happened to me. I justified it by thinking that Harry showed himself to other people differently—to them he was a bitter adult, the man who never forgave, twisting a thorn rope in his dead hands. But for me he was different—a lonely child my own age, my friend.

I marveled at him choosing me, Lucia-the-bad. I knew myself pretty well even then. I had mean thoughts I didn't share with anyone. Sometimes I hated Nan's sharp eyes, the way she could pinch out rebellion like a tender vine shoot. Sometimes I was furious with my sisters—when they left me alone or wouldn't leave me alone, when Ruby was patronizing or Helena was sarcastic. At times I was even irritated with Elphine, if you can believe that. I wanted her attention even more than the others', and yet sometimes I lost patience with her. Her ideas were so unlike most people's, and her strange kindness and pity could be inconvenient. Sometimes I hated how clearly she made me see myself. I saw her gentleness and realized how little I resembled her.

But Harry was my friend, not hers. He would listen when I shared the worst of myself and when I fell silent he would say quickly, *What else?* I would talk and find resentments and misdeeds spilling out. Some of these I hadn't known were there lurking. Some I usually tried not to think about. One time—guilty, wanting someone to absolve me—I told him that I was breaking Nan's rule by visiting him, and asked him if he thought I was bad. He only shrugged. He didn't care if I was ugly inside, I thought, and that was a strange, liberating thing to realize. Talking to him was like digging a hole in the earth and whispering your thoughts into it.

"You can tell me the worst things," he said, once. I did tell him most of them. Once I told him that I imagined sometimes that the rest of the family had just *disappeared* and it was only me left, Blanch Farm all to myself.

"What would you do then?" he said.

I faltered there. I couldn't imagine what would happen after that dizzying moment of revelation—*it's just me left.* I wasn't sure quite who I'd be without the rest of them there.

Once I told him that I hated Brian Last because of the way he looked at me and my sisters and because ever since I'd stolen a handful of sour candies from his shop as a small child, I was never allowed into the post office unless it was empty.

"I'd like to smash his shop windows," I said.

We were in the cage at the heart of the Rose House. The flowers were out; the smell was so sweet it made me feel slightly drunk.

"He'd know it was you," Harry said. "Better do something else."

I thought of the things Brian seemed to love best. He was proud of his garden, I remembered. Most people in the village were content to let their lawns bloom with clover and daisies and purple self-heal, but not Brian. You'd never see a single brazen daisy on that tidy green square.

I asked Harry if there were plants that could invade a neat and well-loved garden and quickly reduce it to chaos. I wanted weeds that stung and bristled with spikes. Things with deep roots.

Harry told me places to dig, he showed me soil and shoots to gather. I found a quiet time—dusk, a rainy evening when nobody was out—and I scattered what Harry had given me over Brian's neat front lawn and flowerbeds.

I waited, and a short while later I had my reward. Nan brought the news back from the village—Brian was in a foul mood, his lawn a mess of horsetail, bindweed creeping through his shrubs, dandelions muscling into every flowerbed. Some of his best-loved and most expensive plants—the ones he would brag about at the village gardeners' club—had been killed.

I told Harry, the next time I saw him. "Nobody understands how it happened so quickly," I said. "Nobody has a *clue.*"

We grinned at each other. If we hadn't been surrounded by thorns, I'd have been tempted to dance with glee.

"Brian would be so mad if he knew," I said, gloating and stupid. "Or he'd be scared—"

I shouldn't have said it. I'd reminded Harry that he was something more than my partner in mischief. He was something to be feared.

He took hold of my wrist without warning. His grip was strong, nothing flimsy about him now.

"Are *you* scared?"

"No." I didn't have to work too hard to convince myself. We were friends, I thought. I was the exception.

He nodded and let me go.

There were moments like that between us. He would be kind, and then abruptly that other side would assert itself. The shadow of the man my friend was going to grow into.

Elphine had felt sorry for Brian and for the ruined garden, the prize plants choked in their prime. She called around a couple of times, offering to help Brian with his weeding (he told her to clear off both times). If she hadn't felt like that, I might have told her what had happened.

Or maybe not. I think I was well past the point of no return by then.

I was older now, and part of the monthly procession to Small Angels. It was troubling to know that I was singing about my friend, that the words were supposed to be *his* words —

I remember yet, Fred Hart,
In the ground you laid me low
You hid my face beneath the earth
In the woods where roses grow.

I wanted to ask Harry if the song was accurate. Had it really happened like that, like Nan said it had?

"They always look so grim when they ring the bells," I said to him, once. "They're all so scared and serious, they don't know you like I do. I could open the door, one of those nights, and you'd be there, waiting. Wouldn't Nan be angry, if I just opened the church door and said hello. Should I do it?"

I wouldn't really have dared—but he scowled, as if I was serious.

"Don't ever do that," he said.

"But it's *you.* I know you now—"

He shook his head.

"There are bad times," he said. "It's bad when the bells ring. I remember then."

I already knew that my friend wasn't always my friend. He made me promise to keep well away if I saw a man walking the woods.

"The dogs, too," he said. "Be careful."

"Are you scared of them?"

He nodded. He looked almost as sad as he had the day we'd first met.

That's when I realized there were things it hurt him to think about. His past was always with him. It was an ache that never went away. Even in our happier times he could never entirely forget how Fred had harmed him, and how he had taken his revenge. We'd be wading the river or playing tic-tac-toe in the Rose House, and then we'd both hear it—a dog barking, far off.

"You could send them away," I said once.

But he shook his head. For him, there was no escape. Even now, Fred's dogs were at his heels.

It hurt me to think of his suffering—so I tried not to. I had small miseries of my own to think about. As I moved into adolescence I waited for my discords to be softened and my family to approve of me wholeheartedly. But it never happened. They still watched me—Nan most of all—and seemed to see me running true to form, Lucia-the-bad, as always.

I had an illicit business, for a while. Did you ever hear about that? Nan had stopped my allowance indefinitely for some infraction or another, and I had no money. If I wanted something—new socks, say—I had to ask Nan for it, and sometimes she'd say yes and sometimes she wouldn't. So I got into the habit of taking a couple of bottles of wine out of the cellar where the last year's vintage was stored, and selling them off to secondary school kids. They'd stop on their way home from the bus stop and I'd be waiting at the bottom of Crockery Hill. I did all right for a while before Nan found out. She was furious but not surprised.

"Please try and keep the peace," Ruby said. "For all our sakes. You know how Nan gets when you set her off—"

She sounded so tired. But she was always tired in those days. She was the eldest, she had more work than the rest of us, and Nan and Grandpa talked to her about worries they didn't share with the rest of us.

I didn't stop to listen to her. When I was in disgrace, I couldn't bear to be around anyone. They all knew and judged, I thought—or if they were Elphine, they worried, and that was worse.

Harry didn't do either. He comforted me by showing me parts of the woods no one else had ever seen.

The deer came close when he was there. They never had eyes for me at those times, it was all for Harry. They were Mockbeggar's creatures, they loved him like the trees loved him. We could sit at the center of the Rose House clearing and they would approach until they were almost within arm's reach, staring at Harry as if they could never get tired of the sight of him.

At other times we lay on the ground and he touched my hand and I heard the trees growing. I heard them whisper his name.

Once he showed me where the wild strawberries grew. Nan had always warned us the fruit of Mockbeggar was poison. And yet the berries were so red, so glossy, that I was tempted to try them anyway.

"Don't," he said. "It'll make you sick."

"How come?"

"The woods soured them all. It happened a long time ago, after they lost me. They thought if I can't eat the fruit anymore, no one can."

This was how Mockbeggar loved him. The bushes poisoned themselves in rage at his death; the trees held him here, attended by dogs, whether he liked it or not.

Sometimes I found him curled up in the Rose House, too tired to cry. I was already older than him—eleven or twelve—and at those times he seemed young in a way that troubled me. I didn't want age to part us.

I told him it would be all right. He couldn't get out, and neither could I, but we had each other.

It was years before he talked about his past with me. I must have been thirteen or so by that time. Still I hadn't tired of Mockbeggar, or of him. One day he took me deeper into the woods than I'd ever been before, down a path that might have been brand-new, the woods parting just for us.

He showed me a glade full of bluebells—it was May then—more flowers than I'd ever seen in one place in Mock beggar before. It was marvelous, I told him, but he only said,

"Wait."

He made me hold out my hands, cupped like he was about to tip water into them, and he touched my palms gently—and suddenly I saw more bluebells, blue everywhere I looked—the flowers that day and the flowers that had been before, a hundred years of springs overlapping each other, memory piled on memory. I lived with him for an instant, spinning around and around with my brother Fred, so that the flowers blurred and no color but blue remained.

When it was over I stared at him for an instant and then we both laughed, breathless.

"I didn't know you could do that," I said. I'd thought it was just the bad things he could share—memories of his last minutes, and what followed.

He grinned at me. "I didn't know either."

It was wonderful, one of our best days—but on the way back I stopped to tie my shoelace, and when I stood up again he had vanished.

He'd done this sort of thing before. Sometimes when we raced each other through the woods or climbed the great trees, there'd be moments when he was gone. Or his outlines would become confused. For a moment he'd be little more than a blurred shape in the edge of my vision. I'd turn my head sharply and there'd be nothing but a crooked sapling or a mossy rock where he'd been standing.

But this time he didn't reappear after a minute as usual. He hadn't slid out of my notice. He was just *gone.*

I called his name a couple of times, before I lost my nerve. It was so quiet.

This was one of the oldest parts of Mockbeggar, the sort of place where my long-vanished relatives might have ended up, I thought.

As a rule, I tried not to think of them—Grandpa's brother and all the others who had been lost in Mockbeggar. It was the other Harry Child who was to blame for all that, not my friend, the boy who was a hand shorter than I was.

Now it struck me that I'd been so stupid I almost deserved what was going to happen to me now. How could I have seriously believed that he liked me and was my friend? Now I was going to die here and never be found.

I called and called until my throat was sore; I turned down one path and took the wrong fork, turned back and went wrong again. I tried my best not to cry. I thought of my family waiting at home, never knowing what had happened—

And then he was back. Just standing in the middle of the path, grinning like he expected me to have enjoyed the joke as much as he did.

There was that cruelty again, you see. That other side to him always threatening to find its way in. Or—I don't know—maybe it was unhappiness. I didn't dwell on it at the time, but he must have been unhappy. In spite of me.

I swore at him. I wanted to hit him. I told him I hated him. I said I wished we'd never met.

I hadn't been reckless enough to get angry with him before. He didn't like it, but thank God he was offended like a child. He clenched his small fists, he yelled back at me in his high boy's voice. He said that I was stupid and ungrateful. I didn't deserve the present he'd given me.

"Show me home," I said. I tried to keep feeling angry, because it was better than being scared. "Show me back *right now.*"

"Damn you, Fred," he said, "you can find your own way back or rot here for all I care—"

We stared at each other. I thought he might hurt me, but instead he stepped back. His expression almost frightened me. I'd never seen such despair, such endless depths.

I thought of saying *I'm not him, I'm* me—because it hurt, that he had confused the two of us, even for a moment. I thought he saw me as someone distinct from all others. But I couldn't say this with him looking like that.

I said, "It's OK. We can go back now."

He nodded.

"Elphine—my sister—she says it can help to find words for things. Sometimes. You can tell me about him if you want. Or about anything you want. I don't mind."

We walked back, and he did tell me.

He told me about his life in the Rose House, the quarrels and the cold and hunger. He told me about the music they had there at nights. When his almost-father came home they would sing his songs—lovers false and lovers true, riddles wisely expounded, criminals' gallows confessions, ghosts denouncing their murderers. He told me about his mother's cleverness in snaring rabbits in the fields, how she had a light step and nimble fingers. He had seen her hook a fish out of a lake with her bare hands. She had dull, rabbit-brown dresses and smooth, rabbit-brown hair, nothing much to look at, people said, and yet men stared at her. Mr. Hart had stared.

He told me about his homesickness at Blanch Farm. How he couldn't sleep, and how Fred disliked him at first, but then, grudgingly, let him sleep curled up in blankets on his bedroom floor. It was better after that, he said—he wasn't used to quiet; he had always been packed into a single room with his family, brothers and sisters snoring and snuffling in the dark. In later years from time to time he would still slip next door to sleep on Fred's floor and they would talk late into the night about the things they would do when they were men.

He told me how Fred envied him the love of the woods. Fred admired Mockbeggar but didn't trust it. It was a place alien to his way of measuring standing in the world—money and land and genteel friends and fine horses. It made him uneasy and he wanted to grasp it. And still Harry was Mockbeggar's favorite and always would be.

He was quiet after that. I thought he'd told me everything he could, but eventually he spoke again and told me about the murder, his death on the steps of Small Angels. He heard Fred so close on the other side of the church door.

"He stood outside and said it could all be mended," he said.

"I know," I said. "It's in the song." And I sang it to him, and it seemed to hurt him and make him feel better at the same time:

Now Fred Hart wept outside the church.
"We were brothers, long ago.
Forgive in memory of our youth
In the woods where roses grow."

And Harry Child unlocked the door.
"We were brothers, long ago.
I remember yet our happiness,
In the woods where the roses grow."

"Yes," he said when I was done. "It happened like that."

I didn't dare say anything.

"I thought it might be different," he went on. "There was a moment before. And there was a moment during when I didn't think he meant what he'd done. It might have ended different, but it didn't, it never does."

"The song, you mean."

He nodded, but he didn't mean just that. I could see the story all around him, he was never free of it. Always just a faint look of surprise at the back of his eyes, the shadow of his brother's betrayal. If I touched him, it would pass to me like fire springing from one burning building to another. When I thought that, it was a struggle not to shrink from him. The idea appalled and fascinated me like a steep drop.

"He used to laugh at the roses," he said. "My family's dog roses, growing near our cottage. *Pretty, but they don't smell, do they.* Those were his words. He couldn't say the same now, though. They're sweet now. He saw them everywhere, just before he died. The scent wouldn't wash off."

I waited for him to tell me more—what happened afterward, what he did to Fred Hart. But he led me to the edge of the woods, in sight of my path home, and then he was gone.

I grew up. Most things stayed the same. My friend didn't change, even as I grew taller. I kept the secret of Rose House well; no one ever spotted me coming or going. But in another way I didn't keep anything hidden. My grandparents and my sisters—even Dad, who took so little interest as a rule—they knew there was something that set me apart. It was like they could smell the roses on me.

They tried to talk to me about it—even Grandpa, who could hardly bear to mention the woods explicitly. I told them that I was fine, there was nothing strange or wrong. I even withstood Nan's interrogations without flinching. And all the time I drifted further from them.

The thing is, that kind of deceit—the kind when you're putting someone at risk without their knowing it—it makes you lonely. Every time I was with them, when they were happy with me, when they shared laughter or kindness, it all had this bitter tang underneath. It wasn't quite real. If they knew what I'd done, how I'd broken the rules, all their affection would vanish. It was my own fault, but I was lonely.

Then I met a girl in the graveyard, and the world changed.

It was early in the year, not quite spring. I was sixteen. I had got up early, intending to go to Mockbeggar and see Harry. But Grandpa was up even earlier, carrying out the small chores he liked to do before the others were awake.

He gave me a piece of his toast, and asked me where I was going. I couldn't say Mockbeggar, so I said I was off to Small Angels.

"You're a bit old for leapfrogging the graves," he said, smiling a little. Even his smiles were sad. His lost brother dogged every step.

"I just want a walk," I said. "Quiet, you know."

He knew about that. He liked quiet. The peace made his grief a bit easier to carry around.

"Better be quick, then," he said. "Unless you want chores from your grandmother."

So I finished my toast and fled, up the hill, past the beacon that stood between our land and Small Angels' graveyard.

I intended to lean against the church door and watch the sun rise. But there was someone there before me. A girl, my own age or slightly older—tall and dark, with a clean, handsome profile like a knight's.

Nobody was allowed in the graveyard. Outside funerals, Small Angels was our place. And yet here was this stranger, wandering fearlessly. As I watched, half-hidden by brambles, I saw her walk up and down the gravestones, stopping from time to time to crouch down and examine an inscription more closely. Then she came to the church door. She touched the marks there—the claw marks Fred Child's dogs had left centuries ago. She tried the door—locked, of course.

Something fascinated me about the care she took, the gentle and certain way she touched the wood and stone. I wondered what it would feel like to have that kind of focus turned on you.

But all the same, I thought—indignant—she was trespassing. Even I couldn't escape Nan and Grandpa's lessons about what was right and proper, you see. I was affronted in spite of myself at this bold defiance of the rules.

I wondered, too, if she would be safe here. Harry could take offense very quickly. Even with me.

I waited until she left, and then I fetched chalk from the house and left a message, in case she came back:

beware

It was the best I could come up with at short notice. Not terribly evocative, but enough to deter the average local. I chalked it on a tombstone close to the church door, where she was sure to see it if she came back. I felt sure she would come back.

I returned the next morning. Ten to one our visits wouldn't coincide, I thought, but if she *was* there, I wanted to see what she'd do.

She was there again. I saw her walk up the path, stop short as she saw my message on the stone.

She paused, stared.

Then she laughed. Her laughter was a shock to me—a dark-gold sound, utterly delighted. I turned and fled back to the house.

I told Harry about her the next time I saw him. I had to tell someone. And with my sisters, I'd have had to tell them why I'd been in the graveyard. It might be complicated. Besides, I wanted something that was just mine. I wanted to keep the sound of her laughter to myself.

Harry was different. In some ways, I thought, he didn't count.

I told him what had happened, and what I imagined she was like. She looked *good,* I said. Noble, like some kind of hero.

"What's she to you, in that case?" he said. "What have you got to do with *good*?"

"I don't know. But I want her to think about me. I could talk to her, next time. I could show her the church."

"Is your grandmother going to lend you her key?"

"Funny." I made a face at him. "I'll work that bit out." I hesitated. "Do you mind, if I talk to her, and show her the church?"

I'd asked him for favors before, but nothing like this. The church was on his domain, and outside family funerals, nobody but our family was supposed to venture there. I thought he might tell me it was out of the question now, but he just shrugged and looked sulky.

"I don't care."

"What about the woods?"

"I don't care." But he was frowning. More irritable than I'd expected. "You're getting boring, you know. Talking about some *girl* all the time. You haven't even spoken to her and already you're stupid about her. You'll forget to come to the Rose House soon, I suppose. Off with *her* instead."

"I won't. Don't be ridiculous." I tried to flatter him. "She's not like you."

"Or like you."

I remembered the sense I had of her—that impression of nobility. He had a point.

"I won't forget," I said. "Promise."

I did mean it. I knew he would always know me best. He had his hands knitted together tight; his face was still set.

I'd seen him that way when his suffering got too much, and I'd seen him that way before he turned dangerous. I held my breath, waited.

"You'll leave me here on my own," he said.

I shook my head, promised again that I wouldn't. He pressed my wrist close enough for his nails to draw blood. (He could leave a mark, if the hour was right and he was in that frame of mind.)

"He left me," he said quietly at last, letting me go. "You'll do it too."

"I won't," I said. I drew back. "Don't scratch me again."

We'd been going to visit one of the green pools, where he said, with childish certainty, that there used to be a mermaid—but now we both wanted to reassure ourselves that all was as it should be. So we stayed where we were and let an hour pass in our favorite way—we lay on the ground in the Rose House, still as two corpses, and watched as the light slowly drained from the sky.

CHAPTER SEVEN

Relics

Chloe had asked everyone to be at Small Angels for ten so that they could make a start on the cleaning. She had already told Kate that her intention was to get the drudgery—the dusting and sweeping and polishing—done in the first couple of days. Then they could move on to beautifying—setting out candles, ribbons, balloons. By Friday the only decorations left to put up would be the flowers, and Chloe had decided to make a little party of this. A number of wedding guests would be arriving that evening to help set out the wreaths and bouquets, and Chloe had promised food and drink to make it worth their while.

As far as Monday went, she would bring the cleaning things with her—masks, polish, cloths—and also refreshments, plenty of sugar and caffeine. They could get some good work done and then down tools well before the light went. Did that sound like a good plan?

Kate agreed that it did. She would walk to the church, she said, so there was no need for Bill and Birdie to worry about collecting her along with Chloe.

She needed to be alone for her first sight of Small Angels. It would be better for everyone that way. Once the initial shock was over, it would be easier to look suitably festive and businesslike.

Dressing in the cool of the morning, she found herself famished, as if she had eaten nothing for weeks. Through the window she saw the sky slowly blueing. The pigeons were softly calling.

Upstairs, the Albatross seemed asleep, but downstairs in the bar there was evidence of activity: in one corner, a number of places had already been laid for breakfast. A smell of coffee and baking drifted from the back room, and cereals and fruit waited on a long table.

As Kate stopped to pocket a couple of apples, John Pauncefoot emerged from the kitchen carrying a fresh loaf on a wooden board.

"Coffee's made," he said. "Will you have one before you go?"

"Thanks." Still standing, she drank the cup he poured for her. She noticed that he set it down on the cloth, rather than handing it to her directly, to avoid their hands accidentally touching. There were some in the village who shook their heads over John's shyness, but his reticence had always suited Kate. During the difficult years, he had been one of the few neighbors to show no inquisitiveness about the health of her parents' marriage.

"You're off to Small Angels?" He was slicing the bread, his back to her as he spoke.

"Yes."

"It didn't worry you, then. That story of Brian's." He didn't quite make it a question, but she heard uncertainty in his voice.

"I didn't think anybody else took that seriously."

"No," John said. "But still."

He hesitated, troubled—but said nothing more, only handing her a slice of warm bread wrapped in a napkin. She thought he might have gone on if she had pressed him, but dawn was long past now and time was running away from her.

This morning she felt as if she was wading through memory like deep water. She shouldn't have gone to Blanch Farm.

But this was the very worst point. Tomorrow would be easier. Next week she would be away from here. She told herself this as she reached Small Angels, paused at the cherry tree which was the unofficial marker between the fields and the graveyard.

She rarely liked places—or people—on first meeting, preferring to take her time deciding what she thought of them. But Small Angels she had liked immediately.

Her first sight had been at one of the Gonnes' funerals—for a cousin, a disappointed man who had lived in the village rather than in Blanch Farm proper. Still, now he was dead, he was entitled to every consideration. The burial would take place after dark, Kate had heard, and there was a rumor that the coffin would be empty. It was tradition for every family in the village to attend, and Kate had pleaded until she was allowed to accompany her mother.

This awful place, Birdie had muttered as they hurried up the path, rain specking their funeral blacks. *I don't know what possessed you to come, Kate.* But Kate had taken in the church—not at its best that rainy night—and loved it immediately and forever: the pale stone, the weathered and crooked graves, the scarred oak door, the trees.

Her first memories of the interior were less certain—a strong smell of cold and dust, the hardness of the pew, her discomfort in the itchy black cardigan Birdie had made her wear. They had to be smart, Birdie had said. The old lady would be sure to notice if they weren't.

The old lady, Kate knew, was the boss of the Gonne family. She was sitting at the front of the church with her granddaughters—four girls in faded black. The smallest of them stared at Kate. Her eyes were bright and green as grave glass—those chippings beneath headstones in the village churchyard which Kate, when she was a little younger, had always wanted to carry away in her pockets. The youngest sister wasn't smiling, and yet Kate had a strange conviction that she was enjoying herself.

I saw you too, Lucia told her later. *You were the only one who looked at us straight on.*

Kate had traveled since that night, she had seen many more beautiful works of stone. She had seen cathedrals, and mended them. But like Blanch Farm, Small Angels still had its old draw.

In the bright late-summer morning she touched the church door—traced the ancient claw marks disfiguring the wood. Other than the fact that she was older—wiser, wearier—there was no sure sign to differentiate this day from the morning she had returned to Small Angels as a teenager, seeking refuge from her parents' latest rancid stalemate. Then she had turned around in the sunlight and found *beware* scrawled on a gravestone.

It was a small, childish thing—but at that moment it meant hope. She need not be confined to life the way her parents lived it. There was romance and mystery left in the world; there were secret messages and sinister warnings. Kate had laughed, surprised and charmed—

Enough, she told herself. That's enough, now. Leave it alone.

There was no more time left to brood. Birdie's car had just turned the corner and was crawling gingerly up the lane. Her parents and Chloe would be upon her in a moment; she would have to agree what an exciting week they were going to have, say a few gracious things to the bride-to-be and reassure her that she hadn't been waiting long.

Gently, she touched the maimed church door again. A long time ago she had asked what had done it, and Lucia had said, *What will you give me if I tell you?*

What do you want? Kate asked.

They had stared at each other, both suddenly uncertain, until at last Kate had looked away and said, *You wouldn't tell me anyway.*

And Lucia had said, *No. I wouldn't.*

At the time, it had felt as if they had endless time to advance and retreat, to be awkward and tender and belligerent by turns. Time to grow together at their leisure, like trees.

Enough. Enough. She shook these thoughts away like a dog shaking water from its coat and went to help the others unload the car.

Chloe seemed to be a planner by nature, and there was plenty to carry—in addition to two plastic crates of cleaning materials there were two handheld vacuum cleaners, a bag of plastic gloves and masks, and the promised bag of refreshments.

"Coffee and donuts," Chloe said. "Ought to help us to power through. I was thinking we could split into two teams—one for the church, one for the Tithe Barn. What do you all think?"

Nobody objected. Birdie quickly volunteered herself and Bill for the Tithe Barn—she had been itching to get a look inside, she said, ever since it was built.

"Are you sure?" Chloe said. "Don't be too noble. There's a lot of stuff to move in the Tithe Barn, the tables need shifting—"

"Oh, no, that's fine." Birdie looked uncomfortable. "We'll be quite all right."

Bill took up the theme, reminded them all that he had a home gym now and was quite possibly in the best shape of his life. Both of them were insistent that Small Angels was best left to Chloe and Kate.

Still that distaste for Small Angels, Kate thought, even now. Neither of them would look at her.

"So," Chloe said. "We'll be Team Church, Kate, if Bill and Birdie are Team Barn. I can't believe we're finally starting. This makes it all real, you know? So exciting."

As she spoke she was digging in her handbag, retrieving Selina Gonne's key to the church.

"Carrying this about is a workout in itself," she said. "I had no idea it'd be so *heavy.* I'll have amazing biceps by the end of the week."

She was owed a reply, Kate thought, struggling against memory. It wasn't kind to leave her to do all the talking. But she watched Chloe struggle with the lock in silence.

There was a special knack to it. Lucia had taught her that long ago. You had to be sure not to twist the key too far.

The Tithe Barn's owner clearly didn't know or had forgotten to pass the secret on. Chloe struggled, first smilingly, and then with a frown.

"It's not as if he could've given me the wrong key . . ." she said, trying not to sound exasperated. "But it just won't—"

"I can try," Kate said. "If you want."

Chloe struggled a couple of moments longer and then stepped back. "Be my guest. But don't hurt yourself, Kate, it's not worth that. I'll give him a call at the office; if this isn't budging he'll have to send someone out to take a look."

But the trick was just as Kate remembered. The key turned. She pushed the door open gently.

"Thanks," Chloe said, moving past her. "Looks like you've saved the day. I thought we'd be trying to climb in through one of the windows."

Relief struggled with annoyance in her voice. She had wanted to be the one to throw open the door this first time, Kate thought. Here comes the bride, here comes light and life.

Small Angels greeted them with the same smell of cold and dust Kate remembered. Though this was more pronounced now than formerly.

The light coming through the open door showed that the floor was coated with dust, the inscriptions on the ledger stones almost obscured in some places. Dust was everywhere, in fact—in the air, catching the back of Kate's throat as she breathed, and clinging to the carved bench ends. Beyond the door the light was dim, so that it was difficult to tell what was grime and what was shadow.

She had wandered here long ago; Lucia had brought her for a secret visit, a gift that was also a boast. (Kate had never asked how she had managed to get hold of Selina's key.) The church had seemed brighter then. She remembered how the stained glass had sent colored splashes of light across the stone floor. She had admired the carvings on the font as Lucia watched her, proud and eager. The church was a wonder and she knew it, and she was hungry for Kate's response.

Kate remembered discovering with delight the carvings of wild men and lions, the words *Criste mete us spede And helpe all at nede.* She remembered a surprising splash of pink on the stone wall on the west side of the nave.

There was a fire, Lucia had said. *Turned the stone pink. That happens with—*

Limestone, Kate finished. *I know.*

Now she felt the urge to go from curiosity to curiosity, forgetting the cold and the shadow—but Chloe was there behind her, setting the box of cleaning things down on the floor, finding space for the provisions on a little table.

"It smells strange," she said. "Not the usual church smell. Do you know what I mean?"

"It's not a usual church, I suppose," Kate said.

Chloe began unpacking dusters, face masks, various kinds of polish. "Brian would say that was an understatement, wouldn't he?"

Kate said nothing. She had said nothing on this topic for ten years. The closest she'd come had been during Sam and Chloe's visit to her last month.

The trip had clearly been Chloe's idea—she had taken it into her head to mend the coolness between her fiancé and his sister, and no doubt meant well. Kate had been surprised Sam had gone along with it, though.

Chloe had been keen to see where Kate worked, and Kate had obliged because it was a good way to kill most of an afternoon. She showed them the workshop, where new grotesques were being shaped to replace those damaged beyond repair by time and the elements. Then she offered to show them the top of the cathedral tower by way of the scaffolding. There was a little lift, it was perfectly safe.

Chloe said that she would remain on the ground. She was scared of heights, but insisted that Sam should get a chance to appreciate Kate's work properly.

So Kate fitted Sam out with a hard hat and together they made the ascent—two hundred feet to the top of the scaffolding, where green plastic netting gave way to wooden boards and metal poles and there was nothing else to hide the view of the city below them.

Kate was up there often—repairing tracery at the windows, replacing buttresses. It was a strange intrusion to have Sam with her too, peering over the rail with a frown.

Chloe was visible below, easy to spot with her bright blond hair and blue coat. She waved up at them and Sam waved back.

"This was her idea, you know," he said. "This trip."

"I guessed. Not that it's not nice to see you."

They had already invited her to the wedding by that point—already announced that it was to be held back home, in the village Kate had barely visited for a decade. There had been a fleeting trip to see her parents' new home—smaller and more central—and several stays in Ipswich, and at a couple of genteel seaside places close to the village for her parents' convenience. She had found ways to see them without spending any significant time near Mockbeggar.

Because Chloe had been excited and well-meaning, Kate had been noncommittal about returning to the village. She would decline the invitation later, by phone. Sam would understand why and wouldn't make a fuss.

But then, to her surprise, he said, "About the wedding—"

"You've got my blessing already." She shifted a little farther down the planking. The cathedral disappeared under scaffolding entirely, here. It would be ten years before they could even think of showing it to the city again.

"The thing is, we're having it at Small Angels."

She stared at him—catching the metal rail to steady herself, all words knocked out of her.

"Don't look like that," he said. "It wasn't my idea. The village church was double-booked, we'd already given the caterers their deposit, we didn't know what to do. Chloe saw the church and she thought why not. She put the deposit down as a surprise, she thought she was helping us both . . ."

"Did you not try to put her off? Even then?"

He shrugged. He must have been a victim of his own discretion. *Best not to talk about all that*, he had said to Kate, long ago.

"I need to know it's all right," he said.

"How do you mean?" Why make this easy for him, all things considered?

"Please, Kate. Just tell me it'll be all right."

She touched the cathedral stone very gently. This section alone had taken sixty years to build, had stood for six centuries. There was something steadying about that.

"I don't know," she said. "Probably."

"Will you be there?"

As she paused, he leaned again over the rail, gave Chloe another wave and a thumbs-up. She was probably watching them talk and assuming that her efforts to get them closer again were already taking effect. He was trying to talk lightly. All the same, she heard an old tone in his voice, a note she hadn't heard for a long time. When they had been very young, he would ask her to tell him that things would be all right. She would shut her bedroom door against the shouts and crying from downstairs and they would crawl under her bed, a makeshift cave, and there she would tell him it would be OK—*here's how this turns out all right.* She would sketch anodyne futures (their parents reconciled, the whole family placidly sharing a takeaway) until he felt better.

He didn't know what it meant, asking her to go back. He didn't know because he had refused to know—when she had needed to share the horror she had seen and the horror she could no longer remember but which had left its mark on her like a scald, he had refused to listen. He had left her alone with her hurt.

She thought of this, and she thought of the two of them lying in the dust on her bedroom floor. *Here's how this turns out all right.* He was worried in spite of himself. And so she had said that she would be there, she would help.

After all, Small Angels would most likely be no trouble. Things were quiet now.

Things were quiet. In the church this morning there was no sound but the soft noise of her and Chloe moving warily through the building.

"I'll light the lamps," Kate said.

Chloe had been warned that Small Angels had no electricity, and that the wedding would be lit by candles and oil lamps only.

"I thought they'd be brighter," Chloe said, following her closer to the altar. "We might have to bring some extra lights in, if only for the photos."

As she stepped closer to the nearest lamp, Kate wondered if Chloe was entirely well. She was pale, and her voice had turned slightly hoarse.

"Are you all right?"

"The dust's getting to me, I think—the sooner it's gone the better. Let's get to work, shall we? Can't have Team Church lagging behind Team Barn."

Chloe grew more cheerful as they set to work. With her mask on, wielding a vacuum cleaner against the worst of Small Angels' grime, she seemed more like herself—calling observations to Kate about the church's beauty, the scandal of its neglect.

To Kate the scandal—the sacrilege—seemed to lie with Chloe herself, barreling into the Gonnes' sanctuary and filling the air with synthetic lemon, sending dust upward and banishing the peace of the uninterrupted past. Here the Gonnes had come monthly, in fear and duty. They had sung their song and lit their candles and waited anxiously for morning. Lucia had told her that much in the early years of their friendship. *It's the most important thing,* she said. Now here was Chloe beating hassocks against the porch wall, collecting rubbish in a black bin-liner.

"There's all sorts here," she told Kate. "Old playing cards, *ancient* cigarette packets—some of this stuff must date back decades."

The Gonnes' possession of Small Angels had dated back far longer, of course. Now they were tidied away, their past was being divided into the recyclable and the non-recyclable.

No point making a big thing about it. They had been here, and now they weren't. That was all. Kate went to work. There were muddy footprints over a ledger stone commemorating a sixteenth-century nobleman—she scrubbed at it until the prints were gone and the words swam in front of her eyes when she blinked. She was used to far more skilled work, but the sensation of restoring something valuable with her hands was familiar and comforting.

"Kate?"

The noise of the vacuum stopped. Chloe had reached a far corner of the nave. Like its neighbor Mockbeggar, Small Angels seemed, at times, to grow larger than it had any right to be. In the uncertain light, there were corners that were hard to penetrate.

"Kate, what's this?" Such distaste in her voice. Had a rat got into the church?

Kate straightened up with some pain—knees cold from the stone floor—and went to see what Chloe was looking at.

Chloe had discovered the Rood Screen, oldest of Small Angels' curiosities, unchanged since Lucia had shown it to Kate a decade ago.

It was leaning against a wall, carefully removed from direct sunlight—a *memento mori* as old as the oldest parts of the church. Two skeletons smiled, and one offered the other a handful of flowers. Their robes were rotting but the colors were warm. In the wrong light the painted dead were horrifying—red-eyed where, centuries ago, a couple of puritan iconoclasts had defaced them, gouging out the jewels once set there. But of all Small Angels curiosities, they were the ones most worth seeing. The mingling of delicate blooms and starkly painted ribcages had made the teenage Kate feel suddenly, gaspingly aware of her own life.

The feeling was the same now. *Use your time,* the dead seemed to whisper. *Your time is very short.*

"Could we cover it, do you think?" Chloe said. "A curtain, or something?"

"You don't like them?"

"I don't want them watching me get married."

Kate felt a slight surprise. Chloe had seemed to enjoy Brian's story so much, Kate had assumed that she must take at least some pleasure from the macabre.

"They don't mean any harm," she said.

"A screen might work," said Chloe. "Or a dust sheet, maybe. We'll think of something."

They broke for refreshments soon afterward. Brian and Birdie were reluctant to eat inside the church—what if they got crumbs on Chloe's clean floor, Birdie said—so they ate in the graveyard.

After the coffee and donuts were disposed of they returned to their work. As Birdie followed Bill back to the Tithe Barn, Kate saw her glance fleetingly back at her and Chloe.

Nobody wants to know, Sam had said once. *Not Mum, not Dad, not anyone.*

The church seemed darker after the brightness of the day outside. She and Chloe returned to work without discussion, coaxing dust out of the intricate whirls of the pew carvings, bringing robins, foxes and hares into clarity.

The dust seemed all around them now. Chloe coughed often. Tight-voiced, she told Kate she was fine.

After this they worked in silence until Chloe spoke suddenly, taking Kate by surprise:

"What do you think the Gonnes *did* up here on moonlit nights? Did you ever wonder?"

"Not really."

"You're like Sam, then—you think it's all nonsense and should be left alone?" She spritzed polish onto a duster, sending the scent of lemons into the air. "The thing I don't understand is that Sam seems to want it both ways—he says it's just silly superstition and at the same time he doesn't want me messing around with it. If there's nothing to it, then what does it matter?"

"It's tradition. I suppose people around here think just because something's made up, doesn't mean it's harmless."

"What do you mean?"

Kate shrugged. Chloe could not be blamed for being curious, especially after Brian's performance at the Albatross. But Kate had lived for so long without talking about these things with anyone.

Chloe was not put off by her silence. She seemed to have something important to say, in fact.

"Look, Kate," she began, "the thing is—"

Someone knocked at the church door, and they both flinched.

"Hello? Kate?"

It was John Pauncefoot. Of course he would knock rather than coming straight in. Kate went to open the door and found him waiting on the doorstep, looking uneasy.

"I'm sorry," he said, looking at Chloe. "Didn't mean to give you a fright."

"You didn't, John." (Though she did still look startled.) "Everything OK?"

"I thought"—he looked beyond them, into the relative gloom of the church. "I thought you might need a hand. There's a lot to do."

He was still worried, Kate thought.

The thought of his concern didn't sit comfortably with her, but Chloe seemed relieved by his arrival. Whatever she had been about to say to Kate seemed to have slipped out of her mind. She didn't bring it up again.

John was a reassuring person to have about. There was something of the shire horse Hector about him. Quietly he set about cleaning under Chloe's instructions, and within an hour they'd made considerable progress.

At last, Chloe told them both that it was time to down tools—they'd both done sterling work, and she was so grateful.

When she spoke, John glanced at Kate, frowning. Chloe's voice sounded worse, dry and harsh.

"Are you feeling all right?" he asked Chloe gently. "I can get some water for you, if you like."

"No," Chloe said—breathless, slightly impatient. "Thanks, John, but I'm fine. I did want to ask you one favor, though. When I booked the church, they told me that the bells were still hanging in the tower. Do you think you could put me in touch with a couple of ringers for the day? It would be so nice to have them chiming out after the wedding."

John shook his head, serious. "I'm sorry."

"You don't know anyone?"

"Nobody would touch the bells. They're not for us, you see."

Kate remembered hearing the bells of Small Angels as a child. She had been sent to bed long before, but the sound had woken her. The bells called across the fields in clear bronze voices, they seemed to say *here, here, here.* She had opened the window and let the lonely music in. The moonlight had made a pale square on the carpet and she had longed for a moment to be out there at Small Angels. The Gonnes were calling someone, she had thought. Who did they think would answer?

"What do you mean?" Chloe said to John. Irritation made the catch in her voice more pronounced.

"It's not for us to ring them. Never was."

"But I've rented this church for the duration, bells and all."

"Even so. It was always the Gonne family's privilege. So you won't find anyone to help, I'm afraid."

"He's right," Kate said. "One of our quaint local customs." Chloe had rented the church on the basis of said customs—she could hardly complain when some of them proved awkward.

"Right." Chloe coughed once, painfully. Then she took a deep breath, appeared to recover herself. "Well, if that's how everyone feels. I don't want to tread on any toes."

In the unpleasant silence, Kate heard an unexpected sound from outside. There were children laughing close by.

Seized by an urgency she didn't quite understand, she went to the church door.

At the edge of the graveyard, three small girls were playing. The mouse children from yesterday. They seemed to be herding or chasing something that Kate couldn't see—an invisible creature moving from one to another, apparently unable to get past them. The girls were talking to it in soft voices: *Don't be scared, it's OK.*

It was too close, too familiar. There had been other children laughing here years ago.

John, following her outside, saw what she saw and shook his head. "Shouldn't be here. Not safe. The little ones—they don't always understand it all."

He went over to the children and (gently, shyly) told them that they ought to play elsewhere.

After the girls were gone, the graveyard seemed quieter than it had before. The three of them packed the cleaning supplies quickly.

Chloe was being gracious with both of them now, eager to show that the business with the bells had left no hard feelings—but for all that, Kate sensed a new constraint in her. She was still trying to hide the croak in her voice. The dust was clinging to all of them, but it seemed to give her the most trouble. As she let Kate lock the door, she took a handkerchief out of her pocket and wiped her hands fastidiously.

"Do you want a lift back?" she said to Kate and John. "I'm sure Birdie could squeeze us all in."

John shook his head. He wasn't bound for the Albatross straightaway. Kate also declined. She wanted fresh air, a walk.

Chloe nodded. "Now, that's a good idea. Blow the cobwebs away." She swallowed a cough. "Well, thank you both so much for today. And see you later, Kate? Maybe we can grab a drink or something when Sam finishes up?"

Kate said that sounded good. She was troubled by the sudden thought that there was spite bound up in her silence as well as caution. She could not tell Chloe anything—but perhaps she wouldn't have in any case, after everything that had happened with Sam. Why save his fiancée from her troubled wonderings, after he had once insisted that Kate keep her mouth shut? And why save Chloe from the consequences of her actions? She had chosen Small Angels freely.

"I hope she's not too disappointed," John said, when it was only the two of them left in the graveyard.

"About the bells? She'll live."

He looked as if Kate's words didn't please him. But all he said was "You'll be back tomorrow, won't you?"

She nodded.

"That's good. Keeping an eye out." Then he changed tack suddenly: "Lucia Gonne's here, you know. Back in the village. Moved home to Blanch Farm three years ago. Have you seen her yet?"

"Once."

"I don't think she's as well as could be. She comes to the Albatross once in a while. Selling off bottles from Selina's old store. Every time I see her she looks more worn out. I sometimes wonder if things might be getting bad again at Blanch Farm. In the wood."

"How?"

"I don't know." He looked uncomfortable now. This conversation might be the longest and most intimate he'd had for several months. "I don't like to interfere. Only I thought it would be good for all of us, maybe, if you looked in on her again whilst you're here. To see how the land lies."

"Lucia doesn't want me around there, John. She told me to keep away."

He shrugged. "I don't suppose that means much. She asks about you, you know. If I've heard anything from your family. Never asks about anyone else. If there was ever a time she needed help, you'd be the only one she'd let near."

"Why might she need help?"

He didn't answer for a moment. Then he said: "Those little girls just now. They were playing with a goose. Said it came out of the woods."

"I don't—" It was suddenly hard to find words. "There are some things I can't think about too much. You have to understand. I don't want to be dragged back."

Not even for Lucia? Not even for Sam? Had she not come here with the suspicion that she might, perhaps, be needed?

"If there's something wrong, the best thing to do is leave well alone," she said. "Let Blanch Farm take care of itself. It always has before."

"It's just Lucia there now, though, isn't it?" John said.

He left her feeling troubled and annoyed. Another visit to Blanch Farm would do nothing but further wreck her peace of mind. John didn't know what he was asking her. Any more than Sam had known what he was doing when he pleaded with her to return to the village.

She walked up and down the graves, shoring up her determination. She was here as a last resort, and for damage control—nothing else, nothing more. She would not see Lucia again; she would forget as much as possible and get back to her cathedral and her peace as soon as she could. She was wiser now. She would never go back to the woods.

CHAPTER EIGHT

Let Me Be Hanged

When she got back from the church it was almost teatime and she thought how nice it would be to see her fiancé. But when she got to their room she found he was gone. She thought that if she went looking for him they might miss each other, so she decided to wait for him there.

She couldn't get the taste of the church dust out of her mouth. It was in her lungs and in her hair. No one else seemed to have noticed it. She felt like the past was *sticking* to her somehow. She was scared she might start coughing and not be able to stop.

That small storytelling voice was troubling Chloe more and more. It seemed, somehow, to know more than she did.

The first thing she did when she was back in her room was wash her face and hands, but it hardly helped. Her chest still felt tight, as it hadn't done since she was a child suffering from asthma. Even as a young girl, she'd kept a close eye on such symptoms—she liked to catch them before her parents did. They had never been good at managing worry, particularly when it concerned their daughter. At school Chloe would allow her friends (she had a lot of friends) to grow dramatic and make a fuss of her whenever she took out her inhaler. Bad lungs became the fashion in their class for a while. But at home she had played down every symptom.

She had thought she had grown out of the asthma entirely. It had been a long time since she used to write *inhaler* at the top of every holiday packing list. She remembered her childhood research, though. An asthma attack could starve the brain of oxygen. She had imagined it, once or twice, wondering if when it happened you'd know it was happening. Was it like fainting? Or was it like watching someone go through a house, turning out the lights one by one?

Now, in the Albatross, she breathed steadily, deliberately, and reminded herself that dust could affect anyone like this. She was out of there now, and Small Angels was cleaner than it had been for years. The worst was over. She opened the window, and sat down on the bed with her lists, her beautiful wedding planner. She tried to concentrate.

She and Sam had first met in a stationer's. The story was a good one—they had perfected it through telling and retelling, twining her memories and his together into one strand.

Sam had been tasked with buying a birthday present for a colleague he barely knew and was having no luck among the diaries, novelty mugs and photo frames.

Chloe had noticed his misery and offered to help; when Sam confessed that he was beginning to loathe the place and everything in it, she leaped to the shop's defense. There was poetry in the crisp, unopened notebooks, she told him, and in the pastel Post-it notes and the tiny memo stickers. Think of writing your plan and crossing things off one by one, and when you're done, the thing you wanted to happen has *happened.* With colored pens and rolls of washi tape you can bring the world to heel.

She realized later that this philosophy would have been alien to him. During Sam's childhood, the Unthanks had never been sure that any plan might not be interrupted by one of Bill's absences, by a poisonous quarrel. If the Unthanks made lists in those days, they were lists of grievances, and these were too jealously kept to require writing down.

After their engagement, Sam had taken her shopping, and together they had picked out an exquisite notebook to start planning the wedding in detail. This final week—beginning on Sunday with the Hag Night and concluding a week later with the Post-Wedding Brunch—had been worked out and finalized months ago. The first draft was still there on the first page of the planner. She turned over pages—irrationally checking that it was all still there, nothing had changed. Her eyes felt tired, dry with dust.

I'll rest awhile, she thought. What's the harm? I've got all the time in the world.

"Shut up," she said.

It was odd and unpleasant to hear her own voice in the empty room. She was not in the habit of talking to herself. But it did not feel like talking to herself, exactly.

She had no answer to her outburst, not even from the pigeons. The Albatross was still and sleepy.

It was almost too warm. Her thoughts were muddling. She turned over a page of the wedding book, listlessly, and thought that she no longer understood the sequence she had planned out in different colored inks. The days had run into each other.

She noticed that the wedding dress—which she had yet to get mended—was hanging a little crooked on the back of the door. She should get up and straighten it, and check on the veil in its box on top of the wardrobe. Perhaps it should be shaken out to avoid creases.

She lay back, intending to stand in another minute. She thought, vaguely, that her hand still hurt where the splinter had lodged itself. The throbbing had subsided before, but now it was growing worse again.

That confused, unhappy feeling followed her into the dream. She was still upstairs in the Albatross, but it was night. The moon cast a sharp square of light on the old wood floor.

She was alone in the room, but there was someone close by, talking in a hoarse voice.

Too much beer, she thought—cross rather than fearful.

But the man's voice grew clearer and clearer through the wall, and she realized that he was not drunk but terrified:

Let me be hanged. Please God let me be hanged.

Nobody answered him. Perhaps he was alone in his room as Chloe was in hers.

He's come out of the woods. Please God keep him away from me and let me be hanged.

She couldn't move—not to comfort him, not to escape the sound of that desperate voice. She could only lie still and listen. The pleading seemed to go on and on.

Let me be hanged. Let me be hanged.

He talked his mouth dry and his throat raw and still he kept on. He talked until Chloe thought he no longer understood the sense of what he was saying.

Then at last he stopped short with a gasp—

He's outside now. Can't you see him?

She woke suddenly. At first she was only aware of a confused knowledge that something needed to be done very quickly, there wasn't a moment to lose.

Then she realized that Sam was back, laptop under one arm. He was staring at her from the doorway with a frown.

"What happened to your notes?" he said.

"Nothing."

She sat up. Loose pages from the notebook were scattered across the bed, out of their right sequence. Her sleep couldn't have been restful. She began gathering the sheets together—disquieted, almost ashamed. She didn't like to think her sleeping self capable of such things. There was a touch of violence in it: a couple of the pages had actually been ripped out.

"How was the church?" Sam asked. "Tiring, by the looks of it."

"It was. Dusty, too. We'll get there, though."

She was glad now that she'd lost her chance to talk to Kate in the church. Sam was obviously the person to ask. He would shake his head over her trip to the woods, and the story voice that was still intruding into her thoughts—but he would tell her it was nothing. All of it was nothing. Small Angels was old and dusty, and she was understandably stressed, and that was all.

"Sam—"

She stopped. He had set two covered plates down on the bedside table. She could smell potatoes and onions.

"What's that?" she asked.

"Tea. Brian had started serving. He insisted on giving me these to take up."

"Are we not going out to eat? Downstairs, at least?"

"I wish there was time. This job is taking longer than I'd thought." He looked tired and strained, she thought. The day spent indoors didn't seem to have agreed with him.

"What's slowing you down?" she asked.

"The Wi-Fi. It's killing me, waiting for things to upload. Nothing *sends*—all my emails keep bouncing back, and I can't get onto our work drive to access anything and when I try to ring the others to see how things are, their end the reception cuts out on me. I was four hours trying to add one PDF to the website. There's about three hours' work left for me to get through *today,* and I'm half-afraid to log back on in case I've lost everything I was working on—" He broke off, catching himself. "This wasn't how I planned this week going."

She stood up, uncovered the plates in turn. Steak-and-kidney pie, piping hot. A minor work of art. She ought to have had an appetite for it, but she didn't. There was still the flavor of church dust in her mouth. She wondered how Sam had missed the asthmatic rasp creeping into her voice.

"Look at this. John's done us proud," she said.

"I don't know what to do."

"Eat first," she said, passing him one of the hot plates. "Then we can work something out."

He looked at her—weary, affectionate. "You always say that. *We can work something out.*"

"It's always true."

There was still time. She could set down her knife and fork and tell him some of it.

He's come out of the woods. He's outside now. Can't you see him?

But Sam looked worse than she had ever seen him. She had always known that he had set his heart on making the business a success—making her proud, making their lives secure—but until now the depth of his need hadn't fully registered with her.

"I think of us losing this account and I feel—strange," he said, after a few moments' silence. "Chills up my arms. I didn't know it was really possible to feel your blood running cold, did you?" He tried to laugh.

She stood up and put her arms around him. She waited for him to realize that she needed comfort too, but he did not notice.

"You're going to have to go to Bill and Birdie's for a few days," she said. "They have better internet. You can get everything fixed from there."

"Really? You're sure?" he said. "I don't have to go." (But she could already see his face relax a little.)

"I'm fine here. You're not meant to see me the night before the wedding anyway, are you? So that'll be easier to manage, at least."

She could ask to accompany him. It would be cramped, and she would have to live with the knowledge that she had wasted money booking a room they didn't use. John's feelings would be hurt. But she could do it, all the same.

Instead she helped Sam pack what he needed. He asked her if she wanted him to stay a bit longer—they could have a drink, or something—but she saw that his thoughts had already run ahead of him. He was in Bill and Birdie's house, coffee at his elbow. He was prioritizing tasks as he spoke.

When he was gone, she behaved very sensibly. She went downstairs, drank a solitary glass of wine. The pub was quiet tonight. John Pauncefoot was elsewhere—behind the bar was John's daughter Meg, pink-haired and no-nonsense. It was a relief not to have to dwell on what he had said about the bells. As if he expected the Gonnes to come back to ring the changes. As if all Chloe's dusting and sweeping was futile.

She came upstairs early, showered and put herself to bed with a cup of tea. The dream lingered, like a stain that had only partly washed out. She wanted to fill her mind with other things before she fell asleep. She picked up the dark, ingenious thriller she had bought herself as a wedding-week treat, and when at last her brain began to skip and stutter over paragraphs she read for a little while from an old copy of *Little Women* which she had found on a shelf in the corridor. John had a good stock of classics, mostly children's fiction.

She had not picked up *Little Women* for a decade. Now she read for half an hour, and put it down feeling steadied, refreshed. It had been one of the books her mother had read to her before she was old enough to read for herself. Good reading for a haunted house, she thought.

Calm now, pleasantly aware of her own good sense, she fell asleep thinking of others you could add to this kind of list. Magazines, perhaps. P. G. Wodehouse almost certainly. What else?

She had—of course—never needed a night-light, not since she was a very small child. She fell asleep in absolute darkness, ignoring the sense that the room was larger and quieter without Sam's presence. When she woke again the darkness was just the same.

But the silence felt different. She could not shake the feeling that somebody had just stopped talking.

It had been decades since she felt real night-dread. It was a part of her childhood she had forgotten. Now it all came back. She knew with utter certainty that she could not roll over in bed; she could not turn her back on the room.

She began to feel that there was somebody standing close to the bed, staring down.

She lay very still. They must not know she was aware of them. It would be much worse if they knew—

The doomed man shifted on the other side of their shared wall.

Please, he said.

She turned the light on then, hastily banishing the dream—it must have been the dream again. Even though it hardly seemed that she had switched between sleeping and waking. Even though it felt as if she had been awake all the time.

She told herself to grow up, to stop being ridiculous. But light on or light off, she couldn't sleep again.

Instead she became furiously productive. She cleared her phone of unwanted photos so that she would have space for new ones taken over the weekend. She set every electric device she had charging. She took out her wedding shoes and walked up and down, clattering on the old wood floor.

Still broken in. She could still run.

It was the quietest part of the night now. She couldn't remember ever seeing this hour in alone before. How endless it seemed, without company.

She took down the veil from its box and shook it out. No creases.

Let me be hanged.

What if she were to knock on the wall, or go out into the corridor and call to him? What if he called back?

She took the veil to the mirror, tried it over her head—first with her face hidden, then visible. The effect, with her pajamas, was disconcerting. The combination made no sense.

Outside now. Can't you see him?

She waited, still wearing the veil. No more sounds followed.

A bird cried far off. Then silence resumed.

At last she crept back into bed, so chilled that she thought that sleep would never come now. And at the same time her injured hand felt very hot.

She must have slept eventually, because the next thing she knew was waking again—waking with dull surprise, dull dread. It was just before dawn, and something bad had been done.

She was sitting up in bed, her wedding veil in her hands. It took her a moment to understand what she was seeing—to grasp the strange ruin of the expensive lace and tulle.

In her sleep she must have taken the veil and twisted it tight, looping it around on itself, knotting it into a strong and slender rope. Now what she held was a noose.

CHAPTER NINE

The Feast of the Ice Saints

Lucia in continuation

Harry told me that the girl in the graveyard would soon tire of her visits. But she kept coming back. She would arrive looking stern and tense, but a few minutes among the graves would soften something in her face. On her third visit she brought a book with her. The time after that she brought not only a book but also apples and crisps and a flask of coffee. She sat in the sun with her back to one of the graves—the same slab where I'd chalked *beware*—and read for about an hour. She was so still that the graveyard birds, bright-eyed robins and blackbirds, hopped close. From time to time I saw her look up from her book and smile faintly, keeping so still that they were not frightened away.

That fourth visit, when she finally departed, she left an unopened packet of crisps behind, just sitting on top of the tombstone, too deliberately placed to have been forgotten.

When I was sure she was gone I approached the grave and stared and stared for a while.

She'd guessed I was there, then. How long had she known? Why hadn't it driven her off? I worried she was making fun of me, but I took the crisps all the same.

We never had crisps at Blanch Farm. (There's fruit in the orchard if you're hungry, Nan used to say.) I thought of the graveyard girl casually picking this bag out of the cupboard that morning. Her family probably kept their cupboards full of such snacks. They probably had sweetened cereal—the kind with plastic toys at the bottom—and a coffee machine, and a fridge that could make its own ice. I knew that these things existed; in those days they were shorthand for a kind of life that was commonplace and yet utterly strange to me. I thought of the graveyard girl living this kind of life, and I wondered if she was happy.

I thought of asking my sisters what I should do, but I knew that it would provoke an avalanche of advice and criticism. We were meant to let Nan know at once if anyone wandered close to Small Angels.

I decided that I wouldn't be driven out of my own graveyard, not by anyone. For three mornings in a row I slipped away to the church at dawn, and on the third day she was there too.

She was standing at the same grave, reading the inscription. On that spot more than a century ago, they had buried Violet Lovell—born 1886, died 1913.

When I drew close, the visitor turned to look at me, and then back to the grave. She did not seem alarmed.

"She's my ancestor," I said. Meaning Violet Lovell, quiet under her headstone.

"I know," the girl said.

I felt an urge to offer her a gift, and at the same time she made me nervous and I was annoyed at that. I wanted to drive her away. So I offered her a small bit of horror, a story Nan had told me once about Violet Lovell:

"She wanted to die, but she couldn't. She was in terrible pain but her pillows were stuffed with pigeon feathers and you can't die on those. The family all knew, but they wouldn't take the pillows away. She languished for a week until she managed to roll out of bed onto the floor, and then she died."

The girl considered me for a moment. Her eyes were very dark. "Why wouldn't they let her die?"

"They were angry. She'd brought the pain on herself. She tried to run away from Blanch Farm and got lost in the woods. That's when she got ill. The family thought she ought to stay alive and put up with her punishment. Besides, they loved her."

"I'd have thought they hated her. Keeping her like that."

"It was both."

Again the girl considered. "Why did she run away?"

She couldn't stand Harry's presence—his watching, the ever-present threat of his displeasure. She didn't know what was good for her, she didn't have the sense to accept the way things were and follow the rules. This was the moral of the story as Nan told it. This was the secret I couldn't tell this graveyard girl with her knight's face and her thoughtful eyes, even though I wanted to. I wanted to tell her so many things, and it alarmed me.

"You're not supposed to be here, you know," I said. "There'd be hell to pay if my grandparents found out."

"I know." She didn't plead or look anxious. She looked like she saw through me entirely.

Harry had been right. I should leave her alone. When I left I told myself I wouldn't go back to the graveyard until she had tired of it.

But she didn't tire of it. I did go back, and she was there—mornings, usually, and weekends. I learned to wait for those times. I offered her more stories—mostly of dark things, the deaths of those relatives of mine lying around us under their headstones.

She had a listening face, even then. It made me want to talk and talk.

In return, she told me about the things she read. She liked geology. One time I remember her describing volcanoes, the molten rock under our feet. I didn't believe her at first, when she told me about how the Earth was made—I had been taught haphazardly at home by my father and older sisters, and my education was patchy. I could believe in ghosts, but not magma. But my graveyard girl didn't laugh at me; she told me to look it up if I didn't believe her. I looked it up and for a while afterward didn't take a step without thinking of the awesome heat below me, rock bubbling.

She told me about the long-dead peoples who had lived in this part of the country before us—Romans and Anglo-Saxons, fighting and farming and building and burying. I still remember little details because it was her that was telling me—odd words like *wergild* and *nomenclator.*

When she had food or cigarettes she would share them. I remember us sitting against Miss Violet's grave, passing a jar of peanut butter back and forth. It was spring by then. The graves were scattered with cherry blossom; some had settled in her hair, and I couldn't look at it for very long. I didn't ask myself why. Instead I asked her if she wanted to see Small Angels.

Of course I had to let her see the church. Seeing her see the inside of Small Angels was worth what followed. I had expected that Nan would find out that I'd taken the key. It was a wonder I'd managed to steal it away from her in the first place.

I got three days in Fred Hart's room for that. She didn't know what to make of me, I think. None of them did. It wasn't my occasional absences—visits to Mockbeggar, or Small Angels—that caused remark. We all liked to wander from time to time, except Grandpa. It was my disregard for the rules. They didn't understand how I could run so headlong into trouble.

But in the end they would shrug, and say that perhaps it was just my way. I was still Lucia-the-bad, pushing things too far. Only Elphine shook her head when they talked like that.

When I was free again, I went to visit Harry, who I knew would be impatient. I hadn't seen him for a week before I was shut in Fred

Hart's room, so that made ten days' absence. He never liked me to leave it so long.

I explained that it was Nan's fault that I'd been away so long. But his disapproval was all for Kate.

"Look where she gets you," he said, frowning. "Nothing but grief and trouble."

"It's not her fault."

I remember thinking for the first time that the thorn cave in the Rose House—still our refuge—was more cramped than it had been. Making my way through the maze of thorns became more complicated the taller I got. Harry never had patience for my struggles. He seemed to think it was my fault for growing.

That day he had no sympathy whatsoever for the scratches and scrapes the thorns inflicted. I remember wiping blood off my forehead as I talked to him. He didn't seem to notice.

"What if I told you not to see her anymore?" he said.

"You wouldn't ask me that," I said.

We stared at each other. For a moment I saw shadows of him at other ages—older, worn down, less friendly. I saw how he must have been as a teenager, and as a man. His face was full of unfamiliar bitterness.

Then he was a boy again—my friend, still, though I had grown older. Sometimes when we were together I felt as if the gulf between us was widening by the day. He wanted to play the same games as he had years ago. At times I was forced into a babysitter's tolerance—not a role I had much taste for. He seemed childish to me, and sometimes that irritated me and sometimes—less often—I felt a tinge of protectiveness. This child-Harry had so much ahead of him, so little of it pleasant. If someone saw us side by side they would have assumed I was his elder sister. And all the while he was not a child at all, and his mind was older than mine, and he had been forced to learn things I had no notion of. Every so often he'd say something and catch me by surprise and I'd remember. He would always be the elder.

We didn't talk about it further. But more than once in the days that followed he complained that I looked different. I was becoming older, boring. I was forgetting how to play.

I went along with the old games. But there were some I no longer enjoyed. He would always be faster; if I hid he would always find me. He could always climb higher, wade deeper.

Sometimes he lost his temper with me. When that happened he might give me a taste of his pain. Suddenly I would hear a snap, feel the sharp, hot sting of a dog's bite and a half-circle of tooth marks would appear on my arm. And then he'd be sorry, and to make amends he would offer me a memory like that memory of the woods in May, shimmering with bluebells. Or a snatch of a song his mother's husband, the ballad seller, used to sing. Or a glimpse of the Fane after a heavy snowfall—he said the snow these days was nothing compared to what it had been in his time—the dark water stark against the soft, gleaming banks. Fragments of his history which were sweet and not poisonous.

Sometimes we would still lie in the Rose House and look up at the sky, and listen to the woods breathing. But these times grew less and less frequent.

There were days when I missed my handsome trespasser, and on those occasions, I would chalk a scrawl on Miss Violet's grave to show that I had been and gone.

Once I got reckless—it was April, she'd been coming to the graveyard for three months now. The woods were racketing with birdsong, I felt a similar din in my thoughts when they dwelled on her. So I wrote in one rush, hands shaking:

hello darling
sweetness
? can't decide which is best
you pick one ©

Then I waited, hidden, to see what she would do. I didn't dare leave her the chalk that day. I thought—what if she reads it and doesn't write anything back?

When she came to the grave and saw the message she stopped short. I saw a hint of color come into her face.

She wiped the words away, but slowly. I thought that might be a good sign.

The next time I saw her I didn't mention the message, and she didn't either. Instead I asked her if she wanted to see Mockbeggar.

Nothing good would come of it, Harry had said to me when I told him my plan. And if my grandmother found out what I was devising I would be sorry I'd been born.

I told him she wouldn't find out. It would only be a brief visit. Barely past the edge of the woods, the merest taste. Not at all like the wanderings he and I shared. Not even like the plays my sisters and I put on.

He was unhappy, but I distracted him—he could be distracted, in spite of everything; there was enough of the child about him for that. I sang him songs, the kind he remembered from his childhood. He was comforted, and I went through tune after tune and thought of Kate the whole time.

I knew that she wouldn't be frightened of the woods—not stupidly frightened, I mean—even as we lost sight of the fields and the trees closed in on all sides. Mockbeggar was in a sweet kind of mood that day. There was birdsong ringing above us, the youngest trees had small, bright green leaves. We found one glade with no mature trees in it, just saplings. You could almost feel them growing before your eyes, you could almost hear them. They were drinking the spring sunlight so gladly. If you stood there it felt as if you could drink along with them.

It was around midday, always Harry's quietest time, always the hour when you were least likely to see him. I wanted to be cautious, that first visit.

I told her Nan's story of the widow's goose. I told her about the plays my sisters and I still staged in our amphitheater. I thought she might think it was silly or childish, but she seemed to understand.

"It must be different, acting out here," she said.

I hadn't told her what the woods could do, but she seemed to suspect it anyway.

We had already gone farther than I'd meant to—we would have gone farther still, all the way to the amphitheater, maybe, if she hadn't fallen.

I don't know how it happened exactly. She was behind me, and then I heard her stumble and fall.

"Kate?"

Her face was grayish. She had slashed both knees open in her fall, ripping her jeans. For a few seconds she was quiet with pain.

"It's all right," she said at last. "Lucia? Stop looking like that. It's all right."

But even when she managed to get to her feet she couldn't walk without limping, and I knew she would have to come back to Blanch Farm with me, and I could see no way that this would turn out well.

It took us a while to get out of the woods. She had to lean on me to walk, when she put her arm around my shoulders I couldn't think of much else. I should have looked around for Harry, I suppose—a movement at the edge of my vision, dull and thin. But I wouldn't have wanted to see him, even if I had been less preoccupied. I was already insisting in my own thoughts that he couldn't have been responsible for the accident.

If Nan and Grandpa had been at home—if Dad hadn't been mixing poisons in the outhouse, ready to defend our vines against insects and fungi—it would all have been over then. Instead, I got her through the orchard without disturbing anyone but the hens.

As it happened, my sisters were outside that afternoon. Ruby was cutting wood for the stove—she was the one Nan trusted most with the axe—Helena was weeding the bed where some of our supply of mint grew, and Elphine was reading aloud to them. *Anne of Green*

Gables, I think. Always one of her favorites. One time I remember her tearing off the tiniest scrap from a blank page of her copy, eating it carefully. She said she'd always have it with her, that way.

She broke off and let the book slip out of her hands when she saw me and Kate coming up the garden path.

"Lucia, what's happened?" She took Kate's other arm without hesitation, began helping her toward the house.

Ruby stared, frozen with the axe mid-swing. Helena frowned.

"Lucia," she said, "what did you do?"

But there was no time for talk just then. Our visitor was in a bad way. She pretended she wasn't, but she looked sick and faint.

Elphine and I brought her into the kitchen—the other two following—and made her sit down.

The bloody mess of her knees was such an ugly shock that I hesitated—Ruby and Helena too. Elphine was the one who said,

"I'll do it. Please can you get me a cloth, Lucia?"

She worked gently, and as she cleaned the blood away Ruby and Helena asked me in low voices what I was thinking, what I supposed Nan was going to have to say about the whole thing.

"She won't find out," I said. "And besides, I could hardly leave Kate in the woods."

"The point is, she had no business being there in the first place," Helena said. She glanced at Kate. "No offense."

Kate nodded—then flinched as Elphine swiped the cloth over her grazes.

"The clean blood's coming now," Elphine said. "I think that's a good sign. Just got to get the grit out." She turned to Helena and Ruby. "Lucia's right. Of course she had to bring Kate back."

When she was done, she stood up and gathered up the bloody rags. She seemed strange to me for an instant—an Elphine who *did* things, who was much less delicate than we always imagined.

"We've got to bury these, not burn," she said. "Otherwise it'll never heal."

One of those old traditions she used to believe. You could never get her to finish a hard-boiled egg without smashing the shell into fragments, in case evil witches should take it and make a boat out of it.

Ruby began to talk reasonably about how it wasn't Kate's fault she had come to the woods or Blanch Farm; that was my doing. Still, it would be best for Kate if she got out of here as soon as possible and kept away afterward. Away from all of us.

I would have protested, but to my surprise, Elphine spoke first:

"I think you're wrong," she said. "I think it's best if she comes back. If she likes."

"You can't be serious," said Helena. "Think what Nan would say—"

"It'll be worth it." Elphine was smiling now, like it was all settled already. She seemed to have forgotten the bloody rags she was holding.

They would never have invited a visitor of their own accord. Nan didn't approve of interlopers—she said they were liable to trouble Harry's peace, and pry into secrets that didn't concern them. But since I had introduced Kate as a *fait accompli*—and since her visit had attracted no notice, caused Harry no offense—the other three accepted that what was done was done. If one visit did no harm, perhaps another one wouldn't hurt. That was how it began.

We had been trained in secret-keeping since we were small. In spite of this, Nan and Dad wondered what was happening with us in the weeks that followed. (We didn't have to hide things from Grandpa. He was always too preoccupied with his own sadness to be inquisitive.)

It was our mood that was different. Kate had troubled the limits of our world. None of us had ever dared break Nan's rule against visitors. But Kate had been in the kitchen, she had talked to us and agreed to return. It made me wonder what other things might not turn out to be possible.

The vines were waking up by this time, the buds were coming. After spending months of winter looking half-dead, the plants had stirred themselves again. Green life meant more work, but we had planning and speculating to occupy us now. How would we meet Kate again without Nan and Grandpa knowing?

We were canny and careful—Ruby, our leader, insisted on that. We went to the woods neither more nor less than usual, and we only met Kate on the safe days when our grandparents were occupied elsewhere.

I knew my sisters would like her, and they did. After her second visit, none of them questioned the decision we'd made. A friend was a novel thing for all of us. We talked about her a lot, in between her visits. We remembered things she'd said, and speculated about her life in the world beyond Blanch Farm.

"She's quite good company," Helena said. "As ordinary people go." She looked quickly at me, smiled. "Don't look like that, Lucia—you know what I mean. From the village. Ignorant."

"She's not ignorant."

"She is about some things," Ruby put in. "And she's going to stay that way, remember? We agreed."

There was no possibility of telling her about Harry. We told her things she needed to know—remedies for Mockbeggar. Besides this we were protective when we played with her in the woods—she was never alone or unwatched for an instant. She knew there was more to know, but she never interrogated us.

I was jealous and happy to see them see the same qualities in her that I had seen. I liked to watch them respond to her—to see her liking them, especially her kindness to Elphine. And it hurt me that she might like one of them better. Or that she might not understand Elphine.

There were a handful of occasions in our lives when we'd met strangers. The kinder sort spoke to Elphine, and you could see in their manner that they thought they were being *good with her*. Tolerant of her oddities.

It was different with Kate. They were good with each other. That's the best way I can describe it. They had a similar capacity for stillness and careful scrutiny. When Kate showed her how to do or make something—how to sew up a rip or change a fuse—Elphine always watched her like she was working magic.

"How did you learn all this?" she said once.

"Books. Magazines. Things break a lot in our house I wanted to be able to fix them myself."

Elphine understood a moment before I did. She was the one to touch Kate's hand, comforting.

She was the one Kate made the kite for—but this made perfect sense, too. They had been talking about kites during one of our walks, Elphine telling Kate how she had made them out of paper and cane for years, but they never worked well.

"I've got a cheat, if you like," Kate told her. And next time she brought Elphine the plastic-bag kite, which anybody could fly, she said, and required no launch whatsoever. Just hold the long ribbon, toss it up into the air, and there you go.

We watched Elphine fly it at the top of the field and all at once I couldn't bear it, losing you to them.

I could hear my heart beating fast. Everything ugly in me came out at once and I snatched the kite away from Elphine. As I took it from her, the ribbon slipped through my fingers and it was off, floating over the trees, far into the woods.

Just a small thing. You could have made her an identical kite in three minutes. What took the others aback was my sudden spite, and Elphine's shocked, hurt look. She never did understand cruelty, or have any resistance to it.

"It's all right," Elphine said. She had knitted her hands together, the way she always did when upset. "It's all right. You didn't mean it, Lucia. I know." There was a red mark on her wrist from my fingers. Had Kate and the others seen?

I didn't apologize, though I could sense Ruby silently imploring me to do so.

"Let's look for it," Kate said. "That's the first thing to do. Maybe it's caught in a tree." I couldn't read her face or voice, but I saw her touch Elphine gently on the arm as we split up to cover more ground. Ruby and Helena went with Elphine, Kate went with me.

We searched in silence. Once she took the path toward the Rose House, and I told her we didn't walk that way. Otherwise we didn't talk for about ten minutes or so.

"You don't have to stay with me," I said at last.

She looked at me steadily but didn't speak. She was weighing me up, and it was unbearable. Better be written off immediately than held in that kind of scrutiny.

We were standing by the green pools. The woods were still, the pools were their same poison-looking selves. I wanted desperately to undo the whole afternoon, but I couldn't. I was still Lucia, still horrible.

"It's all right," I said. "Go back if you want. I know you must hate me right now."

She didn't answer. I wished she was angry. It would have been easier. She was a head taller than me, and strong. She could shake me until my teeth rattled, I thought. Serve me right.

"You do, don't you?" I said. Miserable and angry. One of Nan's old criticisms came back to me. "You think I'm a nasty piece of work."

"Is that what you think?" she said. She didn't move.

It was awful to like her so much, and not to know what she thought. If there had been a moment when she thought of kissing me—I had wondered, sometimes, if this might happen—it was lost. I'd be lucky if she didn't entirely despise me now.

The others were calling. The light was going and we had to get back.

They had found no sign of the kite. Kate said that she would make another one, it was fine—she would make kites for all of us, if we wanted.

We'd have a grand launch, Elphine said. It would be wonderful. Maybe we would have managed it, too, if things had not gone wrong so soon after.

We had planned to stage a play—Kate's first—the following month. Kate had accepted the invitation, even after the fiasco with the kite. Even so, I didn't go to the graveyard for days, afraid of running into her and spoiling things further.

Surprisingly enough, it was Helena who spoke to me about it. We were out lighting the beacons—it was unusual for the two of us to be in one team, but for that night we were. It was late and I wanted to be back, but the gorse and straw wouldn't catch. The wood we'd brought must have been damp.

"You're not going to be awful when Kate comes to the play next week, are you?" Helena said.

"She might not come."

"Of course she will," Helena said, scornful. "Just don't be an idiot this time. We're not going to *steal* her off you, or whatever it is you're thinking."

I dropped the gorse into the flames all in one go, sending up a flurry of light which startled her for a moment and made her step back. She had understood, then—my jealousy, my fear.

"We're her friends," Helena said. "And I'll always be glad you brought her here. But that's it. It's different between the two of you. Just don't invest too much in it."

"What about you and Ruby? She's got that boy she slopes off with whenever they meet at the county fair; you've got people ringing you from town besotted, begging Nan to put you on the phone. Why can't I have—"

"It's not that." She was impatient. "I'm not singling you out. Why do you always think you're being hard done by? You can do what you want, that's not my business. Just don't imagine you're entitled to anything permanent. Not without Harry's say-so. None of us are. If you settle it'll be with someone he chooses. If you ever have a family, it'll be one he gives you."

The gorse was burning up now, the beacon bright in the night.

"Ruby said you'd already realized," Helena said. "And I said you hadn't. So, now you know." She touched my arm briefly. "Come on. One more left to do and we can go home."

On the day of the play, we went to the edge of the woods with our costumes and the wine Ruby had begged from Grandpa—and Kate was there as she'd said she'd be.

Elphine had brought her costume—a magician's robe, to match her part in the story. That plot was one of Helena's concoctions, a fairy tale she shaped for herself, not an adaptation. Unusually simple, for Helena: the story of a kidnapped magician, the scavenging animals that had grown clever and gifted eating scraps from his spells. I had fox ears, Helena had crow wings, Ruby was a bear. I spent years trying to remember Elphine's costume.

We four were already dressed, and Kate changed to match us, pulling off her jumper and shrugging the robe on over her vest. She looked at me as I watched her but she didn't talk to me; all her conversation on the walk to the amphitheater was for the other three.

We had chosen the date deliberately. There are days in May that are particularly prone to frost. Grandpa called them the days of the Ice Saints—Mamertius, Pancras, Servatius, Bonifatius. We all knew to dread these times. A spring frost could easily kill the buds on the vines, and ruin the harvest overnight. If the weather turned cold, we'd have to lug bougies out to the field. These were lanterns—pots full of wax—that would be left out among the vines. If the frost came, you lit the bougie with a blowtorch and it warmed the air a few degrees. Miserable back-breaking work, setting them burning in the coldest part of the night.

The bougies were beautiful, though. Straight lines of small twinkling lights running the length of the field. It was like walking through a field of fallen stars.

Grandpa was always anxious during this season, checking the thermometer frequently. He had a little device that would beep if the temperature fell, but he didn't quite trust it. If you couldn't sleep and went downstairs for some hot milk, you'd probably find him sitting in the kitchen, coat thrown over his pajamas, listening for the frost.

But in the village, those dangerous days were a turning point—once the Ice Saints had departed, summer was only a thought away. Every year they'd throw a bonfire party to mark the occasion, and all the kids in the village went to it.

This year, we would have a celebration of our own—we'd show Kate we could have more fun than they could in the village. I said we should stage our play at dusk, in the woods, with lanterns.

My sisters wouldn't ordinarily have agreed. It was a risk to stay so late, so close to Harry's time. They knew Harry might not like it. But they wanted to impress Kate almost as much as I did.

By the time we reached the amphitheater it was darker than we'd expected. Too late to turn back now, though.

We bowed to our audience—the Dervish and the other trees of Mockbeggar—and we began.

Along with her robe Kate had a wire crown decorated with tinfoil and sweet wrappers, shining silver and red, and her hair was loose. Not a gifted actor, but she said the words like they mattered. I saw her eyes grow wild as she felt the shift, the woods working their old magic.

Halfway through the first act, a deer stepped into the clearing, at the very edge of the light. She stared at us for an instant—and we stared back, frozen mid-dialogue—and then she vanished.

Elphine wanted to go after her a little way. She used to think of the deer like friends, do you remember that? They were gentle like her; perhaps they did understand each other. Ruby and Helena went with her to search—it was too dark now for any of us to stray off alone.

Here was my chance to talk to Kate at last, our first privacy since the day of the kite. Either she despised me or she didn't. Better to know which.

"Are you angry?" I said abruptly.

"No," she said. She was looking at the fire. I studied her profile, handsome as a statue's.

"If you hate me I'll leave you alone." I was trying to think what a noble person—like one of my sisters—would do. "You can still come here and see the others. If you prefer them."

Then she looked at me.

"I like you best," she said. "Better than anyone. You should know that."

"What?"

She didn't repeat herself. So I spoke instead:

"You didn't say anything."

"You've given me so much already. You brought me here. It would be bad to presume." She was looking at her hands now. "Anyway. I don't talk about some things well. The important things—"

Her magician's robe had slipped off one shoulder. I wanted to kiss her bare skin and so I did. I was clumsy, hardly believing my own daring. All the same, she shivered.

I did that, I thought, wondering. She likes me best and she shivers if I touch her.

She kissed me properly then—she gripped my shoulders like she wanted to be sure of me. It was almost too much. To have exactly what you've wanted for a long time—it can be frightening. She made the world different forever.

Remember that? Remember the sound of the fire growing louder, how the trees stretched over us, how the shadows were dark green and welcoming and we could have stayed there for such a long time if there had been no other people in the world?

We had one moment of grace, and then it was gone.

The firelight was broken by a long shadow. Grandpa had stepped into the clearing, carrying a torch—it was properly dark now; I hadn't realized before.

He didn't come to Mockbeggar. After his brother died in the woods, they became off-limits to him. But he was here now. His face, as he looked at me and Kate, was still and sad.

I jumped up, Kate scrambling to her feet beside me. She nearly tripped on her magician's robe. All at once the costume seemed ridiculous. The power was gone. Grandpa had cut us down to size. We were just two silly girls in silly costumes, crouched in front of a badly made bonfire.

"It was my idea to come here," Kate said quickly. "You can't be angry with them."

His face softened. "You're better away from here, girl. Best for everybody that you keep away."

"Grandpa—" Ruby had returned to the clearing, the other two following. She stared at him and I could see her thoughts in her face, disbelief turning to horror.

"You'd better take this one back to the main road, Ruby," Grandpa said, looking at Kate. "Then get back to the house. Understand?"

Kate clasped my face for an instant and her trembling hand felt like a promise; it made the awfulness of the situation a little less.

Then she had gone, following Ruby without a word.

"Come on," Grandpa said. "Back now, Miss Scarlet." He was sorry for me, I think. Sorry for us all.

Nan was in the kitchen, waiting for an explanation.

In times of crisis, we looked to Ruby: if anyone could reason with Nan, it was her. Now she took a breath, and spoke tentatively:

"It was just a play. We didn't do any damage."

Nan slapped her. The sudden brutality of it took us all by surprise.

"You don't lie to me," she said. "Not ever. Understand?"

Ruby nodded, blinking. I hated Nan then—not for the slap, but for reducing Ruby—twenty-one now, good-hearted and responsible—to a meek child.

"You know what you were risking," Nan said. "And for what?"

"Why shouldn't we have a friend for once, like other people?" said Helena. I was surprised. Open defiance wasn't like her—she used to say it was a waste of time to antagonize Nan directly. We were all knocked a little out of our usual orbits that night, I think.

"She's kind," Elphine said. "And she doesn't talk, Nan. She doesn't cause trouble."

Nan didn't seem to hear her. "Do you know what he could do to you, if he had a mind? If he took it into his head to get offended?"

The kitchen seethed with ghosts for a moment. All those relatives who had lost their places here—Violet Lovell, other unfortunates. The ones whose stories had ended in empty-box funerals. They stretched cold hands toward us and whispered *be very careful.*

"He didn't do anything to us, though," Helena said. "We were there at dusk and it was fine, nothing happened—"

"If that meant anything," Nan said. "You can't trust him to be kind. Can't *predict* him. He'll be gentle one day and vicious the next. We can't ever forget the rules, we can't ever push him too far. I thought you had the sense to understand that."

"Is it always going to be this way?" Helena said. "Us living like this? Like outcasts, to keep him happy?"

Nan said nothing.

"Grandpa?" Ruby asked.

But Grandpa didn't answer. He let Nan go about her work. He didn't like this side of things, perhaps, but he didn't intervene, either.

"This is how it is and how it's got to be," Nan said. "You know how lucky we are to have this place, to have his gifts. None of you want to give up that, I suppose? Even if you could?"

None of us spoke. At that point what she suggested was still unthinkable. I saw the identical dread of exile in my sisters' faces. To lose Mockbeggar would be unbearable. We were devoted to our prison.

"Well, then. You don't get something for nothing. You'll all be happier once you accept that."

Then she laid down our punishment: extra work, no allowance, a complete curtailment of all treats and freedoms. Until she was sure our behavior was mended, we wouldn't be stirring out of Blanch Farm without her leave.

"What about the woods?" Ruby asked.

"You can stay out of Mockbeggar for the time being. Might make you appreciate the place more, being kept away from it. Besides, who knows yet what Harry will make of this night jaunt."

"You think he'll be angry?" Elphine said. (I thought she looked at me for an instant then, but that might only have been my guilt.)

Nan shrugged. "No telling what he'll do, in the right mood."

Two evenings later, the frost came. I woke before dawn and Grandpa and Nan had already been out to light the bougies. I felt in a numb, distant way that I would like to be free under the sky for a while, so I slipped out to the field to see the frost lanterns burning.

The lights were small and gold, twinkling in a way that said *come and play*. The beacons said *keep off, keep away*, but the lanterns were different. They wanted you to come closer. Each lantern brightened and dulled according to its own rhythm, producing a constant flicker.

The only things to hear were the noise of the flames—the crackling, bubbling sound of molten wax—and the crunch of my feet on the frozen grass. I moved farther into the field, skirting the burning cans cautiously.

I was alone in the field, and then I wasn't alone.

Harry was close, but not clearly visible. My height, or a little taller. I think this must have been the oldest he'd ever appeared to me since our first meeting years ago.

"Nan thinks you're probably angry with us," I said. "She doesn't know you knew about the play before."

He didn't answer. Put out I hadn't been to see him, I thought.

"Nan won't let us into the woods," I said. "So don't blame me that I haven't been to visit—"

"I saw you with your girl. You said it was nothing. No account. You said you wouldn't forget me. And now you love her."

I felt my throat prickle. "So what?"

"You can't see her anymore. You can't go away and forget."

"What? You can't ask me to do that. It's not fair. I've got a right to—"

"You haven't got a right to anything." His face twisted with rage. "You're mine, like all the rest of them."

Then he took me by the throat. It was the worst he'd ever hurt me. I could hardly breathe and as my vision swam I felt that I was choking underground, buried out of sight.

I tried to plead with him, but I couldn't get the words out.

"You mustn't see her anymore," he said. He loosened his grip a little. "Promise you won't."

I nodded, too hurt to speak.

He let me go and I stepped back, gasping. Then I heard someone call my name. Grandpa had come through the orchard gate, stepping carefully between the flames of the frost lantern.

"Lucia, what are you—"

Then he stopped, seeing the two of us, me still struggling to get my breath back.

"Don't," I tried to say, but he didn't hear me. I saw fear cross his face—he wanted so much to run. But he stepped forward instead and told me to get back.

"Leave her alone," he said to Harry. "She's done no harm."

Harry shook his head.

"It's all right," I said desperately to Grandpa. "He's my friend, we're just talking; he won't really hurt me." I said more, I think. A desperate scrabbling about for explanations. I saw Grandpa trying to take it all in. His eyes were fixed on Harry. He was imagining his brother's death. He was imagining himself and me going the same way. But his voice didn't shake:

"She's young," he said. "Let her be."

Harry stepped closer—seized his wrist.

I heard Grandpa gasp. I could imagine what he was seeing—Harry's worst memories, pain and betrayal.

"Please," I said.

He thought about it—and in the silence I heard Grandpa's breathing—shallow, agonized. At last Harry nodded. Childish, like we had been deciding whether to play hide-and-seek or marbles. He let Grandpa go.

"Don't hurt them," I said. "I'll keep away from her. I'll be your friend like before. I promise."

"All right." His rage had vanished in a moment. "You won't miss her after a while, you know. It'll be like before."

He wanted my agreement, so I nodded. I tried to look like I believed him.

Then there were only two of us left in the field.

I waited for Grandpa's rage, but it didn't come.

"Lucia," he said.

His voice was strange and slurred. There was something wrong with his face. I couldn't understand at first. Weakness didn't belong to him. What I was seeing didn't make sense.

He slumped forward—Grandpa, tall and tireless, the strongest of us all—and still I couldn't understand. I didn't even think fast enough to stop his fall.

CHAPTER TEN

Mint Tea

It was impossible for Kate to return to the Albatross immediately. John Pauncefoot's warning was best considered outside, away from interruptions. Though she was tired—grimy and aching from the day's work at Small Angels—she took a longer route back into the village, winding down lanes where the hedges grew high on both sides, hemming her in.

When she came to the village, she continued her indirect route, taking detours down small lanes. The village was very quiet for this hour. In her memory, the early evening had been a time when strollers and dog walkers would be abroad; people would pause outside each other's gardens to chat and admire. But tonight the lanes had cleared early.

It might only be John's words that made this fact so noticeable. He had made the peace seem ominous.

But whatever his misgivings, he had been unreasonable in his request. Besides, Lucia had told her to keep away. And his fears were groundless. The woods were quiet now. Ruby and Helena had promised Kate that, the last time she saw them.

They had told her to forget all that she could, and not to worry anymore. Mockbeggar would never trouble anyone again. The strange magic of the place was ended. As to how this had been managed, and what had happened to Elphine—these questions were best left alone.

Kate had tried not to wonder. For a long, lonely decade, she had worked hard at obliviousness. But now she remembered a bonfire in the woods, old velvet against her bare skin, a kiss in the green shadows. Beneath that was a deep, shapeless fear.

Restless, she walked farther through the village. The small thatched cottages were like a line of blank white faces which gave nothing away.

There had been a similar kind of hush on the Gonnes' vigil nights, when the bells of Small Angels would ring across the fields. People would wait, pretending not to feel edgy, until it was all over. It was bad taste to talk about it—Bill and Birdie had drummed that into her early on—but nobody could ignore the bells when they sounded.

It's not foreboding, Kate thought. It's hunger. That's what's wrong with me.

She was famished, in fact, as if she had swum for miles. Instead of heading straight back to the Albatross she made a quick detour to the village shop. It was open (Brian always kept late hours, especially when there was anything interesting going on in the village), windows glowing in the dusk. Brian's deputy—a lanky teenager called Ed—was on duty, so there was no reason not to go in and buy supper.

Kate shopped like a child, picking up everything that looked good to her. She bought local raspberries in a cardboard carton, a fresh-made Victoria sponge, soft bread rolls. She picked out penny sweets just as she had twenty years before—with small tongs, dropping them carefully into one of the plastic tubs which Brian left out for the purpose. She had often bought the Gonnes sweets, aware that they rarely had the opportunity to walk to the post office themselves. Tonight she filled the tray with hard pink bonbons and cola bottles and the sour laces which had been Lucia's favorite, and white chocolate buttons covered with hundreds and thousands. She remembered Elphine setting these out into patterns on her lap and then picking them out one by one. She took two strands of the candy necklaces they had all loved, cracking sweet by sweet into their mouths until all they had left were loops of spit-soaked elastic.

She carried her food to the counter, asked Ed to slice her some of the Stilton behind the glass counter. Some cold beef, too.

She guessed that he was curious—about her return, and about the wedding, and probably about her purchases, too.

She didn't explain, and she had already paid when he finally said, "How're you finding Small Angels?"

"Dusty."

"Ah, well, if dust is all you've got to deal with then you're laughing. It'll look great when it's done. And you've got the Tithe Barn ready too, haven't you? Great place for a party."

"Have you been up to see?" she asked.

"Not yet. Haven't had a chance."

"You should come," she said. "We'll be there all week, getting ready. You could have a look round, see how it's all shaping up. Since you're wondering."

He looked down at the counter—brushed a few sugar crystals onto the floor. "Thanks. I'll stop by if I'm free."

She took her food, and left. He wouldn't be happy until she was out of sight, she suspected.

People were wary. Perhaps, like John, they were waiting, even if they pretended otherwise.

Surely she had never been so hungry before. Back in her room, she ate with an eagerness she had forgotten. She had been less interested in food since Elphine's death. Pleasure in sweet and salt had dulled. Now the savor had come back without warning—had she ever tasted such fresh bread? It was all local, if the labels were to be believed. There was a teaspoon on the tea tray; she hacked at the cheese with it, took spoonfuls of red jam, greedy and sticky-fingered. Last came the cake—Victoria sponge, topped with powdered icing sugar. She could taste eggs in it—probably eggs from hens who had wandered over the fields of her childhood.

That night she slept with a soundness she had forgotten, and woke just after dawn. Her small room was lovely in the first light—the sun made the floor and the ceiling beams honey-colored; the white-washed walls were fresh and bright.

Eager to avoid further conversation with John, she went downstairs intending not to stop for breakfast. There was plenty left over from her feast last night—she would take leftovers and enjoy her peace.

But she was later than yesterday, and there was more bustle downstairs. She could smell coffee, bacon, eggs and toast, and John was talking to his daughter Meg as they set the tables.

"—what to make of it," he was saying as Kate came in. "He's never taken on anything like this before."

"Try again this afternoon," said Meg. "Ten to one he'll be fine. If not—"

Both turned to look as Kate came in. John did not seem eager to share the topic of their conversation with her, but Meg—tutting over Kate's refusal of breakfast—explained the problem:

Yesterday afternoon, John had decided to try Hector on the track up to Small Angels. The cart was light and narrow, but even so it wouldn't be the easiest path, and John wanted to be sure that Hector was happy with the journey.

Everything had been fine until they left the main road—here, Hector had stopped and refused to proceed. Something had spooked him. John had a job keeping him from trying to bolt.

"Dad doesn't want to worry Chloe," Meg said. "I know she's excited about having Hector in the wedding. But if that journey's going to upset him for some reason, then—"

"We'll think of something else, if that happens," Kate said. "Can't have Hector frightened."

John said quietly, "He's never been like this before."

"So most likely it's a one-off," Meg said. "Don't panic just yet, Dad.

If he gets upset on the day, we'll have a car waiting." She turned to Kate. "I really don't think it'll be a problem on Saturday. So if you happen to mention it to Chloe, maybe don't make a big deal of it."

Kate said she wouldn't, and avoided John's anxious gaze as she went out.

It was a small thing. Only to have Hector at the wedding would be a kind of guarantee. She had a superstitious feeling that nothing truly wrong could happen while he was there. The idea of being deprived of his strong, kindly presence felt like a bad omen.

The village was not yet properly awake, and this morning's walk to Small Angels was as quiet as yesterday's. It was the hour when she had been accustomed to meet Lucia.

Miss Violet's stone was free of chalk writing, and Kate was a fool if she'd expected or wanted anything different.

Her plan for this half hour was modest: quiet, a rest, a slab of yesterday's cake.

But she had barely unwrapped her food before she was interrupted. One of the mouse girls was pelting through the field toward the graveyard. She looked as if she had come from the woods.

She halted, panting, in front of Kate. It took her a moment to recover enough breath to speak.

"You've got to come with me," she said.

It was the eldest of the three. She looked as if she had been crying. She wouldn't stop to answer Kate's questions, but took her hand and tried to drag her to her feet.

Kate stood up and went with her. They took the graveyard and the field at a run, and were a few yards into the woods before the child came to a stop.

"What have you been doing?" Kate asked softly.

The smallest mouse girl was propped up against the mossy trunk of a fallen oak. Kate's immediate thought was that she was unconscious. But the child's eyes were open, staring fixedly at something no one else could see. The middle sister was alternately talking to her and shaking her, desperately looking for some response.

"Don't," Kate said.

The middle sister turned her head sharply.

"Don't shake her. It won't do any good."

The smallest child was trembling. As Kate went slowly closer, she realized that she was probably too frightened to move.

Lucia and the others had been cautious with Kate, during the days of their friendship. After visits to the woods, they would ask Kate repeatedly if she was all right. Sometimes she had suffered, but only slightly—the woods might outstay their welcome in her mind. A story—even an idea—heard or told under those trees might linger and trouble her. On one occasion—she would never let Lucia know this—even Miss Violet's fate had crept into her nightmares. She had woken one morning with her pillow gripped tight in one hand, convinced that it was full of pigeon feathers.

She had never mentioned these moments to any of the Gonnes, concerned that they might stop allowing her to accompany them on their excursions. She didn't want them to think that Mockbeggar was too much for her.

She had never suffered like the child in front of her, though. This needed expert attention.

"You can make her better, can't you?" said the eldest sister.

"No." Kate stooped and picked up the youngest sister—a very small child and yet a deadweight in her arms. "We'll have to go to Blanch Farm."

If there was another option, she would have taken it. The outrageousness of this bad luck was staggering—to be driven back there after everything she had told herself. Lucia would think Kate was nursing old tenderness, unable to stay away.

Blanch Farm was not a long journey, even with the child in her arms, even with the two older girls running alongside trying to help and almost causing Kate to drop their sister every other second.

The orchard gate was locked today. Of course Lucia would be prudent at the worst possible time.

"Rattle the gate," Kate told the children. "Shout."

They followed her orders with enthusiasm—the middle sister kicking the bars until Kate thought they might actually give way. Still, it seemed a long time before Lucia came through the orchard. Her expression, as she took in Kate and her companions, changed too rapidly for Kate to read it.

"Accident in the woods," said Kate.

"So take them home."

"You know that's no use. You have to do something."

"That's not my job. Especially not now."

The child in Kate's arms was crying now—silently, hopelessly. And there was Lucia posturing beyond the bars, pretending she had nothing decent in her.

You're too old for this, Kate wanted to snap. *Grow up and start looking about you.*

"Open the gate, Lucia," she said.

Lucia glared at her a moment, then dropped her gaze, unfastened the lock.

"This is just for once," she said to the children. "Don't think about coming back."

"OK," said the middle one. In spite of the seriousness of the situation, Kate sensed a ghost of glee in her voice. *Ha. She made you let us in.*

Kate's sole previous visit to the Blanch Farm had been made after her accident in Mockbeggar. She could vaguely recall the kitchen's long wooden table, its red tiled floor. But her most vivid images were the bright, earnest faces of the Gonnes. Lucia frowning over her injuries.

Still, Kate surely would have noticed if the kitchen had been so neglected ten years ago. The Gonnes were largely indifferent to housekeeping, but the sheer movement of people through this room, the heart of the house, would have kept the dust from settling. Now there was grime on the windowsill, and the air smelled of rotten fruit.

Kate avoided Lucia's gaze. She didn't want Lucia to see her reaction to the state of the place. How Lucia lived was none of her business now.

"Put her in that chair," Lucia said to Kate. "And run some water." She turned to the eldest sister. "Put the kettle on."

Both did as they were directed. Lucia's voice had changed, Kate noticed. She had the authority of someone who knew what they were doing.

Lucia tore a handful of leaves from the mint growing in a pot on the windowsill, dropped them into a bowl and poured boiling water over them. She repeated the same process with the large teapot near the sink, and in another moment three cups of mint tea had been poured into two grimy-looking mugs. Then she filled a second bowl with tap water and stirred in a liberal spoonful of white powder from a jar on the counter.

"What's that stuff?" said the eldest sister.

"Bicarbonate of soda. Drink your tea." Lucia looked at Kate. "If I give you a cloth, can you wash her face with it? Wipe it over and then wipe it off with clean water. And help her breathe in some of the mint steam. Best thing for her if she can't drink."

Kate nodded. Lucia lit candles, took a book down from a high shelf.

"Is that spells?" said the eldest sister.

Lucia showed her the spine. *The Wind in the Willows.* A very old copy.

"Listen carefully and don't interrupt," she said. And she began to read. Perhaps for five minutes without a break. Kate had forgotten her skill at this.

At last Lucia stopped. The youngest sister had fallen asleep. The other two had finished their mint tea.

"Will she be OK?" asked the eldest.

"Tell her to wash her hair with more bicarbonate of soda. Keep a candle burning in whatever room she's in. If she's still bad, put a knife under her bed. Just on the floor, understand? Now you'd better tell me what happened. Everything. I'll know if you're lying."

The sisters looked at each other.

"It wasn't my idea," said the middle one, finally.

"It was," said her sister. "It was all of our idea. We were playing with this goose yesterday, in the graveyard. It's there, but it isn't—"

She broke off, looking from Lucia to Kate, not sure if she would be understood.

"Go on," Kate said. "We know what you mean."

"It's friendly, the goose. It's got a bell and a blue ribbon round its neck. We were just playing with it, we didn't mean to scare it away, but it ran off into the woods. So today we decided we'd go back to see if we could find it again and we did, and this time when it ran off we followed it up to the woods. Alice ran in after it, and by the time we found her she was like *that*." She glanced, worried, at her sister. "We could hardly get her to talk."

"Did she say what had happened?" Lucia asked.

"She said there was someone else there."

"Who?"

"I don't know. I didn't see anyone. But Alice said—she said he had something in his hands, she thought it was a rope. She said he was made out of the dark space between the trees. And he was watching us and his eyes were dead. And she said *he doesn't want us here.* Then she started breathing strange and she couldn't talk any more."

Lucia went to the window. The eldest sister looked at Kate.

"I'm sorry," she said quietly. "We didn't know."

"You knew not to go into the woods," Lucia said. "Isn't that the rule with you people? Not a hard rule for anyone who isn't an absolute *moron*—"

"Lucia," Kate said. "They're children. And they're sorry."

Lucia sighed. "Fine." She turned to the eldest sister. "Get out."

"How do we—"

"I don't care. Just get out."

"You can't make them walk back, Lucia," Kate said. "Have some sense." She turned to the eldest sister. "I'll ring your parents."

The landline had been ripped out about five years ago, it

emerged—so Kate called the girls' mother from the orchard, where the reception was the least feeble.

When she hung up after a brief and tense conversation, she found that the middle sister had followed her outside.

"Did you tell our mum about the woods?" she asked.

"No."

"Why?"

"No point. You won't go there again, will you?"

The girl shook her head. Then she said:

"Will Alice be all right? Really?"

"Yes. Just give it a couple of days."

"What about the thing in the woods?"

"What about it?"

"It was real, wasn't it? Not a game, or Alice getting scared over nothing."

"Stay away," Kate said, "and you don't need to worry about whether or not it was real."

The child frowned, but didn't argue. Perhaps she had seen something in Kate's face to give her pause. Kate went back inside without another word.

The girls' mother arrived soon afterward. She took her children from Kate with a minimum of conversation, glancing up at Blanch Farm with distaste.

When they were gone, Kate returned to the kitchen. Lucia was sitting at the table, turning over the pages of *The Wind in the Willows.* Kate caught sight of an illustration of Mole, bound for the river, his chores left undone: *Hang spring-cleaning!*

Lucia looked worse than she had a couple of days ago. Her hands were shaking.

"Have some tea before you go," she said, without looking at Kate. And Kate sat down, waited as Lucia boiled fresh water, added fresh mint leaves, poured a mug for each of them. They drank in silence for another moment.

"It's true, isn't it?" Kate said at last. "What they saw."

"Kids do imagine things. You said yourself the other day—"

"Don't give me that. Don't you *dare*. It's real, it's coming back. Isn't it?"

"All right, then," Lucia said. "Yes. Since you really want to know. I think it is."

Her eyes were on the floor. Kate thought that it would have been beyond her to break the news gently, even if she had wanted to. She had the expression of someone mid-fall.

But now that there was no doubt left, Kate found she was strangely calm. It was a relief, at least, not to have to fight to ignore the signs. Mockbeggar was waking. She was joyful and she was terrified. She wanted to run.

"What happens now?" she said.

"What do you mean?"

"There are dangerous things in the woods. Will you need help? I mean if things go wrong again."

Lucia shook her head, scowling. "You've got no idea what you're saying. You never knew half of what went on here. And you've forgotten things. You've been pretending them away for years."

That same sneer from the other day. Kate lost patience with her:

"What else was I supposed to do? How else was I supposed to live with it? Helena and Ruby wouldn't tell me anything. I had no explanation for what happened, no one who'd listen to me. I didn't know how much was real. *You* wouldn't even see me."

"That was for the best."

"How could it possibly have been for the best?"

Kate took a breath, catching herself. It had happened a long time ago, the hurt should be long gone.

"I knew you'd lost Elphine," she went on, calmer now. "I never forgot what that would have meant for you and the others. But even so. You walked away. Everything we were—you put it aside so easily. It meant so little, in the end."

Lucia was very pale.

"You have no idea what it meant," she said.

Outside, a hen scratched in the yard. There was no other sound, and neither of them could look at the other for a moment.

"You have no idea," Lucia said again. "That's the point. You sit there saying *let me help* and you have no idea what's going to happen now. If you had any sense you'd be out of here already—"

Lucia had stood up, but she seemed to have lost track of where she was and what she intended to do. Kate had never seen her look so lost.

"Lucia." She went to her and took her gently by the shoulders. "Look at me. It's all right."

An impulse seemed to catch Lucia then, and she put her arms around Kate, clinging fiercely, desperate like someone trying to wake from a nightmare. She was trembling.

Kate had forgotten the warmth of her—all spines and burrs in her words and yet in Kate's arms she was soft and yielding; she curled against Kate's chest as if this was where she belonged.

At last Lucia pushed her gently, regretfully away, stepped back. She was still shaking.

"Tell me," Kate said. "Tell me what's going to happen now."

Lucia stared down at her grazed hands and said nothing.

"Don't I at least deserve that? Ruby and Helena said *let it lie.* But if it's not safe anymore then I have a right to know. After what happened—"

"What *did* happen to you, Kate? How much do you even remember?"

Kate searched for an answer and found nothing. There was blankness, and fear. Something had been done to her, and she only had the most shadowy idea what. She had tried to talk to her family, and even Sam wouldn't hear her. She had sought her friends, and the Gonnes had told her to forget. The absence—the tearing away of a part of her history—had been an active hurt for ten years. She did not know how to explain this to Lucia.

"I remember . . ." She struggled, grasped at memories. "I remember the orchard gate. The night of the funeral."

"You're best leaving it at that," Lucia said. "You say *tell me*, but you'd hate me if I did."

And when Kate said nothing she went on, voice shaking:

"Remember being in the woods, the night of the funeral? Remember the dark, and the thorns? Remember *him*?"

The marks on Kate's throat, so easily ignored, were beginning to burn. A sentence—orphaned from anything she remembered before or after—came into her mind then: *Can't comfort him. Can't get out.* Somebody—she was not sure who—had hated Kate deeply.

Lucia gave a slight nod. Her mouth was a wretched line.

"Remember that," she said. "Remember, and run." She touched Kate's hand, gently. "Do me that favor. It'll be nice to think of you safe." She stepped away. "Get out, now."

Don't think about it, Sam used to say. But Kate was thinking of it now. The noose around her neck was tightening.

She needed to get away. She was aware of Lucia saying something—*sorry?*—but she couldn't make it out, she didn't stop to answer.

It was her earlier words that followed Kate as she left, stumbling on the track like someone drunk or sunstruck—*get out, now.*

CHAPTER ELEVEN

What Will You Do with Your History?

Chloe sat and stared at the ruined veil. She waited for the events she had just witnessed to make sense, and they refused to do so:

There was violence in the twisting of the gauze. It had been so beautiful—cathedral-length, two layers of fine gauze edged with lace. She tried to untwist the rope, restore it to some semblance of its proper shape, but the veil was damaged beyond mending.

Perhaps she had allowed herself to become over-tired, over-wrought, and her sleep had been strangely disturbed as a result.

Or—this thought chilled her—perhaps it went deeper. The story-haunting, the voice next door: these might be signs of a serious problem. A psychological unhealthiness she hadn't suspected.

Or it might all be real.

She told herself not to be ridiculous. But fear hung about her like stale perfume. Logic was still a stretch.

There were people awake now. She could hear voices downstairs, and footsteps crossed the hall outside her room. Was it Kate? She had an impulse to open the door, beg Kate to come in and tell her what was wrong with this place or what was wrong with her. But the footsteps died away before she could make herself move.

Birdie picked Chloe up alone this morning. Bill had a dentist's appointment, she explained, and would be out for most of Tuesday.

"He always goes to Ipswich for his teeth. He says the man he sees there is worth the journey. So it'll be just us girls this morning, I'm afraid. Such a shame Sam's still in the toils."

"How's he getting on?" Chloe had hoped for a message from him this morning but had heard nothing. Perhaps he was simply remembering the Albatross's terrible mobile reception and saving himself a wasted effort.

"Not *bad*," Birdie said. "I've overheard a couple of heated phone calls, but they seem to be making progress now."

Chloe had been hoping that one night might be enough to resolve the problem, but apparently not.

"I told him you're an absolute gem, soldiering on like you are," Birdie went on. "He said he's well aware."

Chloe had expected to find Kate waiting in the graveyard—it seemed, somehow, a place that suited her—but there was no one. Birdie told Chloe to fetch her if Kate didn't turn up soon, and disappeared to the Tithe Barn to blow up balloons and unpack glasses.

Chloe was uncharacteristically glad of the solitude. The figment, the narrator—whatever it was—had been quiet this morning but she sensed the story gathering on the periphery. If she concentrated, she could keep it at bay.

Yesterday she had paid attention to Kate's trick with the key. Today after a short struggle she managed to get the church door open, although the key felt colder this morning, and heavier.

She found she was half-expecting all the hard work she and John and Kate had done to have been obliterated overnight. But the stones were scrubbed free of dirty footprints, the pews wiped free of dust. The scent of lemons still hung in the air. The false fuit was an improvement on yesterday, but only just.

If Kate had lived Chloe's childhood, she would have understood better how it felt to have the church smell wrong. When she was young, Chloe had spent Sundays in her father's church, arriving early with her parents. Her father would disappear to the vestry to prepare, her mother would stand at the door to hand out hymn books, and Chloe would insist on standing beside her, intent on allowing *nobody* to pass without their book. After church she would be helpful again—pouring tea, coffee and squash, tipping biscuits onto a plate. When the parishioners had gone and the church was quiet again, she would play hide-and-seek with the verger's children until her parents were ready to leave, crouching behind pews while breathing in the familiar smell of candlewax and coffee and old paper.

She had wanted this smell for her wedding, and along with it, the reassurance of her family's religion, which was kindly and took a hopeful view of the world.

Small Angels smelled wrong, and if there was religion here it was not tame. Not a matter of hymn books and shining tea-urns. The place still felt like the woods' church, or the Gonnes."

But it's mine, now, Chloe thought. At least for the duration.

Furiously, she set to work. As she hoovered and swept, wiping the last vestiges of grime away, she felt as if she were fighting something. After half an hour she realized that she had forgotten to put on a mask—the dust and polish were doing her lungs no favors—but she did not want to break her pace by stopping to fetch one. She would be done soon.

There was no other sound but her breathing and the scratch of her broom. Kate did not appear, and Birdie did not stop by either, though she must surely be wondering how Chloe was getting on. It was as if she would rather avoid the church if she could. And yet it was all *nonsense,* that story of Brian's.

Chloe swept recklessly, sending a little flurry of dust into the air.

If it had been less quiet, she would not have heard that dry little sound from outside.

Something sharp scratched against wood. It sounded like nails or claws. Quiet but insistent on the church door.

She waited, and the noise paused a moment—then began again, slightly louder.

There was no rhythm, she could not predict when the next scrape would sound, but at the same time it was not random. There was intent in that noise. Something was outside, and it wanted to get in.

To go to the door and find nothing would be bad enough. The alternative was unacceptable.

She waited, and in another moment the sound ceased. She was alone again.

Her throat felt tight. What time was it? She had left her watch behind this morning, which was most unlike her. Now she felt forgotten by the world outside, adrift and unsafe.

The door opened without a knock or warning. A dark shape—a man with the light behind him—stood in the doorway.

"Hi," he said. "I've got a delivery here for—"

Her scream startled them both. He had taken her by surprise, but it was most unlike her to react so strongly. It took her a moment to recover herself, and when she did she found she was angry.

"What are you *playing* at? You scared me half to death."

"I'm sorry, I didn't mean to make you jump."

Of course he didn't. Chloe was being unfair. She would get a hold of her thoughts, calm herself, apologize. She tried to take a breath, and found that she could not.

"Chloe?" Birdie had emerged from the Tithe Barn, probably drawn by the noise of the van's arrival. Her face was serious. "Chloe, is everything all right?"

"Fine," Chloe said, "only—"

She should have seen it coming earlier. Only she'd been distracted. She had been careless and missed the signs—the burn and tightness in her chest, the dizziness, the frantic speed of her heartbeat. The asthma attack caught her unprepared.

Beyond her breathlessness and the swimming of her vision, she was aware of them both bending over her with concern.

And beyond that she heard the small narrating voice, watching dispassionately:

Soon there would be no time left.

She apologized as soon as she was able—for the fright she'd given them and for losing her temper. The man with the jars had spooked her, but that was no excuse.

The man—still looking unnerved—said that it was fine. Nobody likes someone barging in and making you jump. He quite understood. He offered a bottle of water from his van, and asked if they wanted to be driven anywhere.

"It's fine," Chloe said. Her voice sounded wrong in her ears. "Thank you, though."

Visibly relieved, he took her signature for receipt of the jars and departed.

"Poor man," Chloe said. "I think I frightened him more than he frightened me."

"You scared *me,* too," said Birdie. "What brought that on?"

"Asthma. I haven't had an attack like that in years. The dust must have triggered it." She stood up slowly. "Or maybe Brian's right, and the church is unlucky."

"It's just easy to imagine things in there," said Birdie. "What with the shadows and the quiet. But that's all there is to it. And it's going to look lovely on Saturday, especially once we pack the place with guests. Now let's get you back and find you some clean clothes. You're absolutely *covered* in dust."

Birdie was pleasant on the journey back—she was always pleasant to Chloe. But whenever Chloe tried to return to the topic of Small Angels, Birdie retreated into positive affirmations: the church was looking beautiful, it would be a wonderful wedding, Chloe was doing a great job.

Eventually her answers to Chloe's comments became shorter, irritation simmering under the platitudes. She did not want to talk about Small Angels' strangeness, or anything Chloe might have witnessed there, and she was put out that Chloe seemed unable to take the hint.

"You still sound so hoarse, dear," she said at last. "Maybe it's better to save your voice, do you think?"

As soon as possible, Chloe thought, she would talk to Sam. She would confess everything—the story-haunting, the nightmare, her trespass in Mockbeggar—and he would roll his eyes affectionately and talk her back into reason: she was not haunted or losing her mind, she was under stress, and her imagination was being unkind. That was all.

Tonight, Birdie had invited everyone for dinner. She had promised to pull out all the stops, a treat to celebrate making such good progress in the wedding preparations.

Chloe would talk to Sam afterward, and then things would be clearer.

But the meal did not begin well. They were delayed by Kate's absence, lingering over their wine and crisps whilst Birdie fretted over the thickening sauce and cooling vegetables.

"This is just plain rude. She *knows* to be here for seven," Bill said. "I say we start without her."

"I hope she's all right, though," said Birdie. "I can't get through to her mobile—"

"That doesn't mean anything. She leaves it turned off most of the time," Sam interrupted.

"I thought of that, so I called the Albatross and John went and knocked on her door for me, and there was no answer."

"She'll be on one of her walks," Sam said. "You know what she's like."

"But if something's happened—"

"What would have happened?" said Sam.

There seemed no answer for this, and none of them mentioned Kate again that evening.

It struck Chloe for the first time how good the three of them were at certain kinds of silence. They talked nimbly over the days that had passed and the wedding that was still to come without ever straying onto the topic of Kate. Or any other difficult subject.

Birdie did bring up Chloe's asthma attack at the church, and Bill and Sam were suitably concerned. Sam advised her to see the doctor tomorrow as an emergency patient, get an inhaler prescribed immediately.

"I thought it might be the curse," Chloe said. "Small Angels, you know. Bad luck."

"Oh, all that stuff Brian Last goes on about," said Bill, smiling. "Poor sod. I think he does really believe it, you know."

"I don't know if I'd feel that sorry for him," Sam said. "He enjoys himself with it, doesn't he? Sometimes, he—"

"Sometimes it feels like you've all taken a vow of silence," Chloe said, cutting him off. "All of you are so careful about Small Angels, but of course there's nothing *really wrong* with it, just tradition."

"But it *is* just tradition," Birdie said gently.

Chloe saw identical distaste on their faces—Bill, Birdie, Sam.

After a brief pause, Birdie mentioned a student of hers who was having a succession of very expensive car troubles—if you *did* believe in curses and ill luck and all that nonsense, you'd believe this poor woman was the victim of it. Bill commented that most of the garages in this part of the world were staffed by crooks. Sam said that was very unlikely. The conversation did not return to Small Angels.

She still meant to tell Sam everything—after dinner, when they had some time to themselves. She meant to suggest a walk, or a drink at the Albatross. But she found that by dessert, she could no longer bring herself to talk to him about it. She was certain, now, that he would not believe her. He would laugh, or worry, or both.

That sound at the church door had felt real. If it was not then there was something very wrong. She might really be losing her mind.

She would have to know, one way or the other. Either there was something to all of this or there wasn't. Either there was a secret, or it was all her own delusion—Brian's story preying on her like a mental parasite. So she would find out, one way or the other. And then she would make a plan of what to do next. You could always make a plan, once you knew what you were dealing with.

That night, the voice talked and begged from the next room, and Chloe lay still. There were moments when the man seemed to know she was there and to be pleading with her directly. She no longer tried to pretend she heard nothing. She lay where she was and tried to stop her hands from twitching, as if they longed to fashion another noose.

Her appointment at the doctor's was early on Wednesday morning. There was plenty of time to go, claim her new inhaler, and have a look around the village before heading back to Bill and Birdie's. Sam—was he worried about her?—had said that he'd break off work for lunch today. They could have fish and chips in the park, just the two of them.

The village surgery was quiet. She was alone in the waiting room but both women at the reception desk watched her. Were they curious, pitying? She could usually guess people's feelings pretty well, but now she felt as if she were interacting with those around her through a billow of fog.

The doctor asked her twice if there was anything else troubling her, apart from the asthma. When she said there wasn't she thought he looked almost disappointed.

She remembered Sam telling her, early on in their relationship, that he came from a place where nothing ever happened. It made her want to laugh, now, that claim. How could he have said such a thing straight-faced? Her hands were sore today, like they had been gripping tight at a rope all night.

Her most promising avenue would be the village library, she had decided. If there were any relics of the community's past—anything to prove that there was *something* to the story—surely this would be the place to find it.

The library stood opposite the post office, close to the heart of the village. It was a small building, with high, narrow windows like a castle. According to the plaque outside, it had been built in 1911 by a charitable subscription, and had originally served as a reading room for working men of the parish.

Inside, it was almost unpleasantly snug. The abiding smell was warm dust (quite different to Small Angels' dust), old paper and human bodies.

Chloe believed in libraries, of course. She was Campaigns Manager for a small literacy charity. But she preferred to buy her books in small independent bookshops, the kind of place she could pick up a coffee and a paperback on a Saturday morning. Here the books looked lived in. On a shelving trolley near the door she saw a dozen paperbacks waiting to be reshelved—plastic jackets sticky from strangers' hands. On a lower shelf was a neat stack of children's books, some torn, some tooth-marked.

At the counter, a beautifully dressed woman in her sixties was listening soberly to a small boy, who was gripping a book and explaining something gravely.

"They don't *normally* eat people," he was saying. "They just get confused sometimes."

"That's understandable," said the librarian. Now Chloe recognized her from the Albatross; they had spoken briefly at the Hag Night. Her name was Elizabeth Daunt. "And I agree with you: they're most interesting creatures and they've been unfairly maligned. But what are you asking me to do, exactly?"

"You could cut out the bits that are wrong," said the boy.

Elizabeth shook her head. "Books aren't like apples, Shaun," she said. "You can't just bite off the rotten bits and spit them out. Any more than you can lop the parts you don't like off human beings."

"You have to stop people reading it, then," said Shaun. "Because people read the book and they saw the film and they got scared. They killed more sharks because of it. The man who wrote the book was sorry afterward."

The book, Chloe saw now, was a copy of *Jaws.*

"They're not *bad,* you know," Shaun added. He obviously wanted Elizabeth to be clear on this point.

"Of course not," Elizabeth said. "But I can't get rid of this book, I'm afraid. Firstly, it belongs to the library, and secondly . . . it's just not a thing to do. I had Brian Last campaigning for weeks last year, wanting me to take down the Halloween display. I told him the same. People should talk over what they read. They should chew their food, I said. What more can I do?"

Shaun looked at her uncomprehendingly.

Elizabeth sighed. "That display of Harvest and Agriculture books is coming down next week. We'll have a Wonders of the Deep display next. Fangtooth, sea urchin, octopus. Sharks. You can check it's accurate."

Shaun nodded—only partly satisfied—and disappeared between the shelves, taking *Jaws* with him.

Moving closer to the counter, Chloe caught sight of a faded hand-drawn poster pinned to the far wall. In thick black letters it demanded: *What Will You Do with Your History?* Underneath were listed the ways in which local and family histories could be acquired, and the uses to which they could be put.

"Brian did that, a while back," said Elizabeth Daunt. She had clearly recognized Chloe. "He visits the school, sometimes. Tries to get the children interested in researching their family trees and the like. The teacher is too polite to ask him to stop." Her expression, when she surveyed Chloe, was sharp but not unfriendly. "I'm glad to see you've managed to escape Small Angels for a little while," she said. "It's a herculean task you've taken on there, by all accounts."

"We're managing OK, thanks. I'm actually treating myself to a morning off."

"Quite right, too. And how can I help you?"

"I was hoping you might have a village archive for me to poke around. I've always been big on history, you see, and—"

"No, I'm sorry. We don't have anything like that here."

"But you're up to your knees in history in this place. Even this building. Surely there's something?"

Elizabeth looked sober. "We're not the memorializing sort of village, I'm afraid."

"So there's absolutely nothing?"

"Was there something specific you wanted to know?"

"No." She thought of telling Elizabeth the truth. What would she say if Chloe admitted she was afraid her mind was failing her? Instead, she breathed deliberately, and said, "I've wiped grime off so many monuments in Small Angels, I suppose it's made me curious. I've got village history under my fingernails by this point."

Elizabeth smiled carefully. "Oh, dear. That sounds unpleasant."

"No, it's interesting. This is a fascinating place, you know."

'Is it? I'm afraid I've been here so long I tend to tune it all out."

"Sam's like that. Is it a village tradition, ignoring history?"

She had, in spite of herself, let her feelings show in her voice.

"Like I said, we're not a memorializing village," said Elizabeth, staring at her. "There's Brian, of course. *He'll* talk history to you. Or pseudo-history, at least. If it's the colorful stuff you're after, he's your man." She paused and then added, as if against her better judgment: "If you're worried about something—"

Shaun returned to the counter without warning: "You should get rid of this one, too," he said, dropping *Man-eaters of the Ocean* onto the counter. Chloe left him and Elizabeth to their debate.

The time was running out. It was Wednesday now and the wedding was Saturday. The key to Small Angels was heavy in her bag. She'd found that she couldn't leave it behind, she took it with her everywhere now.

It was nearly lunchtime but she didn't go home like she'd planned.

She was growing accustomed to that small voice now—forever in her ear. Almost a companion.

It felt galling to have to resort to Brian Last, after his malicious pleasure in spoiling the Hag Night. He had preyed on her ignorance that evening. And now she was crawling back for more information. He would guess that nobody else would talk to her, perhaps even suspect that there was a silence growing between her and Sam.

If the shop was busy, or if he wasn't working today, she would leave it. That would be sign enough that there was nothing to be gained from this (since when had she believed in signs?).

But the shop was deserted when she arrived, and Brian was sitting behind the counter, reading a biography of Churchill.

The bell over the door shrilly announced her arrival; he looked up and nodded unsmilingly.

"Afternoon."

"Hi, Brian."

It was a tiny shop, and yet it held a great deal: magazines, kindling, mousetraps, soup.

In one corner a freezer hummed loudly. The fridge was stocked with soft drinks she had thought long discontinued. It must have been galling for Sam and Kate to come in here as teenagers, bell hanging over their heads like Damocles' sword, well aware that everybody in the village knew their parents' troubles.

"Looking for something in particular?" Brian said.

"I wanted to talk about Small Angels."

"Right." He did not seem surprised. "Want a cup of tea?"

She found that she did. He disappeared into a back room and she heard a kettle start to boil. In a few minutes he reappeared with two mugs of strong tea.

"I left the bag in."

"That's fine. Thank you."

He took a sip of his tea, and said, "So what's brought you to me, then?"

"Nobody else will talk to me." She heard a shake in her voice. Please God let her not start crying. What would he say, if she asked him if he thought she was losing her mind?

"Most of them round here would say it was bad manners, bringing all that up," Brian said. "They don't like to talk about that stuff. It's been the same for generations. Look the other way whenever you can. In my view, that sort of thinking's bound to be dangerous, sooner or later."

"You really believe it, then?" She was leaning forwards in spite of herself—she sounded far too eager but she couldn't hold back. "Seriously?"

"Of course." He looked affronted. "You heard what I told you in the Albatross. Did anyone tell you how Paul Gonne's funeral ended?"

"Yes. But that could be explained, you know—"

"Rubbish. You sound as bad as the rest of them. I've seen things. Not just the night of Paul's funeral. Other things, too. One time I went to Mockbeggar. Just to the very edge."

"Really?"

"I was young, wanted to prove myself." A touch of defensiveness. "Stupid kid like any other stupid kid. I went a couple of yards into those trees, and I heard my mother calling. She'd been dead five years by that point." He set down his mug—tea splashed over the counter, narrowly missing his book, but he didn't seem to notice. "I was never fool enough to go back. The thing about those woods . . . when I got close, I felt like they *knew things.* I wouldn't go near again at any price." A stern look. "Certainly wouldn't be getting married on the Mockbeggar's doorstep."

"But you're talking about the Gonnes' day. That was ten years ago. The family's been gone for ages. It's all quiet, now."

She spoke too quickly. She could see Brian notice it—give her a quick, careful look. Were the horrors she had heard visible in her face?

"Won't last," he said grimly. "And God help us when things kick off again. You think Lucia Gonne is going to be worth a damn if there's trouble?"

"Lucia Gonne?"

"Selina's granddaughter. The one left at Blanch Farm. Worst of the bunch, by all accounts." A tinge of enjoyment colored his voice. He must have few chances to share this choice bit of gossip with a new listener. "I heard there was a big falling-out after Elphine's death. The old lady turned against Lucia. *Livid* with her, by all accounts. And the rest of the family not much better. And what I want to know is, what do you do that's so dreadful it turns *that* lot against you?"

"I don't know."

"Exactly. Take my advice, and steer clear of all of it."

"You really think I should move my wedding because of a legend?"

"You know it's more than that, though, don't you?" His gaze was very sharp, very eager. "You wouldn't have come running to me otherwise. What did you see?"

She didn't answer. He would have pressed her, maybe, but at this point they were interrupted. Three small girls came into the shop, bickering over a pound coin which was to be spent on sweets. She took her chance to escape.

So Brian believed it—that performance in the Albatross had been in earnest. Still she couldn't quite bring herself to put faith in his words. *Steer clear of all of it.* The words chilled and irritated her, caught as she was between doubt and belief.

The only thing left was to see for herself. She made the plan quickly, afraid that if she dwelled too long on it then cowardice or good sense would intervene. She would go back to the woods and she wouldn't leave until she had something decisive. One way or another.

No one could help her, so she would help herself. Always better to *know.* She would rather live like that than live like the locals—even Sam. She would not avert her gaze.

She prepared this time around. She packed water, an emergency mackintosh in a bag, her mobile phone (almost as a talisman—she knew it would be of little use). She dressed for thorns and mud. She borrowed Kate's old bike from Bill and Birdie's—not stopping to ask permission, impatient to settle all this one way or another, and wary of delay.

Even without Brian's warning, this second visit felt more reckless than the first. This occurred to her at Crockery Hill, just as she was about to step through the trees. One visit you might get away with. Risk a second, and you might not be so lucky. If she were a person in a story (and she was, now, wasn't she?) she would have advised herself to turn back whilst she could.

But she saw a flicker of white beyond the first row of trees. Flowers seemed to have sprung up since last time. Was that even possible? She could hear buzzing, as she had the first time she came to the woods. She stepped out of the sunlight.

CHAPTER TWELVE

Harvest

Lucia in continuation

I'm fine. Really. It's just that I can hear their voices when I tell it. I can hear Grandpa saying *Lucia.*

I never found out what he was trying to say to me as we stood in the field with the frost lanterns burning around us. At the time I was sure he was trying to curse me for what I'd done. But perhaps he was just trying to ask what was happening to him.

He seemed to fall slowly, the way a landslide begins. I knelt beside him and tried to get him to his feet again.

Harry was gone. He had let Grandpa go. It should have been all right. I told Grandpa that. I tried to get him to look at me. I told him it was OK, he just needed warmth, tea, coffee, whisky, wine. I told him I was sorry for what I'd done. His mouth made shapes but he couldn't manage the words.

I shouldn't have to see him like this, I thought. He shouldn't have me see him like this. It was cruel, it was indecent.

The ice lanterns seemed to be burning very loud, crackling close to my ears. The lights swam in front of my eyes.

It was a struggle to get him standing. Like holding up a great tree.

His hand was tight on my arm. As if he thought I might run off and leave him.

I called for help as soon as we had passed the orchard gate. I remember I felt as if I hardly knew my family in that strange moment—businesslike and panicking by turns, wide-eyed and pale.

I don't remember doing much between helping Grandpa through the orchard gate and watching the ambulance struggle away down the drive from Blanch Farm. Nan went with Grandpa. She didn't want any of the rest of us there, not even Ruby.

Then they were gone, and the rest of us were left behind in the kitchen. Me and my sisters and our father, all at a loss.

The paramedics had brought mud in. For some reason, the tongue-twister they had wanted Grandpa to say—which he had been unable to manage—was stuck in my head like a tune. *Peter Piper picked a peck of pickled peppers.*

"He looked so frightened," Elphine said softly.

"They know what they're doing. They'll take care of him," said Ruby, with an effort. "We'll be all right, Elphine."

I'd told everyone that the attack had come on suddenly. When Grandpa was better, they'd all know what I'd done, and that it was my fault he had been struck down.

Even if Grandpa's arteries had been conspiring against him for years, it was Harry and I who'd delivered the decisive shock between us. The pain of Harry's attack strained some weak point in him, the knowledge of my betrayal chilled him, and something snapped or burst or broke. I remembered Nan had told me about it long ago—that kind of fear could be too much. It shouldn't have surprised me that it felled Grandpa as it had. There's only a certain amount anyone can withstand, and Harry had taken so much from him already.

"Shit," Helena said suddenly. "The beacons."

It was already past dusk, and none of them were burning yet. We'd never been so neglectful before.

"We'll each light one," Ruby said. "That's the quickest way. I'll take the one by Crockery Hill." That was furthest one, and so the worst journey. It was the one Nan or Grandpa would have taken, if either was there. "Dad, can you do the one opposite Small Angels?"

Our father nodded. "There's gorse in the shed. If you need more."

None of us had expected him to be more use than this. He would do as he was asked, just as he always did—but he couldn't direct or plan.

Dad went out promptly and now it was just the four of us in the kitchen. His departure shouldn't have meant much, only just then it felt as if our ranks were slowly being thinned as the darkness grew.

"We're *us,*" Ruby said softly. "You know?" She touched Elphine's hand. "It'll be all right."

We were four. She wanted us to hang onto that. None of us would have to go through this evening alone.

She said that since I'd had a shock that evening, I could be the one to stay in the house and mind the phone, in case Nan rang with a message. Also I could make a start on tea.

"I'm not hungry," I said.

Ruby set out tins for me on the worktop—chopped tomato, tinned peas, baked beans. "Even so. We should all have something hot. You'll be all right getting on with this?"

I nodded.

"Good. We'll be back before you're done. Then food. Then . . . then we'll see what's best to do. We'll probably have heard from Nan by that time."

"She's going to be livid if she and Grandpa have to fork out for a taxi back," Helena said.

Small smiles all round. That would be our stage direction for the evening: we were going to be brave.

They left, and I emptied cans into a great saucepan alone in the kitchen. I saw my face reflected in the dark window, and I couldn't bear to keep looking.

We were *us,* Ruby had said. They had no idea. Either Grandpa would recover sufficiently to tell them all what I'd done, or the private, poisonous knowledge would sicken me for ever.

Dutiful in small things, I made the best tea I could for them. I scraped blue mold off the bread. I ransacked the freezer and found half a box of fish fingers. I swept crumbs off the table onto the floor, I set out forks and knives and glasses.

When they were all back—all pale, all tired, none of them much inclined to talk—I served it all up on hot plates and poured them wine from a raid on the cellar.

"Well, this is novel," Helena said to me, looking over the makeshift feast.

"I was just trying to do something nice." Of course I took it the worst way. Guilt was making me jumpy, irritable.

"It is nice," Elphine said.

"A treat," Ruby agreed. "You'll have to do this again when Grandpa gets back. For a celebration."

We ate in silence for a few minutes. The phone failed to ring and its silence felt determined and deliberate.

"Where's Dad?" I said finally.

"I don't know," Ruby said. "He didn't want anything, he said. I did try and convince him to come and sit with us, at least, but he wouldn't. Do you think he'll be all right?"

"There's food here when he's hungry, and *he's* not the one who has to work out what to do now," Helena said. "I think he'll be fine."

Our father was never fine, of course, but I saw what she meant. Whatever followed in the weeks to come, Dad would go on as usual, fearful and obedient. There was something blinkered about him: he was never troubled by hopes or fears for the future. Things would stay as they were, assuming we kept our end of the bargain. And of course we would keep the bargain.

So he was probably the best off of any of us, that evening. My sisters and I ate in silence until the meal was mostly done. Still there was no sound from the phone.

"They'll have seen him by now, won't they?" Helena said.

None of us knew much about hospitals—none of us had ever been in one, and even our doctor's visits had been very few.

"They probably will have," Ruby said, not sounding very certain. "It's been a while."

"So why haven't they called?" said Helena.

Ruby sent me to fetch another bottle of wine. When I set it down on the table my hands were shaking. Elphine got up and stood behind me and started braiding my hair, that gentle way she always did when I was upset. You remember how she used to do that when she wanted to comfort you? She used to work in daisies and dandelions which would drop out as the braids came unfastened, so that you found yourself leaving flowers in your wake like a spring goddess.

Usually it helped. Always, in the past, it had helped. But guilt made me edgy that night. I wanted to scream at her to leave me alone.

I suppose she guessed some of that. She could sense my thoughts at times, the way you can make out a shape through a thin curtain. In my memory, she was troubled from that night on. My last months with her were strained, as she waited for me to speak, wondered why I didn't. She would have thought that there was nothing I could tell her which she would be unable to understand or forgive.

"We'll manage," Ruby said suddenly. "We'll be all right."

"Well, obviously," said Helena, bracing. "Let's wash up."

Most unlike us. But we each took a task, we washed and dried and put away like model housekeepers. We told stories as we worked. Ruby began it, recalling something Grandpa had told her a long time ago: when he was a child, his oldest great-aunt had tried to cure him of whooping cough by feeding him a fried mouse. He had eaten it, to avoid hurting her feelings, but had been sick afterward. He'd been soured toward all medicine ever since.

"I hope he's doing what the doctors are telling him," Ruby finished. "Everything will take twice as long if he's awkward."

"Nan's there to keep him in order," Helena said.

We kept up this strange kind of humor as we washed and dried and put the kitchen in unnatural order. I'd never seen us in this mood before. Our jokes were very bland. No one laughed, or mentioned that the phone still hadn't rung.

When the kitchen was done, Ruby said she'd wait downstairs for news. Elphine said we'd sit with her and we did—all through the hours of the evening and night until the call came close to midnight.

Sometimes we were silent during that vigil, and from time to time I thought I'd reached the point where my guilt had become unbearable and I would finally have to tell them. But I said nothing. In the quiet I felt as if I were Grandpa—sitting up late, listening for the frost descending.

It was a stroke. By the time the news came we were all so exhausted that it was difficult to understand exactly what this meant. Nan was brief on the phone: they were keeping Grandpa in the hospital; she'd let Ruby know more when she could. Then came a list of instructions for the vineyard—Ruby had to send Elphine dashing to the kitchen for a pencil and a scrap of paper to note these down—and another list of things Grandpa would require for his stay.

"When's visiting time?" Ruby asked Nan at last. "Or can I bring them before then?"

She listened as Nan spoke. Her face changed.

"Right." She nodded, though Nan could not have seen this. "I understand."

When she hung up, she said, "Nan's going to pick Grandpa's stuff up and then go straight back. She doesn't want us visiting him."

"Why not?" I said. I needed to know as soon as possible what Grandpa remembered and how much trouble I was in. "Can't we see him? Is he talking?"

Ruby said, "I don't know. But Nan said we were to stay here. Stay put, she said. Nothing's changed, we're still in disgrace, apparently."

"That's ridiculous," Helena said. "He's in *hospital*, surely she can give all that a rest."

"It's ridiculous grounding us at all," Ruby said. "When you really get down to it. But it doesn't help to dwell."

We had been obedient—more or less—for a very long time. Nan

had held the threads for all our lives, her rules had kept us safe. The other three would have said that she guessed Harry's moods better than anyone, and so questioning her was pointless recklessness.

The infuriating thing was that I knew better. I knew Harry better than Nan ever would, and still I could only defy her with an effort and with dread of discovery. I was fighting sixteen years of history and custom, you see. She held my threads like she held the others."

"We'll end up like Dad, if we keep on like this," Helena said. She spoke like she despised us all, herself included.

She was right, though I wished she hadn't said it. I had been so good at not thinking far ahead. Now I saw years beginning to stretch out—Kate gone, the vineyard work never finished. A short while ago Harry would have been a consoling thought—my friend waiting in secret, all Mockbeggar's wonders in his gift. Now I couldn't think of him without seeing Grandpa's face, lit by the frost lanterns. How much harm had Harry really meant to do?

Elphine, quietly, said: 'Is that a bad sign, that the doctors want to keep him in?"

Grandpa didn't come home for a long time. The stroke brought pneumonia in its wake, and he didn't seem to be making good progress. When the pneumonia tired of him at last, he went from the hospital to a care home, where he was supposed to be rehabilitated. He stayed there for months.

On the rare occasions when we saw Nan long enough for proper conversation, she seemed irritated with him.

"Not enough *go* to him," she said once. "He'd be back with us by now if he put his mind to it. Strong man like your grandfather, hardly past sixty. He's got no business struggling like this."

He could speak and move again, though only with great effort. Nan said he remembered most of what had happened up to the night of the frost lanterns. But, as far as I could tell, he didn't mention Harry, and he didn't mention me.

Every time Nan returned from hospital, or rang Ruby with further orders, I waited in torment to see if this would be the time it was all uncovered. But nothing changed, the poison stayed buried.

It was probably a mercy that during that time, we were usually too busy to think.

May and June were a growing time in the vineyard. You could see a change almost every day, and when the vines were active so were we, trying our best to manage without Nan and Grandpa. I hadn't realized how much of the work they shouldered before that time. We'd be outside for the greater part of each day.

I mostly remember exhaustion, in those months of late spring and summer. No sooner was the shoot thinning done than we went out one morning and found that the vines were flowering—tiny, unimpressive blooms that meant absolutely everything. Then came fruit set, and more growing and growing—don't you get *tired* like us, I wanted to ask them—and then we were tying vines to the trellises, working one to a row, speaking only if someone needed help or was planning a drinks run.

Ruby tried to make things pleasanter for us, picking up cans and snacks, things Nan wouldn't approve of. But Dad quickly put a stop to that. *Extravagance*, he said. *She wouldn't like it.* No use arguing when he said that. I had wondered if he might relax a fraction whilst Nan was away, but if anything he seemed more feverishly obedient than ever during this time.

I didn't see Harry for a while after Grandpa was taken away. I couldn't be sure how seriously he had intended to harm Grandpa—I think he might not have been sure himself. He dealt these cruelties out without much thought, when the mood came over him. I told myself he wouldn't have meant much harm.

All the same, he had done it. For the first weeks after Grandpa's stroke, I couldn't bear the thought of seeing him.

But I kept my promise. I kept away from Kate, and he watched to see that I kept my word.

He let me know he was watching. My sisters and I were attended, when we worked late in the field, or sat in the orchard (a trip to the garden was all we could manage for leisure). It wasn't constant, but it was noticeable enough for us to agree it was really happening.

Pale shadows. As dusk came it was easy to imagine a creature lying among the roots of a tree, watching.

My sisters said perhaps this was Harry's punishment for our behavior in the woods. Nan must have been right after all. We had gone too far, and offended him.

Ruby tried to cheer us along—she said it wasn't really so bad, all things considered. Perhaps Harry felt some pity for us, given our family's recent trouble, and so he was being lenient.

My sisters and I looked after each other the way that Nan had looked after us when we were small. We took to accompanying each other on journeys into the fields, even for small tasks like fetching in the hens or gathering gorse for the beacons. We closed the shutters early, even before nightfall. Ruby would keep the lights on as long as possible, though Dad would turn them off at every opportunity—Nan would consider it a waste of money, he said. After tea, we would retreat to the attic, and spend our time there together. We might sleep two or more to a room.

I suppose that's a bittersweet time for Ruby and Helena to remember now. Different for me, of course. I was with them but there was a distance. I could be helpful and affectionate—so unlike my usual self that Helena made fun of me—I could hug Elphine and braid her necklaces of dog daisies to wear, and it didn't take the edge off the lonely chill I felt.

As far as the others went, the watching was the worst of Harry's punishment. It was different for me. His story crept into my dreams in strange, ugly ways. I woke one dawn with a faint mark on my hand—a dog bite, which smarted and had to be hidden from my sisters.

Eventually he relented. I went back and spoke to him a couple of times, when I could get away from the others. I told him I couldn't stay long because Nan had said the woods were out of bounds.

I think he thought that I'd learned my lesson, and we could go back to the way we had been. I think he thought that nothing would ever really change.

Once or twice, I volunteered to light the beacon opposite Small Angels. I never crossed the boundary of our land. Harry's land. But you can see Miss Violet's grave from there. I would take my time in getting the fuel arranged, so that I could look across at the church as I worked. Kate was never there. But it was some consolation to see the place where we had met. The physical things—the grass and the graves—made what had happened feel real. In spite of everything, she had been there. She had kissed me, she had changed the world for a short time.

We had been cheated. The thing that had been growing between us—so young and tender I couldn't even put words to it yet—had been uprooted before it had a chance to flower.

I don't think I resented Harry for that yet. Not in my conscious thoughts. Nan had raised me and my sisters in the belief that we had no right to feel angry. Rage was her prerogative—and Harry's, of course.

At Blanch Farm, *good weather* always meant a very precise range of conditions. There are so many things the climate can do to grapes: they can be parched and sunburned, they can be waterlogged. That year, for the first time in Nan's recollection, conditions were perfect—that brush with May frost had been the last serious issue to threaten the crop, and the buds had made it through unscathed. By July, Ruby and Nan began to talk about the possibility of an early harvest.

It was the strangest summer I'd known. Outdoors always seemed lovely, inviting—a world turned gentle. But in the house everything seemed at a subtly wrong angle—wrong enough to *feel* if not to see, sunk a degree or two slanted. We hardly ever went to the woods.

Grandpa had taken a turn for the worse. Nan was with him as much as possible and had less time than ever to spare for us and the vines. Ruby had us all working around the clock, weeding and mowing and generally getting the vineyard into good shape for harvest. If you have everything in a good state beforehand, you'll have an easier time getting the grapes in, she used to remind us. She was out there most days sampling the grapes, measuring sugar. She became obsessive about the logbooks Nan and Grandpa kept. Everything was noted—temperature, rainfall, health of the vines. She used to leaf through the records of earlier years, frowning as she compared their figures to this year's.

By August, the house was too hot to stand in the evenings. Sometimes we'd sleep outside in the orchard, letting the night breeze cool our sunburned faces.

There was a night when I couldn't sleep. I got up, extricated myself from the blankets and cushions we had piled up under the trees, and went down to the orchard gate.

There was a clear moon; it would be time for another night at Small Angels before too long. Without our grandparents these vigils were even more anxious than usual. But we had done all right. We were managing well, Ruby kept telling us.

"If you're waiting for Nan to say *well done*, you'll be waiting a long time," Helena said.

The vineyard beyond the gate was still. I had no sense of Harry that night. The only movement was a small fox padding close to one of the vines, biting a grape or two.

I should have driven it away, but I didn't. It seemed contented, merry, even, carrying out this bit of theft by moonlight. If we could have changed places then—if I could have stepped out of my skin into a fox's pelt and fled into the night—I would have done it.

Elphine joined me softly; she had that way of just being *there,* sometimes. Do you remember that? She wouldn't make you jump, she'd just—she'd just be there.

We watched the fox, colorless in the moonlight, until it had eaten its fill and left.

"I saw Kate," Elphine said, finally. "This evening. She was at Small Angels when I went to light the beacon."

I was furious. Of all the bad luck. And I was jealous that Elphine had been more fortunate.

"Did you talk to her?" I demanded.

"No." Elphine looked shocked. "You know what Nan said. She just waved. Kate waved, I mean. I thought she looked sad. I think she misses you."

It set something right in me to hear that. But to Elphine I said curtly:

"That was never going to work out really, was it?"

"Why?"

"You know how we live. You know me." (I thought of Grandpa.) "I was bound to screw things up, even if Nan hadn't found out."

She looked impatient. "You don't have to . . ."

I waited.

"You don't have to tell it like that. The story of our lives here. The story of you."

I stared at her, not understanding.

"You could tell it different," she said. "Like you did with the song, ages ago. Remember that? You could be a lot of different stories, if you wanted. Not the one Nan tells about you."

I still didn't understand, but I was too proud to say anything. I let her go back to our makeshift campsite and lingered a while longer by the gate—angry with her and myself, running over those words *I think she misses you.* That thought made the rest tolerable.

Harvest came early, just as Nan and Ruby had suspected. People across the country marveled at the weather. There hadn't been a summer like it for fifty years.

Nan was with us a little more frequently by then. She spoke of bringing Grandpa home soon. Whenever Ruby asked if we could see him, Nan told her he'd be back any day now, so there was no point. Our father had been to visit, but we couldn't get much out of him about Grandpa's condition.

I never knew Nan to have much gentleness in her, but now what tenderness she had seemed to have drained away. Gone to Grandpa. Those days must have been a trial for her. She wasn't the sort for bedside watching. When she was at Blanch Farm she was mostly caught up in the money side of things—accounts and bills—and I think she turned to them with a kind of relief.

When Ruby asked about the harvest, Nan told her to use her own good sense. I felt like she was trying to prepare us for taking over the vineyard. Like we were running out of time.

The day was set and the arrangements were made. Ruby chose a week at the start of September—preposterously early for any ordinary year. October would have been the usual time, of course. But that year there was no alternative. The grapes were ripe, already prey for birds and wasps. If we had a rainfall now, the grape juice would be diluted, the wine would be spoiled. Best to seize the moment.

The night before we were due to begin harvest, Ruby couldn't sleep. Helena sat up and reasoned with her for half the night. There would be dozens of harvests. Decades of harvests. This was the first of many. Ruby couldn't afford to agonize like this every time.

We had our usual helpers from the village. Sullen conscripts, brought by tradition—mostly teenage boys. Nan was usually in charge of them, but now Helena had that duty. She had this ice-queen act that came in useful. The village boys were terrified of her and in love with her at the same time; they followed her curt orders without question.

I had seen harvests before, but never one where the weather was so hot so early in the day. Nor one where the workers were so miserable and silent. They talked little to each other, said almost nothing to us. They filled their crates, loaded the trailer. They ate their sandwiches and downed the drinks Elphine brought them. They burned quickly as the sun turned cruel.

Once or twice, during that week, the pickers sensed something amiss; a couple of them were startled by something they thought they saw through the swim of the heat. They were odd and unpleasant, these figments—a man running, dressed in old-fashioned clothes, his face blank with terror. A dog with a bloody muzzle.

A couple of the pickers suffered something more mundane and definite. The wasps came for the fruit, and stung the conscripts' arms and faces as they worked.

That evening, Helena read us facts from one of Nan and Grandpa's books on vineyard maintenance. The best way to deal with wasps was to catch one, tie a piece of white thread around it and track it back to its nest, which you could then set alight—

"No," Elphine interrupted here. "Helena, we couldn't."

"Of course not." She shut the book in disgust. "It's definitely illegal, even if it was safe. The book's out of date. Like most of our books."

Helena was the one who cared the most about the state of our education. It galled her, how little we knew. Elphine told me once that she would have been happier—less abrasive and impatient—if she had been able to study as much as she wanted and push her brain as far as it would go. That smothering harvest week must have brought home to her that this was out of the question now. We would have no more schooling. The vineyard—which might under ordinary circumstances have been developed, transformed into a thriving business—could never change.

That night I dreamed of setting wasps' nests alight. Dingy paper blazing up in a second, wasps pouring out like furious embers.

The days continued flawlessly, pitilessly bright. One of the pickers fainted with sunstroke and was taken home. The rest of us worked feverishly, and at last we were done. The grapes left, loaded onto a truck and driven to the winery four miles away with which Nan and Grandpa had a long-standing arrangement. There was no telling what the vintage would taste like, of course, but there was nothing we could do about that now.

The weather didn't break, but the heat relented slightly as evening came. We were too exhausted to eat—lying on the grass in our orchard campsite, looking at the stars in the dark blue.

I was comfortably sad that evening. I didn't think I could be happy again, but the months had lessened my fear of Grandpa telling everyone what had happened that night in the field. Or at least I had got accustomed to that dread and so it had become easier to ignore. I lay still under the pear trees with my sisters beside me. Ruby said,

"We should eat something. Wash."

But she didn't move. It was a moment away from everything, for all of us. We were cut loose from the past, and from our future—which looked increasingly definite. For half an hour or so we were free of all that.

We lay like that until the car disturbed us. Someone slammed a trunk shut around the front of the house. It was Nan, back from Grandpa's care home. Before she went upstairs, she told us briefly that he was coming home at last.

Nan had been promising his return for so long that we had almost given up. Now, without warning, she had brought him back to die.

I don't think she told us that—she didn't need to. I remember the night before his return: all our futile cleaning, Elphine's flowers. She worked hard all day to keep us cheerful, and then in the evening I heard crying in her bedroom.

I didn't go in. I thought about that a lot afterward. Ruby went to her, I think.

The thing is, I couldn't bear to see Elphine upset like that. It wasn't the way things were supposed to be. It was like the ground shifting, an ebb and surge of the liquid rock under our feet.

The four of us used to have little meetings when we were young. Confabulations, Helena used to call them. On the morning of Grandpa's return we had our last one. We all gathered in the kitchen, one by one, waiting for the sound of the car.

"He'll look different, I suppose," Ruby said. "We can't let him see us noticing."

We went over our preparations. Everything was clean. A bed had been made up in the little sitting room next to the kitchen. Nan and Grandpa would sleep there until Grandpa was well enough to manage the stairs again. (This, we knew, would never happen.)

When the car arrived at last, I almost wanted them to turn around and drive away again. I wondered if the others felt that too.

He was changed. I don't want to talk about it. He seemed to have lost height as well as weight. He struggled, and his new limitations made him angry.

Nan was good with him. No nonsense, no cloying pity. We followed her lead as best we could.

After the first dinner—an hour of watching him trying to eat, increasingly, silently frustrated—we sat with him while Nan went out to light the beacons. He wouldn't light them again, or walk through the night tall and fearless, though we talked about the day soon when things would be different.

When we fell silent, Grandpa finally spoke.

He wasn't usually one for stories. That was more Nan's province. There were hundreds of details from his past that he might mention in passing, and never again.

But that night, without warning, he said, "There's a thing you can do." He was looking at me.

"What, Grandpa?" Ruby said. She was taken aback, we all were. He hadn't spoken so clearly all evening. "What was that?"

"There's a thing you can do. With Harry. To get rid."

When we were children, he could carry two of us on his shoulders at once. But now every word was an effort, and the others couldn't bear to watch, but I did because it was my fault.

"Me and my brother. We were in the woods, long time ago. We went to the Rose House. Looked at the tree. Took some branches away. Idiots. We wanted a trophy to show off."

He was going to betray me, I thought, panicking. Here it was at long last.

"Later, Father found out. Gave us both a hiding. He said *don't go near the tree. If you hurt it, you hurt him.* He said—"

He struggled a moment.

"He said killing the tree would drive Harry away."

"That's impossible," said Helena.

"No. He was sure. Said we'd always known, in the family. Because his strength's in the tree. His story at the heart."

He looked at me and I could hardly bear it because he knew what I'd done and I didn't deserve his kindness, but there was only love and sadness in his face. He was using the last of his strength to give me a fighting chance. I didn't deserve it and yet he wanted to give me this small thread of hope.

I wanted to say something—tell him to stop, I wasn't worth his care and his pain—but he shook his head very slightly.

"I think it's true," he said. "But it would cost you, if you tried it—"

"They don't need to hear about that."

It was our father, listening from the doorway.

"Andrew," Grandpa said.

I don't know if I ever heard him say our father's name before. Dad always had more to do with Nan than Grandpa. It was strange to hear him say *Andrew* now. Worse to hear that note of pleading in his voice. Grandpa didn't beg.

"Mum wouldn't like it," our father said.

"Please, Andrew. Let them hear."

"She'd say you have no business filling their heads with this."

"They have a right to—"

"You're not thinking right, Dad. You've confused yourself, brooding over the past. Small wonder, after all you've been through. Better *shut up* now and take a rest until everything looks clearer. Mum wouldn't want you getting upset and upsetting the girls into the bargain, would she?"

They looked at each other and I felt like I was seeing the end of a story when I'd missed the beginning.

"Time for your bath, anyway, I expect," our father said. He helped Grandpa out of the room, and I heard him calling Nan in the corridor.

When we were alone, Ruby said slowly, "He might have imagined it—it might not have happened like that."

"Then why was Dad so angry?" said Helena. "But what I want to know is, if there's any truth in it, why someone didn't take an axe to that tree long ago?"

"Grandpa said there was a cost," Elphine said, frowning. "It might cost a lot."

"I don't think we should talk about it anymore," Ruby said.

"It's not the right way to do it," said Elphine quietly. "Attacking the tree. There's got to be a better way to help him—" She turned to me. "Don't you think?"

"I don't want to help him," I said.

I didn't want him happy and I didn't want him free. I didn't yet want him gone. I was starting to hate him, but he was still my friend, the boy I had found crying outside the Rose House.

We didn't have a chance to ask Grandpa about what he'd said, even if we'd wanted to. Dad kept a close watch on him after that evening. He sank quickly, and one morning Nan woke up to find him dead beside her.

I tried to think of him as being set free—sitting up just before dawn, slipping through the kitchen and outside, past the henhouse and out into the fields, leaving his suffering body behind him. But I was afraid, all the same, that he had been extinguished and nothing more. Me and Harry had quenched him between us.

There would be a Small Angels funeral, of course. Which was quite different to a run-of-the-mill burial. At our funerals, the living and the dead come close enough to touch. For one evening the everyday world and *our* world would overlap. People from the village would come to Blanch Farm to pay their respects, and for a few hours they would not shrink from its strangeness. They would take a step closer to Mockbeggar.

Here's a selfish thought: I realized that if the whole village was present that night, I would see Kate again.

I don't know how Nan mourned. With the four of us and our father she was impatient, critical, talking always about practical things. She hoarded her grief like she hoarded our income.

But when Nan was out of the way my sisters and I pieced Grandpa together like a torn-up photograph, poring over fragments. *Remember when he—Were you there that time that we*—Sometimes we joked in a particular way I hadn't experienced before. A sad kind of making light. *Imagine what he'd say about that*, pointing out something he'd disapprove of.

But it was all built on shaky ground, as far as I was concerned. If they knew everything about what had happened to Grandpa out in the field, they wouldn't be able to stand my presence.

Sometimes I told myself that it wasn't my fault. I hadn't wanted Harry to do what he'd done. But I'd known there might be bad consequences to our friendship—I'd always known that—and I'd gone on anyway.

Eventually I needed to be away from it all. I might have gone to see Harry, before all this. He would have been my solace. Now, on the afternoon before the funeral, I went back to Small Angels. And you were there—

She was there. My graveyard girl, perched on our tombstone like she'd been waiting for me.

She came over and held me and said nothing. After a moment she kissed me.

There are things that are wild and good at the same time. Summer storms, the taste of raspberries. She was like that; together, we were like that. She took the edge off my loneliness for a moment.

I was selfish even then. She had no idea what we were risking. Nan was busy, but that didn't mean we weren't observed.

I'll leave in another thirty seconds, I told myself. Another minute. Surely I can be allowed that, he may never let me see her again—

She stepped back and let go of me, frowning.

"What is it?"

I couldn't answer because the air was suddenly full of the smell of roses, sweetness stinging the back of my throat. He had found me out.

He knew what the earth knew and the trees and the wind knew. How could I have been so stupid? How could I have imagined I could ever get out from his sight?

"Lucia? Say something." She was curt with fear. My dread of him must be there on my face. Another stupid choice, another catastrophe. What would he do to me now?

"It's all right." My voice sounded like I was drunk. "I need to go home."

"What's happened?"

Perhaps he would be angry with her as well as me.

"You need to stay away from here," I said. "Don't come back, all right? Don't come to the funeral. You have to promise. It's not safe."

She started to stay something, but I couldn't bear to listen. The longer I stayed with her the worse it would be. I kissed her for a final time and I turned away. I made for Mockbeggar.

It was early autumn. There were hawthorn berries out, dotting the bushes like small red baubles. Rosehips, too, and dark, glossy elderberries on red stems. I knew that in secret parts of the woods there would be wild raspberries and strawberries growing. But it was all his, none of us would taste them.

He got close before I realized he was there. I was afraid of what he would do, now I'd broken my promise, but at the same time I'd seen Kate again and half my thoughts were still with her, I couldn't help it.

I had kissed her again, in spite of everything. That warm thought stayed with me even as I walked deeper into Mockbeggar, where the woods turn cool and dark.

Then he was there. Across a clearing he stared at me. He looked older than I was used to. There was a red stain on his shirt. I felt impatience in that first moment—not pity, not fear. Always his sufferings—why could he never think of mine?

He walked through the trees toward me, and as he moved in and out of sight his age flickered. At one moment he was the child who had been my friend the next moment he was older than me, a man set in his ways.

When we were face-to-face at last, he was a child.

"I didn't know she'd be there," I said. "I didn't plan it. I wasn't looking for her."

"Don't lie, you went looking."

"I wasn't doing any harm."

"You're a traitor. You're rotten inside. Always were."

"Nothing's changed," I said. "I'm here, aren't I?"

He took my wrist. He was bone and thorn all at once; I struggled, but he held me. Only a child to look at, as thin and fragile-looking as ever—but he was so strong.

He said, "Listen."

When he tells you his story there's no helping it, no escape. This time was different. The story gripped me closer. I was more than a witness now. He spoke three sentences and the words were already there in my head; I was *in* the story. His fate was my fate, his fear was my fear. I was running desperately through the woods and the dogs were behind me. My lungs burned and I tasted blood in my mouth and my heart was loud in my head and I knew all my running was for nothing I was about to die.

He said something. *Let that be a lesson,* maybe. Then I was alone.

It seemed to take me a long time to get out of the woods. I was dizzy, fighting blind panic. It was a struggle to keep upright. The woods were spinning around me. The trees seemed to whisper and it was all unkindness.

But I got out. I got home. Nan was waiting for me in the orchard. I don't think I'd ever been happier to see her. The dogs—the dream, the story—gradually receded. My mind was my own again. I sank to my knees.

Nan stood looking down at me. I couldn't read her face.

I expected her to help me up. But she didn't move. She didn't ask if I was all right.

"What did you do?" she said.

I was too shaken to lie. I told her everything, from my first meeting with Harry to his jealous rage. There was some relief in it. I suppose I thought by confessing, it was no longer my problem. Nan would manage it, she always did.

"Get up," Nan said when I was done.

I got up. Then came another surprise: she hit me. I don't think she held back much. I almost fell.

"Get back to the house," she said.

That was a bad journey. Almost as bad as what followed. She dragged me upstairs to Fred Hart's room, and locked me in.

CHAPTER THIRTEEN

Man of the House

Selina in conclusion

Morning, midday, night. Food marks the passing of hours. I eat toast and jam, toast and jam. Toast and no jam. The food is running out, but there will be more soon. A boy brings my supply weekly—Helena and Ruby made that arrangement for me, but they don't visit. As for Lucia, I don't even know where she is now.

Yesterday I went back to the woods. Stupid thing to do. I should have contented myself with a gentle dodder around the orchard.

I haven't forgotten the paths. Sometimes I mutter their names to myself like a prayer. The Crow's-Foot, the Elbow, the Blackberry Maze, the Pig's Tail, the Heart Line, the Fate Line. I remember the tracks too small and uncertain to deserve names. In my mind, I stand at the Leap—that sheer drop at the edge of the river—and I stare down and down into the rush of water. I walk there in memory and it's all how it was, everything lush and dangerous. Every trail fitting together beautifully, like lines on the palm of a hand.

There's sense to it. Not human sense, but sense all the same.

I remember the woods as they were. Sometimes I give all my strength to it and when I open my eyes there's a trace of leaf and shadow creeping into the kitchen corners. I can hear birds singing taunts to each other and smell bindweed and heavy elderflower scent and a dozen other growing things in this empty, dusty house.

Yesterday I nearly fell in the woods—the woods as they are now. If I'd fallen I wouldn't have been able to get back up. Might have been weeks before anyone thought to look for me.

I knew it would be hard going and I knew it was a stupid errand. Why see it as it is now, with the heart gone out of it, hiding or sleeping or dead? I knew this and I went anyway. And it was quiet. Hiding or sleeping. But not dead.

It's still there. I felt a hint of it, just for a moment. The sunlight looked deeper. I saw bark frayed off a young tree, like one of the deer had been at it. And I know there have been precious few deer in Mockbeggar since Elphine died.

I smelled roses. Then I didn't. I'm sure it was there, though, for that instant. All around me, I felt things sleeping more lightly than they used to.

I'm almost sure it was there. The color or the romance or the possibility, whatever people used to call it back when the woods were awake. I'm almost sure I felt it for a minute. It felt like that moment just before the rain starts.

Since I got back, I've been too tired to move from this chair in the kitchen. So let me just stay here awhile.

I have no duties these days. I can lie warm in bed till noon, or stay awake until I drop off at the kitchen table.

Most days I tell my stories to myself for company—in my head or sometimes aloud. I miss listeners. It was something to have them looking up at me—brothers and sisters or my granddaughters—and see their faces change when I got to the twist, the exciting or terrible part. Words came so easy once. I could tell my sisters and brothers something to shut them up or tell my father something to drain away some of his anger.

Now I'm faltering. Brain stumbles like my stupid old feet. I try and tell myself the story of our best days and I can't. *One day when Paul and I were not long married, we planted our first vines. Nothing to them until spring, when the first shoot came up bold as hope—*

—Then it fails.

Tonight, this new weakness rankles. I miss having the words come quickly to mind, never doubting that they would. Tonight, I would like to tell the last story. How it ended like it did, why I did what I did. That stupid trip to the woods has raked it all up. I smell roses indoors. I imagine strange things.

I can almost hear them flitting about upstairs—the girls, in and out of each other's rooms. Lingering in the kitchen door, always hungry for something—food or answers. I can see Elphine standing in the doorway, wanting me to help her free some trapped beetle or spider. I see Paul in his chair, carving a bit of wood into a boat, whistling under his breath. I see Andrew leaning against the door. So meek and dutiful, always ready for another task.

I see Lucia. Five years old, seething with questions. Asking me to lift her up, show her our secrets.

We had some good times I try to say to my shadow family, but my voice is going. Been a while since I spoke. So that story fails me too.

What would you do? I want to ask them, *What would you have done?* I want to ask them if they know, if they ever knew, what I really did for them.

Who's the man of the house? my father used to say. A reminder, not a question—because we children all knew and could never forget. Who keeps the money, who eats first, whose opinion matters, who has authority over every thing and every person under the roof—and who owns the roof, every tile of it?

Being the man of the house meant that he could nurse his dark, slow rages like sick children, tend them like he never tended us. He had a right to it. His moods were weather—storms or ice or blazing heat—and we could only wait them out and take whatever shelter we could.

When one of us made him angry, he made us sorry. He never apologized for anything. That was what it meant to be man of the house.

He drank a lot, in a genteel sort of way. Wine, at home, on his own or with the one or two friends who hadn't fallen by the wayside. I thought that it might kill him, eventually. But that was no sure way to freedom. If he sickened, we—and by we, I mean I, the eldest daughter and head servant—would have to tend and nurse, and most likely there would be years of it.

So I got out. Just as far as the next village, at first. He didn't mind me working at the Albatross as long as I was home to help out during the day.

I never bothered with open defiance. One of my brothers did. Maybe it feels good to stand proud in that split second before he gets his hands on you, maybe it's worth what follows, but that was never my style. I said *Yes, Dad, of course Dad,* and I stowed money away here and there and I kept my eyes open and at last I found Paul.

There'd been a funeral not long before. One of his aunts. Empty-box funeral. I hadn't been but I'd heard the stories. Or I'd heard the silence where the story should have been.

Paul showed up at the Albatross three nights in a row, drinking steadily. Mourning came natural to him. You might say it suited him.

Fourth night he set about drinking himself numb, I said he'd be better off at home. He said I should see his home and see if I still thought that afterward. In my memory, it isn't long afterward that I did just that.

He was a gentleman, Paul. I mean about Harry. Makes me smile now to think how careful he was about telling me the story, breaking it all to me. He said it wasn't an easy thing to live with. The woods could be wonderful, but they were never safe. They could leave their mark on you.

He was worried I didn't understand him, but I did. There's violence that tips everything sideways and makes the world strange. Curdles reality like a haunting. *Did that really happen,* you think. You go out into the street and there are people who live safe from such things and they seem hundreds of miles off. You're cut off from them forever because of what you've seen.

After Paul and I were married I came to Blanch Farm and learned and listened. I saw that the Gonnes were living badly. Irresponsible in their ways. Pushed Harry too far on occasion, didn't know what was best for them. I made Paul tell me as much as he knew, as much as any of the family themselves knew. After his brother died, he tried to forget as much as possible. I carried the burden of knowing for both of us from that time on.

I had an idea then. We could plant a vineyard.

Part of the point of it was that it would mean endless work and anxiousness. Grapes wouldn't grow easily in this part of the world. It would mean bloody scratched fingers and frozen feet and sleepless nights. What if we offered Harry this? Something lovely, rooted in drudgery and pain. Perhaps he'd be less inclined to be cruel. Maybe there'd be fewer empty-box funerals.

So I went to the woods and I made my offer.

No cozy chats in the Rose House for me. No ghost child with occasional gentle moods. I went to the Rose House and I spoke to the woods, and I had a sense of Harry at the corner of my eye. He was a shape made of the space between the trees.

I explained what I wanted to do, what the wine could be. I was very respectful.

It was quiet but he was still there. I thought he might hurt me for presumptuousness in coming out to him. I thought he might kill me.

But he said softly, *Show me.*

Nothing else. Not that I wanted to hear more of that voice. If a dead tree could talk, it would have sounded like that.

It was a gamble, of course. If we'd failed, he would have been very angry. All that plowing and planting, disrupting his land for nothing. Digging up the field and getting the vines put in. Nothing but little twigs, at first. Paul worried.

But it worked. I made Blanch Farm safer than it had been for a century at least.

My granddaughters never understood how much of their safety and comfort they owed to me. They didn't understand how you have to be watchful, with certain kinds of men of the house. Can't hurt their pride. Can't let them lose their temper. I carried that knowledge like I carried the key to Small Angels. So cold and heavy, it used to chill me and set my wrist aching.

When Harry was pleased with us, it was like the days in my childhood when my father had money (because he'd just been paid, or found a friend who'd stand a loan, or sold some of our mother's things—it was all the same to him where it came from).

When Harry was pleased with us, we'd find new paths in the woods, like Harry had opened them up for us on purpose. We'd have perfect weather. The orchard would be laden at harvest, and that year's vintage would sell so far and well we'd have people calling from London to ask if there were any bottles left. In those years our wine was a perfect balance, him and us together. His rain, trickling through Mockbeggar and down the slope into the fields, along with our endless work.

With Harry, I could manage. I could keep the threads in hand, keep the money safe, keep us warm and fed, and there was pleasure in that for a long time. But I knew what happens if you relax your guard. Push him too far. You can never presume.

Death at Blanch Farm attracts attention. You feel the ancestors jostling at your elbow at those times, though they're never really far off, all those generations: Harts, Childs and Gonnes, all with their own piece to say, their own oar to stick in. Remember this, remember that. Get it right, or there'll be hell to pay.

I got it right. I kept the beacons burning day and night, the church bells ringing every dawn on the week Paul was to be buried. I ordered him a good oak coffin, and when he was laid out in it I filled his hands with mint leaves.

I was tired. But I thought we were managing. I thought we'd get through the day all right, and be all right in the days that followed. There was Andrew, always useful. There was Ruby, almost fit to take over—already steadier than most at that age.

Then we couldn't find Lucia. Only an hour before the funeral and she was gone. I told the others to keep working, and I went to look for her.

"Keep the others getting ready," I told Andrew. "We can't be leaving late for the church."

"We could all look. It might save time—"

"No. Just do as you're asked." I was sharp with him because I guessed even then that this absence could only mean trouble of some kind. "I'll find her. No point making a big fuss because one silly girl's wandered off."

No long search needed, as it turned out. I found her at the orchard gate. Scratched and bruised, but that wasn't the worst of it. There was fear in her face like I'd never seen. She'd been in the woods, with Harry.

"What happened?" I said.

No answer. She couldn't look at me and I guessed, then, that she had done something. I could have raged like my father then. I could have killed her.

"Tell me," I said. I heard my father there in my voice, man-of-the-house, the one whose anger makes the whole world tremble.

She told me. I think she was partly glad to confess. Ease some of the burden of knowing. So she told me willingly enough. She'd made a *friend* of him and hurt his feelings and now he would be after her and all of us.

She didn't properly understand how things had been before the vineyard. How hard it had been to keep the balance. All my storytelling had gone for nothing because it hadn't borne fruit, she hadn't heard me right. Now we were bound for the old days again, or worse.

I thought of what this place had been to me. So dear it hurt.

Lucia looked at me like she did when she was a child. The way they all used to look for me when something went wrong. She still thought that I'd be able to fix everything. As if I could save her from what she had done.

It was getting dark. The funeral would begin soon, and sooner or later he would be looking for her.

I locked her in the house, out of his gaze. I went downstairs again. Food everywhere, the rest of the family rushing here and there, looking for their funeral clothes, making last preparations. Nothing to be done but leave for church.

Our neighbors were in a fine good humor that evening. Always a big occasion when one of our family dies. Small Angels was busy, loud with chitchat. Only Paul lying quiet in his box.

I remember that I saw a girl staring at us from across the aisle. Dark and sullen. Lucia's sweetheart, the one who came trespassing into the woods and caused so much trouble. She watched me, frowning like she was waiting to speak.

Paul didn't look free, lying in Small Angels for them to come and stare at. Candle flame made him look awake, worrying. Always better to *do* something, I used to say, not just sit there chewing it over and making yourself sick over something that might turn out all right anyway. I would have said it to him there in the church, only he was past hearing. But his look was quite clear to me: he wanted to know what I was going to do.

And I didn't know. The funeral began and there was no time left and I didn't know what to do. My safe place, my home—all lost in an evening. Decades gone in one swoop. One stupid girl was all it took to pull it all to pieces.

All I could think of was that it was dark and Harry would be watching—funerals always drew him—and I had no idea what would happen, and I had no idea what I could do to stop it. That's what was in my thoughts when I did what I did next.

CHAPTER FOURTEEN

Waking

Kate got as far as dressing for dinner at her parents' house on Tuesday evening.

She could do it, she thought, buttoning a clean shirt. She could eat the tender bloody steak Birdie had been promising everybody for days. She could drink and smile and listen to Bill's talk of strength training and house prices.

But when the time came to depart she found that it was beyond her after all. She was good for nothing but sitting at the edge of her bed, watching the shadows cast by the ceiling beams move as the light changed.

They would be happier without her, anyway. Let Sam and Chloe enjoy another night of ignorance. Tomorrow she would have to tell him what had happened to the child in Mockbeggar, and then he would have to decide what to do. No doubt moving the wedding would be hideously complicated. Budgets and friendships would be strained. But she was more concerned with the fear in Lucia's face. Her voice when she had said *get out*.

The absence—that absence where Kate's full memories of that last night in the woods ought to have been—had never been so hard to stand. For the first time in years she tried to remember, sparing herself less than she ever had before.

Her mind shied away, resisted as it would have done if she tried to touch a hot coal—and still she pressed on:

She remembered saying *I'll do it.* At Blanch Farm, after Paul Gonne's funeral. She had been very determined. She wasn't sure now who she'd been talking to. She had been looking for Lucia. There had been a series of questions, and someone had pressed a glass of wine into her hands. Then she had stumbled out into the dark.

Yes, she remembered that. She'd been on a mission. Brave and heedless, not stopping to look ahead. What could she have been thinking? All those promises, all those warnings counted for nothing that night. She ignored instinct and good sense and ran out into the dark with nothing but the moon to guide her.

And then what?

There was nothing clear beyond that point. Only darkness, and endless trees, and a sense of something gone wrong beyond any remedy. *Don't listen to him crying.* She had been desperate to tell somebody that it was life or death that they understood her. The rest of it was lost like a dream.

She shook, alone in her quaint, comfortable room in the Albatross, like someone chilled to their heart. Her car was parked outside. She could pack her things and be gone in half an hour. John would be disappointed in her, but he didn't understand what Mockbeggar had already cost her. She could leave a message for Sam and he could do what he wanted with her advice. Lucia, too, could do what she wanted. Kate was not his keeper, or hers.

She was still shaking. Fear had seized her like a fever now, there was nothing to do but wait it out.

It did pass, eventually, and she was able to think clearly again. She would get out. No one would stop her. But first she would have to talk to Sam.

She could not sleep—yesterday's sense of well-being had vanished—but she was able to crawl under the covers as the light began to return to the sky, and lay cold and still for an hour or so, eyes closed, bedside light on. When the Albatross began to stir, she got up and washed in water so hot it was almost intolerable. She washed the night off and let the water warm her blood. Then she dressed and set off for her parents' house.

Bill and Birdie's cottage was still a surprise to her, despite her brief visit some years ago. Her parents had moved deeper into the village, into a house that was both smaller and more expensive than its predecessor. Sometimes Kate had to catch herself, recall that they no longer lived in her childhood home.

Birdie's first question was what she had been doing yesterday, and whether she had apologized to Chloe for leaving her to deal with Small Angels.

"I will when I see her."

"Well, make sure you do. She had an asthma attack, poor thing. She said it was the dust. I wouldn't wonder if stress had something to do with it, though. All this work she's taken on. We need to look after her. Keep her happy."

"Is she unhappy?"

Birdie frowned. "I didn't mean it like that. I only mean that she's been deprived of Sam for the week. The least we can do is rally round and make sure everything's ready on time."

"I'll talk to her."

"Well, do. You can't just wander off without warning and leave us high and dry—"

"I will talk to her."

"It just isn't fair, Kate."

"No. I know. Is Sam here?"

"He had to do a supermarket run. We're out of printer ink *and* paper, apparently. He said he'd be about an hour."

Kate said she would come back. It was difficult for her to be still anywhere at the moment, and Bill and Birdie's cottage made her restless.

"If you're going to be out and about this morning, maybe you can do me a favor," Birdie said. "Can you let the beer in for me?"

"What beer?"

"The wedding beer, of course. Chloe asked me to sign for delivery at the Tithe Barn—she's had to go to the doctor with this asthma, you see. But I've got a grocery delivery I'd forgotten about, and it's too late to cancel. So it would be very helpful if you could meet the man for us. He's due around one. All you'd have to do would be to help him carry the crates in and sign where he tells you. Just don't accept any bottles that look cracked or suspect—we have to have things perfect from now on, for Chloe's sake."

There was something new in Birdie's voice. Had Kate's desertion yesterday really caused so much upset? She thought of asking about how dinner had gone, but Birdie did not look in a confiding mood.

Kate said she would let the beer in. Birdie gave her the key to the barn, which Chloe had left behind.

"But she went off with the church key still in her handbag," Birdie said. "That big ugly thing. It's so *heavy*, it must be an absolute nightmare to lug around everywhere. I told her to leave it with me, but she wouldn't."

Selina Gonne had been the same about that key, if Brian Last was to be believed. Kate refrained from pointing this out but saw Birdie thinking it.

"You'd better get going," Birdie said, uncharacteristically brusque. "We can't have the beer going astray. I don't think Sam and Chloe would much appreciate that, do you?"

She had thought she might escape without another sight of Small Angels or Mockbeggar. At least she would make a point of averting her gaze from both, focusing only on the Tithe Barn.

The Tithe Barn—Kate could not deny this, though she disapproved of the place on the Gonnes' behalf—had been well built. It was a pleasant echo of Small Angels in its shape and the color of its stone. The great doors opened easily onto a yard half-sheltered by white awning. Inside it smelled of clean wood.

Bill and Birdie had worked hard. The barn already looked almost ready for the wedding. The chairs and the long wooden tables were decked with ribbons. A blackboard had been set up near the door, propped against a bale of straw, the reception itinerary carefully chalked in Birdie's tidy handwriting.

At the top of the barn, the high table was already set with candles. Paper decorations and fairy lights were strung from the wooden beams of the high ceiling.

It would be beautiful, Kate thought, fully grasping Chloe's plan for the first time. For the first time, too, the wedding seemed inevitable. Could Sam and Chloe call a halt to all this now, even if they wanted to?

She heard footsteps outside and went to the door expecting to discover the man with the beer. Instead it was Sam.

This unexpected meeting startled her into a clear vision of her brother: a man closer to thirty than twenty, frowning into his mobile phone.

"Just call me back," he was saying, in a voice she didn't recognize. There was another life where he needed that voice. She knew so little of him now.

But she knew that tired look, the way his hair was sticking up at the back. It was his exam revision look, his fizzing-with-caffeine look. The work crisis was ongoing, then.

"What are you doing here?" he asked her.

"Waiting for the beer."

"Have you seen Chloe?"

"Not today."

He moved past her into the barn, as if hoping that Chloe might be waiting just out of sight.

"She went to the doctor," Kate said. "Something about her asthma."

"I know. But that was ages ago. We were supposed to meet for lunch and she never showed up."

"Have you called her?"

He didn't bother to answer. His attention seemed to have been caught by the barn in its prettiness and anticipation—the place cards, the little candles waiting to be lit.

"Sam." She spoke heavily, awkwardly. She was not good at this kind of conversation. "I need to talk to you about Mockbeggar."

"Can it wait?"

"No," Kate said. "You need to know now. It's waking up."

He sat down at one of the long wood tables, almost knocking a beautifully calligraphed place card to the floor. She wasn't sure if he entirely understood what she was saying.

She sat down across the aisle, turning a chair around to face him, and told him plainly, kindly, what she had experienced yesterday—the state of the girl, Alice, and what she had said.

"She was frightened, then," said Sam when Kate was done. "Hysterical."

"It was more than that. I'm sorry. But I think things are changing."

He straightened the place card in front of him, made no reply.

"Look, Sam, Lucia said—"

"Lucia?" His voice had changed. "You've been to see her?"

"I had to." (He knew Lucia was back, then. Would he have told Kate if she hadn't found out for herself?) "I told you what state this kid was in. She helped her."

"With some hocus-pocus she learned from her grandmother, no doubt."

"Tea and a story, if you really want to know. The point is, this kid was in trouble, and Lucia helped her."

"Which is surprisingly altruistic, but doesn't actually—"

"Just listen. Please. Lucia knows better than anyone what's out there, and she's frightened."

"Or this is all calculated to get your attention. You'll be over there all the time like the past ten years never happened, won't you? No wonder nobody could find you yesterday."

"God, Sam, be reasonable. I went to her for help. And she helped, and then she told me to get out of here."

He straightened the place card again. With his back to her, he felt more familiar—in another time she might have ruffled his exam-hair or smoothed it into respectability, according to her mood. Now she could not imagine touching him with ease.

"You were worried when you came to visit me," she said, calmer. "Remember? You didn't want the wedding here. You wanted to know if it would be all right. Now I can't promise you that it will. If you want me to help you—moving the wedding, changing the date—I'll help. Whatever you need."

He stared at her, mute. She waited, gave him time to think it through, to adjust his plans as she had. The disappointment would take time to manage; she would be patient.

Then, finally, he said, "So you seriously think we should pack up and leave? Just like that?"

She nodded.

"It's three days. That's all. You don't think we can manage that long? It's not as if we're setting up shop for good at Small Angels."

"Why ask me to be here if you're not going to listen to what I say?"

"It's what Lucia says, though, isn't it? That's what you're going on. Have you got any proof yourself?"

"No." She stared at him, trying to understand. "But—"

"We're here, now. And we're so close to the end. Only three days left now. I'm not ruining my wedding because *Lucia Gonne* thinks I should. I've lost enough to those people without losing that as well."

"What are you talking about?"

He stood up, impatient, chair sliding back behind him with a sharp scrape of wood. "I'm wasting time. I need to find Chloe. If you see her, will you tell her I'm looking for her?"

"What will you say to her, if things start to change? This place is so close to the woods. Doesn't she have a right to know?"

"It won't touch her. She's not like that. She doesn't invite that sort of *rubbish* in."

"Like I did."

"She doesn't—she's got good sense. She's logical. She won't get swept up into any of this."

"She deserves to know."

"Don't you dare say a word to her."

The cold anger in his voice troubled her less than the distaste. The resemblance to the Sam she remembered had flickered out.

"She won't believe you if you do talk," he said. "And if she asks me, I'll tell her it's nothing. I'll tell her you had a bad experience, long ago, and it makes you strange about the woods. I'm not having you spoil this for her."

"And if it's spoiled anyway? If things don't want to stay hidden?" She had struck some chord, she was sure of it. He was holding his hands taut, outstretched, the way he used to do when he was upset as a child. 'Is that why you came up here looking for Chloe? Just in case something's happened?"

He turned away, impatient. At the door he spoke rapidly:

"You don't want to put too much trust in Lucia Gonne, you know. There are things they say about her you probably haven't heard, being away from the village for so long. They say she knew more about her sister's death than ever came out at the time. Why don't you ask her about that the next time you call round to Blanch Farm?"

She followed him—full of angry things to say, determined he should hear them all—but outside she was caught by surprise. Sam had stopped short as well.

The yard in front of the Barn seemed to be filling with snow. A shower of petals had blown through the field and settled in little flurries. Others were drifting through the air, white and pale pink. It was lovely, Kate thought, picking a petal out of her hair. It was absolutely unnatural. They were rose petals, and they could only have come from Mockbeggar.

She and Sam stared in silence for another minute, until the wind dropped and the wave of petals ended.

"Well?" she said, quietly.

He looked at her—frantic denial mingling with a dislike she didn't fully understand—and then his phone shrilled from his pocket.

He glanced at the screen, and muttered something that might have been a curse.

'Is that her?" Kate said.

"No. I'm going to keep looking. Let me know if you hear from her." He turned away without another word.

Before she could decide whether or not to follow him, he had already reached the lane where his car was parked. In another moment he was gone, and Kate was left alone, petals clinging to her boots, to await the man with the beer.

It was his last expression which gave her pause. Under the anger, he had looked cut adrift.

She had seen him that way before, when they were children. Trapped in the car, halfway to some distant holiday destination. Bill and Birdie arguing in the front, voices growing steadily louder, Bill driving faster. Sam's look would say: *Do something. Please.* Kate had always done what she could, however small that was. She wouldn't be able to refuse him now, though she wished that she could.

Lucia would call her an idiot. (But if she stayed it would mean seeing Lucia again.) Three days, Sam had said. Not a very long time to be trapped here. Perhaps they would be lucky enough to escape notice.

CHAPTER FIFTEEN

Blackberry Maze

Here was Chloe's proof. Two days ago, she had found Mockbeggar dry at the edges, sad and quiet. Now its colors had deepened. Rabbits ran across the path in front of her, there were birds calling from the trees. Everything was awake. A little farther through the trees and she found herself in a clearing where the ground was vivid green with moss which crept over everything—stones from a ruined wall, fallen trees, stumps and rocks, a green so rich that it lingered when she closed her eyes. Everywhere she looked was outrageous new life.

Relief surprised her into laughter. She was not imagining things, she was not hysterical, she was not losing her grip. Nobody could explain away this transformation.

There was something exultant about it—the heaviness of the blackberries on the bush across the clearing, the drone of wasps on the fruit. One solitary young tree at the center of the clearing was bright with flowers—a dog rose was snaking around the trunk. It had already climbed almost to Chloe's eyeline. She thought of the ruined house where she had found the copper coins. It was overgrown with the very same flowers. The species must agree with Mockbeggar's soil.

The breeze tugged at the flowers and the dog roses shed petals over her head.

She reached out to one of those sweet pink and white flowers, but just before she was about to pick it she had a feeling that she shouldn't, that it would be a huge mistake—

The small storytelling voice had crept back into her mind—she had been too distracted by the woods to guard against it. And in spite of all common sense, she found herself leaving the dog roses alone.

Already she was losing that first giddy sense of relief. If she was not deluded—if everything that had happened existed outside her mind—then the woods were not a safe place.

Brian Last's words returned to her: *I was never fool enough to go back.* She should get out.

But Mockbeggar was lovely. Brian hadn't mentioned that; perhaps he didn't know.

Across the clearing was a path leading through blackberry bushes so tall and dense that when Chloe drew closer, they made her feel as if she had been shrunk to half her normal height. On her last visit there had been no fruit growing, she was sure of that. But now the bushes were laden with glossy berries.

When she was very young, her parents would take her blackberry picking. They would drive into the countryside, fill a Tupperware box with fruit, drive home and make blackberry and apple crumble. It was always a good day, the first day of autumn. She hadn't thought about that for a while. She stepped lightly among the briars, swept up in thoughts of simple happiness she had half forgotten. Five minutes to stop and stare, and then she would get out of here.

She didn't touch the blackberries either.

Don't tell me what to do, she thought. Childishly defiant, she picked a berry.

The taste was a disappointment. She had expected an intense sweetness to match the fruit's ripe beauty. But it was like eating during an illness. The flavor wasn't quite right. Perhaps she needed to go a little farther, try again.

A little way along the track, she stopped to gather her breath. Somehow she was breathless though she exercised regularly and her pace today was a gentle one.

I should have listened, she thought. If only I'd listened! But it was too late by then. She was lost and it was getting dark and nobody was coming to find her.

No, she thought. You're wrong. I am not lost and it isn't too late.

But she should really be going. She had got an answer to her question, after all. She was not deluded. The rest would have to wait a little longer. The mystery of this place was not going to be solved in an hour. She would return with Sam, they could explore together.

She turned back. As she walked she picked and ate berry after berry. The unsatisfying flavor persisted, and yet she couldn't seem to stop herself.

The light must have changed, because it seemed as if the colors of the woods were growing more brilliant. Mockbeggar seemed *happy*.

As soon as this thought came to her, she knew it was absolutely right. What had Brian said? The woods knew things.

There was joy in Mockbeggar's new rich colors, its wealth of fruit. It was waking up, it was full of life again. And something was coming.

Another berry. A gift from the woods, a small piece of Mockbeggar. She felt closer to the woods as she ate. Was that possible? Her head felt strangely tight.

What do you know, Mockbeggar? Another berry.

Somehow she had taken a wrong turning. She ought to have been back at the clearing now, and she wasn't. Perhaps it was understandable because her head was beginning to ache now, and her vision was starting to feel oddly untrustworthy. She stared down at her own hand and for an instant the outlines blurred and doubled—two hands, then one again. The blackberry bushes seemed to press close and then retreat. The bushes were taller here than she could believe possible. She could scarcely see the way she had come.

A few yards more. Then she stopped with a gasp—she had almost stumbled over the corpse of a rabbit which lay stretched out on the track. Its eyes were gone, its belly open. Tiny pink flowers were growing up around it, their petals vivid points of color against the gray-brown fur.

She tried to fill her lungs deeply, then took a puff of her inhaler. She was irritated to have to resort to this—as if she were losing face in front of the woods. She did not want Mockbeggar to see her rattled. She stepped over the rabbit's body and pressed on.

Her watch told her that she had been going for twenty minutes. It wasn't possible for the bushes to continue much further. But five minutes later she was standing again in front of the dead rabbit.

There was no possibility of a mistake. The body's appearance was absolutely identical, the posture—curled, defensive—exactly the same. Chloe had somehow managed to double back on herself.

She shook her aching head and tried to force her vision to stop swimming. She picked a direction, looking left and right with every step. A few yards forwards, and then she almost tripped over the rabbit again.

"Piss *off!*"

The words were spoken before she knew it. She did not sound like someone well-balanced, in spite of her relief of half an hour ago. (No—longer. She had been among the blackberry bushes for nearly an hour, she thought, though the watch face swam when she looked at it.)

She was beginning to feel that the corpse was somehow following her—a slow, sightless crawl, insides trailing.

She was beginning to feel that Mockbeggar was watching her struggles. That the woods were rejoicing in her confusion.

More berries. Why was she still picking them? Juice made her hands sticky. She ate and ate, and Mockbeggar pressed closer. Something was expected. Something was nearly accomplished.

She no longer wanted to know what Mockbeggar knew. Keep your secrets, she thought, just let me out of here, please.

Her efforts always brought her back to the same point. She kept going, through bushes that looked familiar and ones which might have been different. But the exit was gone. There seemed no point looking at her watch anymore. The sky—what she could make out of it beyond the brambles—told her more than enough about the passing of time. It was getting on to late afternoon now.

There was nowhere to sit but the ground—not a single rock or tree stump. She crouched down and did her best to breathe slowly and ignore the sound of her heart drumming in her ears.

She was not trapped. There was no lock between her and the sane human world, only an expanse of leaves and branches. At a pinch these plants could be axed, uprooted, set ablaze. But she was struggling to believe herself now. The path had been so tempting, so easy to begin—and so hard to leave. She had a sense of being held, kept—someone was waiting. A trap had been sprung.

The woods had her and they would keep her until nightfall. And then it would be too late.

Had the voice always been a warning? Had she missed this until now?

Her chest burned; each breath was an effort. If she panicked she would grow too numb and scared to move, or she would start trying to tear her way through the thorns and find herself torn and tangled.

Then she heard a growl. A low, soft sound, with power behind it.

She knew to be afraid now. She'd never known this kind of terror. It felt like a fall backward into nothing.

Chloe didn't move.

The thing—whatever it was—seemed to be padding up and down a few yards off, hidden behind blackberry bushes. Its steps were soft, purposeful.

It knew she was there. It wanted her afraid.

But she heard another sound now beyond the growls—soft but persistent. A woman's voice. Someone was singing.

It wasn't in her mind. Chloe was almost sure of that. The woman sang without stopping, barely pausing for breath. She sounded like she was afraid that if she stopped, she might not be able to start again:

I remember yet, Fred Hart,
In the ground you laid me low
You hid my face beneath the earth
In the woods where roses grow.

The growls had fallen silent, the shape beyond the thorns had ceased to move. Beyond the brambles, the animal seemed to be listening as intently as Chloe.

Then she heard a sudden movement. A rapid drumming of heavy paws on soft woodland earth. It was leaving.

Silence followed. Chloe waited—five minutes, more—but there was no sound now.

Her hands were full of blackberries. When had she gathered them?

No more. She didn't want it. But she raised the fruit to her mouth—

Then someone seized her wrist, took the berries from her.

"Stop that, you *idiot.* Don't you know what you're doing?"

Chloe closed her eyes for an instant, tried to refocus. Then, slowly, she took it all in: the blackberries were scattered at her feet, looking perfectly innocent. In front of her stood a woman of about her own age. The stranger was red-haired, frowning, and unhealthily pale. Her arms were scratched worse than Chloe's, and she carried an axe.

Seeing Chloe's eyes move to the weapon, the woman gave a sharp laugh.

"It's not me you need to worry about. How many did you eat?"

"I don't know."

"Don't you have any sense? Didn't the taste put you off?"

"I couldn't stop." But there were more important things to worry about. "Look, I think there's an animal somewhere close by, I heard—

"I know. It's gone now." Her frown deepened. "God, you look terrible."

"What's wrong with the fruit?"

"It's not meant for you. That's all."

"It did something." Chloe struggled to explain it: "I could hear the woods thinking. They're happy. There's something coming—"

She broke off. If it hadn't been for the shock she would have already realized who this woman must be. Lucia Gonne, the one Brian had mentioned. Worst of the Gonne sisters. She had listened to Chloe talk with a small smile—unhappy, derisive.

"If you were me, you wouldn't find it so amusing," said Chloe, nettled.

"If I were you, I'd have had more sense than to come here. Get out before the light goes, that's my advice." She turned away.

"Wait," Chloe said quickly. "I don't know the way back. Can you show me out?"

Lucia Gonne sighed. "Fine. Keep up, though. I don't have a lot of time."

She led Chloe down two paths in quick succession, walking at such a pace that Chloe—head still pounding, vision still swimming—struggled to keep her in view.

Slowly, she noticed more roses growing here and there along the track. Many had been torn up with violent determination. Some—the taller plants—had been cut down.

"Did you do that?" she asked her guide. But Lucia Gonne did not speak until they reached a place where the trees began to thin, and the light brightened. They were nearly out; Chloe could see fields up ahead. Bare grass had never looked so lovely before.

"There," said Lucia Gonne.

"Thank you," Chloe said—a little grudgingly. The rescue had been so reluctant and charmless. "Before you go—do you know what that thing was? The animal I heard. You heard it too, right? Was that you singing?"

"Take a left," Lucia Gonne said. "Keep walking and you'll get to Crockery Hill."

And then she was gone—back into the woods, where Chloe could not have followed, even if she had wanted to.

More than once, as she made her way back to the road, she had to stop to let her light-headedness pass. Her scrapes and cuts from the blackberry maze were beginning to smart, there was blood seeping through her jeans.

At Crockery Hill, she thought that she wouldn't be able to make it any further. Just then, she heard someone calling her name.

It was Sam. He had parked in the lane and was halfway up the hill, close to where she had abandoned Kate's bike. She was so glad to see him that all other considerations seemed unimportant. She clung to him and felt herself steadied. He was there, warm and solid, holding her, and she was finally out of the woods.

At last he distanced himself enough to look at her.

"Are you all right?"

She nodded.

"I looked all over, I went all around the village and it just kept getting later and later and no one had seen you—"

"I'm really sorry. But I'm all right, I swear."

"You're bleeding."

"I got lost. Had a bit of a shock in there." She took a breath. "It's *real,* Sam. You should see how different it is today to the first time I went in—"

"The *first* time?"

"Yes." She couldn't allow him to get distracted by this revelation. There were more important things for him to know. "I went back today and it's different. Impossibly different. Do you understand? The stuff Brian was talking about—I don't think he's completely wrong."

She waited for him to speak. Maybe he would laugh or try to deny what she'd told him, and then she could walk him to the edge of the woods, offer him her proof.

"Everyone told you," he said at last. He spoke quieter than usual—voice careful, tight, restrained. With a shock she realized that he was making a great effort not to lose his temper. "Everyone said stay away from there. You promised you wouldn't go in. Remember?"

"I know. And I shouldn't have, maybe, but I had to know and no one was talking to me."

"Why did you *have to know*? Why couldn't you just leave it alone?"

"Because it's all around us. It's in the church, in the Albatross—I can feel something close and nobody would explain. I went looking because I thought I was going mad. But I'm not. It's true."

She waited for him to speak, but he didn't. Now she realized that she had made a mistake. She hadn't understood him properly.

"You're not surprised," she said.

He shrugged.

"How long have you known that there was something wrong here?"

"We try not to know," Sam said. "Everybody in the village. Except Brian. We leave it alone and it's better that way. And things were quiet for a long while, ever since the Gonnes left."

"They're not quiet now. Go and look if you don't believe me."

He didn't move.

"You could have said something," she said. "We're getting married, couldn't you trust me with something that the whole *village* knows?"

"They don't know. Or they know as little as possible. It's something people don't talk about. Like a low ceiling we all know to duck. It's mostly second nature to us."

"But you didn't tell me to duck."

"I *did.* I said stay away. What else was I supposed to tell you? That Mockbeggar used to be dangerous and no one knows why but we still give it a wide berth just in case? You think you'd have believed that without question?"

"I would have had questions, obviously, but—"

"That's your mistake," he said. "There's no good in asking questions. People don't know and we don't want to know and it's *fine.*"

"Not any more." A thought came to her. "We're going to have to move the wedding, aren't we? Remember what Brian said—"

"I don't give a—" He stopped, breathed carefully. "I don't care what Brian said. You can't seriously plan to cancel the whole wedding with two days' notice."

"You don't believe me, then."

"That's not what I'm saying. I'm saying it's two days. No one's forcing you to go back to the woods. Can't you just put it to the back of your mind for a short while longer?"

She wanted to tell him that there was more to it than that. The story voice, the man begging for death in the Albatross.

Instead she said, "What if it's not safe?"

"People have been around Small Angels for months, Chloe. The builders were up there for ages working on the Tithe Barn, and nothing happened to them. Don't you think our odds are pretty good?" He was being reasonable with her. Somehow it was worse than his anger. "The problems all came about when people went into Mockbeggar. Remember that bit of Brian's story? So as long as nobody goes into the woods—and I don't think people are going to be tempted to go walking there, to be honest—we'll be all right."

They both knew now and yet it didn't make any difference; she felt more isolated than ever.

"It's not like we're the Gonnes, you know," he went on. "They were the ones the woods always took an interest in. *We* don't matter. As far as we're concerned there's nothing personal. As long as we keep our heads down there's nothing to worry about."

"You're sure?"

"That's how it's always been. Leave it to the Gonnes."

It felt wrong. She disliked the deliberate ignorance he was pressing upon her; she disliked this waving-away of knowledge.

But he did have one good point: the greatest danger seemed confined to the woods. The woods had tried to keep her and they had failed, and she wouldn't go back there. In three days, she and Sam would be miles distant and she would never return.

"Let's get back to the Albatross," Sam said. He picked up the bike, ready to load it into the back of his car. "You must want a wash."

"What do you mean? Do I smell?"

"Just outdoorsy. Flowers and earth." He tried to smile at her. "No offense, you understand. We'll get you back to the Albatross for a bath and a glass of wine and an early night. Don't you think you'll feel like yourself again after that?"

He sounded like Birdie. That same determined ignorance she had treated Chloe to yesterday. She saw that even if she made him listen, he wouldn't believe her. She felt very tired.

"Chloe?"

He was waiting for her answer. There seemed nothing else to do but to nod and say that he was right. She would go back to the Albatross, and rest, and soon feel like herself again.

CHAPTER SIXTEEN

A Noose of Briars

Lucia in continuation

Nan didn't hesitate about imprisoning me. If she'd been a fraction less decisive I might have resisted. But I was still in a bad way from my meeting with Harry. I was in pain and my thoughts were a mess. I let her lead me upstairs without question. I had a vague memory of her putting me to bed when I was very small and sick with flu or whooping cough, and I believed she might be about to do that now. Instead she brought me to Fred Hart's room.

I didn't tell you about Fred Hart's room before. You must have seen the door—first on your left when you get to the top of the stairs. Best room in the house in some ways—fine view over the fields toward the woods. Over the kitchen so it's always warm. But it was always Fred Hart's room. It didn't matter that he'd been dead for over a century. It was still his place, tainted by his thoughts.

We left it alone, for the most part. Nan would go in occasionally to run her handkerchief over the mantelpiece and sweep up the past few months' accumulation of dead spiders and flies. Letting the room gather dust would be a mistake, she used to say. It would look like encouragement.

She'd never used the place for punishment before. If one of us (usually me) needed to be grounded, she'd use our bedrooms. She must have been truly furious to have shut me in Fred Hart's room that night.

Or she might have thought it was the safest place. I wonder if that's possible. I didn't think of it before, but if she thought Harry might be searching for me that night—if he might follow me back to the house—then maybe she'd reasoned that would be the best room. I never thought of it like that before.

As soon as I understood what she'd done I started kicking and hammering at the door, begging to be let out. She couldn't leave me in Fred Hart's room—whatever I'd done, however much punishment I deserved, she couldn't do that. My sisters couldn't let her keep me there.

I called to each of them in turn, and at first I pleaded and then I raged and then I was tearful and frightened. I heard my voice start to sound frantic and demented, the spaces between my words shrinking to almost nothing.

When I fell silent at last, the quiet that followed seemed absolute. For a moment I thought that they'd all left for the funeral.

Then I heard feet clattering up the stairs—someone was in a hurry, taking them two at a time.

"Lucia?" It was Ruby, almost breathless. "Listen, I've only got a second—"

"You've got to let me out."

"I can't. Of course I can't. I just wanted you to know we're going now. We'll be a couple of hours, I suppose."

She knew what I'd done. It was there in her voice. I wanted to see her face—to know how badly she thought of me now—and I was glad that I couldn't.

"Please. You can't leave me shut in here. The funeral's starting."

"You can't go." She didn't sound angry so much as infinitely sad and tired. "Nan says it's too dangerous for you. Maybe not just for you. She says there's no telling what he'll do now."

I couldn't contradict what Nan had said. The time when I could have boasted that I could predict my old friend's moods was long gone.

"She just knows that he'll be angry," Ruby said—she was talking faster now, running out of time—"and he'll be looking for you. She said the first thing is just to get through the funeral. Then we might think of something. But for now you're best inside, out of his sight."

Nowhere was truly out of his sight. Not at Blanch Farm, at least. She knew that as well as I did.

Someone called from downstairs—Helena, sounding edgy.

"I've got to go," Ruby muttered.

I heard her descend the stairs two or three steps at a time, and then conversation—irate—in the hall below. Then the door slammed, and I was alone in the house.

After they'd left me I felt too weak for a while to do anything but sit on the floor with my back to the door, as far removed from the rest of Fred Hart's room as I could manage.

I didn't bother trying the light switch. We all knew that there was no light in that room. Years before, someone had needed a new lightbulb and poached the one from Fred Hart's room, never replacing it. It wouldn't have seemed a pressing matter. Nobody had any business in there after dark.

As the sky darkened, the room seemed to expand. The walls seemed to slide away whenever I took my eyes from them. I couldn't see myself properly anymore.

There's grand furniture in Fred Hart's room—solid, dark wood chest of drawers and bed, dark oil landscapes on the walls. He liked fine things in his day, Fred Hart. He must have thought that gleaming dark furniture suited his position. But it *looms*, if you sit on the floor in the dusk and stare around you. Everything seems slightly larger than it should be.

There were no curtains, and a bit of moonlight came through the small window. It was the sort of night Harry liked. Moon bright enough to cast a shadow.

Then I remembered what he had told me about Fred Hart's death. I had tried not to give it much thought before, but trapped where I was, with Harry's injuries fresh on me, it was impossible to keep it out of my mind.

He told me, once, that he thought often about how long it took Fred Hart to die. He was trying to speak but the rose branches were tight around his throat.

Sometimes I'd find Harry at the Rose House and he'd be frowning over it, wondering what his brother had been trying to say.

He'd have been hanged anyway, he used to tell me. *Noose of rope or noose of briars, what's the difference?* I used to agree with him. I never said that Fred Hart deserved what he got, though—I tried that tack once and Harry didn't like it, somehow.

I knew what he was, really, all along. I knew he was more than a child and I kept on visiting because it made me feel important.

Now he would find me and maybe I'd end up like Fred Hart and maybe someone would say *serves her right* of me, the way I'd once said it of him. Easy to comment on someone else's story.

I decided to get out, if I could. It was probably pointless, but anything was better than sitting in the dark, imagining thorns tightening round my neck.

There was no way out through the door. Nothing in Fred Hart's room would serve as a battering ram. Nothing I could shift, at least.

What if there was a key? It was a remote hope but I told myself it wasn't impossible. Fred Hart's room was left so thoroughly alone, as a rule. There was no telling what might have been left there and forgotten. I began to explore in haste, fumbling in the gloom. I pulled out drawers and opened cupboards and found darkness within and had to feel carefully.

At first I found nothing. A few old clothes. A pair of shoes I put my hands on without realizing it. The leather was soft as skin, molded to the shape of a stranger's feet. Touching them was horribly intimate.

I almost stopped after that. But the idea of a key, an image of it sitting somewhere waiting for me to find it—this had taken hold of me by that point. I kept going. I was the only thing moving in the still house, and if I paused to think I'd begin wondering if someone might be slowly making their way through the garden or the kitchen—Harry come to fetch me. Nan said he had never come to the house before, but after what I'd done, nothing was certain anymore.

I peered as far under the bed as the moonlight would show me. Just dust. I turned over the teapot on the mantelpiece. Nothing.

Would Grandpa mind that I wasn't there at the church? Would he wonder why I hadn't been able to do this small thing for him after all he had done for me?

I retreated to my safe place with my back to the door. As I leaned my head against the wood I felt something soft behind my hair, like there was a person standing behind me.

My breath caught, but it was just a coat, hanging on a hook. I could just make out the shape of it in the moonlight. It was dark and it smelled of ancient tobacco and damp.

I stood up and tried the pockets.

You and Sam had Christmas stockings, didn't you? We didn't, but I can imagine how it must have felt to open one. It was a little like that to go through Fred Hart's pockets in the dark room.

I knew it was his coat. Even before I went through the pockets I knew. The coat belonged to the room. There were pale dog hairs on the sleeves, just showing in the moonlight.

I half-expected to find a dead mouse or a nest of spiders, but the coat only held relics: a handful of conkers, dried out long ago. A deck of cards, unpleasantly soft. A pale piece of wood someone had begun to carve into a boat. Three marbles, a pencil stub, and a clasp knife marked *HC*.

It wasn't incredible that these relics had remained there so long.

Not considering the way we treated Fred Hart's room. What surprised me was that Fred Hart had kept them. There had been time for him to throw away every vestige of Harry, scour the house clean of his brother. But he hadn't. He had kept this small vestige of Harry safe. Even after Fred's dogs had torn his throat out, Fred had needed Harry close. The marbles could have been his—or Fred's—or both of theirs, passing between them as they won and lost games against each other.

I didn't like these signs of affection because it didn't tally with the way my upbringing and Harry had both encouraged me to think of Fred.

Also I didn't like them because they were warm.

I couldn't pretend it away. Both the marbles and the knife still felt warm, like they'd just come from someone's hands.

I was alone in that quiet room, but these tokens held someone else's body heat and I wanted to fling them from me, but I didn't dare.

"Fred Hart?" I whispered.

I wished I hadn't said it. There was no reply, no break in the silence. If he heard me, he wasn't willing to talk.

But the room was full of him. For an instant it seemed to choke me—his ancient thoughts, his complicated love.

I put it all back—marbles, wooden ship, knife. None of it was any use to me. If there was a key here or some other means of escape, I couldn't find it.

I slumped back against the door. My brief moment of hope and energy had burnt itself out. I knew then that there was nothing I could do, and the disaster I had caused was only just beginning.

That's when I heard voices outside. Nan and the others, and most of the village with them.

It was a relief to have something like company, though I knew that none of the guests would come into the house. We never let people inside during our funerals, and nobody from the village would have wanted to venture in anyway.

I was hungry for reassurance that there were other people in the world. The locals I'd always despised were welcome just then. I almost envied them at that moment. Maybe it was better to live dull and safe and ignorant than to do and suffer what I had done and suffered. And this was only the start of it.

I sat close to the window and listened. I heard laughter—they always enjoyed our funerals in the village, you know. I smelled cooking meat. I heard music. Nan would have remembered every tradition.

Then I heard someone come inside and shut the kitchen door. Was it Nan? Had she decided what to do with me?

I pushed back the rug a little way and lay down with my ear pressed to the floorboards. If I didn't breathe too loud, I could just make out what was happening in the room below.

First I heard conversation, too indistinct to decipher. Then a voice spoke louder—Nan:

"—well enough alone," she said.

"I want to see she's all right, that's all."

That voice made me gasp. I hadn't thought you'd be here, Kate. I'd told you to stay away.

"You've got no business here," said Nan. "Never did. Prying where you weren't wanted."

"I don't want your secrets," you said. "I just want to see her."

I was so proud of how you spoke to her. You didn't sound frightened, you didn't posture or get angry. It was a fleeting moment of comfort to think that the girl down there—the one with the grit to stand up to Nan, to dare her rage—she was the same girl who sometimes looked at me like she couldn't bring herself to look away. It was undeserved but it was marvelous, to be chosen by someone like that.

At the same time I was so afraid for you. It wasn't good for you to be talking to Nan like this. You shouldn't have been anywhere near Blanch Farm or Mockbeggar. What were you planning?

Nan—she didn't sound right, she didn't sound like herself—Nan gave a short laugh.

"You don't know when to give up, you don't. Have a drink."

"I don't want to—"

"You want to see her, you want to know what happened, then you'd better be civil. Have a drink, raise a toast to my husband, who we just put in the ground. Not too much to ask, is it?"

You didn't answer, but there was silence for a few minutes. I'd stopped wanting you to come upstairs and find me. I wanted you to get out.

"That's better," Nan said at last. "That's neighborly. Not so bad, our wines. Wouldn't you say?"

"I want to see her," you said. Repetition, water on a rock. "Please. Why wasn't she at the funeral?"

"You don't want to know. Go back to the party and forget all of this. Leave us in peace."

Silence. I suppose you didn't move, but quietly stood your ground.

"You really think she's worth your fretting?" Nan said.

"Yes."

"I suppose I'd better tell you what happened, then. If you're sure. It's your choice. Go back to your neighbors, or stay and listen. Just don't blame me if you don't like what you hear."

Go back, I wanted to call. I stamped on the floor, I pounded with my fists, but neither of you heard me.

You stayed. You wanted to know.

"Fine," Nan said. "You'd best have another drink, then. I know I'm going to."

Then I suppose she poured more Mockbeggar Bacchus for both of you. And she told you all of it. The family secret, and what I had done—how I had wrecked things for us all.

When Nan was done, you didn't speak for a while at first. Finally you said,

"How are you going to fix it?"

Now Nan laughed harsh and loud. "There's no *fixing* it, you stupid girl. No reasoning with him when he's in this mood."

"What if I try?"

"Go and try, then," Nan said. "If you think you're so clever."

"All right, then."

Then I screamed. To both of you. I ran to the door and yelled and kicked and hammered once more, but no one came.

The kitchen door opened and closed. I went to the window and there you were outside, striding through the orchard. You didn't look back. I pounded on the glass until it shattered. I felt the blood, but I couldn't see it in the moonlight.

I shoved, ignoring my injury, and the window gave at last.

But I was too late, you'd gone.

Nan must have followed you out. Now she was alone in the orchard, staring up toward the woods. I was too late, and you were already long gone on your mission, Katherine Joan—bound for Mockbeggar, and Harry.

CHAPTER SEVENTEEN

Dawn Meeting

The beer was safe, stowed away in the kitchen-storeroom at the Tithe Barn. Kate did most of the moving herself, the deliveryman being visibly eager to get away. She didn't mind the work. There was something calming in the simple physical task.

She saw afresh why this venue had appealed to Chloe. Along with the Tithe Barn's kitchen-storeroom with its great fridges—generous enough to hold a whole party's worth of drink—there were also cloakrooms, a lockable office, several well-appointed bathrooms. The guests would enjoy every comfort on Saturday. So little time left now.

That realization shouldn't come as such a shock. It wasn't as if the date of the wedding had been kept a secret. Still, she had thought that somehow it might be averted. That the small candles would never be lit, the arch of paper flowers would be quietly disassembled, the hay bales would be flung onto the back of someone's truck and driven away. But after Sam's refusal to listen to her, the whole thing seemed newly inevitable. Come Saturday, Small Angels would be busy with wedding guests.

Then—easing the final box of bottles onto a shelf in the fridge—she remembered they would gather here even sooner than that.

Chloe had that plan for Friday night: the garland party, the decking of the barn and church with flowers. At least half of the guests would be there to help, and they would make an evening of it. Chloe had promised food and drinks and music.

Kate thought of the Tithe Barn, lit up in the gloom of the evening. A memory—memories were coming back more and more frequently now—returned to her unexpectedly, an image of Blanch Farm on the night of Paul Gonne's funeral. Fires burning outside the house, lanterns strung up along the path. Small lights in the country darkness.

Suddenly feeling cold and sick, she shut the beer carefully away, locked the Tithe Barn up, and left it to await the guests, quiet for a short while longer.

If only she could lose herself in some further wedding chore—collecting the service sheets, confirming the caterers, anything. But her duties didn't resume until tomorrow, when she would be required to attend the wedding rehearsal at Small Angels.

Until then she was left to her own devices. By rights she should be using this time to rest and prepare herself. But she could not rest, and could not think how to prepare. What the next two days held was largely unknowable.

She found herself missing her everyday life—her cathedral, her quaint attic flat with its plants and its skylight. She missed drinking in old pubs with the other stonemasons—their incurious goodwill, their tolerance for her long silences. She missed the ache of missing Lucia. It had all been so manageable.

If all went to plan, then she would be back there in a few days, but that seemed hard to imagine at the moment. Even if she got home unscathed, she would not be the same. All that hard-won forgetfulness had deserted her.

Restless, and unable to think of a better destination, she drove to the big supermarket beyond the village.

This place was Brian Last's hated rival, its shelves stocked with the cheap and non-local. The Gonnes had never shopped there; as children, Lucia and her sisters had regarded it with disapproval and fascination.

Kate brought grass in with her, flecks of green following in her wake. Apparently she had trekked over a fresh-cut lawn without noticing. It only seemed to add to her sense of being unwelcome in the cold, white-lit place.

The supermarket did not feel quite real. She had hoped to draw closer to normality—the world Sam prized so highly—but it felt more distant here than it had at Blanch Farm. She wouldn't get away from Mockbeggar so easily.

She switched on her phone and saw that she had a curt message from Sam, telling her that he had found Chloe and all was well. They were probably already enjoying coffee in the village, Sam having crushed his fears down so small they no longer troubled him.

She bought a bag of Braeburns and a mint plant in a plastic pot, and drove back to the village.

The apples were for Hector, the only other creature she felt minded to see right now. She found him exactly as he had been on that first evening, although today there was mist creeping in, a shade of autumn.

She fed Hector two apples. He watched her as he ate, and when the food was gone, he didn't walk away from the fence but let her stroke him and lean her forehead against his neck for a moment.

Then she heard a cough—or an attempt at a cough:

"A*hem.*"

It was one of the mouse girls. The middle sister, who had interrogated Kate yesterday in the Gonnes' orchard. She was sitting in the saddle of her bike, staring at Kate with a slight frown.

Kate thought of telling the child that you couldn't simply say *ahem*—this wasn't how it worked—and decided against it. The Gonnes—was it *all* going to come back now, every single memory?—the Gonnes had often had that trouble, back in their day. Their library books held so many words they never heard spoken. Lucia, especially, had never liked to be corrected.

"How's Alice?" Kate asked.

"OK."

"I thought you weren't coming back here."

"I'm not back," said the girl. "I'm not stopping. I just wanted to see."

"In case it's getting worse?"

The girl shrugged, sullen. But then the words seemed to burst out of her almost against her will:

"The thing in the woods—I don't think it stays there all the time."

"What?"

"There were petals in the street today. Roses, like the ones in *there.*" She glanced up the hill to Mockbeggar, distant beyond Blanch Farm. "I don't see how they could've come so far. There were so many of them."

"Did anyone else notice?"

"A few people. Mostly they just pretend like it's not there, you know? But they don't like it all the same. Our dad went out to sweep the petals up—"

"There were enough of them to sweep?"

"Obviously. Or why would people be freaking out? There were *loads.* Brian Last came out of his shop and watched and he said something and Dad got mad. I think the flowers made people upset. It never happened before, did it?"

Not as far as Kate knew. But she had never known all the Gonnes' secrets, even when her memories were intact.

"You should get back," she told the middle sister. "You can't keep hanging about here."

"Fine." She looked at Hector, then at Kate's bag of Braeburns. "Didn't he bite you?"

"No. Want to see how to feed him?"

Neither of them should linger here. But Kate gave in to the impulse anyway.

She showed the child how to present Hector with an apple, the importance of a steady, flat hand, fingers kept out of harm's way. Which of the Gonnes had showed Kate this, a decade ago? She thought it might have been Elphine.

The child held her breath as Hector approached—tall enough to make three of her—lowered his head to her outstretched hand. Watching, Kate felt envious of them: both so fully present, so intent on this simple thing.

"He did it!" The girl wiped her hand dry of horse spit, speaking with quiet awe, as if she had been honored by a minor local god. "You saw that, right? He just ate it in one bite."

"Well done," Kate said. "Now you'd better go home."

"Yeah, fine." She sounded unimpressed by Kate's stern tone. "I'll let you know if I see anything," she added. "*Someone* should do something. If it gets worse."

She was gone before Kate could say anything in response—to question, perhaps, the responsibility the child had just thrust on her. If things got worse, Kate would be told. The girl had signed her up for the position without a thought.

But she would have to know more if she was really going to be useful. Her own tattered memories were not enough. She would have to talk to Lucia.

Lucia would know that Kate was still in the village before much longer—assuming she didn't know already. Even the isolation of Blanch Farm was not absolute. Someone would say something. Or Lucia would ask, and then sigh, impatient, when she heard the answer. She would guess what Kate was planning to do.

Better talk to her as soon as possible. But after one more gaze at Blanch Farm, she turned away. The scar around her throat felt as if it had drawn suddenly tight, constricting her throat. She would have to find out. She would do it soon. One more night of ignorance, and then she would look history squarely in the face.

Most unusually, Kate overslept that night. She woke on the day of the wedding rehearsal to hear the Albatross already stirring around her—pigeons cooing, conversation in the passage outside the door, pans clattering from downstairs.

She was still tired. There had been weary times like this just after Elphine's death, when she walked through that last night in the woods in her sleep, retracing her footsteps again and again. When she woke the memories always faded, leaving only dull fear behind.

Downstairs, the pub was almost busy. Three tables were occupied by visitors to the Albatross—walkers, by the look of them—occupied with breakfast. At the fourth table, Chloe sat, sipping a cup of coffee without much apparent enjoyment.

She waved and invited Kate to sit down, assuming that they were both awaiting Birdie's lift to Small Angels. Kate resigned herself, fetched coffee, bacon, fresh bread. Perhaps it was for the best. She was so tired that it might be worth sparing herself the walk.

"What happened yesterday?" she asked Chloe.

Chloe said, "I lost track of the time in the library. Wasn't that stupid? I feel terrible, giving Sam a scare like that."

"He was scared?"

"Well. You know." Chloe shrugged. "Your mind goes places, doesn't it, when you can't find someone. Imagination in overdrive, fifty scenarios running a minute."

"True," said Kate.

"There's one thing," Chloe began. Her face was troubled. "I'm sorry to bring this to you, Kate, it's a strange thing to ask, but you lived in the village for years—"

Kate stood up. "Just getting some more coffee," she said. "I'll be back."

At the buffet table she poured coffee slowly, mind busy with new thoughts. Chloe was still wondering about Small Angels, then. What if Kate were to warn her as she had tried to warn Sam?

No good. Chloe would be incredulous, and Sam would only lose his temper, and that would complicate everything further.

Let Chloe wait, and keep her peace of mind. Let Sam have what he wanted.

Kate lingered at the table a little longer, until Chloe was joined by John Pauncefoot, who had a question to ask her about Hector's cart on the wedding morning. The conversation was a detailed one, and by the time John departed, the time for Chloe to ask anything further was long gone.

The family resemblance was showing, Kate thought, dissatisfied with herself. She was ducking questions like her parents, like Sam.

It was uncomfortably snug in Birdie's car on the journey to the church, five of them packed into a small hatchback, discarded coffee cups and teaching materials rattling around in the footwells.

"It reminds me of when we used to go on holiday," Birdie said, taking a pothole at a fair clip. "You remember that, Sam? Those journeys to Southwold? You two would be crammed in the back with beach balls and sleeping bags and goodness knows what else. It was such a production getting you anywhere when you were small."

Sam said that he remembered. And Kate did, too—her parents' poisonous exchanges, Bill's hands tight on the steering wheel. Do something. Please. She used to make up games to distract Sam: who can spot the ugliest car? Who's the best at pretending to be asleep?

Chloe told them proudly that she had worked out the trick of the church key—as if this were some kind of proof of initiation, Kate thought. But as they waited outside the church porch for Chloe to let them in, her mind was elsewhere: there was a new message on Miss Violet's grave. Chalk letters, crooked as Lucia's writing always was:

don't ©

She was annoyed at the presumption and yet the message—so unexpected—almost shocked her into laughter. Lucia had guessed at her thoughts then.

"What does that mean?" Chloe was studying Miss Violet's grave with some curiosity.

"No idea," Kate said. She wiped the letters away, leaving a pale smudge behind, a ghost mark of her fingers on the stone. As she did so, she was aware of Sam watching. He had that careful blank expression when he looked at her today which meant that he didn't want any more confidences or warnings; he wanted Kate to keep things smooth and civil.

The extent of the church's transformation took Kate by surprise. Chloe and Birdie must have worked frantically during her absence. There were fresh candles, bows at the ends of the pews. The windows—soaped clean now—let in more light. The rood skeletons surveyed it all with interest.

"Damn," Chloe said, looking at the screen. "I forgot to do something about that thing. Could we move it, do you think? Turn it to face the wall?"

"I wouldn't bother," said Sam. "Even if we could shift it, it's probably a bad idea to touch it. There'll be hell to pay if it falls to bits on us. We'll find a screen."

"In the space of a day?"

"We'll find something."

The smell of dust was coming back, the lemony polish was fading. For all their cleaning, all their ribbons and flowers, Chloe and Sam and their guests were only squatters here. They were barely keeping history at bay.

Chloe's father would perform the wedding this weekend. But a parish emergency had forced a delay in traveling, and he and Chloe's mother were not able to arrive until Saturday morning. In his absence the rehearsal was tentative, awkward. Nobody seemed quite sure of what they were doing.

A bad dress rehearsal means a good opening night, Elphine had told Kate once. Perhaps Saturday would go smoother now they had got all the halting and stammering out of the way.

As Chloe and Sam read their vows from the same book, straining to make the old promises out by oil light, they both struck Kate as very young.

She had felt sour toward them a short while ago. It had been there in her refusal to listen to Chloe just now. They had embroiled her in their story, and she resented them for it.

Now she found their ignorance touching as well as infuriating. Their peace and happiness were so fragile.

Sam's failure to listen still rankled, but perhaps he was not capable of behaving another way. Kate had seen the way he looked at Chloe, his beacon of sanity and safety. He loved her and he loved the world that had nurtured her; he was desperate to belong to it. That was another reason he was so eager for this wedding to go ahead as planned, Kate thought. You can never climb far enough out of the bad place not to fear falling back.

She had kept monsters at bay for him before—nightmares, their parents' unhappiness—she would do it again now. She would always do it, if it came down to it.

No more delay. She would ask Lucia for the truth. The idea of talking to someone who at least acknowledged that something was amiss—who might know a remedy—was a hopeful one. She wanted Lucia now, sharply. It would be a relief to talk to her, even to argue.

No hens scratched outside the house today. Blanch Farm looked more desolate than ever.

Lucia didn't answer Kate's knock. Kate went into the garden in case she was there. She found the orchard empty, and as beautiful as she had ever seen it. The rain that fell before dawn had brought out the green of the mossy trees. The fruit was almost ready—plums and greengages in a day or two, apples and pears a little while longer.

The gate into the fields was open. She was surprised by the carelessness of it. They had been religious about keeping it shut in the old days.

Most likely Lucia hadn't gone far. But when Kate went to the gate and looked out into the field, there was no sign of her—only sunflowers, beyond that the woods, and at her feet a scatter of red feathers.

Now the quiet of the yard made new sense. Had a fox tried its luck last night?

So many feathers. Perhaps more than one hen had been taken. She stared up to the still woods a little while longer. It seemed wrong to leave the gate as it was, so she pushed it shut, taking one of the scattered red feathers away in her pocket like a talisman.

She was about to leave—there seemed no point in hanging around if Lucia was away—when a movement through the kitchen window stopped her in her tracks.

It was only a very slight movement. If she had passed by even a little quicker she wouldn't have noticed it. Now she approached the window and saw that Lucia was at home after all.

She was sitting at the kitchen table, head in her hands. She had her coat on, and on the table in front of her, an axe had been set carelessly down among the dirty plates.

Kate knocked and called, and when there was no reply she tried the door.

It was unlocked. Lucia didn't look up as she came in. She was shivering. And she was so pale, Kate thought, feeling something like a kick in her chest.

"Lucia?"

Lucia looked up at her slowly, as if she couldn't comprehend Kate's presence. When she spoke, her voice sounded thick, as if she had been drugged:

"Stupid. Stupid to come back."

Her teeth were chattering. When Kate touched her forehead, it was very hot.

"You're ill. You need to go to bed."

"It'll be all right."

"Rubbish." She put an arm around Lucia's shoulders and forced her to her feet. Her long coat was damp and smelled of rain. She must have been out late or early and when she got home had not even had the energy to take off her outside things and climb upstairs.

Lucia mumbled a protest. She had work to do.

"Later," Kate said. "Rest now."

Beyond the kitchen, Blanch Farm was gloomy, chilly—an old kind of cold, this, as though the house had long ago forgotten what it felt like to be warm. As they crossed the hall, she saw a piano pushed into a corner like a shamed child. There was little else visible in the shadows. Moving through the house felt like exploring a sunken wreck.

The corridor at the top of the stairs led both right and left. Lucia directed them right, to a passage lined with doors. A wooden plaque was fixed to each door, and each plaque was carved with a name: *Ruby, Helena, Elphine, Lucia.*

Lucia's room was small, the ceiling slanted. Its mess wasn't a homely disorder, Kate thought. It was the untidiness of a hotel room in which you didn't plan on staying long. She made Lucia sit down on the bed and fetched her a glass of water from the kitchen.

"Not the way I used to plan it," Lucia said, taking the water.

"Plan what?"

"Having you up to my bedroom." Then she frowned—her thoughts had leaped to a different subject. "What did you do with the axe?"

"It's downstairs." She touched Lucia's forehead again. "I can get a doctor."

"Don't you dare. It's fine."

Her eyes were very bright. Her pallor was gone now, but the flush that had replaced it didn't seem much of an improvement.

"You've been in the woods," Kate said. "Haven't you?"

Lucia didn't answer. Kate pressed on, stern because she was unsettled:

"That's obviously where you got muddy and scratched and tired out of your mind. And you've stayed too long and you've caught a chill. Now you'd better rest awhile."

"Are you going to stay?"

"Yes."

"Won't they miss you at Small Angels?"

"Go to sleep, Lucia."

She did sleep, eventually, and Kate watched her.

According to Chloe's schedule, the rest of Thursday had been left as a kind of buffer in case of unforeseen tasks. Since nothing of this kind had arisen, Kate was free to please herself.

She messaged Sam to let him know where she was, if she was needed. She was not entirely surprised to have no reply.

For the rest of the day, and for the night that followed, she remained with Lucia. More than once she thought of fetching a doctor, but in the evening Lucia's fever broke. She was able to sit up, take a little more water, and berate Kate for coming back before drifting back into unconsciousness.

Kate didn't like to leave her. She did sleep a few hours in a chair in the corner, until Lucia, waking again, told her to go across the hall to Elphine's room.

"I can't." It would be a kind of sacrilege.

"Rubbish. Her room's the only one fit to use right now. Can you imagine her minding, ever? She won't care, she'll be glad to see you again—"

She trailed away, thoughts wandering. Kate held out awhile longer, but as night passed and Lucia seemed to recover by the hour, she did at last venture across the corridor to get some rest.

Elphine's room was as neat as Lucia's was untidy, so carefully kept that Elphine might only just have left it. Kate lay on the bed rather than in it, using her coat as a makeshift blanket. She slept dreamlessly for several hours and awoke as rested as she had ever felt.

Leaving the house at dawn in search of firewood for the kitchen stove, she paused for a moment outside the kitchen door to breathe and order her thoughts.

And there was Elphine, waiting for her in the gray light.

She sat on the old stone bench against the wall. She was wearing the black dress she had worn on the night she died, and her feet were bare. She stared at Kate in the same way she had always stared, that long look that preceded a smile.

She could not be here and yet she was. Gently impossible, entirely herself. There was nothing sensational about the apparition. She was simply come home. In the soft light any injuries were hidden. Her face was a little hard to make out. To Kate, she looked heartbreakingly young.

You have to be the one to break the silence, someone had told her once. It might have been Elphine herself. A story in the woods, long ago. *You should speak first if you meet a ghost, otherwise they might not be able to start.*

What if I don't want to talk to it? Kate had asked.

And Elphine—serious—had said, *Even so. It's better.*

Safer, perhaps—better talk than other things. Or perhaps Elphine had meant that it was the kindest thing, to break the dead's enforced silence and let them talk if they needed to.

Kate was afraid that if she spoke or moved, Elphine would be gone. Or she would come closer and touch her, and though it was Elphine, her friend, Kate found that she couldn't tolerate this idea.

But it was Elphine, all the same. Her friend, who had loved her.

"I missed you," Kate said.

Elphine smiled at her. "She needs to tell it different," she said, as if she and Kate were halfway through a conversation.

"What?"

"Tell Lucia, tell it different, like she did before. If she tells it different, she can find a way out. She can make a door. But she has to do it *soon.*"

"Elphine, I—"

Then a soft noise came from inside the house. Was Lucia awake? Kate turned to look, and when she turned back, Elphine was gone.

She would have to tell Lucia, of course. There had been a message, and Lucia would have to know. But not yet. Lucia was in no state to hear.

Kate found she was glad to keep it to herself for a short while. Seeing Elphine had been a strange, painful happiness. A wonder to keep close. Like seeing that first Mockbeggar deer.

Tell it different. What was Kate to make of that?

She would ask Lucia, but first she needed to get her well again.

Upstairs, she found Lucia had yet to wake. She was flushed, mouth drawn tight shut as if she was afraid of talking in her sleep. Her hair was a dark red tangle, covering the pillow. She was curled up on herself protectively as if shielding an injury.

Why would you do this to yourself, Kate wanted to ask. How can you possibly value yourself so little?

When Lucia woke at last, the blank look in her eyes had gone. She insisted on being helped downstairs to the kitchen, where Kate installed her in the battered easy-chair in the corner. It had been her grandfather's, she said.

Kate looked different, she added. Had something happened?

Kate said nothing was wrong. She read to Lucia—*Wind in the Willows,* which was still out on the kitchen table—and it seemed to help. She dissolved a small measure of bicarbonate of soda in water, and wiped a tissue gently over Lucia's face, then followed it with clean water.

Strange to do this for her, Kate thought. It had always been for the Gonnes to keep Kate safe from Mockbeggar, never the other way around.

Lucia closed her eyes against the water, and Kate was free to scrutinize her face with care—Lucia looked better, she decided. A little rested.

"Tell me about what you've been doing since you left," Lucia said, without opening her eyes.

"What do you want me to tell you?"

"Everything. Every day you weren't here. What did you do, where did you go? John Pauncefoot says you build cathedrals. Brian says you carve tombstones for a living. Tell me all of it. I used to imagine you up among the gargoyles somewhere, but it would be nice to know for sure."

Kate told her. She was not a storyteller, especially not by the Gonnes' standards, but she was able to give Lucia snapshots: the warmth of the stone under sunlight, the heft of the chisel. Sitting perched up among the blue, a coffee flask at her side. A market town below her and beyond that green and golden countryside. The best days were like this. The stone had certainty; it changed very slowly. It kept faith with the dead as best it could; it held their records—names and dates—for centuries.

"Safer than Mockbeggar," Lucia said, when she heard this. "Won't follow you home."

"I suppose not."

"How have you been all this time? Not remembering. Is it easier?"

"It's all right. How have *you* been all this time? What have you been doing with yourself?"

"This and that. Fast food."

"Eating or working in?"

"Both. I did other things, too. Then Nan died and I came back here. The others didn't want to be bothered with it. Now it's mine and I've got quiet if I haven't got anything else." She shifted, struggled to sit up. Her energy seemed to be returning. "So I've done better than I deserve, Nan would say."

"Don't talk like an idiot. You should eat." Impatient, Kate stood up. "Where's the wood for the stove?"

Lucia gestured toward the door. "Shed opposite. But—"

Kate walked out before she could finish. There was the axe by the door, there was the wood in the shed, cobwebbed but dry.

She chopped, brought the wood in, got the fire going.

There were cans of food under the sink. Perhaps the cans had been there since the old days. Lucia and her sisters might have rooted through the same dusty stockpile. After some consideration she added beans to canned spaghetti and heated the mixture on the stove.

When she turned around, Lucia was watching her. Bemused, Kate thought. Or wondering.

"There aren't any forks," was all she said, though. "Or knives, for that matter. Nan must have turned against them, thrown them out."

"Spoons are fine." She poured Lucia's portion into a bowl, left half in the saucepan for herself.

They ate, for a minute or two, in silence. Kate was hungry. The same hunger she'd felt the evening of her first visit to Small Angels with Chloe. The canned beans and spaghetti, ancient though they were, were as good as a feast.

She was pleased to see that Lucia ate, too—eagerly, like someone famished. At last she wiped her mouth and said without warning,

"Elphine used to think we were going to get married. Did she ever tell you that?"

"No."

Should Kate tell her now that she had seen Elphine? She didn't know what it would do to Lucia's equanimity to hear what Kate had seen. Would she be hurt or angry that Elphine had not visited her instead? *Make a door.* What did that mean?

"Elphine had these moods when she'd talk about things that she thought would happen," Lucia went on. "She used to make it sound real. Like a story that hadn't happened yet. Nan had the same trick, only it was more of a snare when she told it." She paused. "Do you think it would've been like this?"

Kate took the room in—the mess, the empty cans, the wine bottles.

"The food would be better," she said.

"You're right. I like to think you'd have spoiled me. Cheese from the farmers' market every Thursday."

"So we're living at Blanch Farm, then?"

"Like you wouldn't have jumped at the chance, back in the day."

They were talking quietly. As if someone might overhear this nonsense story they were spinning out. They didn't look at each other as they spoke.

"That was what Elphine thought about us then, though," Lucia went on. "Not us now. Elphine didn't know the people we are now."

Were they very different now? She looked at Lucia, and Lucia's past and present selves seemed to overlap strangely. The girl she had known was not entirely gone.

But it couldn't be wise to dwell on this. The story was what mattered. She was not here for herself. She had a responsibility to Sam and the others to learn what she could. Lucia seemed mended enough to talk seriously now.

"I need to know," she said abruptly. "Everything that happened back then."

"Why? Why go into all that if you don't have to?"

"The wedding. It's still happening. Besides, there's the village."

"What do you care about *them*?"

"Someone has to look out. Isn't that what you're doing? Whatever it was you all used to do here in the old days? You're obviously working to fix things. And it's not going well, is it? Because it's just you left to handle things on your own. But I'm here now too. So."

Lucia stared at her bleakly, as if watching her from very far away.

"Say something," Kate said. "Don't look like that."

"You're good. I didn't forget, exactly, but—all the same."

She was considering it. That was something. Maybe she would make up her mind to talk to Kate if she had time to get used to the idea.

"Let me sort your hands out," Kate said.

Lucia looked down at her hands as if she had forgotten the grazes—scratched afresh from her last visit to Mockbeggar. After a moment she nodded.

Kate cleaned the injuries in silence. In the quiet, she could hear Lucia's pain—one soft hiss, one shuddering breath. She worked gently, bathing away the dirt and dried blood until the cuts were clean.

As Kate stood up to rinse the cloth, Lucia said:

"All right. If you want. I'll tell you. Probably better you should know. Just wait awhile. Until I can talk without getting dizzy."

"Fine. Of course."

"You won't thank me, though. You'll hate me when I've told you."

"Don't be ridiculous. You want to go back upstairs and sleep?"

"No, I'm OK here."

"Fine. Then rest here, and I'll go and see if there's any fruit ready. Don't do anything stupid whilst I'm not looking."

"What do you mean?"

"I don't know. Running off to the woods without me, getting sick again. We can go together, next time."

"You're bullying an invalid, but all right, since you're so insistent. We can go together."

Kate had no wedding duties that day, but tonight was the wedding eve and she could hardly avoid attending the garland party with the rest of Sam and Chloe's guests. She had intended to return to the Albatross for a wash and a change of clothes, but Lucia had been worse again in the afternoon, feverish and insisting that she needed to go to the woods. Kate had read to her, brought her water and cool mint tea, and watched with relief as the unhealthy glitter faded from her eyes.

Lucia spoke little for a couple of hours. At last, however, she seemed rested enough to sit up in bed and look at Kate with a slight frown.

"I thought you had a party tonight. You were supposed to go back to the Albatross before, weren't you?"

"Sam will have to take me as I am. Mud and all." Her appearance would probably be the least of Sam's grievances.

"You can borrow something if you want. There'll be shirts upstairs. There are towels, too. If you want to wash."

Kate hesitated. She was half-inclined to stay at Blanch Farm. Would Sam and the others miss her among so many other guests? What if Lucia grew worse while she was away? She might go to the woods, if Kate was not there to watch her. Or the woods might come to her.

But there were Sam and Chloe to think about. She couldn't leave them so close to the woods without at least seeing that they were all right.

"I'll have to go," she said to Lucia. "Just in case."

"I know." She smiled—a small, private expression. "Go and get ready, Katherine Joan. I'll be fine here."

To take anything from Elphine's room would be unthinkable. She tried Ruby's room and then Helena's, and found them both in a mess—socks and books discarded on the floor, drawers still open. They had each filled a couple of bags, Kate thought, and abandoned what wouldn't fit. It was like they were fleeing an oncoming disaster, flood or fire. Village wisdom was that they had left hastily after Elphine's death.

She was not comfortable going through Ruby and Helena's wardrobes. But in Ruby's room she found a shirt hanging behind the door. It was soft cotton, dark red. She thought that Ruby—at least the Ruby of a decade ago, who had been her friend—would not mind her borrowing it.

Even in late afternoon, Blanch Farm seemed to be preparing for dusk. The bathroom was cold. There were some signs of Lucia's presence here—a damp towel on the floor, a comb on the sink with red hair caught in its teeth. There were other relics too: in a jumble on the windowsill Kate discovered a wealth of half-empty shampoos and soaps, far too many for one person. By the sink was a jar of toothbrushes. In the shower, four razors sat in a pile—handles bright plastic, blades long rusted.

Kate washed quickly in tepid water. Outside a bird was calling. A pigeon—distant relative to the Small Angels flock, perhaps.

Shivering in the dim light, she found herself oddly expectant, awake from head to foot.

There was music coming from far off. They must be already beginning at Small Angels. Fleetingly, she thought about taking Lucia with her. Lucia would be brightest of the guests, her laugh turning heads. She would dance and her moss-stained red dress would swirl around her, and Kate would keep an eye on her and know that she was safe. She had said once—a long time ago—*I like how you watch me.* Other things had changed, Kate thought, but not this.

Dressing, she managed to knock against a bottle of shampoo and send it clattering into the bath. The sound was so loud it made her jump.

From outside she heard Lucia call her name. A moment later and Lucia had flung the door open. Her eyes were frightened.

"Kate? Are you all right?"

"I'm fine. Knocked something over."

Lucia sank down at the edge of the bath, leaning against it for support. She looked about to faint. The fever was still on her.

"You should be in bed," Kate said, disapproving.

"I was. Then I heard that and I thought—" She broke off. "Your shirt's wrong."

Hasty in the half-light, Kate had made a mistake with the buttons. Lucia made her stoop down and unbuttoned, buttoned again, her hands unsteady.

"I won't be long," Kate said. Lucia's hand was at her throat, gentle as if she thought Kate might vanish. She was suddenly aware of her own breath.

"Coming back here? You should know better."

Too late for that, Kate thought. "You'll be all right for a short while?"

"Safe as houses. Go and enjoy your party, Katherine Joan. I'll be here when you get back."

CHAPTER EIGHTEEN

Dusk at the Rose House

The woods are sweet this evening. Mockbeggar is happy, the joy spills over. I can hear music a short way off, drifting from Small Angels. The people there will feel the change in Mockbeggar. The mood of the woods will flow over them like a tide rising.

She notices too. Lucia, red girl, my old friend. She has been hunting me for days. She looked for me on the old paths, and found roses. She tore up the plants, she struck the branches with her axe and ripped at the small pale flowers. Petals fell in her hair and she shook them out as if they were filth. She worked and fought until her strength was used up. At last she struggled to stand, limbs stiffened and cold from crouching on the ground, wrenching briars up by the roots. She staggered like an old woman when she got to her feet. I saw her begin to despair.

After that last time, I thought she might not return. I thought she might have made herself ill with too much work and a want of food and sleep. Or I thought her heart might have failed her.

But she is back this evening—same as ever with her wild red hair and her slatternly red dress and her axe. She walks with a new purpose. I know where she is bound.

She was afraid to come and see the Rose House before. I suppose she will have said to herself that she would rip out the small roses first, and then turn her gaze to my ruin. She is here now, though, stepping across the Fane less nimbly than she used to. There is fever in her eyes.

See what you have done to yourself, I want to tell her. *And see how little you have accomplished.*

When she arrives at the Rose House she does see it. She stands in the clearing and stares. She sees that my ruin is as lovely now as it ever was. The leaves are opening and the flowers are budding out of season. Most of the blooms are already out. The house is all green leaves and thorns winding above the rubble. I wonder if she could find her way through to the heart of it now, like she used to.

She draws in one breath, one gasp. She sees it all now.

I think she is about to cry or scream or curse, but she only lets the axe fall from her hand and wraps her arms about herself as if she is cold.

She cannot pretend any longer that I can be uprooted. She has only hurt herself trying.

It won't happen like last time, with red girl and her sisters. Years ago I was injured, I was lost. The tree at the Rose House withered. She has been hoping that the same could happen again. But I am planted throughout the woods now, not only in one place. There are roses and roses and roses—she could never hope to destroy them all. I'm here for good.

I see her realize that. At last she speaks:

I know you're here.

She waits, and there's no sound but the wind. She tries again:

Come and look at me.

It is like we're playing one of our old games. She was fond of me then. She would laugh when I appeared. Now I say nothing and she grows angry.

Look at me, damn you!

At first I was glad when she returned, but now I don't think I like to have her here after all. She brings back a past I don't care for. She made me remember being young, happy in the woods with my brother, and that time is past and buried and I don't want to think of it. If she talks much more I will quiet her.

But she stands silent in the clearing. She takes a briar in a hand and squeezes down tight, drawing blood. I don't know which of us she most wants to hurt. She is shaking.

We should have burned you, she said. *Burned this whole place.*

She turns suddenly, stumbling forward like her eyes are failing. She crosses the Fane with a stagger. She doesn't look back, but she wants to. She will be longing to see me now; she will be watching the depths of the bushes and wondering what face she may see staring back, her friend the boy, or the man she dreads. She is trying not to run.

When I was lost, my thoughts were scattered like dry earth on the winds. I was like one dreaming, neither here nor there.

But I came back to myself little by little. I know my name now. There was a song sung and I was in it. Fred Hart and Harry Child once met. I remember our meeting.

When I was dead, he hid me underground, he let earth fill my eyes and mouth. He imagined he was done with me, but he was not done. He buried me too close to the woods. Mockbeggar heard my story, and the trees loved me enough to find me.

When I was driven out, betrayed again, the trees found me a second time. They remembered me as they remembered me once before. They remembered and they bound my history into a hundred fresh shoots, a hundred thorns. Roots and flowers all over Mockbeggar, roses climbing. I will not be cut down again. I will not be driven out.

The trees worked patiently. Now they rejoice in me. *Here he is back at last, the child we love.* Two centuries and their love has not changed. I am like a rock wrapped about by tree roots. They will never give me up.

This evening the woods are full of delight. There has not been such life in Mockbeggar for a long time. Soon the woods' work will be completed and I will be as strong as I ever was.

The dogs are with me, they wake when I wake. When I remember my old hurts they grow restless—their ears set back, their teeth showing. They are here and gone and then here again, padding through the shadows of the woods, soft, fog-colored shapes. They are always hungry.

Lucia, red girl, my friend—she kept them from me for a time. I found myself different with her. I was young with her, many things could be forgotten awhile. It all tasted less bitter: Fred and his betrayal, the vengeance which has been a shadow of satisfaction, like food eaten in a dream.

I am like the dogs, I am still hungry. I remember my brother's wedding day, the bells pealing over my head, the toasts drunk while I choked on my mouthful of earth.

There's another wedding now. Another bride. I've seen her twice in the woods. The second time I would have kept her if I could, as a revenge for the joy and life she carried with her like sunlight too bright, and revenge for opening the church and letting the air in, for trespassing in my ruin and prying the coins from my tree.

That was the last thing needed to wake me. Without a thought the bride brought me back to this place where my thoughts can collect again, like a swarm of flies. I can act now, and suffer. My wounds feel fresh as they did when they were first inflicted. This pain and history must needs be shared.

Fred Hart's family have failed in their duty, and I am growing stronger. I can wander further every evening. I have been through the village already.

The dogs are stronger too. They have killed hens at Blanch Farm. Small prey, but it reminded them of larger kills. They delighted in it. They remember more and more, they grow impatient for the hunt.

It is almost enough. One more night, and I will be ready.

CHAPTER NINETEEN

Mockbeggar Bacchus

Sam walked Chloe back to the Albatross after the wedding rehearsal. He talked mostly about work, and the tasks yet to be done before the wedding. She was not sorry when he left her to make a start on these. After their conversation at the edge of Mockbeggar, she was finding his company unusually difficult. She had never felt lonely with him before.

She ate dinner upstairs, reluctant to see anyone. Then she curled up on the bed, dirty plates discarded on the floor, and tried to rest.

Her thorn scratches from the day before still stung; the tormented whispering from next door might be about to start at any moment. Hours passed, and she was still awake. At last she went downstairs to the bar.

It was so late by this time that even the pub regulars had departed. John, stacking glasses behind the bar, looked surprised to see her.

"I thought that you were out," he said.

"No. Having an early night, only I can't sleep."

"Can I get you something to help?" he said.

She suspected he was offering an extra feather pillow, or hot chocolate on a tray. But she ordered wine, the second-cheapest red, which was her and Sam's usual choice.

She took her drink to a corner near the fireplace, a remove from John's anxious glances. There was no fire—the days weren't cold enough yet, though tonight she felt a promise in the air that the time for fires was not far off. In the meantime, because there was a fog coming down and the night was dreary, John had filled the little fireplace with candles, which flickered comfortingly.

The chair was high-backed, padded with cushions. The second-cheapest red was reassuring company. It told her gently but firmly that the wedding would be all right. She was all right. Everything was all right. She sat in quiet comfort, watched the candle flames. John locked up, and—still unhappy, though she felt now (a second drink in) that there was no need—told her that he was going to bed, and could she please turn the light off when she was done.

"I wouldn't be too long," he said. "Don't want to fall asleep down here. Not a good place for dreaming."

"How do you mean?"

"There are strong dreams in the village. Or they say that. People think—people used to think the Albatross is the worst for it. Because it's an old building, I suppose. There might be echoes here of things that happened a while ago. And they can find their way in when you're sleeping." He looked as if he already regretted his words. "It's just a thing people say. But still, you shouldn't sit up. There's a draft. Not healthy, you know."

It wasn't lonely, being downstairs alone. The door of the pub was locked, the old-fashioned bolts pulled across, and in spite of John's warning, the wine had already done its work. She felt snugger, safer, than she had done for a while.

How long was it since she had felt entirely at ease? Before she first had a sense of the story voice in her ear, perhaps. Or perhaps the moment before she had first heard Brian's story.

The night was quiet—so quiet she could hear one of the candle flames guttering. Her head was very heavy.

Without intending to, she slept. When she woke the candles—all except one—had burned out, and the Albatross was dark. John must have come down and turned the light off, not liking to wake her.

There was moonlight coming through the window, making the whole room strange.

Hardly a breath of wind tonight, and yet she could hear the roses outside tapping the window. Less a tapping, really, more of a scratching. Like thorns or nails drawn across the glass.

She was too sleepy to move. Looking at the squares of pale moonlight on the floor, she wondered if this was not still a dream.

The light changed. Something broke the squares of moonlight. Something cast a shadow on the floor.

A person outside? The scratching grew louder. Something was trying to get in.

Rustling. A sigh. She was as still as she had been in the blackberry maze.

At last the shadow moved, and the pale squares of moonlight returned to their right place on the floor.

It's over, she thought. It had moved on. It was trying other houses, other windows—

Then something heavy slammed against the door, shaking the lock, almost shivering the wood into bits.

She expected someone to rush downstairs. But everyone else in the Albatross seemed to be sleeping like stones and it was only Chloe left awake to hear.

It knew. The thing on the other side, it knew she was here and it was here for her. It wanted her and it was going to get in.

The door shook again. She heard herself whimpering. She might have been making the sound for a while.

Then came silence. She heard a scratch on stone. Footsteps retreating. It was leaving. But it had heard her. It had followed, and now it knew for certain, and she knew it would come back.

The next morning she lay listlessly in bed, listening to the world wake around her. At last it was Friday—the eve of the wedding, the night of the garland party. Soon the caterers would be at the Tithe Barn, delivering cake and flowers and wine. John Pauncefoot would be decking Hector's cart out with ribbons. Cars and taxis full of guests would make the country lanes busy. The noise of the Albatross seemed louder than usual today, the voices from downstairs more urgent.

She had been looking forward to this morning for eighteen months, but now she couldn't even bring herself to sit up in bed.

Her phone beeped. Miraculously, a message from Sam had got through. He told her, elated, that he had finished his work project, everything was safely handled.

In her head she drafted a reply. She would respond when she found sufficient energy.

She had slept little last night. It had taken her some time to get the nerve to leave the Albatross bar after the sounds at the door had ended. She had kept the lights on in her wake, unable to tolerate moving in darkness even for a handful of seconds.

Upstairs, she had propped herself up in bed, back to the wall. She read *Little Women* until just before dawn, when exhaustion finally took her.

She was usually a prompt and early riser. Now she discovered that you could lie in bed almost indefinitely. You could fall back among the feather pillows and drift. It was possible to let a full hour pass without moving.

The day after tomorrow, she was supposed to be leaving this place. She tried to imagine herself and Sam in two days' time, sitting safe and happy in a taxi, honeymoon ahead of them. It didn't feel convincing.

That thing at the Albatross door had been looking for her. She was as certain of that this morning as she had been last night.

She wanted to speak of what had happened, confirm that it *had* happened, and she found that she couldn't. Who would believe her? Brian Last, perhaps. And what could he say other than *I told you so*?

Loneliness was new to her. She found that it made it harder to be sure of what was real.

What if she were to ring Sam up now and tell him that something had come out of Mockbeggar and it wished her harm. Would he listen? *Run,* she would say, if she was watching this happen to someone else. *Get out while you can.*

But Sam would never forgive her—and canceling now would mean disappointment, strained friendships, money lost.

Besides, she did not like to think of herself driven out. This was her wedding—*her* church, *her* barn, rented fair and square—and she had a right to them. The thing from the woods wanted her cowed, but it had failed to get into the Albatross. She could be careful for two more nights.

Someone knocked gently at the door, startling her into action. Her legs ached as if she had been walking all night, and by the time she opened the door there was nobody waiting outside. But John Pauncefoot had left her a breakfast tray: coffee, bread and butter, two soft-boiled eggs, and raspberries in a blue china ramekin. Invalid fare, she thought. Food to tempt an uncertain appetite.

John's concern, coming unexpectedly like this, was almost too much. She carried the tray inside and set it down on the chest of drawers, then walked up and down the room trying to get herself under control.

She reminded herself that John, like the rest, must have known more than he had let on. They had all watched her wander close to the edge—Sam and Kate and Bill and Birdie. Oh, they had warned her—or Sam had, in his way—but they hadn't talked to her like an insider. *It's nothing, but all the same . . .*

It was then that she noticed her story companion was gone. It was as if last night's visitor had frightened it into silence. It didn't seem to know what would happen to Chloe next.

It was probably an indication of how far she had strayed that the loss made her feel bereft. She would have been glad of any company.

The story had warned her before, in its way; it might have warned her again.

She had no appetite but she made herself eat, and then take a shower.

Afterward, she caught a glimpse of herself in the mirror—wet hair dripping down her bare shoulders—and was not reassured. She looked slightly wild. Ready to bite or bolt. Maybe Sam was right, and Mockbeggar had done something to her.

Too late to worry about that now. Too late to do anything but put on the dress she had chosen last week—in a smart boutique, in another life—and make herself ready.

Her low heels, chosen with a view to managing the easier kind of country lane, clip-clopped the old wood floor as she took out her favorite perfume and coaxed her hair into civilized curls. The noise seemed excessive. As if she were treading without due respect for the old building. Or as if she were saying rashly, *here I am.*

Still no word from her story friend, no noise from the dead man in the room next door. She felt increasingly bereft, and also as if she had failed a test. She had been given fair warning. What happened next would be her own fault.

According to today's schedule, Chloe, Sam and his family would arrive at the Tithe Barn early to set out the snacks and take delivery of the wine. Chloe had ordered a few cases of a local supplier's second-cheapest white and the second-cheapest red—just to tide them over, she told Sam. They would keep the quality stuff for tomorrow.

When Birdie collected her, Bill and Sam were already packed onto the backseat with a box of ribbon for the bouquets, but there was no sign of Kate. Sam looked gloomy when Chloe mentioned her absence. There was another failure. She had been so sure that this week would make things better between the two of them.

At the Tithe Barn, she busied herself with opening the boxes of flowers, which had arrived an hour before. She had forbidden her parents from paying for the wedding—some traditions should be left in the past—and other than the dress, the flowers were the one gift she had allowed them to bestow.

Now she saw that they had taken advantage of this loophole to indulge her. As they came out of their boxes, the flowers made Birdie exclaim in delight, and Bill mutter something approving about the price. Even Sam's face relaxed a fraction as the bunches of cut flowers were brought out and laid on the tables.

There were sunflowers, with thick, furry green stems. There were pinks and cornflowers, brilliant yellow poppies. There were vivid dark-red ranunculus, neat four-petaled daphnes, delicate blue blooms of ragged lady.

Her parents' gift, arriving ahead of them, felt like a promise that they would be here soon. They had been lavish; they must know that she would scold them for spending more than they could afford. They had planned it as a surprise, she thought, imagining them plotting it—heads bent over the catalogue like two mischievous children.

"It looks like a real wedding now, doesn't it?" Birdie said.

Chloe couldn't help turning to Sam. She wasn't quite sure how to read his expression, and there was no time to ask what he was thinking because a car was pulling up outside—the first of the guests were already here.

Beth and Nicole both hugged her as if they had been apart for far longer than five days. They brought a new atmosphere with them—a dear and familiar echo of her old life. The respite they offered, the safety and sanity, was so sudden that it almost brought her to tears.

She excused herself, saying that she would fetch the drinks. The wine was in the Tithe Barn kitchen—red in a cupboard, white in one of the tall fridges. All to plan.

She had a chilled bottle out and opened before she took in the name on the label: *Mockbeggar Bacchus.* Under the white printed letters was a small white outline of a running dog.

Impossible. Surely the Gonnes' wine couldn't be drinkable anymore.

But the opened bottle breathed a smell into the kitchen that was like hedgerows, green growing things. The wine filled the room with summer. An old summer. Mockbeggar was here—

"Chloe?"

It was Beth, smart in a peony-pink dress, her expression worried. Perhaps Chloe had been here in the kitchen—staring at the open wine bottle—for longer than she'd realized. Through the opened door she could hear voices, laughter. More guests had arrived while she was in the kitchen.

She opened her mouth to answer Beth and found that she didn't know what to say.

"I thought you might need a hand with the drinks," Beth said after a moment, her voice kind and worried.

"It just took me a while to get the bottle open."

Beth looked at her carefully. "You're all right, then?"

"A bit jittery, I suppose. It's all been leading up to this—" She broke off.

"Do you want to talk about it?"

"No. Thanks, but it's not worth making a fuss about."

She filled the first glasses with Mockbeggar Bacchus, a wine almost as pale as water.

"Let's have a drink," she said. She was weary with fighting and resisting. Why not try it, since it had come here almost as if it had a will of its own?

The number of guests had already doubled by the time she and Beth returned to the main room. A handful of Sam's friends were happily bickering over the sound system in the corner. Some guests were already seated at the long tables—drinking, laughing, binding sunflowers with string, slotting cornflowers into jam jars. There were children playing under the tables and climbing over the hay bales stacked by the entrance. From outside she smelled cigarette smoke.

There were so many of them. Nicole, prowling about taking photos, Bill holding forth, Birdie nodding and dropping *you're right*s and *exactly*s into the conversation whenever he paused for breath. There was Elizabeth Daunt, the librarian. John Pauncefoot hanging a string of lights. Even Brian Last, gloomy near the door. Friends and well-wishers, but strangers too: people she might have passed in the village street, people who had stared at her from their gardens or across the Albatross bar. She had issued an open invitation to the garland party—it had seemed like a kind gesture given the village's vested interest in the opening of the Tithe Barn—but she had not expected so many to take her up on the offer, especially knowing what she knew now.

Maybe it was curiosity that brought them, or the promise of free food and drink. She would have liked to think it was goodwill, an impulse to look out for her and Sam, to make sure the wedding was accomplished safely. It felt more like the pull of something about to happen. It was the same anticipation she felt at the beginning of a novel she knew would take her out of herself—the thrill of the lights going down in the cinema. These people were laughing and talking and drinking just a fraction too much, she thought. The festivity was already slightly hectic—they were waiting.

Nicole appeared, insisted on crowning her with flowers—she had sourced them locally, she said with some pride—and taking her picture before Chloe had time to compose her features.

"Does it look all right?" she said, anxious.

"Perfect," said Nicole, frowning. She might have said something else, but here she was distracted—the camera's battery seemed to be running low—and Chloe was left alone in the crowd.

She wanted to take off the wreath—she didn't recognize the flowers, where on earth had Nicole found them?—but was worried about hurting her friend's feelings.

The party was growing louder now. Too loud, almost. She felt a flash of panic and looked around for Sam. She couldn't find him at first; for a moment she was afraid that he had left, out of patience with all of this. But then she spotted him at the heart of things—his arms full of flowers, barely still for a moment.

To her surprise, she realized that he was enjoying himself. His smile was easy, he was pointing out refreshments, offering advice on the flower arrangements, welcoming newcomers without any appearance of effort.

She took a long sip of wine. She tasted greenness in it—nettle, cut grass, sunlight on vine leaves. All nourished with Mockbeggar rain, water rolling down the hill and into the earth of the Gonnes' fields.

Beth told her a story, but Chloe had no idea what she was saying. She drank another sip, and another.

The party seemed to recede; the noise became distant. The people moving before her eyes seemed flimsy as paper—then it all came back to her in a loud, bright rush.

Why did the air smell so green all of a sudden? Had anybody else noticed?

"Chloe?" Beth was still there at her elbow, smiling with worried eyes. "I said, the food's here. Are you hungry?"

A man had just arrived bearing boxes of pizza and garlic bread, olives and sautéed mushrooms and stuffed peppers. She had chosen it all so carefully and it smelled good, but she couldn't bring herself to try a bite of it.

"I'm good," she said. She finished her wine.

Definitely there was green in the air now. Rose-sweetness, too. The scent was so strong it ought to have been visible. Had *nobody* else noticed?

"I'm good," she told Beth again. "You go."

Sam met her eyes at last. He was holding an open box of garlic bread to Birdie, trying to get her to have some (Birdie was always wary of calories), and he was laughing. His smile didn't fail when he looked at Chloe.

It was his old look, the way he would catch her eye when they were out together—dinner at a friend's house, a concert where music was too loud for conversation—so steady and affectionate. It didn't mean much more than *I'm still here, we're still us,* but it was important. It had been one of the things that had first made her imagine spending the rest of her life with him.

Someone moved past roughly, almost knocking into her. It was Kate. She stopped to apologize—for the near-collision, for her lateness.

"Time got away," she said.

Chloe thought of the woods, where time had slipped through her fingers with terrifying ease.

"Better late than never," she said. She did not want Kate to realize how relieved she was to see her. Sam would have been so hurt by her absence. Besides this, it felt better—safer?—to have Kate close by. She might have little time for Chloe or the wedding, but Chloe suspected that there was strength under her rough manner. If something were to go wrong, she would be a helpful person to have at hand.

Kate frowned, and then did something unexpected: she straightened the wreath on Chloe's head with delicate precision. "You've been all right?"

Strange question from Kate. But Kate didn't look entirely like herself. Her long, dark hair was loose, and she was wearing red, the first color Chloe remembered seeing her in. As she moved through the crowd, people had stared at her with grudging admiration. She seemed as much an oddity in the village as she was among her own family.

Perhaps Kate felt differently to them about all of this—Small Angels, Mockbeggar. Chloe thought, fleetingly, of telling her what she had seen and done. But it was no time for talking about that. Besides, she was feeling better. She had decided to feel better.

"All all right, thanks," she said to Kate. "I like your shirt, by the way."

Kate nodded—unaccountably sheepish—and turned away. She was lost in the party crowd before Chloe could decide whether she should have spoken to her or not.

The green in the air was still there, but it had become less oppressive. If you didn't know much about the woods, you'd call it pleasant.

Here was Beth back from the buffet. She had a piece of pizza on a paper plate for Chloe.

"Just in case," she said, looking hopeful, and then pleased when Chloe thanked her and took the food.

She had forgotten the simple delight of pizza almost too hot to eat, laden with cheese and fragrant with garlic, heavy with pepperoni and mushrooms.

She refilled her glass and drank again, breathed in the leaf-and-rose smell of the evening air. It was all delicious, she decided.

People approached her, eager to congratulate and compliment—she was the bride, the heroine of the hour. And she must look better now, she thought, because Beth's face had relaxed. Across the room, someone turned up the music.

Ordinarily the untidiness might have bothered her. Now she reflected that if the children had caused a little mess then it could be handled tomorrow. If the dancing meant people moved chairs out of position, she would put them back later. She had grown tired of worrying and planning. She was exhausted, in fact. She felt curious now to know what would happen if she let events carry her for a while.

The night was warm as summer. Moonlight was coming in through the open barn door, and the dancers' shadows made strange shapes in the light—like tree branches, Chloe thought, if you looked out of the corner of your eye.

She found herself dancing, though she couldn't remember when she had joined the others. Sam had his arms around her, and she could feel his hands hot through her thin dress. The bride's wreath was tight against her hair, flower stems scratching, but she would not take it off.

Some guests—the older ones, and those with children—had taken their leave by this point, but everyone else was still here. It was strange but she didn't mind it now, just like she didn't mind the feeling that had been coming over her slowly: that the woods seemed to be coming closer and closer, as if they wanted to attend the party too. Soon, if she looked outside, she would see them creeping slowly among the graves, roots plowing up bones and coffin wood.

The thought made her laugh, and Sam smiled back at her, mistaking near-hysteria for delight. There was no possibility of talking; the music was much too loud. Sam held her tight for a moment and then spun her so suddenly that she almost tripped.

He paused, worried, and then he saw that she was still laughing, the sound lost in the music. The Tithe Barn would be lit up from outside, glowing bright in the night. They must be able to hear the party from down in the village, she thought. Even from the heart of Mockbeggar, if there was anyone in the woods to hear.

She let go of Sam's hands. He looked surprised, but was immediately seized by a couple of his friends, who had a bottle of whisky with them and were insisting that he take a shot. She smiled, slipped away before Sam could protest.

She needed to be outside now. Her heart was beating fast and she was dizzy with wine, and above all she wanted to see the moonlight.

The Tithe Barn yard was quiet. There were torches burning in brackets, casting inviting pools of light, but it seemed that nobody wanted to stray from the music and feasting. Even the smokers had gone in. It was just Chloe and the night now.

The sky seemed to have known what she wanted her wedding eve to look like. Above her was a clear sweep of stars. No night for sleeping.

She thought—a little fuzzily—that she loved all of it. For now she could forget what the woods had done and love them, those not-very-distant beeches, their sympathetic rustle. She loved Small Angels, she loved the Tithe Barn and everyone in it.

She loved them but she wanted to be by herself for a time. This feeling required all her attention. The air was fresh out here. She wandered a little way down the lane, savoring the night world around her.

Lulled by the steady sound of her own footsteps on the quiet track, she had almost reached the main road before she realized how far she had strayed from the Tithe Barn. She was swallowed in night.

Something dry moved behind her. Whirling around, she told herself it was nothing but a couple of dead leaves blowing along the road. But the dry sound grew louder.

How could she be certain she was alone out here? How—even wine-drunk and music-drunk—could she have been so *stupid*?

If she wasn't running, nothing was wrong. A fast walk was a different matter. It didn't imply panic or flight. She didn't look around but strode back in the direction of the Tithe Barn. There were more dead leaves stirring in the breeze, more than she thought was possible.

She wasn't running. And if she wasn't running, nothing was wrong.

But she wasn't alone on the path. There was something moving behind her.

The approaching lights startled her into a gasp. It took her a couple of seconds to realize that they belonged to a taxi, driving carefully up the lane toward her. The beams dipped every so often as the car plowed into a pothole or navigated a dip in the road.

It was ten o'clock, and this was the first lift of the night—booked for guests who wanted to retire early, though as it turned out she was the only one tired of the celebrations.

The driver—John Pauncefoot's son-in-law, she remembered—stopped beside her, looking curious and mildly concerned.

"Do you want me to drive up to the barn?" he said as she got in.

"That's all right. The others will be a while, I think."

He nodded. "Do seem to be enjoying themselves." He glanced back at her. "That's pretty."

She didn't understand at first. Then she remembered the flowers in her hair.

"Oh." Embarrassed, she took off the garland, held it awkwardly. "Thanks."

He seemed glad to get away, she thought; they took the road quicker than he had on the approach. He didn't talk, and she was grateful. If he noticed anything amiss in her appearance then he gave no sign of it.

"You take care, now," he said as he dropped her in front of the Albatross—a welcome sight in the dark, its lamps shining bright on either side of the door.

The sensible thing would be to go to bed. She had intended to be asleep by eleven at the latest, so as to be fresh for the day ahead. But she was restless, feverish. In her bedroom she drank a glass of water, and then another. It did nothing. Her ears felt strange—the music still echoing through her head, though the Albatross was very quiet. The room spun if she turned her head too fast.

The wreath had survived the party without the slightest damage. It was beautifully made—she would have to tell Nicole how impressed she was—and it would match her dress perfectly. She always did like to use local suppliers when she could, she thought with desperate levity.

Thinking of the dress reminded her of the tear. Beth had offered to stitch it for her, but they were running out of time to make the repair.

The damage might not be obvious. Or perhaps they could mend it tomorrow, early.

She must be as mad as any of them up at the barn, she thought, stripping off her clothes, kicking off her muddy shoes. But now that the thought had come to mind, she needed to know the full extent of the damage.

Another trial run, then. The silk draped as easily as it had last weekend. The shoes fitted as comfortably as they had then. She twisted her hair into the same style—rustic, charming, half-up-half-down. She painted her mouth the same color with shaking hands. Her perfume had worn off, so she sprayed on more.

When she looked at herself in the mirror, she found that, in spite of all her care, she looked different from how she had five days ago. The rent was visible. There was a trace of dirt on her temple—how had that got there? And that wild look she had noticed earlier had not gone away.

To hell with it. She put on the flower crown again.

There, damn it, that was what they all wanted—what the woods wanted, what that awful story wanted from her. Bride dragged through a hedge, bride half haunted. She looked like somebody on the run.

All at once, the wine she had already drunk wasn't enough. She threw a jacket over her shoulders and—still in her wedding dress—went back downstairs.

John had told her on her arrival that she could take what she wanted from the fridge behind the bar when the Albatross was closed; he asked only that she write down what she'd taken in a notebook he'd left out for the purpose.

She had nodded but thought it was unlikely she would need to take advantage of what seemed to her a rather trusting arrangement.

Now she carelessly selected a cold bottle, found herself a glass, and sat by the empty fireplace to drink.

When opened, the bottle breathed a gentle smell of summer into the dusty pub air. It was Mockbeggar Bacchus. Of course.

She poured herself a large glass, sat back in the armchair, and drank.

The knock at the door startled her so much that she almost choked.

She froze. Please let it pass by. Please let it stay outside—

Another knock, louder. And someone called her name.

It was Sam. His voice sounded strange. For an instant, she wondered if it was really him. What if someone—something—was imitating him, trying to get her to open the door?

Was that a sane thing to wonder? Or had she begun to lose her grip? She stood up to let him in.

He was shivering, eager to get inside. Only when she had secured the door and turned to look at him did he properly take in her appearance.

"Why are you dressed like that?"

She thought how she would look to him—wild-eyed, head still wreathed with flowers, alone in a dark pub in her ripped wedding dress.

"Trial run," she said. Another thought occurred to her. "Oh God, you shouldn't look at me. Bad luck." But perhaps it didn't matter anymore. So much else had gone wrong or turned crooked; why shouldn't they mess up one more tradition?

"You didn't say you were leaving," he said. "I was looking all over—"

"I didn't want to disturb you."

"Chloe," he said. He sounded more at a loss than she had ever heard him, in all the time they had known each other. "What's happening?"

"You don't want to know. You've already made that clear."

"I thought you were happy tonight."

"I was. So happy I thought it would be a good idea to go wandering through the fields on my own in the dark of night. Doesn't that seem odd to you?"

He didn't answer.

"Why are you so desperate to pretend that nothing's wrong?"

"What do you mean?"

"I needed someone to listen and you wouldn't—I was so lonely, Sam, and I was *scared*—"

He began to speak, but there was another sound too, now.

"Quiet." She heard her own voice—the harsh urgency in that one word—and was almost afraid of herself.

Something was moving outside. The same shadow in the moonlight, searching for her.

She thought, with a sudden plummeting horror, that Sam wouldn't understand. He would say *we'd better see who it is*, he'd get up to open the door—

But he didn't move. It was strange what fear could do to a face. Changes the features like death, she thought.

They waited in the quiet. It felt as if their air was running out. As if these quiet seconds would never be over.

Then the noise came again:

Scratch, scratch. A rasp that might be the sound of breathing.

Another scratch, another rustle. A low growl. The same sound she had heard in the woods, Chloe thought, shivering in her wedding silk.

Then silence returned. Innocent as if there had been nothing outside at all.

For about a minute neither of them could speak. At last she found she was able to sigh. She sat back in her chair.

"Don't move," Sam said, as low as if he had hardly any breath left. "Please, just—"

They both waited. Outside, a rabbit screamed far off. A car went by.

At last Chloe breathed fully again. Across from her, Sam's face was still fixed, horrified.

"It probably won't come back," she said.

"How do you know?"

"It didn't last time."

Silence as he took that in. At last he said,

"You should've told me."

Just now she was too drained by relief to resent this reproach. "I don't think you would have believed me. I don't know if I believed it myself, before. John says there are vivid dreams in these parts."

"Especially in the Albatross." He spoke with a sigh. "They say that."

All things considered, it might not be the best remedy, but his face and voice made her push her glass of wine across the table to him.

He drained the Mockbeggar Bacchus as if he was painfully thirsty.

"I think . . ." Once she said it aloud there would be no unsaying it. But she needed to voice this fact, no matter what he said, no matter how certain the words made it. "I think it's following me."

He set down the glass with a clatter, like he wasn't seeing the table in front of him.

"Tell me all of it," he said.

And she saw he finally did want to know.

So she told him all of it, from her first visit to Mockbeggar up to this evening. She paused only once, to pour herself another glass of wine, and when she had drained it, he followed suit, drained the glass in turn. When she finished at last, he was quiet.

Finally he said, "I'm sorry."

She nodded, and he stood up and went to her. When he embraced her she felt that something had shifted. There was a new closeness between them. They knew each other better now.

"It's how it's always been, you see," he said. "It's the only way we know how to manage. In the village, and the same at home. Mum and Dad and Kate . . ."

She had been disappointed by him a few days earlier, but this desperate straightforwardness made him dearer to her. He was frightened and off balance and yet he was still his old thinking self—that was there in the considering look he had in his face. And he proved her right a moment later because he said,

"I think you need to get out. Quick as possible."

"But the wedding. All those people."

"I'll deal with that. I'm good at finding explanations." He smiled faintly. "I'll give Dad a call now and ask him to drop the car round—"

"We're driving?"

"No train till the morning. We can be off in half an hour. All you need to do is go upstairs and get your things."

She wanted to thank him, assure him that she understood why he had found it so hard to accept her story, and say that she forgave him.

But instead she found herself coughing. Something was pressing strangely at her lungs, clenching at her throat. She couldn't breathe. It felt as if something in her chest was about to tear.

Sam was watching her—first in confusion, and then in alarm.

"Chloe . . ."

The flowers were pressing tight against her head, the wreath seemed to be contracting; her head felt like it was held in a vise.

Sam was saying something but she couldn't hear him now, she couldn't see. Her hands didn't feel as if they belonged to her. She struggled to take the flowers away; she couldn't bear them close.

The stems broke but she was only distantly aware of it. She was going to die. If she didn't get breath soon it would be the end.

Then something eased. The vise had loosened a fraction. She could take a gulp of air. She could inhale, shuddering. There were tears on her face but the spasm seemed to be passing.

Only there was a strange feeling at the back of her throat. Something foul and wrong—

Retching, she spat something out onto the floor.

"Oh my God . . ." Sam muttered. He sounded far away.

Earth. It was on her tongue, sticking at the back of her throat, catching in her teeth. Her mouth would never be clean again, she thought. And she would never get away from here now.

CHAPTER TWENTY

SUNFLOWER, MOONLIGHT

Kate took the Gonnes' old path to Small Angels. The vigil-track could barely have been used for a decade, and yet the grass had not grown up, the way showed clear.

The air this evening was like a gift. She could smell dry grass and ripening fields. It had been one of her favorite scents as a child, but until tonight she had forgotten how, in summer, she used to open her bedroom window at nine or ten at night and lean perilously far out, trying to fill her lungs with it. It was as delicious now as it had been then. Chloe and Sam had been gifted with perfect weather for the garland party, at the very least.

Kate had an obligation to be there. She would hurt Sam by staying away, and she was duty-bound to see how he and Chloe were managing. If it had not been for this knowledge, which she held sternly at the forefront of her mind, she might have turned back.

She was still half in Blanch Farm in spite of herself—upstairs in the dim bathroom, the pigeons calling, Lucia's hands unsteady at her throat.

An old craving was one thing. She could excuse nostalgia—thinking over three kisses ten years ago—as harmless weakness.

What she felt now was not harmless. She knew she would go back, all the same.

Over the years she had wondered how things might have played out between them if their childish romance hadn't been cut short. She wondered if Lucia had also imagined this alternate history, and if so, whether it resembled Kate's at all.

Was it the adult Kate or the teenage Kate she had looked at just now under the skylight, eyes wide?

Perhaps she saw both of them, the way Kate saw Lucia-then overlaid with Lucia-now, grimmer and wiser, aged into moments of weary grace, oblivious to her own well-being.

It shouldn't matter. Kate hadn't come back for this. She quickened her pace.

It had crossed Kate's mind that the party might not be well attended. Chloe and Sam's guests would be there, of course, but Kate had doubted that the evening would appeal to the rest—the locals invited out of courtesy, to mark the opening of the Tithe Barn. She thought that they would be squeamish, as Ed from the post office had been. But apparently most of the village had got over their wariness, because she found Small Angels and the Tithe Barn transformed.

There were cars parked along the lane and in the field beyond. The massive doors of the Tithe Barn were flung open, and a great bonfire was burning in the yard. Inside, the tables were spread with flowers and ribbons, chairs pushed carelessly against the wall. The room was hectic with color, cut flowers sitting in boxes and spread out for arranging, filling the barn with a smell of growing things. People were stringing lights around the beams, shouting to make themselves heard above the laughter and music.

A handful of children were chasing one another around Small Angels' graveyard as if it were a playground, passing Miss Violet's grave without a glance. Selina Gonne would have been appalled.

A couple of Chloe's guests were smoking at the church door, admiring the claw marks in the wood. They stared at Kate as she passed. She had been almost two days at Blanch Farm. Perhaps some trace of the place lingered about her.

She was late. The important thing was to see Sam and Chloe—to let them see her and know she was here—but she couldn't find either of them in the crowd.

Bill and Birdie were sitting in a corner next to a display of oversized lanterns. They looked perfectly content, and Kate didn't approach them.

Now she was collared by a neat, dark woman in green—one of Chloe's bridesmaids, whose name Kate had forgotten. Her expression was disapproving; Kate's lateness had clearly not escaped her.

"Glad you made it," she said.

Kate nodded. "Have you seen Sam? Or Chloe?"

"They're about—here and there, you know. There's so much to do. We're tying the sunflowers now. Are you all right to lend us a hand?"

Kate let the green bridesmaid press the sunflowers into her hands and deliver a few instructions about binding them together with ribbon (five blooms per bunch) and setting them in one of the vases already waiting on a table in the corner.

"Call me if you get stuck," she said, and was gone before Kate could answer.

Impatient, she set the flowers down on the closest table and looked about her. There was Sam—surrounded by friends, hanging balloons from one of the high beams. He nodded when he saw her, gave a brief wave and turned back to his guests. He had a smile for them though not for her. But he was happy. He was happy and safe, and he wouldn't welcome her warnings or questions. Better to leave him alone.

She found Chloe elated and untroubled. She was wearing her bride-wreath already, which didn't seem like her—she was running a risk of damaging it before tomorrow—but Kate supposed she was entitled to giddy recklessness tonight. She seemed to have forgotten her earlier anxious curiosity about Small Angels. Better for Kate to keep silent tonight as Sam had asked, rather than alarm her with a warning she would probably disbelieve. Let her enjoy her party.

She was all right. Safe and happy, like Sam. Kate could rest easy.

The woods felt closer, kinder. She could hear the breeze moving the leaves outside.

Had the world shifted slightly as the dusk came on? It was that old Mockbeggar feeling, Kate thought—the barrier between what was possible and what wasn't turning flimsy and uncertain. The music had grown loud; it seemed to be coming from outside as well as within, as if the trees were echoing the drums and violins. She could almost taste the romance, subtle like dead-nettle nectar.

Her mind returned to Lucia, despite her best efforts. She had run next door, frantic, when she thought Kate was in trouble. She had pulled at Kate's borrowed shirt to get her to stoop; her eyes had been bright, avid and alarmed. She troubled Kate as she had always troubled her.

Why did you come back? she had asked. And Kate's reasons were sound: the safety of her brother and Chloe and the mouse girls and the whole village.

But now her imagined Lucia insisted: *Why did you come back?*

And Kate's answers had all run out; she was forgetting them.

You can want things for yourself too, Katherine Joan. You know that, don't you?

She arranged sunflowers carefully, binding thick green stems with red ribbon. She was good at this—better than most of the other guests, who were drinking, fighting over the last few slices of pizza, or had slipped away to join the dancing. Outside the children were laughing, singing an old song and supplying their own lyrics when they forgot the words.

There was something slow, dreamy about it all. Sitting with the flowers all around her, listening to the talk of her neighbors, Kate let the mood overtake her.

She had forgotten how things could be around Mockbeggar. That sensation of slipping free of everyday concerns. The romance, the way life seemed to fill with grand possibilities. The colors around her had become richer. Was it possible that the sweetness of the woods had returned tonight? Could it be that there was more than danger to Mockbeggar's waking?

In the moonlight—for the moon had risen without her noticing, time had slipped away—it seemed impossible to say how many people were here now. Surely there were more in the Tithe Barn than before? The dancers cast faint shadows on the barn floor, and as she watched them she found herself almost hypnotized. The flowers she held seemed to move and twist in her hands.

The trees felt closer to the Tithe Barn than they had ever been before, as though Kate and the others were at the very heart of the wood. Don't go to the woods, people said. But tonight, the woods had come to them. And yet their presence seemed gentle—a hint of green in the air, a subtle sound of leaves in the wind.

This evening felt like a respite. Or a gift. A wedding present for Chloe and Sam. Mockbeggar could be generous, sometimes. She had almost forgotten that.

Still people danced—perhaps they couldn't stop now. Sam and Chloe were among them. Chloe had her fair hair loose and Sam held her tightly. Their dance was slow; they stumbled often, laughed often.

There's nothing to dread just now, the moon and Mockbeggar seemed to say. Be easy, tonight is a night for sweet dreaming.

Kate sat alone at the long table, dozy with a blissful kind of tiredness. There were too many sunflowers in the vase in front of her, she thought. Six—not five, as the green bridesmaid had instructed. One flower wouldn't be missed.

Ten years ago, she was used to country walks after dark. There had been evenings when she had lingered recklessly late in Small Angels graveyard, smoking and waiting until the stars came out, just in case Lucia might appear. Tonight, the bright moonlight cast soft shadows, the air was warm and leaf-scented. It had been a long time since she had found it so easy to believe the possibility of strange good things.

She found Lucia waiting for her at the orchard gate. The unlit beacon threw a shadow toward her, cage-like. She was fastidiously keeping her feet out of the shade, as if it had a kind of substance. Her gaze was fixed on Mockbeggar. Her expression troubled Kate's easy mood.

"What's wrong?" she said.

Lucia looked sharply toward her. Her expression—more open than Kate had ever known it—was hopeful and uncertain and bitterly self-derisive. The intimacy was like watching her unbutton her dress and let it fall to the floor, and Kate stopped short a few paces from her.

"I went to the woods," Lucia said.

"What? Are you all right?" Her first impulse was to draw close and reassure herself that Lucia was unharmed, but she was still wary of eliminating the distance between them.

Lucia shrugged.

"Lucia, are you *all right*?"

Now, losing patience, she did go closer. There were fresh scratches on Lucia's arms, and she stood as if she required the support of the orchard wall to keep upright. Kate touched her forehead—no return of the fever—nothing amiss, no need for Kate's hand to shake.

"You should be indoors," she said, finding words with a struggle.

"It was stupid, wasn't it?" Lucia said. "I know I promised not to go back alone. Go ahead and yell if you like, I understand if you're angry—"

She stopped talking so suddenly that Kate guessed that her own thoughts must be clear in her face—how wrong and ludicrous it was to talk of Kate being *angry* in that flat, simple way, as if she'd ever felt anything simple for Lucia, as if the only important thing right now was not Lucia's wellbeing. Perhaps Lucia finally understood the exasperated tenderness that had dogged Kate for a decade, the way she still felt for Lucia—this Lucia and the Lucias before her and all the Lucias that would follow.

They stared at each other, faces strange by moonlight. Lucia said unsteadily:

"You could do better, you know."

But all the same she caught Kate's hands and kissed them and then she clutched at her shoulders—desperate, almost blindly—and stood on tiptoe and kissed her forehead and her throat, haphazard and greedy, kissed Kate's lips as she gasped.

A decade had seemed a long space between embraces. Now the interval felt like a few bars' rest in a melody. It felt as if this was always meant to resume.

Now Lucia shivered, and Kate took her by the hand.

"Come on. It's not good for you out here."

The kitchen was cold. Lucia—however recovered she seemed—probably shouldn't be spending a long time there.

'Is that from the party?" she asked, as Kate shut and locked the door behind them.

She was looking at the sunflower—pale as everything was in this light.

Kate held it out to her. "Here. Since you're convalescing."

"That's sweet of you. No one's ever bought me flowers before."

"It's stolen, not bought," Kate said. (She thought that Lucia was looking rather too pleased with herself.)

"That's even better. You know me."

Lucia found an empty wine bottle, rinsed it and filled it with clean water, set the flower carefully in to drink.

Now was the time for a story. Kate had a duty and a right to hear the truth, to know exactly how bad things were—and Lucia knew as much.

But when she turned around, she was thinking of kissing Kate again—Kate could see it in her face as clearly as if she had spoken.

"It's late," Kate said.

"Are you tired?"

"No." She touched Lucia's wrist very gently and felt her shiver. "Are you?"

Lucia's bedroom was at the end of the hall. They passed the other rooms, doors closed now: *Ruby, Helena, Elphine.* Memories flared up as they passed—brilliant for a moment—and then died away. At last it was just the two of them.

Between dusk and dawn, Kate found, it was possible to slip free of time, to drift here and there like a small boat on a wide dark sea. At some point in the night there was a storm. Kate heard rain on the roof but she had no idea of the hour it began or ended.

It grew cooler with the rain. Kate sat at the edge of the bed—back to the wall, her long coat draped over her shoulders—and watched Lucia sleep.

Rest ought to do her good. But she did not look restful. She slept as if ready to spring into action at the least sound.

It was nothing o'clock in the long moonlit night, an hour that was no hour. Kate was free to brood over what had just occurred, and yet she could not quite think of it as memory. It was still too close. In this strange, drifting, numberless hour, it was still happening.

Lucia had undressed with a matter-of-factness that had taken her by surprise. Nothing coy, nothing self-conscious. No vanity then—but there was a glitter of wondering pride in her face at every sound Kate made, every stifled gasp. *Look what I did. Look what I did to you.*

Kate clutched at her with a kind of desperation—she was *there,* finally, at last, thank God—and when Lucia had said *don't you dare be kind* Kate shook her head. She had been kind until Lucia's eyes were dazed and her curses and endearments had collapsed into one long stream of nonsense.

It was still happening. Kate echoed with it. She sat and listened to the rain and watched Lucia.

When Lucia awoke it was with a sudden movement, as if blindly reaching about for a weapon. Then she met Kate's eyes, breathed out a long sigh.

"All right?" Kate said.

She considered a moment. "Better than that. You agree with me." Then her expression changed. "What time is it?"

"I don't know. Three, maybe."

"We should talk, then. I owe you a story, and there's not much time left." She stood up, threw off the covers. "Let's go downstairs. We can have some coffee." She began to dress, not troubling to switch on the light, then added: "Do you want to talk about before?"

"Last night? Not if you don't."

"I'll tell you the story first. You might think— You should hear first. After that it's up to you."

It took Kate a moment to make sense of what she was saying. The change in her was jarring, like missing a stair. Her face was sad and distant.

"Fine," Kate said.

Lucia nodded, and went downstairs to begin the coffee without waiting for Kate to follow.

By the time Kate arrived downstairs, the lights were already on—brilliant, too bright, hurting Kate's eyes—and two almost-clean cups of coffee were set out on the kitchen table. Kate sat down.

Lucia took the seat opposite, studied her across the mess.

"I need to tell it my own way," she said. 'Is that all right? Because it wasn't beautiful, the way it happened. No style, just mess. It's easier if I tell it like a story. One of Nan's. You don't mind, do you?"

"That's fine."

She nodded, and began:

"In the beginning"—she stopped, took a long sip of coffee, and then continued—"in the beginning were the woods."

Time was still moving strangely. Otherwise Kate was sure Lucia would have run out of night before she finally paused in her long and tangled story.

As it was, when she did finally halt, it was not yet quite dawn. Soon it would be morning, the day of the wedding. But for now, they were still in the between-time, the overhead light almost unnecessary but not quite.

Kate had never liked this hour. Dawn was all very fine and hopeful, but the light immediately before it was sickly and unkind, showing up everything the night had graciously hidden. Blanch Farm kitchen had never looked so dismal. She and Lucia must look as old and haggard as she felt.

"Bearing up?" Lucia said.

She didn't know how to answer. She had lived through years of her own history and Lucia's; she had revisited scenes she remembered and scenes she could hardly believe had happened. She had seen herself in Lucia's words, through Lucia's eyes. She had heard herself yearned for and admired. To hear it had been like feeling Lucia's hands on her again.

But this had been swallowed up in one cold dark thought:

The man in the woods was dead. That had never really been in question, perhaps, but now she knew it for certain, she knew his name.

She knew his name *again.* She had learned the secret on the night of Elphine's death. She had gone running into Mockbeggar in search of Harry Child. What had she found, or what had found her?

"Kate." Lucia was watching her with concern. "Look at me."

"It's all right."

"You're remembering?"

"Some of it. I think it'll keep waking up the more I hear."

She was like Mockbeggar. Thoughts and memories blooming and greening like young branches. Fresh leaves rustling. It was coming back.

"You want me to go on?" Lucia said.

"Yes. Just give it a minute."

Lucia took a sip of cold coffee. Her hands were shaking. Her face had changed in the telling of the story—some energy seemed to have gone out of her. But it was more than that, Kate thought. Her features seemed to have shifted or sharpened in focus. Kate saw her more clearly: the hurt, the hunger, the terrible errors, the great love.

"Bear in mind, I made myself as miserable as anyone," Lucia said quietly, without warning. "If you're judging me, you should remember that."

"I'm not judging you."

"Then you've not been listening properly. You heard what I did."

"You were a child. How could you have stood a chance, with your grandmother and Harry looming over you since before you could speak?"

"The others didn't turn out like me. *They* didn't screw everything up."

Kate winced at the hurt and rage in her voice. "Lucia—"

"Just listen. Let me tell you the rest, then you'll understand."

CHAPTER TWENTY-ONE

Cruel Sister

Lucia in continuation

After you'd left, Nan stood motionless in the orchard for a while, staring up toward Mockbeggar. At last she began walking the same way you'd taken, away from the house. She went slower than usual. I'd never seen her move like an old person before. She paused at the orchard gate and for a moment I thought she was going to go after you. But then she pulled the gate closed and turned back toward the house.

She saw me staring down from Fred Hart's window. In the lantern light, I saw that her shoulders were sagging. Her face was hollow. Her expression didn't change when she looked at me. She moved down the garden path out of sight.

I knew what was going to happen. That was the worst thing. I knew exactly how it would play out, as clearly as if I was there watching. I saw you, brave and defenseless, striding into the woods, closer and closer to Harry, who hated you because you meant so much to me.

I screamed after you but you didn't hear me. Outside the funeral party was getting louder and louder. Our guests had been drinking a while, and at this point they were still having a good time.

Desperate, I crossed back to the door. I hammered and called and begged my sisters—

And then, finally, I heard someone outside. Footsteps approached timidly. I knew it was Elphine before she spoke. I should have guessed she would be the one to come.

"Lucia?" she whispered. Wary in case Nan might overhear.

"Elphine, you've got to let me out *right now.* Kate's gone to the woods."

She didn't understand at first. I struggled to explain—I couldn't get the words and the sense out right, my voice was hoarse from screaming.

But the moment she grasped what had happened, she left me without a word. I heard her racing away downstairs. I pictured her dashing through the shadows of Blanch Farm, fair hair flying behind her, savior of the hour. She would get Ruby and Helena, they would get the key, together we would stop you, Kate, before you even got to the woods.

I tried to believe that. But so much time had elapsed since Nan spoke to you, and you weren't one to hesitate. You'd be at the top of the fields by this time. I had a vision of you at the edge of the woods, vine fields dark and empty behind you, Blanch Farm and its lights far off. Nobody near to help you or hold you back.

When the others finally came and let me out, I could hardly bear to delay to explain what had happened. Elphine had to help me tell it—enough for them to understand that you were bound for the woods and for danger.

"All right," Ruby said, serious and determined. I'd rarely seen her look so grim. I'd forgotten you were so dear to all of us, not just to me. "Let's go, then."

None of us mentioned Nan. Her anger would have to be weathered later. My excuses would come later.

The hurt of my betrayal was there in the way they spoke. Even with Elphine, I think. They addressed each other—*fetch the torches, don't forget your gloves*—but not me. If any of them noticed me taking the axe from beside the kitchen door, they didn't mention it. They would have been trying to make sense of me. Perhaps they wondered how I could have risked so much. Perhaps they thought it was typical of me. Lucia-the-bad through and through.

Nan would have noticed our absence, if it hadn't been for the fact that the funeral was in full, terrible swing by now. We heard voices raised in fear and confusion—shouts coming around from the other side of the house—but none of us looked back as we made for the orchard gate and out into the fields. You were the thing that mattered most, Kate. We were united in that, at least.

They don't like to talk about that party in the village, do they? None of them except Brian Last. Thanks to me, Harry was angry that night. I suppose the noise of the party grated on him; he wanted to shut people up, or at least stop them laughing and enjoying themselves.

You know how the woods loved him. They would shift to accommodate his mood. Their influence drifted downhill like dust on the breeze. It swept through Blanch Farm and people breathed in fear.

Imagine the party you just left, only that wild feeling is malicious instead of joyful. That's what Harry brought with him, when he came to watch Grandpa's funeral.

The guests began seeing things at the edge of the circle of lantern light. Faint animal shapes. Pale coats and bloody muzzles.

He would have heard the buzz of enjoyment turn anxious, he would have seen Nan and Dad trying to restore order.

Then he would have seen you heading through the orchard, Kate. He would have seen and followed. He would have been behind you in the field, just a few paces behind.

I don't know exactly how it happened, everything he did. But my sisters and I followed you that night as quickly as we could, and we saw two fresh sets of footsteps in the earth of the vine fields. You were moving quickly, it looked like—but you weren't running. You didn't know he was there.

"Quicker," Helena said, when we saw the tracks. And we ran. The axe was getting heavy in my hand, the handle slippery with sweat.

At the edge of the woods we stopped, breathless. The footprints disappeared among ferns and dead leaves.

"Lucia," Ruby said, "where would he go? The Rose House?" Her voice was flat and businesslike—and so much anger underneath, curbed until a more convenient time.

"Yes." I thought of Fred Hart, strung up among the roses, close to Harry's ruin.

"You'd better show the way, then," said Helena. "Since you probably know it best."

So I led them to the Rose House. If the situation had been less dire, I would have been humiliated to have them see me so clearly. But just then I didn't care. None of it mattered compared with finding you.

I looked for you as we went, desperately hoping that you weren't where I knew you would be. I shone my torch around, let tree after tree loom strange and close in the unnatural light. But there wasn't a trace of you.

I thought the ones who had never been found—our family's empty-box funerals, those ancestors who were never seen again. I thought of you lost like them.

I'd never hated Mockbeggar before. The woods had frightened me often, but that had never killed my love and gratitude. It had been a fair exchange, I thought, for the joy of the place, for all our games and stories—for Harry. Now I trembled with hatred that could go nowhere and find no expression. My hands shook as I held the torch.

I didn't know what he was doing to you. I was blundering uselessly through the dark and I *didn't know what he was doing to you* at that very moment.

He must have followed you from the house. You'd have had no idea. You wouldn't even have looked back, I don't think—you'd have been too taken up thinking about what you were going to do to save me and my family.

Even if you had looked back, you wouldn't have seen much. In the moonlight, his shape would have been almost nothing—perhaps an old crabbed shrub among the hedgerow.

You wouldn't have stopped, probably, until the top of the field, the edge of the woods. Then you would have paused. Some instinct of self-preservation would have whispered *don't.*

That's when he'd have come close to you, so soft you wouldn't have noticed more than a deeper cold in the night air. He'd have put his hands around your throat and his nails would have scratched you like thorns. He would have whispered in your ear. I can guess what he might have said:

Thief. Trespasser. Let her be hanged.

Then he'd have released his grip, and let fear take you.

I don't know what part of his story he used to poison you, what horror in particular. I think—I think it might have been the time he lay underground, listening to the living trample the ground above.

You were shivering when we found you. You didn't seem able to see, like your eyes were full of earth.

That's my guess at least. When we found you near the Rose House—

No, I'm all right. Let me go on, I've got to finish this now.

When we found you near the Rose House you were snarled up among the rose thorns, brambles binding your throat and wrists tight against an oak at the edge of the clearing. I thought you were dead.

I can't stop remembering the way you looked. There was blood at the corner of your mouth, and your head was hanging down. Your weight was pulling against the thorns and I could see your blood, dark in the moonlight.

It was quiet. No sign of Harry, or the dogs.

Ruby took my wrist—she didn't want me rushing over to you, I suppose. Until we knew what we were dealing with.

"Where is he?" Helena said to me.

I didn't know. The silence felt wrong.

"Better get her out quickly—" Ruby began.

Then you startled us by looking up. Your eyes didn't look right. Horror swallowing sanity whole. Harry had done that to you.

You were mumbling and we couldn't understand you at first. Ruby took the axe from me; she and Helena set about trying to free you without making too much noise.

Still no sign of Harry. Nothing keeping you there, it seemed, but the brambles and the waking nightmare that had swallowed you up.

He wasn't far off—I could already sense his approach. And you were talking and talking, trying to explain something to us. I thought of Grandpa out in the vine field.

Ruby got one of your wrists free. Helena was tearing at the branches and leaves, giving Ruby the clearest space to work. Elphine was holding you up, talking to you gently, telling you that we were here, it was going to be all right. And I did nothing. I stared and couldn't take in what Harry had done. *Come out,* I thought to him—like I had in the old days when we played hide-and-seek. *Come and look me in the face.*

"She can't hear us properly," Elphine whispered to me, dismayed. "I don't know if she knows we're here . . ."

But then you looked right at me. I don't know if you could see me, but you knew I was there.

"Pale child," you said. Your voice was slurred. "He's not right. Can't comfort him, you have to get away."

"We will," Helena said. "It's all right, Kate, we're almost there—"

"Don't listen to him crying. Can't comfort him. Can't get out, there are dogs all around . . ."

You lapsed back into mumbling. Ruby stared at me, at the other two—for an instant it was as if we were one unit again—*us*, united in disaster.

Then: "Lucia . . ." Elphine said faintly.

She was facing in the opposite direction to the rest of us, away from the Rose House.

The dogs were a few yards away, watching from the edge of the trees—ugly, pale shapes. They seemed flimsy as smoke, but I knew their bite was cruel. Harry had warned me of that.

They hadn't approached closer—yet—because they recognized us. They were accustomed to giving us a wide berth. Part of the old arrangement. Harry let us into the woods without let or hindrance, and his companions did the same.

But the bargain didn't extend to you. And slowly the dogs came nearer, teeth bared.

Ruby and Helena resumed their desperate struggle to free you. But I saw that it was too late. The dogs were moving closer, eyes curious and hungry. Another moment and they would spring.

I took a step toward the dogs—Elphine tried to hold me back, but I pulled away, went closer still. I called for Harry. I screamed his name. The dogs flinched and growled but they didn't spring; they knew *me* better than they knew anyone but him.

I knew he was there before I saw him. Always that same feeling, a sense of someone watching from the periphery. He came quietly out of the trees, like he'd been watching just out of view ever since we got to the clearing.

The others stopped when they saw him. Ruby let the axe slip out of her hands.

He looked exactly as he had the first day I'd met him. Small and thin, far too young to be out in the woods alone after dark.

At the sight of him, you began to struggle, Kate—fighting the roses that still held you.

He watched you, face full of childish spite.

"Let her go," I said. "She's got nothing to do with it."

"Of course she has." He spoke as if the others weren't there. "You were *my* friend and now all you can think about is *her.* You said you'd stay away from her and you didn't." He took me by the wrist in his old way—nails digging in. "You left me by myself. You broke your word."

You were choking now. The noose around your neck seemed to

have tightened. I couldn't keep my eyes away from him for more than a second so I could just hear you struggling to breathe.

"It's all your fault," Harry said.

I didn't answer him because I couldn't argue with that.

"Weren't you happy?" he said. The anger had gone for a moment. He sounded younger, like the boy I'd first met. "Didn't we have fun in our games? What call did you have to go betraying me after so long?"

"I didn't betray you."

"You did. As if *she* could ever know you as well as I do. Like any of them know you like I do." He looked at my sisters, at you—unconscious, now, or almost. "None of them know your ugliness like I do. I kept your bad thoughts safe, don't you remember? I was there when you wanted to do what you wanted and damn the consequences to anybody else. None of them will love you now they see all that."

"I know," I said.

I remembered then what you'd almost made me forget, Kate. I was Lucia-the-bad and I'd never really stood a chance of being anything else. I was never going to be Elphine, or even Ruby or Helena. I made up my mind.

"What if I stay?" I said. "Let her go and I'll stay as long as you want. It'll be like before. Even better."

I saw him hesitate. Because it was what he wanted. I'd been talking partly at random but now I saw it, mingled with his fury—an old and desperate hunger. I had reached to the heart of his loneliness and he was taken aback for a moment. The dogs slunk back a little way—and now I took my chance. I turned and ran to the Rose House. As I passed Ruby, I snatched up the axe she'd dropped. She called something to me, but I didn't turn to listen. I was already in the maze.

He'd taught me the way so carefully. No one else would have dared try to get through those briars, but I knew where to duck, where to step right and left, where to tread carefully over snaring branches.

I found my way to the heart of the place, I raised the axe and I struck the trunk of the rose tree with all my strength.

Then he was with me. That first axe-stroke had already weakened him. I hadn't realized I could do such damage so quickly. He reached for me, but I don't think he could see me properly; he seemed dizzy.

I struck again at the tree, and he gasped.

"Please," he said. He sounded breathless, a little surprised. Like he couldn't believe in what was happening. "Lucia, it *hurts*—"

I tried not to hear—I thought of you and what he'd done to you—but he kept pleading. He was crying with pain and fear.

And now the story was with me.

That story—his life and death and revenge—it was his weapon. You know that. He could give you a taste of it and it was like you were living his story, his hurts became your hurts.

When I struck the tree the story struck back; it filled my head and my heart like I was a seed and his story was growing out of me.

For a moment I *was* Harry. I was twisting on the ground trying to shield my face as the dogs tore at me. I hadn't realized that kind of pain was possible.

I had thought that my other tastes of his history were bad enough. But they were nothing to this. This was enough to kill. I felt something wet on my face and didn't realize until later that my nose had begun to bleed. My heart was beating painfully.

I tried to keep striking the tree. The trunk was half severed now, there wasn't so much to go. But I was weak and it hurt to go on. I could feel blood—Harry's blood, not mine—trickling down my arms where the dogs' teeth had bitten, I had forgotten my own name. And all the time he was there, that pale, whimpering child who had been my friend, and his eyes didn't leave my face for a moment.

I tried to force myself to keep going, but he kept *staring* and my arms were shaking and I was so frightened. If I kept on it would kill both of us and I was too weak for the task. Even as I struggled, I knew I was going to fail this test as I'd failed so many others.

Then there was a rustle of branches behind me. Twigs snapped. Someone took the axe from my hands.

It was Elphine. I didn't understand how she could be there. It should have been impossible to find a way through the maze. But Elphine had done it. She had forced through the thorns, and even in the moonlight, I could see that she had been cut terribly in the process. She was bleeding across her face and hands; a branch had caught her mouth and scratched deep and I was almost afraid of her.

But she smiled at me—sweet, gentle, wiping blood out of her eyes.

"Don't look," she said to me. "It's going to be all right."

Then she swung the axe, and Harry began to scream.

CHAPTER TWENTY-TWO

Elphine

Do you remember the ladybirds, Lucia?

Remember that day they got into the kitchen, a great multitude pouring in from some lair in the wall or under the floorboards. They clustered together in the corner of the window as if they thought their numbers would protect them, poor things.

Nan told Grandpa to kill them. Can't have an infestation, she said. This house is full enough as it is.

(She always used to make Grandpa do the killing, did you ever notice that? Rabbits and mice and the other things. It confused me. Because she wasn't sentimental, was she? She used to tell me there was nothing to be gained from a bleeding heart. I used to wonder sometimes if we really knew her at all.)

Kill them all, Nan said, but I was upset at the thought of it. So many lives swept away in one go. Even if they only had one thought between them, surely it was a pity to snuff it out. They seemed happy, at times, when they fluttered against the glass. Sometimes they looked like they took flight just for the fun of it.

They didn't know what was going to happen to them. They had no time to prepare, to think *this is my last moment of sunlight, I must be sure to enjoy it.*

You always said that kind of musing was dust and moonshine. But you saw me thinking it just the same and you said to Grandpa no, don't kill them yet, we'll get them out.

Nan said it was a stupid plan. But Grandpa said let them try, what harm can they do? And you said don't worry, Elphine, it'll be fine.

Do you remember that?

You hated ladybirds. You never did like things crawling on you. And still you helped me catch them in jars and carry them outside. It took hours but we freed every single one, not a ladybird-soul left in peril; they fluttered up and away in a red cloud.

Too stupid to feel grateful, you said, but I don't think that was true. They looked happy to be safe and free.

I've seen you, Lucia. You helped me save the ladybirds, just like you helped the child Kate brought to you, just like you saved the woman in the woods and it felt right, didn't it? It felt like something rightly aligned. You felt like you were coming home.

Here I am. Here I am. My thoughts are fluttering and scattered like the ladybirds, tapping against the window and crawling in your hair. Do you guess I'm here? Do you remember the ladybirds? Do you remember your kindness and grace?

I wonder if it surprised you, what I did in the woods. It was necessary because I couldn't have you die, but all the same—he screamed. I hurt him terribly.

We're alike, you see. Not Lucia-the-bad and Elphine-the-good. Not really. Perhaps we are made differently but we are made of the same stuff.

When Mockbeggar woke again, the trees began to remember what they heard of me. You told my story—all of you, after my death, even if I think I was told better than I really was. I drifted here and there, in and out of the woods' memory. I found my way home.

Now you've told our story properly, start to finish, and here I am—vivid, *happening,* for a time. Elphine again.

I'm glad I heard it. Me and you and Ruby and Helena, playing in the woods.

I think it will continue always, the story of us. Somewhere we are still happening—the four of us, children, running among the trees.

Dearest Lucia, I am here but you won't listen to me. You won't hear me when I say *find a way out, tell it different.*

You have to show Nan that she was wrong. Her story of you doesn't fit. You have to kick it off like shoes that are too small. You have to save yourself.

Tell it different. No one was ever so good at that as you. Remember how easy it used to be? Like with our books. Or with the song, remember? You found different words that day and you sang them, and Nan was so angry. How dare you meddle, she said. How dare you trouble the universe. You have to do it again now, Lucia. Tell it with grace, while you still have time.

CHAPTER TWENTY-THREE

THE BROKEN PLEDGE

No more time now. Dawn had caught up with them. Sam's wedding day had come at last—no chance of a rest for Kate now, no chance to sit with what she had heard and was beginning to remember. She felt as weary as if she had lived the night of Elphine's death all over again.

Lucia looked equally exhausted. In the unsparing morning light she had an unwholesome pallor that Kate didn't like. She sat very still, empty coffee cup in front of her, and stared at Kate.

"So now you know," she said.

Kate knew and she didn't—what Lucia had told her was too much to understand at once. She had never been able to picture Elphine dying. Whenever, in the past, she had tried to reconstruct her memory of that night, this moment had always been the most elusive. Now the truth of Elphine's last minutes drifted in and out of her grasp. She could imagine it and then she couldn't: Elphine with her face wrecked by the thorns, swinging the axe with a terrible certainty.

Her idea of Elphine had altered. This was a new side of her, Kate thought—ruthless and loving. But of course she would be like that, if Lucia's safety was in question.

"I suppose I should finish the story," Lucia went on. "Unless you want a break."

"No. I'm fine."

She was more worried about Lucia than herself, though it felt impossible to say this now. The night's closeness was gone. Lucia wasn't even looking at her.

"I didn't realize at first what had happened," Lucia said. Her voice was unnaturally level. She was trying to imagine that this had happened to someone else, Kate thought. Perhaps it helped to tell it like a story. "I heard screaming and the axe and Elphine was whispering something but I couldn't make it out. Then all the noise stopped. I was lying on the ground and she was there too, close by. I thought of us lying in the attic. We'd find a patch of sunlight and share it. I don't know why that came into my head just then. I spoke to her but I already knew she was dead."

She was pressing her hands together so hard that her grazed palms must have hurt.

"The story was too much for her. It took her over for a few seconds and in that time she felt Harry's wounds and she died his death. It all happened to her, the way it had been happening to me before she took over. After she—afterward they said it was her lungs. But it was the story that really killed her. The fear of it. And I should have been the one to bear that, and I wasn't."

"You can stop now," Kate said. "You don't have to tell me the rest."

But Lucia pressed on, ignoring her:

"It was so quiet, after the rose tree was felled. Harry was gone and I knew I wouldn't see him again. I stayed with Elphine until Ruby and Helena came. It took them a long time to get through the roses and when they saw Elphine they didn't—it took them a minute or so to understand.

"We couldn't get her out. That place was a cage at the best of times. So in the end we left her there.

"I remember Ruby saying *we'll have to, nothing else to do,* and she sounded so reasonable but wrong at the same time. She talked and talked as we got out of the Rose House. I remember that. Talking and planning. I don't think she cared whether we were listening or not.

"When we were out in the clearing again, I had some crisis of conscience—I'd failed Elphine so thoroughly I didn't want to let her down again, even though it didn't matter now, not really—I tried to convince them we shouldn't leave her out there. Helena started to reply but Ruby spoke over her:

Just do the right thing for once in your life, she said to me. *Just shut up and help.*

"You were waiting for us, hardly conscious at that point, sitting propped against a tree. I couldn't work out how they'd got you loose. Ruby said later that the rose seemed to give up the moment Harry screamed.

"But it took us a while to help you back to Blanch Farm. I think they thought you might be dead, too—or as good as. I know I did."

Now, faintly, Kate remembered a walk through the woods that never seemed to end. Ruby and Helena were holding her upright. Her throat was raw with pain and her head was swimming. She could hear her heart beating in her ears but nothing else. None of the sisters spoke. It had seemed like a nightmare, at the time and afterward. For a long time, she had tried to believe it was nothing more.

"It was quiet when we got home," Lucia went on. "We'd left to screams and angry voices and when we came back there was nothing. The rain was just starting, wind was stirring the lanterns. All the guests were gone. Helena sat with you in the kitchen and Ruby and I ran to look for Nan and Dad.

Around the back of the house I found Nan sitting at the deserted table, the remains of the feast before her. There was rain falling into the wineglasses.

"I thought she'd be able to guess what had happened but she didn't. I had to tell her.

"*Elphine's dead in the woods.* I couldn't get it to sound real. And she didn't believe me. She told Dad to drive you to the hospital. Meanwhile she and Ruby and Helena would go back to the woods to see what was really going on.

"Ruby and Helena told her that they had seen what I saw. It was all true.

"But still Nan wouldn't quite believe it. *You girls don't know what you're talking about,* she said. *Elphine won't be—I'll have to go and see her myself, sort this business out. Like I sort everything else out . . .*

"Then there was activity for a while—people running here and there, everyone with a job to do. Ruby called an ambulance for Elphine, though Nan said there was no call for it. Her face was so strange that Ruby didn't argue with her.

"Do you remember any of this? Sitting waiting in Grandpa's old chair in the kitchen and all this happening around you?"

"No."

Helena said it might have been because of what happened. What he did. She said you were better not remembering. Like your mind was trying to keep you safe. I remember I kept looking at you as you sat there because I had this stupid idea that you couldn't die with me watching.

"Nan, Ruby and Helena went racing back up to the woods. Dad drove you to the hospital. I stayed in the kitchen.

"They wouldn't let me come with them. I suppose they didn't want me touching Elphine, helping to bring her home. So I was left there alone."

"Lucia." Kate leaned across the table. "You can leave it. That's enough."

"No. It's nearly finished. You need to hear it all." She pressed her hands closer together, looked around the kitchen as if she couldn't quite make it out. "They wouldn't let me touch her. They said I'd done enough.

"They didn't know the full extent of what I'd done, though. That emerged later, in the days that followed. That time isn't clear in my memory anymore. I remember crumbs, pieces that don't fit together.

"The clearest thing I remember is going to the woods and walking for hours. I thought there'd be some sign of her, after all the stories we'd told. That was how they *worked.* I was certain I'd find her. I didn't want to be in Mockbeggar—it was Harry's place—but it would be worth it to see her again.

"But there was nothing. It was like a different wood. The magic was all gone. I walked and walked and searched and listened, and there was nothing. Tame and ordinary. Dull as the rest of the world was now that Elphine was gone.

"That's when I realized that there was another price to pay for banishing Harry. Killing the tree claimed a life, and spoiled the woods in the bargain. Mockbeggar's trees were mourning the one they had lost. Harry was gone, but he had taken the wonder of the woods with him.

"I kept away from Helena and Ruby. I knew they'd look at me and see everything I'd done—all the lies which had led to Grandpa's death and to Elphine's. I kept away from everyone. I know you called to see me, I heard your voice downstairs, but I couldn't bear to have you look at me and ask for an explanation. If I saw you, you'd know who I really was.

"Helena and Ruby never told me they were leaving. I only found out when Dad mentioned it to me in passing. He was the one who told me things in those days—the others seemed to have elected him their go-between. He told me that there was a relative, someone from our mother's family, who was going to give them a home for a while.

"Ruby, always dutiful, wanted to extend the invitation to me. I told Dad she could save herself the worry, I'd be fine. I know, I knew they couldn't bear to see me.

"Our mother's relative was the one to arrange for Elphine's burial at Small Angels. An eleven o'clock ceremony. No regard for custom, though this hardly mattered now. We were lucky Elphine didn't end up in the village churchyard. Our mother's relative suggested cremation—Nan wouldn't hold with that, of course, though I thought there was something to be said for the idea. I liked the idea of Elphine free of everything heavy. Free of our family, and Small Angels.

"After her burial, Ruby and Helena and I were together only once, and that was our trip back to the Rose House. Helena said it was important that we make as certain as possible that the tree would not grow back.

"Nan would have nothing to do with this. She had seen the woods by then, and this last loss was enough for her. She washed her hands of it all, she despaired.

"She was dangerous in that state of mind. I kept out of her way. But even with Ruby and Helena her temper was unreliable—she flung glasses, spoke more than once about how much better it would have been if one of us had been taken instead of Elphine. Dad attended her.

"So we went back to the Rose House, where the flowers had all died back and the maze had vanished."

She paused. Her face twisted. For a moment she seemed to smile strangely.

She doesn't cry, Kate thought, chilled. It's not something she does.

Before she could stand up and put her arms around Lucia—whatever the consequences would be—Lucia spoke again:

"I thought I'd find them," she said shakily. "In spite of everything, I had this stupid idea that Elphine would be there. And Harry. But it was so quiet. And so dead. Helena and Ruby couldn't stand to look at me much as we went to work.

"We hammered copper coins into the tree—the plan was to poison it, if there was any life left. One of our books—those ancient schoolbooks that were supposed to teach us about the outside world—said that copper was fatal to trees. We wanted to take every precaution.

"They left that day, rushing like the house was on fire. Nan turned me out soon afterward. Helena and Ruby didn't look for me and I didn't expect them to.

"You know how it ends. The woods were quiet. Then they stopped being quiet. He's here again. It was all for nothing. Because of me, she died for nothing."

"She died to save you," Kate said. "She fought for you and she *won.* You're here because she loves you."

Lucia didn't answer.

"So what's our plan now?" Kate said.

"I don't know what you're talking about."

"Are you going back to the woods today? How do you want me to help? Do you have to go to the Rose House at night, or—"

But Lucia was laughing, dry and horrible.

"You don't change, Katherine Joan," she said softly. "God, you're consistent. But it's no good. You can't fix this. What do you think I've been doing all this time? The roses are *everywhere* now—not just in the Rose House, all over the woods. There's no tearing them all out. I take an axe to them and there's more and more; there's too many for anyone now. Mockbeggar learned from last time. And Harry's been getting stronger for days. Why do you think the woods were so happy yesterday? They're celebrating because they've got him back at long last."

"What happens next?"

"I don't know. The agreement's over. Our family broke our promise to be dutiful, to remember and keep him company. No telling what he'll do now."

"But that means everyone in the village is at risk. Including you."

Lucia shrugged. "There's nothing to be done."

"Elphine doesn't think that," Kate said.

"How would you know?" Then Lucia put a hand to her mouth. "You've seen her."

"Yesterday. I didn't tell you then because you were still recovering and I didn't know if I believed what I'd seen, and I didn't understand what she was telling me. But maybe you'll understand. She said *tell it different before it's too late.* Do you know what that means?"

Lucia stood up, impatient. "It doesn't matter."

"Of course it matters, if there's a way for us to fix this."

"But there isn't."

"I know it's difficult, but we at least have to—"

"No, we don't. *You* need to go to your wedding and get shot of this place."

"People may get hurt. People at the wedding, maybe."

Lucia said nothing.

"You're just planning to let everything in the village go to hell, then, without lifting a finger to help?"

"You'd be happier if you could give up this idea that I'm secretly a kind person."

"You used to be," Kate said. "I remember. The way you were with Elphine, and with me. You were kind, and you were brave. You'd never have said *that's that* and gone along with all this without trying to mend things."

"That was ten years ago," Lucia said. "You're nostalgic for someone who's been gone a long time. If she ever existed at all. And if last night didn't get her out of your system then I can't help you."

Kate got hastily to her feet, hands shaking. Sudden anger made it hard to think. But Lucia wanted her to lose her temper, so she would not—not even now, as she witnessed Lucia's determination to live as her worst self, to let others suffer rather than rewrite the role her grandmother had written for her decades ago.

"Elphine thought you were better than this," she said. Her voice was shaking, but she did not want her last words to Lucia to be clumsy or ill-considered. "So do I. If you think differently, then I'm sorry for you."

She left Lucia alone in the desolate house, empty wine bottles in front of her, empty rooms on every side. Outside in the quiet yard (no hens pecking about now) Kate quickened her pace. She was needed in the village, and there was nothing more she could do here now.

CHAPTER TWENTY-FOUR

The Bells of Small Angels

"Don't look," Sam said. But Chloe couldn't look away from the earth scattered across the floorboards. She could taste it in her mouth. Blood too. If she thought about it a moment longer she would start screaming.

"Look at me," Sam said. "Please, Chloe."

She stared at him, unable to speak.

"It's all right," he said shakily. He gripped her hand tightly. "Just give it a minute—"

Gently he helped her to her feet, guided her to a chair. She was dimly aware of him disposing of the disgusting mess on the floor and fetching her a glass of water.

Then he waited, watched as her breathing slowed, and after a few minutes the room stopped spinning. Nothing was all right, but she could start to think again.

"As soon as you're ready," he said, "I'll bring the car round."

She shook her head. "Can't. Too late."

She had been spared, but only for the time being. She would not get out of the village unscathed. She knew this with absolute certainty—her injured, shaking body knew this. Whoever was doing this to her had not gone very far away. She had a sense of them in the periphery now, an unfriendly watcher. There was no slipping the noose. If she tried to stir from the village, that pressure around her throat would tighten again, she would spit up earth until it choked her. She would die the sort of death she had imagined as a child—the helpless coughing, the burning in her chest, the frantic struggle for air.

She tried to explain this to Sam. He listened intently, without interruptions and without skepticism. At another time she might have smiled over the reversal.

Here was one comfort, at least: she was no longer alone in all this. He had his eyes open now, and he would share the danger with her.

When she had explained what she understood of the situation, he sighed, and sat back in his chair.

"So. That's what we're dealing with, then."

"I should never have brought the wedding here."

He shook his head. "I should've talked to you properly. I'm sorry."

Without warning, the door rattled. A key turned in the lock and Kate entered, shivering in the dawn cold. She was still wearing the clothes she had worn to the party, and her hair was wild.

She stared at the two of them—Sam, rigid with alarm, Chloe in her creased and wine-splashed wedding dress.

"What?" she said sharply. She shut and locked the door with haste, turned back to them with a frown. "Sam? What's happened?"

To Chloe's surprise, he told her the truth—and told her as if he had no doubt that he would be believed:

"Something followed Chloe out of Mockbeggar. It's angry, and it won't let her leave the village."

Kate sighed. She looked tired, but—Chloe thought, startled—rather as if she had expected to hear news of this kind.

"You'd better tell me everything," she said to Chloe.

But Chloe hesitated. It was one thing to tell Sam. But she barely knew Kate, and much of what she had experienced had been difficult to fit into words. It was not an easy thing to share with a stranger.

"She'll understand what you're talking about," Sam told her gently. His eyes were on Kate, and his expression was pleading. "She knows about Mockbeggar. She'll be able to help us."

And Kate said, "You can tell me. You don't have to worry." Absently, she put a hand to her throat. "I'll believe you."

In one respect it was easier to tell the story a second time. Chloe had Sam now to prompt her if she lost her train of thought or got confused about the sequence of events. This was helpful because her mind was feeling less clear just now; she was growing cold and shaky.

Halfway through the story (about the time Chloe escaped the Blackberry Maze) Sam took off his coat and draped it around her shoulders. He muttered something about getting changed into warmer clothes, but she shook her head. If she stopped now she might never find her thread again.

Kate listened without comment, almost without moving. Only once, when Chloe described her meeting with the last Gonne sister in the woods, did she stir—reaching across the table for the bottle of Bacchus.

When Chloe was finished, she nodded, quiet a moment.

"I'm sorry this happened to you," she said at last.

"What are we going to do now?" Sam asked. "Do you think if we talked to Lucia—"

"No. That's no good."

"But what other options do we have? Surely if *you* ask she'll do something?"

"No." Kate's voice had sharpened. "Trust me. We're on our own."

A light came on in the back room, and John Pauncefoot appeared in the doorway wearing slippers and a navy wool dressing gown.

"It's quite early," he said mildly. "Chloe, is that your wedding dress you're wearing?"

"Yes." In spite of Sam's coat she was trembling. "That's bad luck, isn't it."

She clearly wasn't talking normally. They were all staring at her now.

"Kate," John said, "I've got some mint growing in the kitchen. Some tea would be a good idea, wouldn't it?"

"We could do with some mint leaves, too," Kate said, standing up. "And do you have any bicarbonate of soda? And a bowl of clean water?"

John looked surprised, but nodded.

"I can help you feel better," she said to Chloe. "If you want."

Anything. Anything that might wash the foul taste from her mouth and the green and rose scent from her nostrils. She nodded.

"Good," John said. "That's a good start. Whilst you're doing that, I'll give Brian and Elizabeth a call. They might be able to lend us a hand."

"Waste of time," Kate said. "Even if they could help, they wouldn't. You know how people in this village are about Mockbeggar. *Leave it to the Gonnes.* You've all been happy to let them handle all the strain and the danger for decades."

"But we shouldn't have been," said John. "We've come to see that. Brian and Elizabeth and I . . . It hasn't sat right with any of us for a while, the way things went on with the Gonnes. After Elphine's death, we used to wonder if there wasn't something we should've done to help, somewhere along the line. Or something we could do in the future, if the time came to it. Apart from the Gonnes, the three of us have been in the village the longest. We know this place. Maybe we can be some use. So if you don't mind I'll invite Brian and Elizabeth round now and we can talk all this over."

Chloe followed Kate upstairs in silence, too tired and shaky to ask questions. John had brought Kate the mint tea and other things on a tray, as if Chloe were having another breakfast in bed. Clearing a space for it on the dressing table, Chloe discovered the key to Small Angels—colder now, and heavier than it had been the day before.

"I feel like dropping this into the nearest river," she said, showing it to Kate. "But I suppose that would only bring worse things down on my head, wouldn't it?"

"You'd lose your deposit, certainly," Kate said. "Sit down, keep that coat around you. I need to fetch some things."

She wasn't long—from her own room she fetched cotton wool pads and a thick gray hoodie.

"Put that around your shoulders until you can get changed," she said. "I don't want to spill anything on your dress."

"I think the dress is a lost cause."

"Absolutely not." She sat down at the dressing table, and went to work. At another time Chloe would have been curious about the strange collection of supplies that John had assembled. Now she was content to let Kate stir bicarbonate of soda into the water, stir briskly.

"Drink your tea," she said. "Crush the mint leaf and smell it. Then we'll do your face."

Chloe did as she was told without question. The tea was almost too hot to drink, the mint stronger than she had expected.

When she had finished about half the cup, Kate brought the water over to the bed and crouched in front of her.

"Close your eyes," she said. "I'm going to wipe this over. Not much. It'll help."

Chloe shut her eyes. If nothing else, it was comforting to be treated like a child for a while. Kate washed her face with water-and-soda-bic, wiped it clean with a flannel. She worked steadily, as if Chloe were one of her damaged gargoyles.

"There. Now finish your tea," she said, when she was done.

Chloe drank, and by the time she had finished, found that she did feel steadier.

"How does all this work?" she asked Kate.

"The mint's good if you're panicky, wrapped up in a bad story. It brings you back to yourself. Or that's what I was told once, anyway."

"What about the bicarbonate of soda?"

"It cleans off a lot of things. Mockbeggar's just one of them." She put the bowl back on the tray.

"Who taught you all of this?"

"The Gonnes."

"So you've seen this sort of thing before?"

"Once or twice." Kate's expression was bleak. Her tone made further questions impossible.

They were upstairs about a quarter of an hour, but in this short space of time, John Pauncefoot had worked a small transformation. There was coffee and fresh bread set out on the bar, and Elizabeth and Brian (and John Aubrey) had already arrived.

"I said something would happen," Brian said, as soon as he saw Chloe. "Didn't I say?"

"Hardly constructive to point that out *now*, Brian," said Elizabeth Daunt. "We're not here for recriminations. We're here to come up with a plan of action."

"Strange thing to hear from someone in this village," said Kate. "You've all been content to leave things to the Gonnes for so long."

"Well, we're not content anymore," John Pauncefoot said. "You know the most, don't you, Kate—about what's wrong in Mockbeggar. If you tell us what you know, we can share now. Share the burden."

Kate glanced around the little assembly, taking in their faces one by one. She looked serious, pitying.

"Fine," she said.

She began in a rush, but as she went on her pace slowed a little. She spoke succinctly—Chloe had the idea that she was leaving many things out—but then she had a great deal to cover.

She told them about an old murder which was paid for again and again; she told them about the Gonnes' secret happiness and danger, the strain of living by the dead man's rules, the strange and lovely transformations that Mockbeggar could produce. She told them about an attack on the ghost of the Rose House, and how this went terribly wrong.

"Why would they do it, though?" Brian Last said, when Kate paused for breath.

"What?"

"Why would they try getting rid of him after so long?"

Kate hesitated. Finally, she said, "They wanted something more. Something else."

"They were very young, those girls," said Elizabeth Daunt. "It's not so surprising."

"What happened afterward?" John Pauncefoot asked.

Disaster for the family, Kate told them, but quiet for Mockbeggar and for Harry, until now. She told them how the woods had mourned, and how Lucia and her sisters had driven copper coins into Harry's tree in the hopes of preventing any chance of his return.

"It was my fault, then," Chloe said. "I woke him up."

To Brian and Elizabeth, who had not heard the story she'd told to Sam and Kate, she explained about her visit to the ruined cottage, the removal of the remaining copper coins.

She looked at Kate. "I did wake him, didn't I? You didn't tell me that before."

"It was always going to happen. Sooner or later. Most of the coins were already gone, weren't they? So I think you can spare yourself the guilt."

"But that's why he chose me, isn't it? That's why he did all this."

"Maybe," Kate said. "Maybe it's because the church was opened. Or just because you were happy and he didn't like to see it. Or because he's got hate in him and it has to go somewhere and you were there. I don't know if you'll ever get an answer for sure."

"The point is, it's done," Elizabeth said. "What matters now is that we decide what to do tomorrow. Or today, rather. From what you've said, Kate, it sounds like things are likely to revert to how they were in the bad old days, before any of us were born. This Harry Child roaming where he likes, a menace to everyone. Especially a menace to Chloe. That's pretty much how things stand, isn't it?"

Kate nodded.

"We'll have to get away, somehow," Sam said. "I just can't work out how."

"What does Lucia Gonne have to say for herself?" Brian asked.

"Nothing," Kate said. "She won't have anything to do with this. I told Sam. We'll just have to manage. Get Chloe and Sam away from here somehow. I heard—someone told me once that he's quietest around noon. I think that's your best chance. Make a run for it then."

"Do we go along with the wedding beforehand?" Sam asked.

It took Chloe aback to think how inconsequential the ceremony had become. All that planning, all that expense—all insignificant now.

"Better had," Kate said, looking at Chloe. "If you can bear it. You don't want him getting wind of anything amiss."

"Is he really likely to suspect?" Brian said.

"He hears things," Kate said. "He knows what the earth and wind and rain know. I wouldn't risk it."

"What about afterward, though?" Chloe said. "Suppose we do get away. What about the village?"

Brian and Elizabeth exchanged a glance. John Pauncefoot busied himself with the coffee cups.

"We'll see about that in due course," Elizabeth said, finally.

"How, though?" Sam said. "What will you do?"

The Albatross was quiet for a moment. Outside, one of the pigeons called softly.

After the plan had been made, Elizabeth insisted that Chloe and the others try to take an hour or so of rest before the day began.

Sam said he would come back to the Albatross to be with Chloe and keep an eye on her—he just needed half an hour to run to his parents' house and fetch a few things.

"You can stay here until he's back," John Pauncefoot said. "Or there's a sofa in the back room you can lie down on—"

But Chloe shook her head. She would be all right upstairs in her bedroom for a short while. She wanted to sleep if she could.

She couldn't sleep, though. It was fully day now, the bedroom was light and entirely unalarming, and yet she found that she didn't like to be alone. She couldn't close her eyes without having to open them a moment later, convinced she heard the scratching—from inside the Albatross this time. She would have liked to be able to turn to somebody and say *did you hear that too?*

It was worse knowing what was hunting her. Kate had avoided describing the dogs too extensively, but Chloe could imagine them all the same. She could put a face to the man who had called to her from next door, begging to be hanged. Fred Hart, terrified out of his mind. Perhaps Chloe would find herself in the same state before too long.

Her thoughts were interrupted by a knock at the door. She expected Sam, but it was Kate, already dressed for the wedding. The suit had been Chloe's gift—a goodwill gesture to cultivate the friendship that had never blossomed. Six months ago, she had sent Kate a list of shops and detailed instructions as to color palette and style (nothing too sleek or citified, please) and asked her to pick out something she liked and send Chloe the receipt.

Kate had dutifully realized Chloe's vision for the wedding. The suit was soft, earthy tweed, she had her hair loose and wore a soft blue tie which would match Sam's precisely.

"Nicole's going to want to take your photo," Chloe said, trying to smile. "For her portfolio."

She had almost forgotten that Nicole and Beth would be with her soon to help her get ready. She wasn't sure she would be able to stand their kindness and concern.

"Couldn't sleep," Kate said. "Thought I might as well get ready. I can sort your dress out, if you like."

"Seriously? Be my guest. It's not like you could make it any worse."

She was being melodramatic but surely she was entitled, all things considered. Kate nodded and went to work, unhanging the dress from the door and sitting herself in a chair in the lightest corner of the room. Without ceremony she took out a small sewing kit and set about mending the rent in the skirt.

It looked like a soothing thing to do—to focus on this single task for a while. Perhaps that was why Kate had volunteered to help. She must be grappling with some ugly memories. Chloe suspected that she had underplayed the extent of her suffering the night of Elphine Gonne's death.

Perhaps she had underplayed other things too: how things stood between her and Lucia Gonne, for one.

Kate's face was calm but her mouth was tight and unhappy. Had Mockbeggar marked her deeply? Would it change Chloe, too? Even if she got away from the village in one piece, would she ever be quite the same person again?

Chloe said, "I'm sorry to drag you back into all of this."

"You couldn't have known."

"But I know what the wood's like now. I know what Harry Child can do to people . . ." There was a faint relief in saying his name—in knowing that other people had been hurt as she had been hurt. She was not alone. And she added, without intending to ask: "How did you manage, afterward?"

Kate said, "Not well." She snipped a thread, held the dress up to the light. "Don't bury it alive. That's what I learned." She inspected her work with a frown. From where Chloe sat, the tear had vanished as if it had never existed. "I don't think you're likely to do that, though," Kate went on. "You're better balanced than the rest of us. Sam must like that about you."

Chloe thought back to a story Sam had told her, a rare glimpse into a chaotic childhood. *She used to sew name tags on for me*, Sam had said. *Back when we were friends.*

The bouquet was resting in a glass of water. Chloe took a sprig of cornflower, pinned it to Kate's waistcoat. She would have thanked her again, but there was no time. There were people outside the door—her parents and bridesmaids, excited to share this happiest of days.

In the hour that followed, she was too busy to think much about what lay ahead. The exertion of smiling, chatting, feigning appropriate joy—this was enough to take up most of her thoughts.

They guessed that something was amiss, all the same. Her parents, Beth and Nicole—they heard that strained note in her voice, saw her reluctance for photographs, but none of them mentioned it. They could tell she didn't want to discuss it and no doubt they imagined some minor and mundane problem: a little tiff with Sam, a guest who had forgotten to RSVP, a problem with the caterers. They seemed to have agreed among themselves to accept her pretense at normality, and their tact made her want to cry.

It was a relief to be away from them all at last, waiting at the door of the Albatross for John Pauncefoot to bring the cart around.

Sam and Kate had already left for Small Angels; Brian and Elizabeth would be ready at the church too. They were all business this morning and yet Chloe suspected that, like her, they half-thought that this was all for nothing.

Her mouth still tasted of earth. Harry Child could strike her down at any time and there was nothing that anybody could do about it. If he decided to choke the life out of her at her wedding, in front of everyone who loved her best, then he could do it.

There was a mist coming on, unusually heavy for this time of year. She heard the clip of Hector's hooves well before she saw him and John emerge from the fog. John must have worked hard in decorating the little cart—it was as beautiful and quaint as she had imagined. Even Hector had flowers strung around his neck; he wore them gravely, like chains of office.

"You look very beautiful," John Pauncefoot said. "Are you ready to go?"

She nodded.

"We'll see you right," John said. "Just remember to be ready, when it's time to go."

She and Sam would go through the wedding ceremony as planned, and at the end of the service they would step briskly out of the church and be on the road in an instant. Kate would have the car ready. All they had to do was run.

The journey to the church felt very brief this morning. There was barely enough time for her to get used to her high position in the cart—John at her side, the air catching her hair—before they were moving gingerly up the track to Small Angels.

"All right?" John said softly. Not to her, Chloe realized, but to Hector. The horse climbed the slight slope to the church without hesitation. There was something comforting in his steady pace. She felt that he was intelligent enough to know if there was something to fear.

She was glad to arrive—eager now for this all to be done with, whatever the outcome. This time tomorrow, at least, she wouldn't have to wonder anymore.

John helped her out of the cart, and Chloe walked into Small Angels as she had already done a score of times in her imagination.

The church was exquisite, its quaint beauties no longer lost in dust. The flowers lining the aisle were fresh. The little candles flickered in their jars. Even the rood skeletons' smiles seemed friendly today—Chloe was glad she had forgotten to screen them after all.

The Albatross's musician had brought his band, and their music belonged in that place as organ music would not have done. The band steered the wedding guests gently through unfamiliar hymns. There was gladness in the music, and in the faces of the congregation. A trace of last evening's hectic enjoyment still lingered.

Chloe's vision had been perfectly realized in almost every detail. The weather was the only snag. Even inside, the onset of autumn felt inescapable. The lamps and candles did their best, but there was little light coming through the windows. The air had a damp chill to it.

In spite of this, Small Angels was as lovely as Chloe had hoped—and she had been robbed, she thought. She and Sam both had. They ought to have been fully present now, enjoying the music, the gentle humor of her father's sermon. Instead it was all a test of patience, something to endure before they could make their escape. The music and prayers seemed to come from a distance.

She had forgotten that Kate was to do one of the readings. One of Chloe's favorite passages: *Stay me with flagons, comfort me with apples, for I am sick of love.* She read steadily, but her eyes kept flicking toward the back of the church, as if expecting to find someone standing there.

Now was the time at last. Five minutes till noon. Chloe and Sam—married now, though Chloe hardly felt it—had signed the register. During their first kiss as a married couple, she had felt his tension, the fear barely held in check. But he pressed her hand, smiled in the old way. *Still here, still us.*

Kate was already outside. The car was waiting. They were nearly through.

The music started up again. Time for the procession out. Sam's hand was cold in hers. She didn't look about her. It would do no good to see the dear and ignorant faces of her friends and family.

The mist had grown heavier during the service. The church path was almost hidden, the shape of the cart only vague. John had unhitched Hector and was walking him up and down, muttering in a low voice.

"All all right?" John said to Brian, who had followed Chloe and Sam from the church. Inside, the band was playing—there was a short space now before the guests would leave their pews.

"So far, so good," Brian said. "What's up with Hector?"

"Restless. I think he's—"

Hector screamed.

A shape moved in the mist, farther up the road. A pale creature, there for an instant and then gone. Hector reared—screamed again, his voice full of fear and rage—and let his hooves thud down on the track. John was desperately trying to quiet him.

"Easy," he muttered, "we'll be all right now—"

But Hector didn't seem to hear him. His eyes were wide, his ears back. He seemed about to rear up again.

"Go," Brian said, shoving Sam forwards. "We'll deal with this."

They couldn't possibly deal with this, Chloe thought. She saw the same horrified conviction on Sam's face. But Brian yelled at them again to get out, and at last they turned and ran, Sam pulling at her hand to speed her onward, ducking around graves. Running in the wedding shoes after all, she thought, with a flicker of desperate hilarity. Running but probably not fast enough—

Behind them, Hector screamed again. She had to force herself not to look back. They were almost at the lane now and Kate was waiting for them, car lights shining in the fog. Her face showed pale through the windscreen.

The dog came out of the mist without a sound. It should have made some noise, Chloe thought, her breath catching. An animal that size.

What she had heard in Mockbeggar hadn't prepared her for this. The creature was large—all dense, ugly muscle—with a short muzzle, bared teeth. Its eyes were fixed on her. It snarled.

She turned to Sam but he was looking at Kate, watching powerless from the driver's seat. Then he leaned close to her, muttered *keep going, no matter what*. He shoved her forward toward the car.

Then he was yelling, running in the opposite direction—back toward the church—and the creature's old hunting instincts must have been prompted because it was behind him, pursuing, and in another instant, they were both lost in the mist.

Chloe stood motionless, uncomprehending. Then someone took her hand and dragged her forward; she was pushed into a car seat. In another moment Kate was climbing in beside her.

"Seat belt."

"What are you doing? We can't just *go*—"

Kate started the car. Before Chloe could object further, they were speeding away from Small Angels at a reckless pace. Another moment and the church was lost in the mist.

"Kate." It was hard to talk, Chloe discovered. She was shivering, her teeth had started to chatter. "*Kate*. Stop, for God's sake. We've got to go back."

"He wanted to get you out of here. If we go back now it'll make everything worse." She wouldn't look at Chloe.

They passed the village in an instant. There were windows lit up against the fog—then it was all behind them, and they were crossing open country, driving fast toward the woods.

Sam just had to get back to the church, Chloe thought. That great door had kept the dogs out once. Please God let it stand fast now, she thought, if it comes to that.

The deer crossed their path so suddenly that Chloe gasped. The creature was racing, panicked, entirely blind to the car.

Kate swerved sharply to avoid the collision. The deer leaped free, but it was too late to correct her course.

The car crashed through brambles and nettles, sliding into a ditch and at last hitting a tree with a dull crash of metal.

For a moment neither Kate nor Chloe moved. The woods around them were silent. Chloe felt as if they, too, were struggling to understand what had just happened.

The barking came from the woods, close to the place where the deer had emerged. It was being hunted, Chloe thought, half-stunned and unable to move.

Kate said something, but Chloe couldn't make it out. A warning?

Something moved outside the car. A dog came out of the fog, and beside it came another figure. She tried to move her head to see more clearly.

A human shape. All dull colors, like a dead tree. She couldn't see well enough to make him out clearly. There was something red down the front of his shirt, a long stain.

He was close to Chloe's window now, watching her struggle to breathe.

It was Harry Child. The tightness at her throat was coming back, the taste of earth in her mouth.

She tried to look at Kate but she couldn't find the strength to turn her head, and when she opened her mouth she began coughing, helpless.

Her vision was blurring. The man outside the window was a vague shape now, but she thought she saw him move his fingers a fraction. There was something in his hands. A circle of briars.

There would be no respite this time. He was going to kill her.

Then a sound pierced the fog. At first Chloe wasn't sure whether or not it was taking place in her own mind.

Then she understood it: the bells of Small Angels were ringing as they hadn't done for ten years.

The notes were very clear. Dizzy—too far from herself now to feel much fear—she thought that the chime was beautiful and yet it set her teeth on edge.

The dog snarled, and the man outside Chloe's window turned his head sharply.

The bells went on, and Chloe continued to struggle for breath. As she neared unconsciousness, she thought she heard Kate say hoarsely:

"Lucia, what have you done?"

CHAPTER TWENTY-FIVE

A Pale Child Waiting

The dog was right behind him. It was nowhere. It was—

Oh God it was ahead of him now, it was circling.

Sam stumbled, almost fell. The fog was so thick that the road and Small Angels were both hidden. All he could make out were the gravestones, soft under gray cloud.

The animal had gone quiet. Was it playing with him?

Then the growls resumed—louder, and from both ahead and behind. There were two of them.

He tried to remember Kate's story. There were three dogs, weren't there? Fred Hart had three dogs. Where was the third one now?

He took a step forward, edged around a crooked stone cross.

Too risky to run. No clue where they might emerge from the fog next.

Fucking things weren't *real.* They were nothing but history. But they didn't know it, that was the thing, or they knew and they didn't care. He was going to die ripped apart by history. Impossible things. Figments with teeth.

He inched forward, hoping that Small Angels might appear out of the fog. Nothing.

It was so quiet. What was happening in the church?

A growl—*shit*—something rushed past him and was gone in a blur of white.

They *were* playing. Toying with him, trying out their new strength. Kate had said they were getting stronger. If he got out of this then he'd apologize to his sister for not listening before. For every mistake that might have contributed to him being here now while Chloe was God knew where, already choked to death or caught in the woods, Kate doomed alongside her.

He imagined them so clearly it felt like he was actually seeing it: Kate slumped over the driver's seat, face hidden by her long, dark hair. Chloe sitting with her head thrown back, eyes staring blankly ahead.

Two dogs at Small Angels. Where was the third?

Another snarl. This time when the monster came out of the mist it was almost solid, outlines clear unless you looked at it face-on. This time it lingered in his vision a fraction longer.

The dogs weren't hurrying. It wasn't as if there was any real urgency to this hunt. Sam wasn't going anywhere.

A scream—tearing through the fog without warning, drowning the dogs' snarling—made him cringe. It was high and unhuman, a horrible mingling of terror and anger. Every instinct told him to run from the sound.

But it was Hector, Sam told himself. Up ahead, not far off. The horse was frightened and furious but he was *there*.

Sam started in the direction of the scream, moving as fast as he dared.

Fog and tombstones and wild grass—it was going on forever; he wanted to sob and he didn't dare make a noise.

He went a yard farther. A dark mass slowly became visible. Small Angels. He must have circled around and around, disoriented, five yards from the church door without seeing it.

No sign of the dogs now, but they would spring if he tried to get inside, he thought. Rip his throat out right at the verge of safety.

He heard himself swearing under his breath without a break. They'd be on him in a second. Any moment now—

Something moved close to his right, pale and very fast. A growl. Then it sprang toward him.

Pointless to run. But Sam darted forward anyway, driven by instinct.

And there was the church door swinging open; there was Brian Last staring at him, white-faced, yelling something Sam couldn't make out.

In. Get inside. His mind had narrowed down to that one thought.

Get inside, slam the door. God, it was too late, it was behind him, it was on him—

The church door slammed shut. He was back in Small Angels.

Brian had barely turned the key in the lock before something large crashed against the wood.

"Steady," someone said. "Sam, take a minute. Breathe."

Elizabeth Daunt. She spoke as if asking him to pay a small library fine. He breathed, as she had instructed him, and then looked around him.

There were his guests—his friends, his parents, Chloe's parents—all huddled together at the back of the church. White faces and wedding finery. Close to the font were John Pauncefoot—bleeding from a nasty bite on his leg—and Hector.

"Couldn't leave him outside," Brian said, seeing where Sam was looking.

"No. Of course not."

The door shook. Something solid and definite—muscle and bone—slammed against it again and again.

"There's two of them," Sam said.

Another crash. In Harry Child's time, the door had held the dogs off. Or so the song had said. The barrier didn't seem as effective now.

"That's not going to last long," Brian said. "I'd give us five minutes."

"I'm sorry you got involved in this," Sam said—to Bill and Birdie, to Chloe's parents, to everyone.

"We're not finished yet," said Elizabeth. "Door's holding so far—"

Another crash, louder than any that had gone before. Somewhere at the back of the church, a child was crying.

The villagers had been dodging the secrets of Small Angels all their lives. Now they would know, whether they liked it or not. Even if it killed them.

When Sam looked around, he saw that knowledge on his parents' faces, on Brian and Elizabeth's faces.

Unwarily, his gaze was caught by the rood skeletons—bare bones still smiling. He felt a surge of dislike—Chloe's antipathy. There was a smugness to their grins. They knew too much. Had they been waiting for this all along?

"Sam? Sam Unthank? You in here?" The voice was brisk and unfriendly, and it came from just outside the church. "It's Lucia Gonne. Let me in."

"Careful," Brian muttered, a trace of his old self returning. "You don't know if she's in league with those things . . ."

But Sam let her in. Kate wouldn't have forgiven him if he'd done otherwise.

In spite of himself, he was taken aback by Lucia's appearance. She was shaking and pale, and her arms were scratched as if she had been crawling through brambles.

"Where is she?" she said.

"Kate? She's gone with Chloe."

"What are you talking about?"

When he told her what had happened, she looked as if he'd hit her. For an instant she didn't seem able to speak.

Small Angels was silent. Around him he felt the others—his co-conspirators, Brian and Elizabeth—react with dismay. Elizabeth had raised a hand to her mouth.

"What?" he said to Lucia—curt with alarm. "Won't it work? Don't they stand a chance of—"

"He'll be with her by now," Lucia said flatly. She was pressing her hands tight together as if she was holding desperately to something Sam couldn't see. "There's no getting away from him that easily."

It was like seeing the dog emerge from the mist, only worse. In spite of himself, he had hoped that it might work, he might be able to get Chloe away.

Lucia's face had changed. Despair had abruptly given way to something else.

"The bells," she said. "We've got to ring them. Now. Only thing that might make him turn back. It's the way we always called him in the old days. It might get his interest—he might come and see—"

She was frightened and desperate, voice shaking. Her haughtiness had all fallen away. Sam realized that she was ill—she could barely stand—but she didn't care. Her only thought was of Kate. It was disorienting. He had disliked this woman for over a decade—for her family's ostentatious strangeness, for taking Kate's attention, and (worst of all) for hurting her. Now he looked into Lucia's face and saw love and terror as deep as his own there. The strength of feeling didn't fit in with his idea of her at all.

But even as he thought this, he was wrenching open the door to the bell tower, seizing one of the ropes. Lucia—struggling to stand, struggling to keep hold of the rope—was there beside him, and together they went to work.

After a few minutes he was dimly aware that someone else had taken Lucia's place, that Lucia was watching from the corner now. Eventually someone took his place, too, seizing the rope when he was too tired to go on. It was Bill, it was Brian, it was Elizabeth—friends and family and neighbors stepped forward one by one.

There was quiet outside. Did that mean something? Did it mean something good?

He took another turn; the rope burned his hands and his back began to ache.

When someone put a hand on his arm, he shook them off. But it was Brian, and he was not so easily deterred.

"Stop a moment," he said. "She's up to something."

She was Lucia—Brian's tone made that quite clear. She had gone to the door, leaving the village to continue with the bells a little while longer. She was waiting, Sam realized. Listening?

At last the bells fell silent, and a great hush followed. The child at the back of the church had subsided into whimpering. But other than this it was quiet. No growls from outside.

Lucia turned at last, looked around at them all. Her expression was strange.

"What's happened?" Sam demanded. "Did it work?"

"I think she'll be all right, now." She looked around the congregation again, and then back to him. "The rest of you, too."

Then she opened the door and stepped outside.

The fog had not lifted. But it had receded a little way, so that the first few rows of tombstones were visible.

The white dogs waited among the graves, eyes watchful. On the path ahead of them stood a child.

He was dead, Sam thought. The child standing only a few yards away—so thin and ragged, shivering in a bloodstained shirt—was dead. No living person had such a face, so still and bloodless.

The child held something strange. A briar, twisted into a noose.

Lucia went to him. She stopped only once. Pausing on the path, she stooped to one of the gravestones, retrieved a tiny piece of chalk from the base of the stone, and marked something with shaking fingers.

The child and Lucia spoke a moment. Sam caught only a sentence of Lucia's, spoken like a promise—*I'll come back to stay.*

The child stared at her, searching her face. Finally he nodded, and held out his hand to her.

Sam was about to call to her to wait, but it was too late for that—she had taken the pale child's hand, and the two of them disappeared into the mist, the dogs in their wake.

CHAPTER TWENTY-SIX

In the Woods Where Roses Grow

When Harry Child appeared outside the car, Kate realized that she and Chloe were about to die.

Her seat belt had stretched taut, holding her tight in place. But she forced herself to twist as far as she could, to look at him straight.

His face was sallow and twisted and wretched. He had one hand against the glass. The other held a snarl of brambles. A thorn noose.

Chloe's eyes were wide, horrified. "Kate, I can't—"

No chance to say anything more. The attack took her, and her words were lost in coughing, a desperate struggle for air.

Not much longer, Kate thought. The faint mark around her neck was cold.

Then came the bells. It was so long since she had heard them that she couldn't believe it at first. The bells of Small Angels. How could they be ringing now?

Then she understood. It was Lucia—who else could it be? What reckless thing was she doing now, and why?

Outside the car she saw him startle, too. In spite of every thing, she might almost have said that he looked surprised.

A moment's consideration. Beside her, Chloe still struggled for air.

Then he turned away—strode into the trees without a backward glance.

For a few seconds she didn't dare move, afraid that he might return. Beside her, Chloe was still coughing—but less violently. The wheezing had lessened. In a matter of minutes, she was breathing more normally.

The dog had gone too. It seemed to Kate that she and Chloe had been forgotten. The bells had driven them out of Harry Child's thoughts. At least for a time.

It was very quiet. Chloe had subsided into near-silence. Kate began struggling with her seat belt.

She caught sight of a movement outside the car. The doe had returned. From the edge of the trees it considered the wreck of the car with interest but no pity. Its movements were easy now. It knew that the dog was long gone, the danger had passed.

And Harry Child was bound for Small Angels, for Lucia and Sam and the others.

The car was stuck in a ditch, tilted to the driver's side. Kate's door was pinned shut by the brambles which had slowed their crash. They were going to have to climb out, and she wasn't sure if Chloe even had the strength to open the door on her side from this angle. Was it worth turning on the engine to get the window open? Could she possibly smash the glass?

The church bells sounded louder and louder—jangling, haphazardly rung—and then stopped abruptly.

As if it were a signal, the deer turned and disappeared into the trees.

"Kate," Chloe muttered. "Look."

There were lights on the road ahead, moving steadily nearer.

In the quiet and the fog, the possibility of another car hadn't occurred to her. It felt like an envoy from another country. The fog was so thick that she could make out nothing but the beam of the headlights until it drew level and stopped, hazard lights blinking.

Someone pushed through the brambles with as little thought as if they were grass. They wrenched Chloe's door open.

It was Ruby Gonne. She looked from Kate to Chloe, her face taut with concern.

"Where's Lucia?"

"With Harry Child, I think," Kate said. "She rang the bells just now. She must have wanted to get his attention."

Ruby swore. Kate could not, in her childhood memory, find an instance of Ruby swearing. It had been so important for her to set a good example in those days.

Ruby turned to her companion—Helena Gonne, who had rolled down the window on the driver's side. "She's at Small Angels."

"Oh, for God's sake. What is she thinking?"

"We'll have to get up there and find out," said Ruby. She turned back to Kate and Chloe and took in Chloe's ghastly appearance, the blood and dirt on her white dress. "Are you hurt? Can you get out?"

"We're OK," Chloe said. She held out a hand for Ruby to help her out of the car. "Come on, let's get moving."

They were already in Helena's car and bound for the church when Ruby said,

"I take it the escape didn't go so well."

"How do you know about that?" said Kate, surprised.

"Sam," Chloe said, before Helena or Ruby could answer. "He tracked you down, didn't he? Last night? I thought he was keeping something to himself. I just assumed he'd lost the rings." She was quite obviously struggling to keep her voice from shaking. "Did he tell you everything?"

"More or less," Ruby said. "He said Lucia hasn't been much help in all this. Until now, apparently."

Kate remembered her last words to Lucia, the reproach and anger. She had challenged Lucia to live a different story. Had Lucia decided to take her advice after all, had she gone to Small Angels to help?

Kate couldn't quite believe it. Only yesterday Lucia had despaired of herself. How could she have experienced such a reversal in so short a time?

"We shouldn't have let it get to this point," Ruby said, as Helena turned onto the Small Angels track. "We should have come down here . . ."

"Would she have seen us?" Helena said, sending gravel flying up in their wake.

Driving through the fog, it took them until they were only a few yards away from Small Angels to make anything out clearly.

Then Chloe gave a stifled exclamation. Hector's cart had been knocked onto its side and smashed, flower garlands ripped to pieces.

Some of the wedding guests were standing in the graveyard, looking at a loss. Brian seemed to be trying to organize something; people were going in and out of the church as if there were some crisis inside that required attention.

Sam stood on the church steps—the door was open, and it looked as if he had just ventured out. When he saw the car he froze, seemingly unable to believe it for an instant—then he was racing through the graves toward them, wrenching open the door on Chloe's side.

"Are you all right? Why are you back? What *happened*?"

"It's all right." Chloe spoke firmly, though her voice was tired. "He let me go. What happened here?"

Now Sam glanced at the rest of them—Kate and Ruby and Helena. "Lucia. She came and got us to ring the bells. Harry Child was here and then the two of them left."

"How long ago?" Ruby demanded.

"Just now. Five minutes, maybe."

"She went with him?" Kate said. "How did he—"

"She took his hand." Sam's voice was strange. He was still coming to terms with it, she realized. "He was dead but he was here, and she took his hand like he was a child. Really a child. She said she'd come back to stay."

Kate thought back to Lucia's story from the night before. To stay with Harry for ever. What would that really mean? How could that promise be kept?

There was a new mark on Miss Violet's grave, smudged like it was done in haste —

©

"We need to go," Kate said. Her voice was so hoarse that she barely recognized it. "We have to get out there, *now*."

The mist was retreating. Was that a good sign? She couldn't bring herself to ask. None of them had spoken since passing beyond the graveyard.

Helena carried a rucksack—supplies, she had told Kate with a half-mocking twist of the mouth. In the old days the Gonnes had rarely ventured into the woods without tools for emergencies. Matches, Swiss army knives, a torch apiece. These accompanied them even when they entered the woods dressed up in their acting finery.

In spite of Helena's preparation, in spite of being older and stronger, she and Ruby seemed hesitant compared to their child-selves. They no longer believed that they were capable of handling whatever Mockbeggar dealt them.

At the edge of the woods, they paused. The Rose House was their obvious destination, but in the fog, after so many years, they needed to confer about the journey. Which path was best, the Elbow or the Pig's Tail?

They had grown old, Kate thought. Ten years ago they would have run into the woods to find Lucia, wary but bold. Losing Elphine had changed them. The past decade must have changed them too. They had lived in the world, beyond Mockbeggar. Perhaps, like Kate, they had done their best to forget.

They know what they're doing, don't they? Sam had said to her as they parted at Small Angels, and she had nodded.

Watch yourself all the same, he told her. In her last glimpse of her brother, he was standing watching her, Chloe beside him. His expression was clear as it had been before he diverted the dog. *Watch yourself.*

Neither of Lucia's sisters was prepared for what had happened to the woods in the past few days. The last time they had been here, it had been dormant and dull. Now, even in the fog, the greenness of the place was obvious. Roses grew high alongside the path.

"How could she let it get like this?" Ruby said. "Why didn't she call us?"

"What did she say to you?" Helena asked Kate.

Kate didn't answer, and Helena added, impatient:

"Oh, come on, she's obviously told you the whole story. What did she say about us? Why didn't she tell us this was happening?"

"I don't think she thought you'd want to see her."

Ruby stopped for an instant, looked back. "Seriously? What else did she say?"

"It's your story. You know it already."

"Please, Kate. We need to know. How is she? What's she going to do now?"

So Kate told it—plainly, roughly, losing track of her narrative more than once. They were patient with her.

She told them what she had seen and guessed and worried over—Lucia's imprisonment in the story of herself, her inability to escape or help Harry find his own way out. She told them Elphine's warning.

This moment—as they moved through deeper fog—was the only part of the story that they made her repeat.

"Elphine *would* have said that," Helena said softly. "She always thought the best of Lucia."

"She wouldn't have given up on her," said Ruby.

"We didn't give up on her." Helena was frowning. "It wasn't like that."

Ruby turned to Kate. "What did Lucia say, when you told her Elphine's message?"

"She wouldn't listen. She didn't think she had it in her to change things."

"So what's she doing out here now?" Helena said.

"I think— She talked about making herself useful, before."

"Useful how?" Helena said sharply.

"I think she might be coming back to the woods to stay. With Harry."

They understood her. She saw it in Helena's suddenly rigid expression, the way Ruby pressed a hand to her mouth.

If only Lucia could see them, Kate thought. If only she could see what it did to her sisters when they thought she might come to harm.

They pressed on through the trees—more urgent, and yet still cautious. Slowly, Kate began to realize that neither Ruby nor Helena was quite sure of the way.

"It's grown up," Ruby said, kicking her way through ferns. "This way used to be easier."

"Did it?" said Helena. "This is the Life, right?"

Ruby stared at her. "No. Can't be. We passed Heart Line back there, didn't we?"

"We didn't."

"We can't go back and see," Kate said. She was beginning to panic. "We can't be wasting time like that—"

"We won't. We'll be all right," Ruby said. "We'll take a left here and no matter who's right, we'll be at the Fane, and then we can . . ."

They were at the Fane. But not exactly where they had intended to emerge. They had taken the wrong track, and arrived now at a steep and dangerous place where the banks rose high and the river, far below, ran deep and fast. Instinctively, Kate drew back from the dark rush of the water.

This place was called the Leap. One of the Gonnes' ancestors had named it in a sardonic mood. The distance between one bank and the other was just a thought too far for even the tallest or most agile to jump. To try would mean falling, and a fall would mean death. The fog had brought them almost to the dreadful edge without their realizing.

"Oh for fuck's sake," Helena said, "how did we—"

She didn't finish—and neither of the others spoke—because on the opposite bank was Lucia. She was standing perilously close to the drop. One footstep more and she would be falling, smashed and drowned in an instant, lost forever.

Kate moved forward to beg her to step back and to safety. But the words failed her, because Lucia was not alone.

She stood hand-in-hand with a thin child. His eyes were on hers and he was leading her toward the edge and he was whispering to her.

Just one step more, Kate seemed to hear him say in his high, small voice. *One step, and it's done.*

CHAPTER TWENTY-SEVEN

Lucia in Conclusion

They shouldn't be here. I don't know what they're here for. Damn it, Kate, you should be far away, you shouldn't have to see this.

They're scared to move suddenly in case they startle me. Scared to speak. My brave Kate, my clever sisters, all at a loss. I can see in their faces that they know what I'm about to do.

This morning, Kate wouldn't even give me her anger. I didn't even deserve that much. And that was worse than the contempt and dislike I've so often felt for myself. I want to be worth her anger. I don't want her to lose hope in me, even if I have lost hope in myself.

I haven't changed in ten years, apparently. Still so *hungry* for her to like me.

I wish I could have been the person she and Elphine thought I was.

After Kate left Blanch Farm this morning, I found myself thinking backward. I hadn't told our story for a long time and telling it brought back things I'd forgotten. It was strange to think of me and him in the woods again, playing almost like ordinary children. I'd forgotten those moments.

If there's a way out for him, I can't find it, any more than I can find a way out for myself. We're still two of a kind. No wonder he chose me. No wonder I chose him. I don't know if we deserve to be free of this. A story wears a groove if it's told often enough. It wears you away like pacing feet on stone.

Village rumor has it that Nan walked the house a lot toward the end, after Dad died and there was no one left to keep her company. She would tread endless circuits, night and day, room after room, as long as her strength lasted. Around and around the empty house.

Sometimes I dream I'm her, walking the same circles.

I sat at the kitchen table after Kate left me and I thought of what they say about Nan's last days, and I touched the table without thinking because it's comfort, that solid wood.

Small comfort. I heard Nan say, *You'll come to a bad end one of these days.*

I remembered the first time she made that prediction. Twenty years ago. I was sitting with my family at the same table, in the same chair. Nan was retelling my latest misdeed: my persecution of the grape pickers.

Everyone knew already, of course, but that hardly mattered.

I think Grandpa might have tried to make light of it. No one else said anything. There was no point, I suppose. Nan would have her say. But they couldn't have understood how it felt to have that story told again, in front of everyone, months afterward, when I thought I'd lived it down. I wanted to cry; I wanted to run away and never see any of them again.

Under the table Elphine took my hand and gently squeezed. Thanks to that, I kept the tears back. I sat with my head bowed and scratched at the table with my thumbnail:

I

I had planned a full sentence of rebellion—*I am not like you say*—but Helena had seen what I was doing and made me stop.

It was still there, though, two decades later. If I leaned back in my chair, I could just make it out. *I* scratched deep by a heartsore child.

Harry seemed to be a way of being different, something other than Nan's picture of me—a way of being more. But in the end, he only helped to confirm everyone's suspicions of me.

You could tell it different.

I had believed that, once. I heard Harry's song and I went to work as if the story were soft like hand-warmed clay, as if it could be shaped as I wanted. Child-Lucia, so brave and ignorant. I remembered her without contempt for the first time in a long while.

I had spent years at that kitchen table listening to the story of myself. Lucia-the-bad, sure to come to a bad end. This morning I sat in the same place and thought of how I would finally settle my accounts.

I saw that I could twist things a little. I might be a lost cause but I can still do something useful before the end. I can make my life into a story with a point. I can keep Kate safe, and the others.

No one knows Harry's loneliness like I do. No one else made it so bearable. I knew that even if things were bad between us, if I went to him and promised to stay in the woods with him, he would probably accept. And this would be better for everyone.

I knew then what I would do, as clearly as if I'd already done it.

He will want proof that I'm really going to stay, of course. He'll need it to be impossible for me to leave, ever. But he'll help me there. He'll help me manage it.

Not the noose. Something quicker and kinder.

I can see it now, laid out ahead of me. It's clear what I'll do—one good thing at the very last. I will stay with him and Kate will be well and safe. They all will. Those people in the church . . . it'll be all right.

I'll prove Nan wrong, after all. It will not be a bad ending, really.

I made my decision in the gray dawn, and that's when Elphine came to me. I felt her hand, gentle on the back of my head, the way it used to be when she would braid my hair. Same delicate touch. Like she could be my lightning rod, carrying all bad thoughts safely away.

Not like that, she said. *Please, Lucia, don't.*

But I have my story now, and I'm telling it at the edge of the Fane. *I am not like you say.* I ignore the horror in Kate's face, my sisters' voices calling, pleading.

This is the story of Lucia who was, at the last, capable of one good thing.

I needed to draw him to me, away from the village and more importantly from Kate. I had an inkling, even then, that she might have something stupid and admirable in mind.

So I lit the beacons. I'd forgotten the knack, and it took me longer than I'd expected to get the first and second—Blanch Farm gate and the orchard gate—blazing properly. But by the time the flames were burning at the edge of Crockery Hill, hardly visible in the morning light, I thought I would soon have his attention.

When I got to the church to light the Small Angels' beacon, the last, the dogs were waiting outside. They let me pass out of old habit.

I hadn't expected to find such chaos. My first thought was of Kate—but she'd gone, driving straight into danger. Yet again I'd failed to stop her running into harm.

For a minute I didn't know what to do, I was lost. I saw Harry finding her, hurting her.

We rang the bells, we called Harry straight to us.

It was a strange thing. I couldn't have done it alone. But her brother was there, and others, too. If I hadn't come to Small Angels to light the beacon, I wouldn't have known she was in danger until it was too late. I wouldn't have got his attention in time.

But we rang the bells, and he knew it was me calling, and he came.

He looked very young, when he stepped out of the mist. It took me aback for a moment. But I know his strength very well. I knew that his appearance meant nothing.

"Is she safe?" I said.

"Who?"

He knew who I meant, of course. I didn't show my impatience:

"Kate. Is she all right? And the other one, too?"

"Yes. Both." He didn't like that this was my first question. But I'd had to know. "What do you want? Why did you call me here?"

I had the words ready, the script I had settled on:

"I've got a bargain for you."

"I don't want your bargain." But he stayed to listen.

"If you leave them alone—all of them—I'll stay with you forever."

He was shivering. I don't think I'd seen him do that before.

"I'll come back to stay. I'll be company at the Rose House, in the woods, for always. You won't have to be on your own."

I thought he'd be eager. But his face didn't change. Still he said,

"Do you promise?"

"Yes. The two of us, like you wanted."

At last he agreed. Maybe he's troubled because he's getting what he might have wanted once, but the circumstances are different, I'm different, things are not right between us anymore. Still he won't refuse what I'm offering.

And so we came here, to a place where I can end this story well.

As we walked through the mist to the river, he kept his hand in mine—it felt like both comfort and capture.

Closer. One step more and that's it. There's spray in my face and I can hear the rush of water and my heart beating loud in my ears and I think of strange, unconnected things: the color of our bathroom at home, Grandpa burning the toast, Helena finding a toad in her shoe one autumn morning. Tiny instants of my life flutter close, like ladybirds.

Far off, someone is talking. Kate and my sisters.

"Don't listen," Harry says. Petulant now. "You promised. Don't listen to them."

I'm not listening. But they don't stop.

Their voices drift across the river to me. I'm not listening. But the words find their way in all the same, like sunlight through heavy curtains.

They are telling a story.

Or it's not that exactly. But they're speaking by turns, offering memories, pleas, words of love. They are begging me to make something different out of these—a new story of myself.

It's a story of me but not one I know. Not one I have ever told or heard.

In their words, I am young, terrifyingly fragile—barely able to hold my head up. I am jaded and bewitching. I am infuriating, a teenage thorn-in-the-side. I am a thief of food and clothes and wine, I am generous in sharing the spoils of my crimes. I am wild and joyous company, I am a co-conspirator. I am selfish, I am Elphine's tender guardian.

There are so many stories, they say. The past is vast, the future is infinite possibility. They beg me to choose again, to shape a kinder narrative.

And I can tell that they believe it. They believe everything they are saying.

"Don't," Harry mutters. "Don't."

I take a step back. His hand tightens in mine.

"You said." He sounds so young. "You promised you'd stay." He is frightened, disappointed. But it could change to anger in an instant.

"There's another way." I risk one glance back across the river. Three pale faces watching, intent. They have shown me it can be done. There's a chance, even now. "I think there's a way out."

"Liar." Some part of him still craves my friendship, I think, because he's haphazard when he attacks; his violence lacks conviction. He scratches me, he takes my throat in one hand and squeezes, but I can still breathe, just about.

"There's a way," I say, choking. "There's a way out."

I don't think he hears me. And why would he listen, after so much time has passed and he still thinks of me as a traitor?

But I hear a whisper now. I don't know if it's in my head or not but I think it's Elphine:

Your pocket, Lucia. Quick.

The marbles are there in my dress pocket. Not glass, no shine on them. They're pale ceramic, unpainted. Unspectacular things, unless you happen to know their full meaning.

"Look," I say. I've sunk to my knees now—I don't know when that happened—and he's standing over me, frowning as I hold out my hands.

"Where did you find those?"

"He kept them. Even afterward."

He doesn't answer. I keep going:

"I can get you out of here. I can make it all right between you and Fred."

He doesn't release me, but he doesn't tighten his grip any further. It must have been so long since he's heard Fred's name. After a moment he steps back and he's crying; he has wrapped his arms around himself and he looks helplessly and wretchedly alone.

I remember now how it felt to pity him. I feel Elphine prompting. She always said how unhappy he must be.

"You can't," he says. "Nobody can."

But my sisters' words—Kate's words—still ring in my mind. I try to do for Harry what they did for me. I offer him a chance to tell his story differently.

I tell him what he doesn't know. I tell him how I found the childhood relics, how carefully Fred cherished them. He was loved, and mourned, even afterward.

He doesn't seem to understand me. But then he lets go of my throat.

"He kept them?" he says. "Truly?"

"They felt warm when I first found them. Like he still remembers."

Here is the material for another story. Love, even after everything. A wish that things could be different, and better.

"You could free yourself and him," I say. "You could make it all right."

"All right between us?" he says. "Truly?"

"I think so." My voice is raw, it doesn't sound like mine.

I realize that he wanted this always. I wouldn't notice it before because I was selfish, I wanted my friend to be *mine*, I couldn't bear the thought of him leaving.

Now I'm ready. I'll show him the way out, if I can.

Something shifts in the woods. Mockbeggar—the trees are paying attention. I sense ancient minds, slow and powerful, all turning toward us at once.

It's dreadful. Someone calls from the opposite bank but the mist is thickening again and I couldn't answer now anyway; I just want to cringe away from that attention. I didn't think Mockbeggar could pay such interest. All my life here and I didn't know.

Harry helps me up. His hand is very cold. There are tears on his face but he's calm now.

He leads me to the Rose House. The fog is thicker than ever. The roses seem to be thicker too. I know they can grow fast. Perhaps it isn't my imagination.

He has to help me into the heart of the house. Even with him guiding me it's not easy. These flowers are definitely thicker since I was last here. The smell is dizzying.

We sit in our old place. He's frightened now. Around us the woods are pressing close. They are listening hard.

I think it will take the others a while to find me. I think that's probably just as well.

Harry and I aren't quite alone, though. I feel Elphine close, whispering, urgent.

Tell it different, while there's still time.

"I don't know what to do," he says.

So I tell him what I was told, what I've learned. Tell it differently. Tell it so this time it doesn't end with revenge, Fred Hart's family paying and paying and paying, Harry all the while trapped in the woods, remembering. Tell it with grace, so we can all be free at last.

Then I sing to him, the rough verse I made up for Elphine long ago:

But maybe one day things will change
And he'll be free to go
And history will be laid to rest
In the woods where roses grow

He's still confused, frightened. He doesn't entirely understand what to do.

"Think of how it hurts," I say. "The way you hate him, and yourself. The way you tell yourself that same story over and over. How would it feel to put it all down and just walk away?"

He's struggling. I'm worried that he'll get angry again in a minute; he doesn't like to feel at a loss, and he's frightened into the bargain.

But now he's changing—his face shifts, he is old and young, happy and wretched at once. He is my friend and my enemy, and dozens of other people I don't recognize.

"Just tell me," I say quietly. "Tell me how it used to be. How he was your brother."

He's still frightened, but I see now he's been waiting to tell this for decades. Centuries, maybe. He's reviewed his wrongs over and over, and all the while this other story has waited underground, buried but not gone.

Now he remembers. He tells me of Fred's kindness, when Harry first came to Blanch Farm. Fred was the one who arranged things so Harry could spend time in Mockbeggar. Fred was the one who spoke up for Harry when the village boys mocked his family.

When they sang together in the Albatross, or on the walk home to the farm in the moonlight, their voices balanced perfectly. There was harmony there that he thought would never be broken.

He talks and talks—more things return as he tells the story, small details shining into view like gems.

He changes as he talks. I see him shift and age. The woods change too. It's getting dark.

Once he stops, looks about him. "They're angry," he says. I don't recognize this tone. He sounds older. He is frightened, but not for himself. "They won't want to lose me again."

"Keep on, though."

"They'll do you harm, if they can. If I go—"

Of course. I should have seen that coming. No one has defied Mockbeggar quite like this before. For an instant I am afraid—with crushing terror, like the clutch of a giant's hand. For a few seconds I can do nothing but suffer.

Then it's all gone. One way or another, it was bound to turn out like this.

"You could run," he suggests.

"No. Keep going."

He touches my hand briefly. Still so cold.

"Will you remember being my friend?" he says. "Not just the things that went badly?"

"Yes. I promise. Tell the rest."

He keeps going, remembering harvest suppers, games of marbles, jokes that made no sense to anybody but the two of them. His voice is fainter now. He remembers the pair of them spinning round and round in a clearing full of bluebells.

I blink, and then I can't see him. There are only dark green leaves and pale flowers swimming in front of my eyes.

Run, Lucia.

Elphine? Her voice, gentle in my ear, but when I look about in the leafy shadow there's no one. Just me and the woods now.

Run, Lucia.

Too late for that, I think. The fog's too thick, and what I am able to see doesn't look right: petals falling in front of my eyes, petals everywhere, bright white specks in the gloom.

Just me and the woods, and Mockbeggar won't let me go.

CHAPTER TWENTY-EIGHT

MOCKBEGGAR'S CHILDREN

Kate pushed through roses and waded through ferns, careless of mud and injury. Ahead of her, Helena and Ruby were struggling too: ducking under branches, tripping over roots in their haste. They had left the river behind them only five minutes ago and already the sound of the water was lost.

They were already too late. Lucia and Harry had left the Fane in the direction of the Rose House. Kate had no doubt it would be the place of their final confrontation. By the time Kate and the others got there, it would be finished, one way or another.

They didn't speak, except to briefly confer about directions. Ruby and Helena were only half-certain what path they were on. Kate didn't trouble to ask them how much longer the journey would take.

Nor did she ask them if they thought that the woods were changing. There was no need for confirmation.

No animal noises, no birds calling. The ground was softening. In some places they were struggling through slippery mud. The oaks and beeches seemed closer together than they ought to have been. The trees were closing ranks.

She thought of the Gonnes' empty-box funerals. How long had those lost unfortunates wandered, before the family gave up on them? How long had they survived Mockbeggar?

Ruby came to a sudden halt. "Helena," she whispered. "Look there—"

Up ahead, just where the narrow and uncertain path vanished into mist and branches, stood a teenage girl. She stood as though she had been there for a long time, waiting for them to notice her.

"Elphine," said Helena, voice broken.

They didn't try to get closer. Somehow, they knew that this would be impossible. But they followed that flitting shape onward through the trees.

Sometimes she was nowhere. Sometimes she was a soft smudge of black, fair hair bright against her funeral dress. Sometimes she looked back as if she wanted them to hurry.

When they heard rushing water, they quickened their pace. The breeze moving through the branches seemed to whisper disapproval. But Elphine was there, leading the way.

She stayed with them until they came close to the edge of the Fane again. Then she stepped ahead of them into the mist, and when they hurried down the path after her she was gone.

This part of the Fane was nothing like the Leap. Here the river ran shallow, and halfway across a flat brown stone emerged from the water. This was the crossing that led to the Rose House.

It was so quiet, Kate thought. How could that silence mean anything good?

Ruby touched her hand gently. Elphine had brought them here, her expression said. That had to mean something.

The place did not feel unfamiliar. Perhaps she had remembered the Rose House without realizing it. Perhaps Lucia had simply described it well. Either way the place was as Kate had pictured it. Only the rose tree was wrong—

"The flowers," Helena breathed. "Look."

The roses had shed their petals—all at once, like a snowfall. The ground was dotted with pink and white, spots of color drifting across the clearing, caught by the breeze.

"She managed it," Ruby said wonderingly. "He got out."

Something moved in the Rose House. Kate saw a flash of red like hope and there was Lucia. She was scratched and bleeding and moving like someone drunk—but she was there, she was alive.

Kate went to her without any other thought, caught her as she stumbled at the step to the ruin.

"You shouldn't . . ." She looked at Kate with dull confusion. She spoke like a sleepwalker. "You've got to get out."

"Well, obviously." Helena's voice was shaking, sharp with relief. Ruby did not seem able to speak at all. "Let's get moving."

"Should've gone before. Too late now." Lucia was mumbling. Cold as she leaned against Kate's shoulder. "I rang the bells. Did you hear? Called him."

"I know. I heard."

Lucia spoke quietly, with a brief and weary smile: "Heroic. Wasn't it?"

"Very. Scared me half to death. Don't do anything like that again, please." She smoothed the hair from Lucia's face. "I saw the gravestone."

Lucia didn't seem strong enough to speak further. But she took Kate's hand, raised it clumsily, for a moment, to her mouth.

On the way back, they took a wrong turning, tried to correct the mistake and ended up going even further wrong.

The thing was, they had cheated the woods. Lucia had robbed them of Harry, the one they loved best. Now Mockbeggar was angry—rage gathering slowly, silently, two centuries of deep unhuman love suddenly thwarted—and Mockbeggar planned to keep them.

Lucia alone seemed not to know or care what this meant. Her eyes were cast down as if she didn't trust her feet to carry her. She hadn't spoken since they left the clearing.

"She's cold," Helena said, as she took Lucia by the elbow. "Lucia, do you want a coat?"

Lucia didn't answer. She was shivering. They draped a coat around her shoulders, but she didn't seem to notice.

After about an hour, they found themselves in a clearing none of them remembered. There was nothing remarkable to it except the wild plum trees growing at the center—three of them, as neat and healthy as if they belonged to a well-kept orchard. They were heavy with fruit, most of it ripe.

Kate remembered the buzz of the Blackberry Maze in autumn, but there was no sound here. Not a wasp or fly crawled over this fruit. Mockbeggar was taunting them with this show of poisoned delicacies. In spite of all she knew, Kate might—if she had been alone—have been tempted to take a plum and try it. She was suddenly thirsty and the fruit looked very sweet.

They walked, walled in with green, without a word between them. It seemed to Kate that they were wandering through the very heart of the woods now—trees which should not have existed, which could not be still standing. Monstrous, beautiful old oaks stretched above them. The paths were all gone. It did not feel like any human had set foot here before. It was as if they had strayed into a part of Mockbeggar's memory.

According to Kate's watch, three hours had passed. Sam and Chloe and their wedding—all the waiting people in Small Angels—seemed to belong to another life now. Mockbeggar was all there was or would ever be.

When Ruby, who was leading the way, stopped walking, Kate's first response was alarm. Was there something worse ahead? The next part of Mockbeggar's revenge?

But Ruby gave a hoarse half-laugh—not amused, but not terrified either. Kate saw that they were back at the old clearing where the plays had been performed. The amphitheater.

They had stumbled across familiar places before in the past few hours; it didn't mean much—the usual landmarks were no help in navigating. Still, it was some comfort to stand where they had been happy and safe for a time.

They made Lucia sit down on a fallen tree. Helena sat beside her. Kate stood close by, watching Lucia's face for any change. Ruby paced up and down.

"It doesn't feel smaller," she said. "I thought it might."

They were quiet for a moment. They had been so many different people here. For a brief time, they had remade themselves and their world. Even now, the possibility lingered. In the shade of the Dervish, it seemed to Kate that Lucia and her sisters looked a fraction younger.

This place was still a stage, Kate thought. Elphine might have been crouched in the shadow of the twisted Dervish, waiting for them to begin.

"Tell a story," Lucia said.

"What?" Helena spoke sharply. It was startling to hear Lucia say anything after so long.

"If we tell a story, they might let us out," Lucia said. "We have to offer something in exchange. For what I took." When none of them understood her she added irritably: "Tell it to the trees. Don't you remember?"

"Give something to make up for losing Harry, you mean," Ruby said slowly.

Lucia didn't speak again. The effort of talking seemed to have exhausted her.

"We may as well try," Helena said. Lucia had slumped against her, head on her shoulder. "I don't have a better idea."

Ruby said, "All right. Shall I go first?"

"You always used to," Helena said. "You start off, and we'll join in as you go."

To Kate—leaning exhausted against the trunk of the Dervish, her eyes never leaving Lucia's set face—the story the sisters made resembled a braid. One of Elphine's loose, unreliable plaits, perhaps. It was something she had liked to do for all of them, Kate remembered. It was a way of persuading you to sit quiet, wait and think and breathe.

Ruby and Helena told the woods what it had meant to grow up in their shadow. They remembered the fear and love they had for Mockbeggar. The pull which endured, even now. It had been a gift to grow and play here. And hadn't they been a gift to the woods, in their turn?

Remember, they said to Mockbeggar. Remember how we lived. Remember Grandpa calling the hens home at night, his voice ringing like a great bell. Remember Nan, watchful and tireless, scratching sums at the kitchen table, gin in a glass at her elbow. Remember our mother fleeing even as her last baby kicked inside her. Remember our father letting her go. Remember our songs and games—we were witches and horses and queens. Remember how our voices filled this theater in the woods. Remember the stories we made.

The leaves of the Dervish rustled faintly. A bird was singing far off. A rabbit stared at them from beyond the briars.

Together—faltering, now, their voices starting to tire—they continued. They told the woods stories of what might happen, bright possibilities which were not yet wholly out of reach.

They told Mockbeggar how they might return—Helena with her wife, Ruby with her young son—to see the places they still loved. They told Mockbeggar of the stories that they would hear if they let the village back onto the woodland paths. They told Mockbeggar of games and plays not yet begun, children not yet born, plots and intrigues still unformed.

Remember us, they said to the woods. We were your children, too.

And now even Lucia spoke. Harry would not be forgotten, she said. He would be a memory still, but a memory at peace. People would talk about him but there would be no grief and fear now, he would be free. The story had ended better this time.

They talked until there were no words or breath left to them. In the pause that followed, the birdsong sounded louder. A cloud had shifted somewhere. Kate thought—did not trust the thought and yet could not ignore it either—that she remembered the way back.

The others felt the same. She could see it in the sudden energy in Ruby's face, Helena's bright look. Lucia, who had sat so still for so long, now looked up.

"You want to try?" said Ruby.

"No point sitting here wondering," Helena said.

Kate went to Lucia and helped her to her feet. "Time to go home," she said.

This time the journey felt different. They were all still exhausted, but their slow progress no longer felt pointless. At every step, Kate saw something she recognized. The memories attached to these sights were happy ones—some she had lost without realizing it.

At last they saw white up ahead: the silver birches waiting for them. Beyond that, the fields, Blanch Farm, the village.

It had never seemed so dear and lovely to Kate before. Tomorrow she would walk every lane, study every commonplace house with affection, impressing it all on her memory. She would be in the post office every day, the library too, she would never grow tired of the Albatross—

She glanced at Lucia. She was still very pale.

"Look," she said gently. "See? We're out."

Lucia nodded—she understood, Kate was certain—but as they reached the fields, her strength failed utterly. If Helena and Kate had not held her up, she would have fallen.

"We can take a break here," Ruby said. "Rest our legs."

"You make it sound like we've been on a hike," Helena said, with a trace of her usual sarcasm. But she helped Lucia sit down on the grassy bank that divided the plowed earth from the start of the woods.

The other three sat down beside her. For a moment, none of them spoke. The sun had passed its height and would be setting soon. In a short while Kate would marvel at that, and work out how much time had been lost in the wood, and discover what had happened in her absence.

But it was enough for now to sit with Lucia and her sisters, watching the sun cast their shadows across the dark plowed earth. Blanch Farm lay below them—innocent-looking, from this distance, unchanged from their childhood.

"This *place*, though," Helena said softly.

A pause.

"I brought wine," she added, in a different tone. She rummaged in her rucksack, brought out a bottle of Mockbeggar Bacchus.

"Were you planning a party?" Ruby said.

"I was panicking, throwing things in. I didn't know what to expect." She turned the bottle in her hands, tracing the dog drawing on the label. "Does anybody want some?"

For the time being, there were no more words between them—they had talked long enough in the woods. It was bliss to be allowed to sit in quiet, and drink the wine—which was still cold, though it should not have been by this time. Perhaps a chill from the Fane had crept in, or perhaps the woods meant this small wonder as a pledge of friendship. Mockbeggar had taken new histories to its heart: their child-selves, the fear and joy of their play here. The brief brightness of Elphine's life. And the story of two boys who had walked here together, two hundred years ago.

They drank in silence, and the sun sank further. For a moment, Kate counted not four but five shadows stretching over the dark earth.

CHAPTER TWENTY-NINE

Comfort Me with Apples

Those who had witnessed the attack at Small Angels struggled to explain it to those who had not. In the days after the wedding, Chloe and Sam's guests, locals and visitors alike, found themselves unable to make themselves understood. They could tell their friends and neighbors that dread had filled the church like smoke, that Hector had screamed with fear and rage, and that unseen claws had raked the strong wood of the church door. But they faltered in their descriptions. Accounts differed, people squabbled over the sequence of events. Was it before or after Hector's first scream that the bride and groom had fled?

The important thing, Chloe stressed to her parents, was that everyone was safe. She would be back in town next week. She loved them, and she was fine. There was really no need to worry.

Once out of sight of Small Angels, most strangers were content to leave the mystery alone. One or two thought regretfully of the green-scented night at the Tithe Barn, the pull of the music, the woods—but in a short while their everyday lives reclaimed their full attention.

The locals couldn't forget so easily. The woods were still there, surrounding the road in and out of the village. Small Angels still looked down on them all. There was no getting away from any of it, and their curiosity was not so easily left unsatisfied.

A few facts were definite enough: some kind of animal had come out of the mist that morning. There were John's injuries to bear that out, as well as the fresh marks on the church door. (Almost identical to the old claw-marks of two centuries ago, people noticed. And what was to be made of that?)

It was also generally known that the bride had fled the church, in spite of whatever had been going on outside. She hadn't got far, true—Kate Unthank's crashed car was proof of that. Someone said that they had later seen the just-married couple driving to Blanch Farm, which seemed of a piece with the whole strangeness of that day.

People wondered, but they were reluctant to press the pair too closely—especially Chloe, who had seen her wedding so thoroughly spoiled, poor thing.

Autumn came on quickly in the days following the wedding—the mornings turned crisp, the green began to slip away from the leaves. The wheat was cut and baled, and at sunset the gold stubble had blue shadows. The world began to change—as autumn always changed the world—and a feeling of waiting persisted. Something more was needed, people felt. They kept an eye on the woods, on Blanch Farm, on Small Angels.

There were no more rose petals drifting from Mockbeggar. No more dreadful apparitions, either. Hector returned to his field, peaceful as he had been before the wedding. Once his leg mended, John Pauncefoot visited him often, feeding him apples in companionable silence. Sometimes three children—sisters on pink bicycles—visited too, though they never went past the gate to Blanch Farm.

Lucia Gonne was still at home. She had been seen walking up the drive more than once, red hair and red dress unmistakable. The peculiar thing was that there were others there now, too—her older sisters had come back. Nobody could guess what they wanted or how long they intended to stay.

Brian would have speculated in the old days. Now, astonishingly, he seemed to have taken a vow of reticence. The Gonnes had a right to enjoy their family home, he would say if anyone asked his thoughts on the matter. What more was there to say?

He was too busy for much gossip anyway. The local entrepreneur, horrified at the disastrous launch of the Tithe Barn and Small Angels, had gratefully agreed to take Brian on in an advisory capacity. The church required a local eye, Brian told him firmly. If the entrepreneur wanted his investment to prosper, he'd do well to remember that.

A relieved Chloe passed the key and its attendant responsibilities on to Brian, and now he was stopping by every day to tend to the place. There was mud, dried rose petals, and other debris left behind by the wedding guests. The dust was coming back. Brian dealt with all of this uncomplainingly. Apart from practical maintenance, it also seemed wise to him simply to stop by from time to time and remind the church that it was not forgotten. The rood skeletons watched him cheerfully, and whenever he lit a candle, the shadows were soft and delightful.

To Sam's surprise, the entrepreneur also sought out him and Chloe.

The pair of them had remained in the village after the wedding, staying on at the Albatross. Chloe, despite her protests, was too shaken and exhausted to travel immediately. It didn't matter, Sam told her. Better that she rest and mend where she was. He didn't give a damn if they lost their hotel deposit.

Then the entrepreneur had stopped by to see them. In a lather of anxiety about the Tithe Barn's disastrous grand opening—already imagining the hostile online reviews, the failure of his investment—he offered Sam and Chloe a partial refund to make up for their disappointment.

Sam insisted that they had no intention of blaming him, or publicly criticizing the Tithe Barn. It hadn't been his fault.

But the entrepreneur insisted. A partial refund, in exchange for Sam and Chloe's goodwill. He wouldn't hear of them declining.

At last Sam had given up trying to convince him the gesture was unnecessary, and taken the money.

It meant he and Chloe could afford to rebook their honeymoon at a more expensive hotel, he told his parents. So you couldn't say that they had got *nothing* out of their whole experience.

He and Chloe—and even Kate—were gentle with Bill and Birdie that week. It was an uncomfortable time for them. The wedding had been a bewildering experience—Sam and Kate in danger from something neither of them understood or felt able to discuss. Now it seemed that the village's calm, oblivious old way of life, to which both of them had clung, was beginning to shift.

Mockbeggar had changed—that was increasingly clear. The deer had returned. The blackberries edging the road were flourishing outrageously. Birds called from deep in the woods. More than one person found themselves lingering at Crockery Hill, looking up into the trees. The foxgloves looked marvelously bright from a distance. How would it be to go closer, or even to step into the woods a little way?

"People need to know," Chloe said. "They need to know *properly.* Like we do."

They had come back to Small Angels—Sam, Chloe and Kate—to talk without Bill or Birdie overhearing. And to be sure that all was as it should be.

The marks on the door were already fading. Soon it would be hard to tell which set of scrapes were the most recent.

Sam said, "It's not what we're used to, though. You have to understand, ever since we were kids, it was always—"

"Leave it to the Gonnes. I know. But it's all different now. You have to share it, the good and the bad. And I think you have to go back to the woods."

"As a right, or as a duty?" Kate said.

"Both. Or that's how it feels to me. You told us how wonderful it used to be. Dangerous too. If it's like that again then it'll bear watching. I think it could do with some more stories. Happy ones, this time."

But not from Chloe. She was reluctant to return to Mockbeggar just yet.

When she went to the church door to see the claw marks up close, Kate took the opportunity to say to Sam,

"She's doing well. You both are."

"Good of you to say."

"I'm not patronizing you. It's true. Not everyone would manage so well. And Chloe had no idea about any of this a week ago."

"You like her, then?"

Kate nodded.

"She's going to organize you within an inch of your life, but you won't mind that, will you?"

"Not everyone craves poetic chaos."

She didn't answer.

"Don't feel sorry for us," Sam went on. "It's still romance. Just because it's not some . . . I don't know, some wild adventure. Nothing epic, just the two of us. With her, just a cup of coffee is romance. Just talking about stupid things. It doesn't have to be any more than that, because it's her."

Kate said, "I don't feel sorry for you."

When Chloe returned to them, she seemed to think her idea had been adopted without the need for further debate.

"You can ask the Gonnes, can't you, Kate? See what they think about telling the village the story. I mean, you'll be seeing Lucia today, won't you?"

"Maybe."

"There you go, then." Her smile was bright, guileless. "Talk to Lucia, see what she says."

Kate had been to Blanch Farm several times already that week. She had gone to offer help and had instead found herself installed in a chair in the kitchen as Helena and Ruby offered her tea, coffee, wine, insisted that she stay for dinner. They seemed anxious to open up, Kate discovered. They talked to her about everything—their past, the woods' past. They talked about Selina, and Paul, and Andrew. Most of all they talked about Elphine.

She watched Helena and Ruby clear a small island of order in the house. The kitchen was tidied, the mold was scraped away from the window frames and inside the fridge. Helena stacked the empty shelves with oats, dried fruits, canned vegetables, canned fish. Convenient, restorative foods. For her part, Kate brought fresh bread, fresh cheese, beautiful pots of jam, and the four of them had long, easy meals, supplemented with fruit from the orchard—plums and greengages, apples and pears all ripe now. This harvest would be a kind one.

Sometimes Ruby and Helena found relics as they tidied: a hair-ribbon of Elphine's, an unopened packet of their grandmother's cigarettes. Some of these things they kept, and some they threw away.

Ruby and Helena asked Kate about her family, how people were managing in the village. They remembered things that she had told them ten years ago—individual remarks prized as if very important. They made her describe her work in detail. There was no distance now, no closing of ranks against the outsider. At the end of every visit, they asked her when she could come to Blanch Farm next.

Lucia, curled in the low chair in the corner, was often silent. The other three had come to the conclusion that this was the best thing for her. She rested, healed, rolled her eyes from time to time at her sisters' cleaning efforts.

"It won't last," she said to Kate. "This isn't the kind of house you can keep tidy."

The kitchen door was open, letting in the gold autumn sunshine. The surviving Blanch Farm hens were scratching the step where Kate had last seen Elphine.

"No excuse for laziness, all the same," Helena said without rancor. They were being careful with Lucia, Kate thought. They wanted her to see there was no grudge left.

"We were so young," Ruby said one afternoon, when Lucia was asleep in her chair. "We couldn't win, growing up like we did."

When she and Helena talked about Lucia, it was with affectionate patience, a special kind of care. They were almost treating her like Elphine. Perhaps that was how they had managed to forgive her.

During Kate's visits, Ruby and Helena also described the lives they had made away from Blanch Farm. Both were happy, for the most part. But when Helena talked about her wife, her training as a doctor, when Ruby described her son's quaint games and sayings, and the free and perfect happiness in his laughter, there was sometimes a note of unease. They had been afraid that Blanch Farm would not leave them alone. They had fled, but could never get quite far enough. For years they had been waiting for the woods to creep into their hard-won new lives and take everything away. Now they would be free to leave, the past no longer following close at their heels.

And they would leave before too many more days had passed, Kate suspected. They missed their lives away from the village. As soon as Lucia was well, they would go.

Lucia was welcome to come with them, Ruby said. She could visit as long as she wanted.

Lucia smiled, but shook her head.

Kate watched her carefully. She watched her a lot that week, though it was rare that they spoke directly.

Lucia looked better and better by the day. Her color came back, and her face began to look fuller. She had recovered enough to show off a little, to argue with Helena about the mess upstairs. Still, she only spoke to Kate when the others were present.

One afternoon, Kate went to Blanch Farm a little later than usual. She found Ruby and Helena at work on the drive, battling against the encroaching grass. Ruby had found a scythe; the two were absorbed in debate over how it should be used.

Lucia was dozing in the kitchen. When Kate came in, she looked up and smiled like her old self.

"I pressed your sunflower," she said. "The one you stole from the party. I forgot to tell you. Elphine showed me how to do it, ages ago. The petals are shut up in *Wind in the Willows* right now. Give it a few more days and they'll be ready."

Kate was suddenly at a loss, unsure of whether to sit or stand. "One was stingy. I should have brought more."

"It was just right. You did everything right." Lucia looked at her hands. "You and Elphine."

"It was her idea."

"Even so. Thank you, Katherine Joan. It's been good seeing you again, you know. I meant it before. You do me good."

Why this tone of finality? Why, in spite of that glow of returned health, did she look so sad?

Before Kate could ask, Ruby and Helena returned, bringing the smell of cut grass with them.

"I need to ask you all something," Kate said.

"You look serious," said Helena. "You're not leaving the village yet, are you, Kate? Lucia would be inconsolable."

Ruby, standing at the sink, turned to flick water at her.

"I still say it would've been a good thing if you'd been stuck in Mockbeggar awhile longer," Lucia said. "I think it would've done you the world of good."

They were easier with each other, Kate saw. The play had become a little rougher. They would argue all their lives, and all their lives they would return to each other whenever there was trouble or joy to share.

"I need to ask you about the village," Kate said. "Chloe thinks—"

"Chloe?" Helena said.

"The one who was getting married," Ruby said. "The bride-in-the-mist."

"Oh, the bride-in-the-mist. Sorry, Kate, carry on."

(The name would spread, Kate thought. It would make its way to the village, and Chloe would become a story. The woman who fled into the fog, ghost hounds at her heels. After all she had endured, she deserved this kind of alchemy. Perhaps—if Mockbeggar was truly restored—Kate would come across a shade of Chloe decades from now, standing at the drive to Blanch Farm in her wedding dress, her expression hopeful and disbelieving.)

"Chloe thinks the village should know all about Mockbeggar," she said. "She thinks that it should go back to how things were. Before Harry, when everything was shared. When people took stories to the woods."

"There's danger in that," Helena said. "Even now. Mockbeggar's never going to be tame."

"I know. But even so."

The three sisters shared a glance. Ruby was the first to speak.

"I think they've got a right to know," she said.

"I think we've got a right to share it," said Lucia. "If there's ever danger again. It shouldn't be just us dealing with it. It didn't do us good."

Helena sighed. "If they want to know, then we need to tell them," she said. "I'll draw you a map, Kate, before I leave. Neither of these two can draw worth a damn, you know."

They agreed that they would visit the Albatross tomorrow, let anybody who wanted hear what they had to say.

Before she left that evening, Kate went to the Gonnes' orchard. Ruby had begged her to take some fruit away; the trees were laden, and she was worried that it would start to waste. As Kate picked her way through the long grass, she found that the process had begun already. Under the plum trees, fallen fruit was rotting; wasps crawled over too-sweet flesh.

When Lucia found her, she was reaching for a branch that was a little too high, where a cluster of greengages hung, golden-green in the sunset.

"People used to say our fruit was cursed," Lucia said.

It was a pleasant shock to see her standing. She wore her old red dress, with a cardigan thrown over her shoulders. A loan from Ruby or Helena—they still told her off for getting too cold in her weakened state.

"Liar," said Kate.

"I swear, they did. Eat Blanch Farm fruit and you'll have to keep coming back for more. No one with sense would risk it."

Kate took a pear from the basket, bit into it carefully.

Lucia—voice catching just a little—said, "You never did know when to leave well enough alone."

Kate let her take the pear from her and finish it. Three careful bites. She dropped the core into the long grass, wiped her hands on her dress.

"Why did you say *it's been good seeing you again*?" Kate asked after a moment.

"Because it's true," said Lucia. "You're going away soon, and I wanted to be sure I'd said it before you did."

Very reasonable, but her hands were shaking.

"I don't want to say goodbye to you," Kate said. "Once was enough."

"I ruined it all, though, didn't I? After that night you stayed and I told you the story, it was all spoiled. You haven't talked to me properly since then. You only even look at me when you think I don't notice."

"That last morning, you said it was nostalgia. The two of us, that night I stayed. Getting it out of my system. I thought maybe that's what it might be for you."

"No. Of course not. I wanted you to go somewhere safe, that's all." She frowned. "Why, was that how it was for you?"

"You know it wasn't."

"Then you should've said something before. It's been days."

"You nearly died. Of course I'm not going to trouble you with questions. *What are we, do you like me really, where are we headed.* You've had bigger things to—"

"Rubbish. As if I didn't want you to trouble me. As if there was anything I'd ever want more than that. What do you think we are, Kate?"

They were friends and distant unfriendly acquaintances and lovers, they were tentative children and they were sad, tired women, and in all of these facets and faces Kate thought now that she loved her. The fact of Lucia—alive and well in the orchard in spite of everything—was a thought as glad as any she had ever had.

But to find words for this would be a slow undertaking. Her thoughts had been walled up alive in her head for half her life. To tell it all would take a long time.

Lucia understood, she thought, because she stood on tiptoe to kiss her very gently on the mouth.

"Better than anyone?" she said. "Still?"

Kate nodded. Lucia touched her mouth gently, fingers sticky with pear juice.

"Me too," she said. She was shaking and when Kate pulled her closer she smelled of outdoors, the chill and the dead leaves, and the fruit that meant harvest.

The following evening, the Albatross was so full that people sat outdoors on the picnic benches, though the day was a cold one. Meg Pauncefoot had sternly warned her father against overwork. Still John managed to be everywhere, setting out heaters for the outside drinkers, taking orders, answering questions as well as he could.

The invitation had gone around the village earlier in the day. Elizabeth displayed a notice in the library and told every patron what was happening. Brian had told everyone who called into his shop, and posted several times on the village's online community forum, so nobody could say they hadn't been invited. A few had elected to stay away, though. Bill and Birdie Unthank were two of these.

"They'll find out sooner or later, won't they?" Chloe said.

Sam shrugged. "Maybe not. You'd be amazed at what they can ignore."

"I suppose if they're happier that way," said Kate. "They are, aren't they?" she added, when the others looked at her in surprise.

Sam was about to answer her when the conversation in the Albatross ended abruptly. The Gonnes were here at last.

They were adults now, not the girls that some people remembered from Paul Gonne's funeral. Still Blanch Farm lingered in their faces. You felt as if they were still not entirely at home in large gatherings. They did not seem quite tame.

The youngest, Lucia Gonne, looked haughty as she stared around the Albatross. Only Kate could have guessed at her nervousness.

All three women carried gifts: two great baskets of fruit—apples and plums, blackberries and raspberries—and a bunch of flowers. Not a rose among them; instead they carried dog daisies and honeysuckle, ragged robin and honesty.

"Thanks for coming to listen," said Ruby Gonne. "We thought it was time to talk to everybody face-to-face. We brought you some gifts from home. Blanch Farm and the woods."

"And they're all safe," said Helena. "In case you were wondering."

"For a long while—as long as any of us can remember—Mockbeggar was just for us," Ruby went on. "The rest of you didn't get a chance to visit, to find out what it's like. Now things are different. It's safe to go back, if you want to."

A murmur. John Aubrey, sitting at Brian's feet, considered Ruby with his head on one side. Lucia was staring at Kate.

"You know there's a secret," Ruby went on. "A story we always kept to ourselves. Now we want you to know everything." She turned to Brian. "A couple of people already know. We've decided we want them to tell everybody. If you don't mind filling people in, Brian?"

Brian said, "I don't mind."

"Try the fruit," Helena said. "Take a flower. Make your minds up. We're leaving it up to you."

The Gonnes set down their gifts. Duty done, they looked about to depart.

"Won't you stay for a drink?" John Pauncefoot said.

Ruby—surprised, gratified—hesitated for a moment, then glanced at Helena.

"Thank you."

"Will you be coming back in the future?" Elizabeth said. "Keeping an eye on things?"

The sisters shared a look.

"We will be coming back," Ruby said, "but not for that. Mockbeggar is for everyone now. The paths are open. Listen to Brian. Then go and see."

"Brian's going to love this, isn't he?" Sam muttered to his sister. But Kate was gone. (Lucia, too, seemed to have departed, leaving her sisters to hear the story.)

"She does that, you know," Chloe told him. "I wouldn't worry. It's just her way." She poured more wine for both of them, and set a quartered Blanch Farm apple on his plate. "Hush now, the story's about to start."

Outside the Albatross, the yard had cleared, drinkers crowding inside to hear the long-kept secret.

Kate found Lucia waiting for her at the church porch, wearing her old red dress. The moon would be rising soon, the cornfields were all cut. It was a night for wandering, and they could walk where they liked as the stars came out. Nobody would part them.

Kate caught Lucia's hands and kissed her, and led her into the cloudless dusk.

In the Albatross, the hubbub continued. The fruit had been eaten, the flowers had been divided. The world was a little lovelier than before. A few people had left but most remained. They had tried the Gonnes' gifts, and now they were ready for their story.

The music paused. Drinks and conversations were forgotten. John

Pauncefoot put down the glass he was cleaning, and Elizabeth set aside her book.

Brian let them settle down a little before beginning. He let them grow impatient, sipped his beer and opened his salt-and-vinegar crisps with a pretense of thought, as if he was asking himself where and how he should start his story. In fact, he knew—he had known for a while now—how he would begin.

All right, he would say, *so*:

Acknowledgments

A big thank you to Dr. Gareth Morgan and James Townsend for their generous help in answering my questions about vineyards—any mistakes in this area are entirely mine. Many thanks also to Mandy Townsend of Dunesforde Vineyard.

I'm hugely grateful to have had Mary-Anne Harrington and Caitlin McKenna in my corner during the editing process. Thank you both for your wise and inspiring feedback. It's been a delight to work with you on *Small Angels* and I'm going to miss our Thursday Zooms.

I think writing a book must always be a kind of adventure—and I feel extremely lucky to have had Jenny Hewson at my side during this one. Thank you so much Jenny for your patience and astute judgment as *Small Angels* took shape, for clearing away the dead wood and letting the tiny shoots breathe.

Thanks also to Amy Perkins at Tinder Press, and Francesca Davies at Lutyens & Rubinstein.

Thank you Gran for your abiding interest in this book, and for keeping me from lollygagging.

Thank you Rachel for all your encouragement.

Thank you George for two and a half years of sage and honest critique.

Thank you Amie and Grace, for coming into the woods with me.

Thank you Mum and Dad, for everything.

About the Author

Lauren Owen is the author of *The Quick* and *Small Angels*. She studied at St. Hilda's College, Oxford, and holds an MA in Victorian literature from Leeds University and an MA in creative writing from the University of East Anglia, where she was awarded the Curtis Brown Prize.

About the Type

This book was set in Caslon, a typeface first designed in 1722 by William Caslon (1692–1766). Its widespread use by most English printers in the early eighteenth century soon supplanted the Dutch typefaces that had formerly prevailed. The roman is considered a "workhorse" typeface due to its pleasant, open appearance, while the italic is exceedingly decorative.